Praise for

HAMMER

"Unfailingly entertaining . . . *Hammer* has the smoothness of a good cable drama."

—Sam Sacks, *The Wall Street Journal*

"Hammer has a lot to say about the role that art plays in the world at large. . . . The novel gains lamentable timeliness from a late plot twist involving Ukrainian independence and Vladimir Putin's 2014 invasion of Crimea, but Reed sensitively handles those issues while steadily raveling his characters' increasingly disparate lives into an intricate look at politics, morality, and coming to terms with one's past."

—Cory Oldweiler, *The Washington Post*

"Hammer is a many-layered slow-burn of a novel . . . A tragedy of manners, should such a thing exist (perhaps *Les Liaisons Dangereuses*). It is also a timely document of a world in which corruption and sincerity, lofty intentions and craven pursuits, can be impossible even for the perpetrators to tell apart."

—Bethanne Patrick, *Los Angeles Times*

"Reed casts his appraising eye on the equally cutthroat worlds of modern art and Russian politics . . . [He] is consistently excellent in his takes on art, money, and the ruthlessness of the auction house business."

—*Publishers Weekly*

"Reed's riveting second novel is at once a romance, a geopolitical thriller, a meditation on art, and an investigation of the moral compromises that everyone makes in the gravitational presence of wealth. Reed does a masterful job of complicating his characters' motivations. . . . Richly textured, compulsively readable, and brilliant throughout."

—*Kirkus Reviews* (starred review)

"A timely tale in its outlying politics and a hardened critique of the ever-commodified world."

—*Booklist*

"Reed's great gift is to write about the contemporary art market, about the relationship between beauty and rapacious wealth, without cynicism or easy satire. By the time you finish *Hammer*, you'll feel like it all makes a kind of sense. Not to mention that—as one of Reed's characters observes, and as *Hammer* amply demonstrates—there are way more destructive things the super-rich could be doing with their money."

—Jonathan Dee, author of *The Locals* and *The Privileges*

"For the second time, Joe Mungo Reed has found a way to entice readers into the intricacies and beauty of a world at first niche, which in his careful hands quickly becomes familiar, then thrilling. *Hammer* displays an artist's uncanny ability to pay attention to the fine moments and meticulously weave them into a stunning work of fiction. Joe Mungo Reed has solidified himself as a novelist of great poise and power."

—Nana Kwame Adjei-Brenyah, author of the
New York Times bestseller *Friday Black*

"Art is among the most manipulated markets in the world, and no novel since Michael Cunningham's *By Nightfall* captures this truth better, or in more exquisite prose, than *Hammer*. Joe Mungo Reed makes good on the promise of *We Begin Our Ascent*, dispelling the myth of the sophomore slump and proving that a writer's second book can be his best. I was captivated from the gorgeous opening to the thrilling end."

—David James Poissant, author of *Lake Life*
and *The Heaven of Animals*

ALSO BY JOE MUNGO REED

We Begin Our Ascent

HAMMER

Joe Mungo Reed

SIMON & SCHUSTER PAPERBACKS

New York   London   Toronto   Sydney   New Delhi

Simon & Schuster Paperbacks
An Imprint of Simon & Schuster, Inc.
1230 Avenue of the Americas
New York, NY 10020

First Simon & Schuster trade paperback edition March 2023

SIMON & SCHUSTER PAPERBACKS and colophon are registered trademarks of Simon & Schuster, Inc.

For information about special discounts for bulk purchases, please contact Simon & Schuster Special Sales at 1-866-506-1949 or business@simonandschuster.com.

The Simon & Schuster Speakers Bureau can bring authors to your live event. For more information or to book an event, contact the Simon & Schuster Speakers Bureau at 1-866-248-3049 or visit our website at www.simonspeakers.com.

Interior design by Ruth Lee-Mui

Manufactured in the United States of America

1 3 5 7 9 10 8 6 4 2

The Library of Congress has cataloged the hardcover edition as follows:

Names: Reed, Joe Mungo, author.
Title: Hammer / Joe Mungo Reed.
Description: First Simon & Schuster hardcover edition. |
New York : Simon & Schuster, 2022.
Identifiers: LCCN 2021030017 | ISBN 9781982121624 (hardcover) |
ISBN 9781982121631 (paperback) | ISBN 9781982121648 (ebook)
Classification: LCC PR6118.E4547 H35 2022 | DDC 823/.92—dc23
LC record available at https://lccn.loc.gov/2021030017

ISBN 978-1-9821-2162-4
ISBN 978-1-9821-2163-1 (pbk)
ISBN 978-1-9821-2164-8 (ebook)

To my mother, Nicki

We are then charmed with the beauty of that accommodation, which reigns in the palaces and economy of the great; and admire how everything is adapted to promote their ease, to prevent their wants, to gratify their wishes, and to amuse and entertain their most frivolous desires. If we consider the real satisfaction which all these things are capable of affording, by itself and separated from the beauty of that arrangement which is fitted to promote it, it will always appear in the highest degree contemptible and trifling. But we rarely view it in this abstract and philosophical light. We naturally confound it in our imagination with the order, the regular and harmonious movement of the system, the machine or economy by means of which it is produced.

ADAM SMITH

Art does not need us, and it never did.

KAZIMIR MALEVICH

I

Autumn 2013

1

OCTOBER LIGHT. Afternoon light. He strides back to work along Mayfair streets with his sandwich in its little triangular piece of packaging.

Summer, when it came, came late, but now the good weather is hanging on into these shortened autumnal days. He walks through Berkeley Square, across the small park in the middle of it. The plane trees rustle with a breeze unfelt at street level, shedding substantial leaves, which descend slowly enough to surprise the eye, as though through liquid. Businessmen out, eating lunches, their ties removed, collars loosened. A woman with her back against the trunk of a tree in her skirt suit, her shoes off, her feet placed together on the dry dirt beneath the spreading roots. A couple cross-legged on the grass, each on a plastic bag rent open to its maximum extent.

It is a wishful performance, Martin thinks, as if Londoners hope that the embrace of these fine days can somehow prolong them, as if the inhabitants of the city think that they can dream it southward.

At the exit of the square, a bustle of pigeons peck at crumbs beneath a bench, brazen, flapping off only as he is almost upon them, and then taking back the space with their Mick Jagger struts as soon as he has passed. He pauses at the road as a taxi accelerates to beat the lights. He crosses, heads for the auction house.

The afternoon trade is picking up in the boutiques and the art shops. He sees the assistants at work. Greeting, straining to not strain. Working to facilitate, to go unnoticed until needed. See-through men and women like him. Chameleons or shades. Some classical category of the damned or forgotten.

ONE CAN feel the imminence of the contemporary sale as soon as one is through the doors. Thronging of people taking their last looks at the lots—a few prospective buyers, and then the enthusiasts, the art students, the odd tourist wandered in. The clatter of the end of lunch service in the restaurant. The clip at which the other staff go about their tasks. The phones ringing. The clanking of the freight elevator, audible from the reception area, as tables, chairs, and pieces of camera equipment are moved for tonight's event.

Martin climbs the crème-carpeted stairs toward the upper galleries. The first time he came to the auction house he was surprised by the homeliness of the décor—not the sterile white finish of the contemporary gallery, but something closer to a decent regional hotel. Part of the house's ethos is expressed in this choice, Martin supposes: the assertion of its existence before the modern gallery, prior to the reverential emptiness of the contemporary space.

He passes through another door toward the offices, climbs a set of steep stairs. An anxiety has been rising through him all week, as is normal when sales approach. He sits at his desk and eats his sandwich—a damp prawn mayonnaise that clags around his gums. It is the last he will eat until after the auction is done.

He will be bidding on behalf of one of the house's clients, and he broods on this as the afternoon stretches on. One must simply raise one's paddle and speak clearly, and yet in such simplicity lie old anxieties: the voiceless cries of bad dreams, the wince of answering a roll call at a new school.

AT FIVE, a text from James, his housemate and childhood friend. Have you done your team yet? Martin has forgotten about fantasy football, about the midweek round of Premier League fixtures. Despite all the bustle around him, he logs onto the website for a moment, makes a couple of substitutions. James will have spent hours this morning poring over his selections, and Martin feels he must make some effort of his own.

At six, he changes in the men's toilets with a couple of other junior specialists. The smell of hair gel and cologne. The plumbing whispering and choking. A collective giddiness as the sale approaches. He puts on a fresh shirt. He likes to dress well, a charge given to this pleasure, he feels, by the way that in the household he grew up in such care over one's appearance was considered unnecessary, vaguely suspicious.

Martin's parents are hippies. The home in which he was raised, in which his parents still live, is part of a Jacobean manor divided up in the seventies. Semicommunal living, they call it. "We still have normal day jobs," Martin's mother would say to parents of Martin's friends, as if such a thing should even need underlining. "We still have our own units." It's a slightly bashful utopianism: communal garden work, meals together at the weekends, still the smell of lentils about the place, the odd beard or pair of clogs, children running free through the hall and outbuildings, half-clothed on summer days. Residents tend to leave when their kids grow up, but Martin's mother and father have stayed, the longest-serving tenants, sources of lore, guardians of tradition.

It was a good childhood. Only occasionally embarrassing. They were ahead of the world in their environmentalism (far enough, Martin sometimes thinks, for him to have seen the ineffectiveness of it all). To not reuse a plastic bag was a cardinal sin in his childhood home. After Martin's dad broke his wrist falling from the roof of a toolshed, Martin took his sandwiches out of his rucksack at school one day and found them wrapped in a polythene bag that read PATIENT'S BELONGINGS.

Perhaps it is reaction against this background that inclined Martin toward the auction house, with its ostentatious neatness, with the daily need to talk calmly of millions of pounds as a butcher talks of kilos of mince.

He takes some time at the mirror applying wax to his hair. Henry, another junior specialist, hums a phrase from Vivaldi's *Four Seasons* from one of the toilet stalls.

WHEN THE public start to arrive, Martin is up in the offices: fielding calls from clients, fetching documents on behalf of his boss, Julian, who will be conducting the sale tonight.

When he descends toward the reception area, it's busy. Chatter rises up the stairwell, surging and then ebbing as voices compete to be heard. He pauses on the stairs and watches the crowd in the entranceway: clusters of people, growing and collapsing according to the competing gravities of the powerful and renowned. Client relations staff move between the punters, handing out bidding paddles and catalogues, greeting potential buyers, making their practiced small talk. He is not unable to see the scene as his mother might, to be nauseated by the sheer good taste of the attire, the frivolous timbre of the chatter, the whiteness of the teeth of a man who throws back his head and laughs.

Still, it's too easy to condemn the art market with reference to its worst participants. There is the work, and then there are the people with the money necessary to buy that work, and the house has no choice in the latter. That is the realm of politics and business and financial markets. Martin is able to induce a sense of vertigo in himself by considering the manner in which money finds its way into the room. Determined by what? By stocks or oil or decisions of the Chinese treasury?

He goes down into the hubbub smiling benignly. Henry, at the foot of the stairs, speaks with a collector, snaking his arm through the air, probably talking about some powder encountered in Courchevel last winter.

Martin moves into the crowd. The smell of dry-cleaned clothes. A woman ahead steps back from a splash of wine, spilled from the glass of the person addressing her. "She sold the beach house," a man says, "and the cash is going into the collection."

"Sashimi," says a woman in another group. "Sashimi is a different matter."

JULIAN IS in conversation with a dealer friend of his, Peter Beaufort. If Julian is in any way nervous about handling the sale, it doesn't show in his body language. He has a thumb hooked in his waistcoat pocket. He inclines his head to listen to Beaufort, the smaller man, speak. As Martin approaches, Julian laughs at something the dealer has said, ruffles his hand through his own disordered white hair.

Martin hands his boss a couple of pages. The smell of Beaufort's aftershave is thickly floral, fecund. The dealer looks at Martin without seeming to see him. Julian nods, winks, turns his attention seamlessly back to Beaufort. In seeing this gesture, a familiar wish returns to Martin: that he could carry himself as easily in this world as his colleagues do. And yet, he should be mindful that the appearance of ease does not preclude effort—a thought that should be native to a specialist in contemporary art.

Martin is liked well enough in this world, but this is a liking he has no control over. His raw earnestness earns him some credit, yet he is not nimble in his flattery. He leaves too much of himself exposed.

HE MOVES again, past caterers, past a woman weighing a bidding paddle in her hand like a tennis racket. He seeks clients he knows, faces open to greeting, to blandishments and reassurance. People are pressed so close he can smell their dinners on their breath, make out the marks of combs across scalps, the layering of foundation on cheeks. Martin keeps a green Moleskine upstairs on his desk with details of those he has dealt with—their interests, their purchases, their jobs and children. This work is not unlike matchmaking, finding a piece for a client, a client for a piece. A caterer moves past carrying glasses above her head.

He stops to talk with Alex Philpot, an executive at a pharmaceutical company (which Martin's mother once picketed). He is tall, blond. He looks German, even though he is not. Martin enjoys talking with Philpot, who is acute in what he likes, mannerly and considerate: no doubt once a boy considered a credit to his school and family. Tonight, Philpot wants to talk about the Ed Ruscha in the catalogue. "He's mastered the vernacular of the commercial culture," he says to Martin.

"Certainly."

"He is playing with the question of whether we may be charmed by this vernacular. The issue is not is it compelling, but is it *permissible*. There is a meta question of judgment in the pieces that is open, I think. Which is actually, to my mind, generous."

Behind Philpot's shoulder Martin catches sight of a client, Mrs. Dempsey, making her slow way through the crowd. With reluctance, Martin excuses himself.

Mrs. Dempsey walks with a stick. She is wearing a neck brace and, under that, pearls. "How wonderful that you are here tonight," says Martin.

She looks up sharply, studies him. He wonders whether there is a genuine recognition there. "You can't just give up at my age," she says. "You can't just lie down and wait to die."

"Yes." He tries to think of something agreeable to say. Or not agreeable, exactly, because Mrs. Dempsey is not the kind of woman who tolerates agreeableness.

She grips her stick with knobbly hands. "Hot in here," she says.

"It's a busy night," says Martin. "It's all the body heat of this crowd."

Mrs. Dempsey frowns. "I'd have thought you'd have accounted for that and not run the heaters earlier in the day."

"Yes," says Martin. "I suppose we should have."

Martin wonders what else to say. He looks at the people around, sees a profile that he knows, waits for the resemblance to break, for a turn of mouth or eye to betray the fact that he is watching a stranger. Yet it is Marina, a friend from university, the ex-girlfriend of Martin's housemate James. She's married to a rich Russian, a collector, and Martin has expected her at auctions before, has seen this expectation disappointed enough that now her presence here is a surprise.

She sees him and grins. He feels a slight jolt at this confirmation. He smiles back, or he is smiling already (because a slightly idiotic beam is his default expression on nights like these), and then she is moving toward Martin, making space with an arm held out ahead of her.

He says, "So nice to see you," to Mrs. Dempsey, in a way that he hopes conveys his need to move on.

"If you say so," says Mrs. Dempsey.

He steps toward Marina's approach, away from the old lady. Not the best practice, of course, to leave her so abruptly. Marina slips past a group of dealers. They haven't had direct contact since university. Martin read about her marriage to Oleg Gorelov in the papers. The house invites the man to each auction they hold, but since Martin has been working here Gorelov has never come.

Martin is struck newly by Marina's tallness. She has a long forehead, a slightly snub nose. Hers is an odd kind of prettiness, he has thought before, that seems on the edge of something else. She hasn't changed, he thinks, and finds himself wondering with concern whether she will think the same of him. The last time he saw her he was still an immature student: a boy, really, with a helix ear piercing and a Penguin introduction to Nietzsche. There is an ironic sort of smile on her lips, but she was always like that. She was tolerant, he thinks, was more kind and patient than she ever needed to be. She embraces him when she arrives, says, "How long?"

They do the calculations together, settle on sometime in summer nine years before. She studies him, and he is glad to sense that she is noting differences from the boy she previously knew.

"Very smart," she says. She nods up and down to indicate his attire.

"Yes," he says "Thank you. You too."

She ignores the compliment. He is too slow with her still. Flat-footed. "You work here?" she says.

He nods.

"You're going to ask about me?"

He smiles. "I know a bit about you."

"Oh yes? My husband?"

"My bosses are interested in your husband."

"Right," she says. "I'm sure they are. And you too, I suppose?"

"You're here with him?"

"I am."

"He's going to bid tonight?"

"Who knows?"

He recalls Marina in those university days in his and James's old flat. Her sitting with her legs tucked under her in an old rattan chair they'd dragged off the street. Her levering open a window that had been painted shut by the landlord and hunching to blow cigarette smoke through the crack she had worked. She was studying music and literature. She explained poststructuralism to him, alternately exasperated with him and with the theorists she spoke of. She was always confident, embodied, vaguely regal in the certainty of her choices. He was a nervous boy, rushing about, trying to please. She was good at cutting through his chatter, his frantic affect. She'd already done a lot of the things other students were trying for the first time, and so she was interested in actually studying. She would listen to him talk and offer back a spare response that undid him. He read books like a teen, with a hunger for fine phrases and nubs of wisdom. She read properly, widely, and with care. He wants to crack the seal on these old memories, but this is not the place, he thinks. It was a long time ago. There is something in the way she is watching him that makes him think she is glad to see him, though it seems unlikely.

On the back of this pleasure, he feels a slight dread, however.

James has never gotten over her, and as they talk Martin already feels the onus of having to relay what is said to James, to describe Marina, who looks so well, who puts out a hand and clasps Martin's forearm to interrupt him and repeat a thought: "Nearly a decade," she says. "Christ!"

He wants to concur with the appropriate enthusiasm, yet he doesn't quite know what to say, can't shake the thought of James. Involuntarily, he looks toward the doors of the sale room, and Marina sees this, says, "Of course you have work to do."

He assents to this with the requisite amount of apology, a click back into the automatic manners of the night. She suggests they should meet sometime, and he agrees, though he knows the suggestion is made only to be polite. She turns in the direction by which she arrived, a professional care intruding on Martin's awareness now: the desire to see the group she moves back to and to locate Gorelov. She presses back through the crowd, and Martin cranes his neck to see her approach a heavyset man with a sun-spotted head, who turns to take in her approach and turns back to Julian to whom he has been talking. Beaufort is there too. It is, of course, a major opportunity to have Gorelov here. He used to buy a lot from auction houses and private dealers, apparently, but hasn't been active in the art market recently. Julian speaks, fluttering his hands, and the man listens, strikingly still and offering a curt nod only occasionally.

THE SALE room is bright—lit for cameras already—empty but for the staff setting up: specialists, client relations people, and the porters in their black aprons and white shirts. Pictures, lots in the sale, line the walls. Behind the podium at which the phone bidders will stand hangs a large Gerhard Richter abstract, all metal and air and hurry.

Martin takes a breath, enjoys the emptiness of the space, the readiness.

He goes over to claim a position at the phone bidding desk,

unfolds the piece of paper on which is noted the phone number of the client he will be bidding for and the lots that the client would like to follow. The client is after two more minor works: a Cy Twombly sketch and an Anish Kapoor sculpture. That is why Martin and not a more senior member of staff or a private dealer has been assigned to offer on the pieces. Still, both will sell for many multiples of Martin's annual salary. Earlier, Martin could have used the house database to link this customer number to an actual identity. He chose not to, however, sensing this would be a distraction, a source of unnecessary pressure. It is useful, anyway, not to prejudge a client's resources, but to leave them to demonstrate their wealth in the only way that matters: by placing a successful bid.

THE DOORS of the auction room open to admit the punters, who come in carrying their conversations with them, taking time to seat themselves, an effort to observe the room concealed behind their casual talk. The specialists stand ready at their desks, the large white phones they will use to dial out to clients in front of them. The Internet people are tapping at laptops on a podium to the left of the block. Everyone is well-dressed. Among the younger staff there are hints of those already trying to distinguish themselves sartorially by leaning into the eccentricities of an expert: red socks, a colorful pocket square, a striking brooch. The porters stand with their hands clasped in front of them, blank passport-photo faces: the handsome children of good families with degrees from the best universities in the country waiting only to heft pictures. This is all a key part of the sale, of course: the superfluity, the sense projected in every possible respect of elegant casualness, of easy underuse.

Up above the hall, Martin knows, a handful of bidders are being shown into private booths, where they can watch the auction from behind smoked glass. The cameras in the corners of the sale room will transmit video of the proceedings to another smaller room in which those unable to fit into the main space will watch the auction play out on flat-screen TVs. The stream will be transmitted out over the Internet, available to anyone who wants to tune in to follow the pictures sold, to watch the prices ascending on the ticker behind Julian.

Many of the punters are quieter now, whispering if they talk at all. There is an anxiety in the air that is not unwelcome. People do not come to this room solely to acquire artworks, but also for the chase, the outmaneuvering of others, the zero-sum game.

Julian enters the hall through a door behind the block, and the hum of the crowd falls away completely.

Martin spots Marina in the middle of the rows of chairs. She sits straight, Gorelov next to her. Gorelov lifts up and examines his paddle very carefully. There is a resoluteness about the man that is compelling. Marina seems to watch him from the corner of her eye.

JULIAN REACHES the block, takes out some notes from a leather satchel, places them down. He takes his time. He is careful, performing already. It is not easy for a salesman to bear himself completely without apology. Julian's first remarks are firm, steady. Martin is a believer in atmosphere, in small actions that make or destroy a night, and he already feels that this night is going well. Julian indicates the first lot on the right wall of the auction room, which is a Christopher Wool work on paper: a smaller offering to draw the room in. The word *spokesman* is spelled out in stenciled letters, broken, running across three lines, chopped into arresting incoherence. Julian sets off the bidding at £300,000, raises the price in increments of £50,000. His gaze is steady and concentrated. The number appears on the projector screen to his right, beneath it other currencies—the dollar, the euro, the yen, the renminbi, and the ruble—churning along.

Every auctioneer is a self-caricature at the block, and in front of the room Julian is erudite, impatient, and slightly blunt. "Are you bidding, or are you not bidding?" he says to Henry, as Henry's phone bidder seems to hesitate. He looks over his glasses at the room. He sends his arms out ahead of him to acknowledge bids from the floor, like a man swimming a slow front crawl. He takes the piece easily above its reserve.

The Wool sells to a phone bidder represented by Ella, the Chinese market specialist, who is working three phones from the middle of the desk.

A Hockney watercolor comes and goes, a small Warhol painting of a dollar sign, a Wade Guyton, a Jeff Wall photograph. Some punters hold catalogues on their knees, noting down the price of each lot as it sells. It's good sport to predict the realized prices. Martin himself has played this game as an observer, enjoyed the brief sensation of omniscience born of seeing a piece go for what he'd guessed.

MARTIN CALLS his client before the Twombly sketch is on the block. The man who picks up the phone has an American accent. He is inside a vehicle. Martin hears shaking metal, the rumble of tires on a road.

Martin clarifies the sum the man is prepared to pay. He waits for the previous lot, the Ed Ruscha, to finish. Philpot has his arm up in the middle of the room, but the price churns up ceaselessly until the lot is fought only between Ella's client and Beaufort. They swap the leading bid until, at £1.5 million, the dealer slumps back into his chair and the hammer comes down on Ella's offer.

There is a murmur in the room. The auction is surpassing expectations, a sense rising in those present that this could be a significant night, the kind of sale noted in the popular press tomorrow.

When the Twombly starts, Martin can't get in a single bid before it is beyond his client's maximum. The action in the hall is so quick. He asks if the man wants to raise his offer, but the lot is rising further away from them as Martin is posing the question. He makes his apologies as the price passes half a million.

Ella takes the Twombly, and then three of the next five pieces. In intervals between the lots, punters on the floor lean together, speculating as to the identity of the client she is working for, trying to find a line of taste in the pieces bought. They are blue-chip works, hard to gauge a particular sensibility from. Perhaps it is just an art investment fund, the acquisitions made upon the advice of a few experts, money buying money. Even in this, though, there is some conflicted excitement on the part of the art community, as in a village at which mining prospectors have arrived, confirming suspicions the locals have long held about the unique value of their land.

THE ELEVENTH lot—a small, uncharacteristic Anselm Kiefer— doesn't sell. Julian doesn't push it, however, but lets it go, placing the hammer down quietly on its side. The room gains more energy from this, if anything. The next lot goes for more than its high estimate.

Martin calls the client again. Something goes wrong in the middle of the process. "The number you have dialed has not been recognized," says the message. In the desire to not have the man waiting on the line, Martin has left the call later than he should have. On the second attempt, the phone rings eight times before the client answers. Martin, flustered, explains that lot fifteen is about to begin.

"Yes, yes," says the man.

Julian is drawing clients through the bidding on item fourteen, and already the pace of that sale has tailed off.

The item Martin is to bid on is an Anish Kapoor sculpture: a giant metal disc, like a satellite dish, that is to be hung on the wall. It is buffed to a mirrored finish, the surface divided into inch-wide octagons, which break any reflection that falls upon it to incoherence, like a pixelated image. It is a fantastic piece, Martin thinks: double in the way of great works. The object and the image that object creates. The play of them both. A thing that cannot be examined without meeting one's own reflection.

The previous lot is finished. A pause as the room absorbs this, a rising giddiness out there. "How much would you like to bid?" says Martin.

"This thing will appreciate, right?" says the man.

Martin hedges: "I wouldn't like to speculate. But this is a blue-chip work, from a blue-chip artist. He is represented in major museums, famous collections—"

"He did the twisty sculpture for the London Olympics?"

"Yes."

A picture of the Kapoor looms upon the screen, like a cold planet.

"What is that called, that Olympics sculpture?"

"The *ArcelorMittal Orbit*, I believe."

"Right."

"I will start the bidding at five hundred thousand pounds," says Julian.

"Go to two and a half," says the man.

Julian begins. He moves in increments of £50,000.

Beaufort is bidding. Martin looks to his left to see Ella talking earnestly into her phone, her right hand twitching at her side. Bids come through from the Internet. Martin gets his hand up at £1.1 million, holds it for a moment.

The leading bid is taken back by a man in the middle of the room. Martin has never bid more than a million on anyone's behalf. He talks rapidly into the receiver, describing the progress of the sale.

At £1.8 million, Julian takes another of Martin's bids.

It is important for experts to know their place, to facilitate, to advise humbly. There are paintings that come through the storerooms again and again, stamped with the house's brand from previous sales, and it is tempting to feel that some acquisitions are wasted on their buyers, valued more by those who sell them, those who've known them over decades. Though covetousness in an expert is never befitting. This is a point held to with pride by Martin's superiors. Yet putting his hand up at £2.2 million, Martin senses that whatever their denials, his bosses must sometimes feel, as he does now, an illicit thrill to take part in an acquisition, to join in the lavish, potlatch spectacle.

He holds the top bid for a time. Julian looks around. "Do I have two-point-three?"

A paddle goes up, eventually, in the middle of the room. Then another, behind that. It's Gorelov. He raises his paddle in the air patiently. Marina tracks her husband's movement with a very slight turn of her head: a complicated spousal glance, Martin thinks. He loses himself for a moment, is brought back by Julian saying, "Two-point-five? Two million, five hundred thousand?"

Martin puts up his hand, says, "Yes."

Julian turns. "Martin. I have two-point-five from Martin."

"We have it at two-point-five," says Martin to the man on the phone.

Meanwhile, Julian waits on £2.6 million, gets it from Gorelov.

"Do you want to raise your maximum?" Martin says.

Julian is looking at Martin.

Martin gestures to show that he is awaiting an answer. Julian takes the hint, makes some remarks about the Kapoor to the crowd.

"Two-point-seven," says the client on the phone.

"Yes," says Martin. He raises a hand.

The woman in the front row takes two-point-eight.

"Do you want to bid two-point-nine?" says Martin into the receiver.

"I need to check something," says the client. There is a buzz, the rustle of movement. *Don't cut out,* Martin thinks. He feels the eyes of the room on him. He realizes that he is no longer nervous.

"This is a wonderful piece in the artist's catalogue," says Julian to the room, stalling.

Another rustling on the end of the line. "Okay," says the man.

"Two-point-nine," says Martin firmly. Julian smiles.

"Three million?" says Julian. The woman shakes her head. Julian looks around the room.

Gorelov has not bid again, and for a moment, ascertaining this, Martin's eye catches the gaze of Marina, who along with much of the room has been watching him. The telephone receiver is damp with the sweat of Martin's hand. Julian points at him, strikes the gavel off the block. The picture of the item disappears from the screen.

Just like that—£2.9 million. Martin imagines it all physicalized, the sheer ridiculous extent: the oily tang of notes, the grub of so much currency. He feels he can taste it in his mouth.

"You won," Martin says to the client. "Congratulations." His voice is not quite his own.

"Great."

"It is a fantastic sculpture," says Martin.

"Yes," the client says. "Yes. Yes."

"It's a great work," says Martin again.

"Yes."

Martin cannot take the client with him in his enthusiasm. *Don't force it,* he thinks. He consults his notes. Reads through the formalities to be worked out when the auction has concluded. He puts down the phone. He is giddy. He feels the energy of the room to have been raised further. The punters look alert, even this far into the sale. They watch Julian like children at a puppet show.

THE HEADLINE lot of the night is a Basquiat, titled *Hannibal*. The canvas is painted orange, drawn across a spiky homemade stretcher, motifs and words scratched over it, overlapping. In the bottom right corner, a skull-like head stands out, highlighted in blue. In the top left is Basquiat's signature crown.

There is all sorts of high-flown analysis in the catalogue, as Martin knows, having assisted Julian in his drafting of the text. You could look at it and talk of Picasso, and African art, and the early graffiti scene of New York City. Yet that would miss the main fact, which is that it is, as Julian said, examining the picture for the first time in the storeroom, "a fucking great painting." It is luminous and raw, a picture that creates its own terms of success, that invents itself before you.

Martin knows, as the porters carry the painting up to the block, gripping it with their white gloves, that it is going to sell well.

And it does. It starts at £3 million, and breaks the high estimate of £4.5 million easily. Julian raises the bids in increments with which one could buy a house. Martin looks at the painting, and back to his boss, who is tracking the movement of the crowd before him, reaching out a hand to acknowledge a bid, closing his fingers and drawing back.

The picture makes five and then six, and still the bids show no sign of slowing. Gorelov and another man are going for it in the middle of the hall, and a third person bids through Ella's phone line.

That this should be a thing of such value is thrilling to Martin: this artifact of a lost New York, this piece of wounded weirdness. Martin's mother would call the success of this picture tokenistic. She'd say that the work represents nothing more to these people than any other luxury good. And yet, Martin has met clients such as these, knows them at least to be skeptical when it comes to claims of value. And this homemade bundle of sticks and canvas, acrylic paint and scraps of paper has what value? What value beyond what the conjunction of these items presumes to do? Which is—excuse Martin for being too sincere—to tell a tale about what it is like to be a human being.

The price passes £7 million.

Ella is calling out more loudly, speaking sharply into the phone, snapping a finger to indicate a bid. There is a sense out on the floor that the auction is justifying itself, Martin thinks, that there is nowhere in the city that it would be better to be tonight.

The fact is that Martin never stopped believing any of the truths of his parents, but just wearied. Wearied of recycling, and boycotting Nestlé, and hoping that one day the British public would turn against a cynical tabloid culture. He got tired of losing, of the sense that integrity inhered in standing outside an important building with a placard and a flask of tea.

And yet there are places in the culture where humanity is celebrated. Where the complexity and strangeness of life is acknowledged. These works challenge. These works may be understood only in snatches. They solve nothing, maybe. But they exist. They speak of other worlds, of life on other terms. Ella snaps her fingers again, and in the middle of the room Gorelov slowly raises his hand. Martin imagines his mother's response to all this. "It's a feeding frenzy," he can almost hear her saying. Within himself, he tells her that this is the market trying to understand its limits. "This hysteria?" he imagines his mother asking, exasperated. *Yes*, he thinks. *This is money confronted by something beyond itself.* Would she prefer the market to never be confounded?

Julian acknowledges Gorelov's bid, grasping the air, drawing his closed fist back toward him. Ella snaps her fingers. The man raises his heavy arm again.

The picture goes past £8.5 million. The bids, slowing now, push it toward nine. Julian is delivering his patter with a wryness. He doesn't disguise his surprise, his sense that such resolve on the part of the bidders is a little ridiculous. Nor does he disguise his pleasure in it, though. *You'll regret this tomorrow*, his smile seems to say, and that is, of course, perfect, because what surer sign is there that you are having a good time? He draws his hand down from the air, points it to a dealer in the fourth row from the front. He draws the other hand up, the finger already pointed. He is looking out for the next bid, holding an upraised finger in the air in front of him, ready to bring it down above Gorelov, as if he knows the oligarch's thoughts before Gorelov himself does. It comes refreshed to Martin as he watches: this is what he wants to do. He wants to stand up there and do that.

Marina looks at her husband. He sits there solidly.

Julian waits, his finger still raised, smiling. Something about that smile makes the crowd laugh, giddied and euphoric.

The man's hand comes up.

2

OUTSIDE THE auction house, the street is quiet. They stayed late, settling the business of the picture, and now Oleg feels he is emerging onto a different pavement from the one he alighted to three hours previously. The boutique next door to the auction house is dark, an alarm system blinking within, behind the shadowed profiles of mannequins. The traffic on the road is sparse: a couple of taxis, a white van. Down the road a handful of people are traversing the pedestrian crossing, shouting back to someone following them. The bars and clubs and fancy restaurants are not far away from here. Oleg has spent enough time in this part of the city late at night, though his desire for all that is limited these days. His stomach doesn't feel totally right tonight. Quiet streets always unnerve him, the stillness seeming like a prelude to drama. He glances around to locate Marina, who has been talking to a girl from school whom she bumped into on her way out of the auction hall. Nearby, Victor has started up the car in anticipation of their departure. This area, with its designer clothes shops, was the hunting ground of Katya, Oleg's ex-wife. He accompanied her occasionally then, when this was all new, when there was some pleasure to be had in taking out his card, working to shock those shop assistants, forcing through sheer excess a change in their pinched expressions.

He steps a pace toward Marina, reneges on his internal vow of patience. She gives him a glance that says, *Just one moment.* She puts an arm out to grasp the elbow of the woman she is talking to, beginning a complex choreography of good-byes.

•   •   •

IN THE car, after they have set off, Marina says, "We're going where?"

"Home," he says. "Of course."

"In times past, you would want to go out after this," she says, "to lavishly celebrate your new picture." Her Russian can still be jarringly antique, even now: that of the old novels she read as a teenager.

"And you would have liked that?" Sometimes he feels that his slowing down is infuriating her, as if his abandonment of old habits has left her nothing to push against.

She says nothing. She leans toward the window. Streetlights play into the vehicle. Her hands in her lap clasp and unclasp.

They've barely moved since they set off: they crawl through traffic just yards from the auction house. He could walk home quicker than this. He speaks in a raised voice: "Is the horn broken?" Victor's eyes in the mirror meet his own. An apology, then, and the horn. A surprised pedestrian steps back as she waits at the crossing. He feels the heat of Marina's glare on the side of his face.

They move unsteadily northwest, across Oxford Street, pedestrians peering at the tinted windows of the car as they creep by. He reaches a hand to the back of his collar and massages his own neck. He moves his head sideways and something clicks horribly. Marina looks up from scrolling her phone and says, "Ruslan is dead."

"Dead?" he says.

"Heart attack, it says."

"Oh."

She's watching him carefully. "You think . . . ?"

"I don't know."

Ruslan was another expat Russian, who made his fortune in car dealerships. A bad industry, which Oleg steered clear of. The man had enemies, of course. Yet it's a surprise. Oleg saw Ruslan at some charity event only a couple of months ago. Oleg speaks firmly, trying to convince himself: "It can happen at his age, a heart attack."

"Of course," Marina says.

"The simple answer is the best, no?" Oleg recalls a vague rumor from a year back that the man was winding people up in Moscow, not quite playing the game. Still, this would be a lot. This would be an intensification.

Marina is still looking at him. "Are you sure?" she says. "It seems suspicious."

He says, "People die all the time for ordinary reasons."

Marina watches him warily.

"Anyway," he says, "I take precautions. You know this. I take my medicine when I'm told to."

AT THE house, Marina gets out. Victor opens the other door for Oleg. She is starting toward the steps already.

"I'll go to the country house," he says as he emerges from the car. "It's quieter there. Perhaps I will sleep." Also, he thinks, the city makes him uneasy tonight.

She looks back at him, and he catches it: a moment of relief on her part. He doesn't begrudge her this, though it saddens him. She is doing her best to look concerned, though she doesn't move back toward him. "If you really think it'll help," she says.

"I do," he snaps. "That's why I say it." He climbs back into the vehicle. He wonders at that impulse in him to sour things so readily.

"The world keeps on running happily when you sleep," she says. "Remember that. Okay?" It is a sharp little joke, and the reciprocity of it relieves him.

He nods. Victor closes the door behind him. Carla, the housekeeper, greets Marina at the threshold, silhouetted by the warm light of the hall. Oleg experiences a twinge of doubt. Perhaps he should stay. Yet Victor has started to drive. The windows of the homes in the square are predominantly dark. They negotiate the tight streets, passing showrooms, closed-up restaurants.

In the outskirts of London, Oleg thinks of Ruslan, imagines the
man falling facedown in a gaudy living room. He was that kind of
man, Ruslan. Bad teeth. Never got them fixed, however much money
he made. He was a big fan of prostitutes, lived like it was still 1995,
as far as Oleg could tell. He was heedless, incautious, and whether it
was his health or his political judgment that failed him, it all amounts
to the same thing, Oleg thinks. Yes. A particular case, he tells himself.
No need to brood on it tonight. This evening was a success. He thinks
of his picture. The price. Did he get carried away? He recalls talking to the auctioneer afterward; the man's congratulations were delivered as if Oleg had actually achieved something, as if in exceeding the
high valuation of the picture he had exhibited truly superlative taste.
A funny man, whose politeness seems to have some structure behind
it, some game of his that he is inflicting. He wore a Breguet—vintage,
sixties, of a value clear only to those who know about such things.

They pass down a short high street, all of the shops closed but for a
minicab business where two fat men sit in padded chairs, backlit, looking out of the window, watching vehicles pass. He thinks of his father.
The impatient waiting of unlucky men.

Still, the Basquiat *is* marvelous. He's not insensitive to that. Such
fucking energy. Young man's energy. He's buying it, of course, because he no longer has such energy himself. Yet who—in these days
of eternal weariness, of pausing on the staircase to catch his breath, of
kneading at his flaccid dick—who could begrudge him that?

They are speeding up again now. Out in the countryside. Hedges.
Trees overhanging the tarmac. Some leaves fallen onto the road,
squashed down by tires. Autumn held off for now, but ready to come
down like a curtain.

They are chasing him these days, the auction people. The dealers
also try so hard to talk to him. Still, he will not forget that snootiness
he first encountered. He never got a decent deal from those who did
private sales, and yet on the auction floor he could always buy what he
wanted. A thin victory, perhaps, but a victory nonetheless. With those

first acquisitions he played into their perception of him, used what he had—his money—and made himself vulgar for them. And yet here is the thing about cash: people *want* it. The man thought to be greedy is supposed only to hold a fault common to all. Yes, he is acquisitive, but so is everyone else. His money, his barbaric money, keeps this world running as it does.

He moves his head closer to the window and looks up. The moon is thin tonight, the sky very dark. *Fuck them,* he thinks. What does he care what they thought of him then, what they think of him now?

Victor's eyes meet his in the mirror: checking on him. A large truck comes by the other way, taking a shortcut on this smaller road, delivering some essential to the city for tomorrow morning: bread or fruit or dairy. The car sways a little with the air pounded toward it by the larger vehicle.

Marina is probably in bed now. She liked the picture. She said nothing about the price, did not look at him as she did when he bought that kitsch Murakami sculpture. That means something. Even if she is unbearable sometimes, she is acute. Acuity is her primary virtue and fault. Her work each day is making up lies and exaggerations for her employer, and yet at home she batters him with her relentless truths.

The picture is wonderful, he tells himself. There is nothing more to be said about it. The road is like a tunnel now: tall hedges by the sides, just the headlights tracing the tarmac. He leaves his concern about the money he spent right there, on the anonymous lane. The picture is great. The right choice. The right direction. The picture is just what he needs.

3

MARTIN LEAVES the house late, delayed by the usual postauction things—the press releases, the tying up of business, the glad-handing of clients.

He walks along quiet pavements to Bond Street station. He arrives down at the platform just as his train pulls in, breaks into the funny half-run one does to hurry in a city. He gets into the carriage before the doors close behind him and the train moves, the station stuttering and blurring and then darkness and the faintest glimpse of the wires running along the walls of the tunnel, going up and down like a sound wave.

AT HOME, Martin kicks the door where it jams against the warped doorframe. The flat is a basement, christened Château Shin by James in honor of the legs they see striding by the front window.

James is on the sofa, a Penguin classic and a glass of wine on the coffee table in front of him, his laptop open on his knees. Martin can smell a hint of smoke in the air, though it's agreed between them that James should smoke outside. Martin decides not to mention this. James puts his laptop on the table, lies back, looks at Martin standing in the doorway.

"Congratulations," James says.

"Thanks," says Martin. "You followed it?"

James nods.

"Crazy, eh?"

"I was thinking of going to the pub to watch," says James, "but I found a couple of decent online streams."

Martin suffers a second's confusion before realizing that his friend is talking not about the auction but about the midweek football and their fantasy teams. He tries to mask his curtailed satisfaction at James's unlikely interest in his work. "How many points did I get?" he says.

"You destroyed me," says James. "Even John Terry got a goal."

James and Martin grew up together. James lived next door in the big house. He's one of the people for whom Martin's childhood needs no explanation. They could talk about that—about the gardens, the neighbors, the suspicion with which the other kids at school viewed them—but they do not. They talk about football, their liking for which is doubtless part compensation for the strangeness of their background.

"How was work?" says Martin.

James shrugs without taking his eyes from the screen. He plays the piano by the hour. For the past week he's been playing in Westfield Mall, in the window of the Burberry store. "The shop manager asked if I could play 'something like James Bond music,'" he says. "What the fuck is 'James Bond music'?"

"I have no clue," says Martin.

"It's a good commute," says James. "I suppose."

He still wears his dinner jacket from his day's playing, the bow tie off, the buttons of his shirt undone. Because of work, it's James's most common outfit. The suit has acquired an oily sheen through persistent use. James's contention is that it has begun to wash itself, "like hair does."

Martin goes into the kitchen. There is a jumble of dishes in the sink. He opens the fridge and inventories: some shriveled tomatoes; a jar of peanut butter; a bottle of ketchup, emptied but replaced in the refrigerator for some reason; a tiny jar of anchovies, the salt scum around the top gray.

"Have you eaten?" he calls.

"No."

"Are you hungry?"

James pauses, as if the possibility has only then occurred to him, as if he must consult within himself. "Yes," he says slowly. "Pretty hungry." James's skinniness is more a product of omission than restraint. He will eat ravenously when he does eat, but between those times he'll skip meals for want of the motivation to feed himself.

"I'm going to go and get something," says Martin. "You want to come?"

"Give me a minute to get dressed down."

At Huntley Hall, the sound of James's piano leaked through the gaps in the stonework and the blocked-up doorways between their homes for three hours each night. They'd play football on the lawn together before James's parents got home. Then James got his scholarship and went to boarding school and Martin would only see him in the summer holidays and the odd weekend when James didn't have a recital. James came back home for his last year of school. Things weren't going well at Millfield. A freak-out. A friend's suicide. At the local comprehensive school in town, which Martin had attended all the while, no one knew what to make of James: a wan, solitary kid, with no embarrassment about that solitude. He smoked roll-ups already. He sat on the steps outside the gym and read Merleau-Ponty. He seldom spoke in class, not for lacking the confidence to do so, because he could talk to adults as one of them, but out of a cool indifference which even the teachers chose not to challenge.

The book on the cup-ringed coffee table is a tattered anthology. *The New Poetry*. For such a regular reader, James returns to the same books so often. A limited circulation. A nest made of things close to hand. James comes out of his room, throws his keys into the air but fails to catch them, kicks them across the carpet, and then picks them up again as he follows Martin out the door.

In the last months before they left school, James rallied academically, became again the boy to whom Martin had been compared unfavorably by his mother. He stayed behind after classes to talk to teachers. He sat in the library through lunch. He got an offer of a university place at York, as Martin happened to also, and then, come summer, he got three As in his A-levels. When he collected his exam results, teachers asked him whether he shouldn't revise his aspirations, take a gap year and a shot at Oxbridge. He grinned and refused. The other way James seemed grown-up was that he had a serious girlfriend. Marina came to visit Huntley Hall that summer: a slender Russian girl, who walked confidently, and like James talked easily to adults, and seemed to enjoy her visit. She helped in the garden. She and James took long walks. Martin asked her, shyly, what she was doing next year, and her answer explained James's grin when he picked up that envelope of his A-level grades. "The same as you," she said. "Going to York."

They eat in a Turkish place. The restaurant is a standard after-hours stop, a location for banter and loudness and pub business unfinished, but for now it's quiet. The men behind the counter work slowly, sawing slivers from the rotating elephant legs of kebab meat, preparing for the rush. Martin and James sit at a table in the window. James eats a kebab with a knife and fork, some contrariness in the care with which he goes about it. Martin lifts his own pita, and the thing crumples. A rivulet of grease and garlic sauce flows across his palm, begins to make its way down his wrist. He puts the mess down, sets to work plucking napkins from the dispenser, cleaning his hands.

"You remember Istanbul Grill?" says Martin.

"Sure," says James.

"We went there, like, three times a week when we were students."

"Yes."

Martin has been letting himself talk, thinking only glancingly of his aim, which, he now reflects, is what? To lead the conversation to Marina, he supposes. To approach the subject softly.

James knows she is married to a rich Russian man now, knows, presumably, that her husband collects art and so might cross Martin's path. Yet they haven't discussed this, and it feels daunting now to speak of it.

"It's funny," says Martin. "Tonight, at the auction . . ."

James's expression changes. He looks suddenly and unguardedly severe. Does he anticipate what Martin will say? He's been hunched over his meal, but he draws himself up now. He exhales heavily through his nose. Martin has paused, and his friend now prompts him: "At the auction?"

Martin can't do it. Not now, at least. He says, "A Basquiat painting went for ten million."

"Right."

"It's just funny that people spend that kind of money."

"Yes," says James. He raises his eyebrows to assent. Martin feels relief, though it's wounding that James accepts this invented banality as something Martin might have wanted to exclaim over.

JAMES TAKES out a roll-up when they're outside, gets out his lighter. He takes a prolonged look at Martin. There's a wind on the street now. The hiss of the Westway in the distance. He holds his cigarette with his thumb and forefinger, the rest of his hand shielded around it. His hair is blowing around as he hunches into the task. What would Marina think? Martin wonders. James has been the same for so many years now, but for the smallest signs of aging: his hair retreating above his temples a little, his face pinching a bit, a tiredness around the eyes. Contemplating him now, Martin wonders whether this aging doesn't change some crucial aspect of his look, however; whether the scruffiness, the apparent indifference to clothes, which previously served to underline James's handsomeness, has now flattened into nothing more than dishevelment. The cigarette catches. James pulls on it. He straightens. He blows out smoke. "Let's do things backwards," he says.

"Backwards?" says Martin.

"A kebab and then a pint."

"I'm working tomorrow," says Martin.

"Of course," says James. "If you're going to have a hangover, why not get paid while you're having it?"

"A pint, you said. Who said anything about a hangover?"

James shrugs. "It's a good night for you. Your place sold all of those pictures." He drags hard on the cigarette again. "You need to enjoy it."

Martin looks at his friend. "Okay," he says.

The night eats itself then, as James seems to wish it to. Martin doesn't deny him this. James can be infuriating, but the thing Martin always credits him with is a sincerity, a neediness that churns along beneath all of James's playacting and manners.

They spend a little over an hour squashed into the pub, drinking lagers and then whiskies. James, voluble, emphatic: chafing at the edge of what those around them will tolerate. His is an earnestness that reads, sometimes, like irony. His conversation tends to drift toward a cleverness that puts people on edge. James rolls a cigarette and puts it behind his ear. He rolls another, and then another.

The two of them walk to a different place, which is closing up as they arrive. They go back to the first bar, which in their absence has ceased to admit people and is beginning to shut down. James remonstrates with the bouncer, mentions Wittgenstein for no apparent reason. Then they are back on the street, tramping home, James stopping to examine a bookcase that someone has left out on the curb.

The flat, then. The sticky door. A smell of dampness, of earth, ever present in these basements, gouged beneath the shallow foundations of the Edwardian grid. The sofa with its linen throw over it. The lamp with its wonky shade. The chipboard Ikea coffee table.

James and Martin were living together when James's relationship with Marina fell apart. It was the third year of university. They lived in a two-bedroom flat in a terraced house divided into three. It happened early in the year, and Martin remembers standing in the kitchen feeling a new light thrown on everything around him. Martin never felt that he could tease out the specifics of the breakup. A mutual friend

said that Marina had gotten together with someone else, but that had
never seemed a likely explanation. Marina and James were wearyingly
proud of their frankness, and infidelity seemed to Martin more likely
to be a consequence than a cause of their breakup. At the time, he
could sense the view of the apartment altering through James's eyes.
No more Marina sitting at the table in the early evening. A coconut
shampoo removed from the bathroom. An electric heater—bought because she felt the cold—now an artifact of a particular kind of winter
that wouldn't come.

James stopped playing. Martin no longer witnessed that strange
morning sight: James in the living room hunched over his digital piano,
insect-like, all elbows and shoulders, headphones on, and pressing into
the keys with such vigor that the keyboard, though transmitting only
through the headphones, still creaked and clicked and shuddered with
a peculiar and sometimes pleasing rhythm.

"It was a vehicle," James said when he stopped. He'd played the
past years to get him through university, he said, and because it was expected by Marina. In his accounting, he reverted to an adolescent gran-
diosity of the kind that a few years before had so impressed Martin:
he'd known at seventeen that he wasn't going to make it, James said,
and so he'd merely gone through the motions after that. There was no-
bility still, he argued, in making up the numbers, being the background
to those who would be truly great. After Marina broke with him, he
pushed the piano into the corner of the room, behind the door. He
did just enough that year (or perhaps little enough, because Martin
suspected there was some pride in his decline) to scrape a third-class
degree.

James sits heavily on the sofa, his eyes drunk. He looks at the coffee table in front of him. "That's the best-selling item of furniture of
all time," he says, indicating the table. "There have been more feet on
this type of table than any in history. Think where it's been." He waves
his hands. "It's been in palaces, prisons, murder scenes. You want to
sell something significant at your auction house? This is significant."

"We look for a different kind of significance," says Martin.

"Scarcity," says James. "I know. Scarcity. Originality. A vanguard form."

He scratches the side of his head, and in doing so dislodges a cigarette from behind his ear, which tumbles onto the sofa and which he regards for a slow second and then picks up, inordinately satisfied, and lights.

4

SHE WAKES before the light, the bed to herself. There's a delayed quality to her thought. She remembers that Oleg went on to the country house, considers the solemn way he announced this: the weary prince in exile from his kingdom. She lies still for a moment. She had wine last night, at dinner and then before the auction. She feels that in a hint of grogginess. She looks around the room as her eyes adjust to the glow of the bedside lamp. She prefers the calm of this London house, particularly the upper floors, where the designers have had less of an impact. The bed is nude wood, the desk and the wardrobe matching. The alarm goes again. She pivots, puts a foot down to the white-painted floorboards.

There is no moon visible when she parts the curtains, no hint yet of the dawn. A drizzle darkens the pavement under the streetlights. A taxi idles as it drops someone outside the house two doors down. At a party years before, some bore said that the square is the most haunted in London. Oleg likes this idea, has repeated it to those who have visited since. The haunters are apparently serial: a ghostly horseman, a maid who drowned herself in grief, a couple of murdered children (always some murdered children in these tales). Her husband often passes on these stories with relish. He is a resolute materialist, but even more so he is a man who does not doubt his own logic, who doesn't worry about self-contradiction.

As she descends to the kitchen, she thinks of his picture, of the auction last night, and of the surprise of meeting Martin there in that warm, close room. She was pleased by it, she realized. She felt, what? A presence to a version of herself she had forgotten. He was a respite from the dealers and acquaintances swarming her husband. At such events she's more than once been called Katya, mistaken for her husband's previous wife.

When the car comes to the curb, there is a bluish softening to the night sky. The streets are quiet now: a few delivery vans out, cabs, shift workers hurrying home.

Seated in the back of the vehicle, she takes out a tablet and reads e-mails. Most are queries that may be answered thoughtlessly. She taps at the screen and thinks idly as she does so of the Basquiat. It's a picture she would linger over in a museum, though considering it in their home disquiets her. There is too much life in it. It's too vivid a thing to buy and lock away. Oleg will still be sleeping now, if he has actually made it to sleep. It was a pleasure last night to be alone and not to have to witness his insomnia. She can't cope with these newly itchy days, this diminished masculinity of his. Certainly, there were times before when he was too full of himself, a little out of control. "He wants to be the best man at every wedding," a friend of his once told her. Now, though, she would struggle to get him out to a wedding. He's paranoid. He is becoming a man of strange and unpredictable impulses, a seeker of something he can't articulate. There is a thirsty way that he looks in his unguarded moments that kindles an unreasonable sense of dread in her.

The car rolls past St. Pancras station. Commuters are just starting to mass. A homeless man walks across the road dragging a filthy beige sleeping bag. There is light breaking into the streets now. Gulls on a quiet side street fight over some food left behind from the night before. The driver beeps a white van pulling into the lane ahead. The drizzle has stopped. When they come to the Old Street roundabout, they turn toward the City.

She works for a financial services firm: one of those large companies that people recognize only as something they don't really know about. Familiar names that furnish the world, that connote little. She rises before dawn each day to make money she doesn't really need.

She's not unaware that this situation is ridiculous, though talking of needing the money, of the necessity of the work, is also to miss part of the point. Strictly, no one she works with needs all the money. The money is just a sign of the firm's purpose, its centrality to events.

In actuality, she is often surprised at the approval with which people greet her income. They like the children of the wealthy to earn for themselves. Further acquisition signals seriousness, she thinks, some attentiveness to the value of all they already have. And yet, what of all this extra cash piling into her well-filled bank account? What of such obscene consolidation of resources? Sometimes she speculates a further logic at play: the collective wish for a contingent state to be a law of the world. Do people believe that a talent for profit-making is woven through her chromosomes? If so, it is an unpleasant model of events that obscures an even worse one: that she was simply lucky, has continued to be lucky; that it has all fallen on her like a pile of bricks.

Her mother tuts and rolls her eyes at those children of other émigrés who occupy themselves with fashionable parties and unprofitable vanity businesses. "All they have," she says, more Russian than usual in these moments, "and what they choose to do is this?"

Marina feels differently. Their mothers and fathers have sweated and connived to get them so much, and what seems odd is to push on, to still want more.

IT'S ASFAL working at the security desk today. There is a giant artwork hung from the high beams of the atrium: a cascade of bottle tops woven together into a colorful sheet, perpetually falling in calculated ripples and billows. Asfal seems always to await its crashing down around him with an expression of laconic resignation. The artist is West African. Marina wrote a press release about him. This was his biggest piece at the time of its unveiling.

"Early," says Asfal. "Even for you." He rubs his jowls. He hacks a phlegmy cough.

"I get things done like this," she says. "No distractions."

"Not a people person," he says. "I get it. There's a limit. I do the night shift for a reason."

"People are fine," she says.

"Of course," he says. "So are penguins. I love penguins. Do I go to the zoo every day though?"

HER FLOOR—the twentieth—is empty when she emerges from the elevator. Beyond the green glass, the city spreads beneath: tiles, vents, balconies, roof gardens, streets grooved through the blocks of architecture with the logic of ages past, the river shining like molten metal in the dawn. She walks to her terminal. She inputs her passwords and waits for the computer to wake. Her department within the company is communications. She tells the story of people's money. She dislikes the framing of her work, the sense that what she does merely supplements the trading activities of the firm. The truth is that her work is the central activity of the firm at large, whether management concedes it or not. The company itself is a story spun on a massive scale. Soon the cubicles around her will fill with men and women who do economics, science, prediction, analytics; who think their work objective, self-propelling. They'll consider the African markets, the recent dry weather in the east, the pension liabilities of certain large American retailers. They'll consider the effect of changes within the House of Saud on the short-term price of crude. They are working so diligently on a picture of the future, not reflecting on the fact that their picture only has value as far as it convinces others: the markets, the hobbyist stock-pickers, the hemorrhoidal men sipping coffee and aware of business op-ed deadlines. Their expertise is valuable if it is believed to be.

The company's CEO wakes at 3:30 a.m. This is widely known,

important. The firm has algorithms, fields of computer processing centers in the west of America. They profile risk, predict opportunities. They're telling stories to themselves, and Marina just carries these stories to the rest of the world. The placement of the data centers is optimized for environmental stability, ease of maintenance, energy costs. Each choice is gridded logically into the system. They are seeking a perfect model of the future, while knowing that the only perfect model of the future is the future itself. The company's aims are immodest. When she describes the firm, she plays to that part of people that wants to be dominated, that dreams of a tyrant working on their behalf.

People trickle into the office slowly. The noise rises. Phones ring. The patter of keyboards builds into ambience. People exchange greetings with Marina as they pass her workstation. Some here are scared of her, she suspects. Her work rate, her firm way of being, gives rise to wariness, if not also admiration. This used to bother her, but she's come to accept it. She doesn't ever eat in the office, doesn't linger making tea. Her husband has always modeled such self-containment. "At most you can control what others *do*," she recalls him saying. He was some Russian archetype in the moment, some blunt holy sage. He waved his hand in front of his face, gesturing. "What they *think*? Forget about it. Their thinking is not your problem."

"But what if they act on their thoughts?" she had said.

He'd scoffed. "Here is a secret: people very seldom do this."

What she liked in those early days of loving him was his resolve, his certainty about who he was and what he thought. And yet there was something playful in this: an understanding that it was, on some level, a game. "People know nothing," he said, "so I act as if I know it all." He had made himself a character with such earnestness that she had to credit him.

At nine-thirty, Lawrence arrives at Marina's desk brandishing some pages of catalogue proofs. They explain a new emerging market fund the company is starting. Accompanying the text is a glossy image of a busy Indian road: a silver Mercedes passing a line of rickshaws, crowds streaming from a station entrance, Western branding on the buildings in the distance, Hindi signs in the foreground, steam rising from street stalls. It is almost too obvious, which is usually a signal that it is pitched just right.

She runs her finger over the picture. When she was younger, she would have relished pulling apart such an image placed in such a context, uncovering the questionable assumptions and stereotypes inherent in this choice of photograph. Yet if she has learned anything since university, it is the limits of such reasoning.

The point is reaching the consumer's gut. The rising crowds of the unwashed other, thin men in weirdly cut suits, the possibility of all that desire and need.

"Isn't it rather good?" says Lawrence. "I really think that it's come out well." Lawrence is six foot four, a polite man of good breeding. He has a horsey manner: all restlessness and floppy hair. "Jackie thinks that it's a little too dirty. She doesn't like the pollution, the grubby signs."

Marina is studying the text, marking an awkward line break where the word *consistency* is broken with a hyphen. "Pictures of Switzerland are clean," she says. "European market presentations are clean. They are about stability, incremental progress. Emerging markets shouldn't be clean. This fund is for a different investor. The point is the edge, the potential. You go to trendy restaurants?"

"Sometimes."

"You want realness in those places, don't you? Food that has come from the earth. Meat that looks like something dead. You want to be pushed a little, to get away from the plebs who can't pronounce *nduja*. It's about openness to experience."

"Yes. I see," says Lawrence, though she isn't sure he does. Hearty enthusiasm, however, is one of his talents.

She gestures at the picture. "Tell Jackie that it's only just dirty enough."

5

MARTIN PASSES the morning with a hangover. The Tube carriage is quiet, prerush. He travels amongst some of the truly driven, and those compelled by their roles to be in before most—baristas and cleaners and maintenance men. Odors of deodorant and Red Bull mix in the carriage.

In the office, he sits at his terminal and tries to work on the catalogue for a forthcoming British Contemporary sale. He sips his coffee, looks out of the window, thinks of the night before, of Marina grasping his arm and exclaiming over time gone by. He types some words, erases them again. Eventually, people arrive around him. It's another clear autumn day, and he has been watching the light change as the morning sun creeps across the brickwork of the buildings on the opposite side of the street.

He hears Julian laughing from his office, speaking into the telephone. His boss has arrived buoyed by the success of the auction. In the kitchen, Henry is speaking even more volubly than usual.

At ten, Martin rises from his seat. He's making notes on a Chris Ofili, and he is tired of sitting in his imitation Aeron chair trying to conjure words about the painting. The sentences on his screen feel awkward. He decides to go to the storeroom. He heads for the hallway, ducks under the lintel, turns down the stairs.

The auction house offices are cramped up in the rafters of the building. This is the house at which typewriters were banned until after the Second World War. The sterility of modern offices can be left to newcomers to the business. The need to duck one's head on entry to the private rooms attests to nothing less than the venerability of the house. It hardly matters that the building used to be a telegraph exchange, a location to which the company only moved in the sixties. A lesson of the trade in that: the most convincing antiquity is often counterfeit.

He taps the storeroom keypad. The heavy door releases. Inside, he passes a couple of guys packaging up paintings sold last night. He moves toward the racks, locates the Chris Ofili picture that he's been writing about. He slides out the board to which it is attached with a sureness he has had to train himself in. Martin recalls his first week on the job, watching Henry pick up a Gwen John sketch, and feeling that the confidence with which his colleague held the picture attested to a childhood surrounded by beautiful and expensive things.

Propping up the picture and stepping back, he thinks of what he has been noting down: colors recalling Marcus Garvey's Pan-African flag, Black identity, a reimagining of the subjects of Gauguin and Picasso. It is all true, important to the description, but underpinning those things is the object itself. There is always, at base, a work. And if he is lucky, Martin can find his way back to that. The picture is as tall as he is. It's a collage in dyed and distressed leather. He can smell the faint tang of the hide, a note of adhesive behind that scent. Close to the picture, he can study creases in the surface, running in organic rivulets: the perfect inconsistency of living tissue. Three women, nude but for fig leaves, hold grapes to their mouths; dark air behind them, the moon above, a plant to their left rippling like kelp in a current, a hint of the shimmer of an early Bridget Riley. It's a dream picture, all varied density and shift. The sway of leaves. The tectonic grinding of all that dark blue behind the figures. It's detailed in gold leaf, giving the whole image a shivering precision.

They talk of having "an eye" in the business. An expert should recognize the range of an artist: the way a painter draws a line or lifts the brush from a canvas; their symbols and compositional logics. Yet Martin dislikes the notion of the eye. There's an insistence that it can't be taught, and this innatism strikes Martin as just the kind of aristocratic nonsense you would expect from an industry full of toffs. There are geniuses, certainly, with photographic memories and cognizance of minute details. They are not numerous, though, and beyond them are the others: those who are fluent in the right language, comfortable lifting up a picture and putting a price on the thing; who use the right terminology, and look and dress alike; and whose skills must only be regarded as congenital out of an aversion to the simpler explanation, that they were all born to the same station in the world.

AT NOON, Martin meets his mother for lunch. Waiting outside the house, he watches her amble up the pavement between the Mayfair shoppers. Despite the mild weather, she wears her waxed jacket and cords—more rural than anything she would have on at home. It must have been all she could bear, he thinks, to leave her wellies behind.

She'd be surprised, however, by how much she'd fit in at the auction house. She could easily be mistaken for a lady from a mothballed estate making a rare trip to town, a Victorian watercolor in hand for presentation at the front desk.

She works part-time as a school librarian, and today, on one of her days off, she has come up to the city to protest against the delay in the Iraq report. She is one of those Iraq people, still preoccupied with the injustices of 2003 beyond all others, absorbed, ten years later, with details once widely discussed and now forgotten: WMDs, the forty-five-minute claim, Hans Blix, and Resolution 1441.

He bends to embrace her. She smells of beeswax. She steps back, looks at him. "Smart," she says, a hint of wryness to temper the assessment.

"What shall we eat?" he says.

"Indian," she says. "Shall we go to the vegetarian buffet?" She likes a cheap Indian restaurant to the north of Euston Square.

"It's a taxi ride," says Martin.

"It's your lunch hour," she says. "Take an hour, for once."

Normally he would argue, but today the office is quiet after the sale. "I'll get an Uber," he says. His mother frowns a no, and turns to flag a taxi.

At their destination, she insists on paying the fare, which is about the same as lunch for both of them will cost.

They queue for the buffet with grad students, railway workers, and regulars from the British Library: men in corduroy suit jackets too big for them, with creased pieces of newspaper to read as they eat. There are posters extolling the benefits of vegetarianism on the walls.

"How's the house?" says Martin, when they are both sitting with plates of pulses and rice in front of them.

"Harvest time. I've been pulling up onions."

"Yes?"

"It's all well. We chug along."

"Good."

"The lime tree by the tithe barn had to come down." She wrinkles her nose. "Disease."

"That's a shame."

"Your father rethatched the round house."

"Good."

"The younger ones wouldn't be able to do that. They lack for skills." She digs a poppadum into a puddle of sag aloo. "How are you? Are you selling anything interesting?"

"As always," says Martin.

"Yes?"

His mother has good taste. She prefers a particular British color palette: that of half-warm summer days. She likes the St. Ives school. In the school holidays, she and Martin would come into London to go to the museums. He remembers the Tate Modern when it had just opened. The surprise of it, then. It was the kind of tasteful monument one didn't expect Britain to produce. He took a penny and rolled it down the ramp that led into the building. He recalls the shock of those busy yet quiet rooms, all that reverence new to a boy who had never been taken to church.

Something about the auction house hits her wrongly, however. She talks as if all Martin sells is Jeff Koons: a man who is, in her mind, the art world's Tony Blair. Martin has taken her into the storeroom and shown her pictures she has liked—an ecstatic Cecily Brown, all movement and color, for instance—but somehow she returns, outside those moments, to the idea that he flogs endless editions of *Balloon Dog*.

"Some good pictures," Martin says.

"Well, I'm glad."

"I'll send you the catalogue."

"Maybe I'll buy a few."

"Sure," he says.

"I'll have to find a few million quid," she says.

"Not all of them cost so much," he says. "But yes. They're not affordable for us."

"It's a bubble," she says.

"People see these pictures as investments now. It's true. Perhaps that's good, though. Isn't it better that people value creative work as well as gold?"

"It's our money fueling this," she says. "The people's money. Quantitative easing. Cheap credit. The banks have more cash than they know what to do with. This is where it's going."

"I'm sure you're right."

"I am."

"Didn't they need to do it to prop up the system?"

"This system? You want this system propped up?"

"I eat three meals a day. Maybe there are worse systems."

"I'll send you an article about it."

"What am I to do?" He sighs exaggeratedly. "Do I go back to work? Shall I call them from here and tell them I quit?"

"I'm discharging what I know," she says, laughing with him. She gives a faux-modest shrug. "That's all."

• • •

THEY PART outside Euston station. She stops near the entrance, and people stream around them. "You don't want to come?" she says.

"Come where?" he says.

"The protest," she says. "They're dragging their heels on the report. It's going to be a stitch-up."

"I have to work," says Martin.

"Five years, it's been, this inquiry," she says. "Eight million pounds. They're going to hide it away. It won't change a thing."

"Yes," he says, he agrees. But that is also why he will not be there, amongst the small crowd of scruffy baby boomers, with their placards and their anoraks, their same old posters about war crimes, and dead babies, and B-liar.

How does she not get tired? he wonders.

"Maybe next time," he says.

She nods. "Don't work too hard," she says. She kisses him on the cheek. She moves through the station doors in her distinctive shambling way. He is struck, once again, by the proud shabbiness, that of those who feel they have no need to impress. The hall has got into her after all this time. She is the lady of the manor, despite all she might protest.

AT THREE, Martin is at his desk when a rainstorm comes in. Dark clouds stutter high over the city, and then break suddenly. People hustle around the office shutting windows. Martin wonders whether his mother's protest is still going. He imagines her huddling into that waxed jacket as she hurries off the street.

Julian prowls around, still animated by the thrill of the previous night's sale. He comes past Martin's desk, rubs Martin's back momentarily. "Can we have a chat in the office?" he says.

Julian's office is a jumbled mess, strangely aromatic, as if someone has spilled a jar of spices somewhere under the piles of paper and mounds of old catalogues. Julian's chair faces the door, behind it the window, against which fat raindrops smatter like handfuls of pebbles. There are a couple of pictures on the wall to the right: a Paul Klee sketch, and a kitschy nautical painting. Julian clambers through the debris toward the chair. He settles in his seat and takes a moment to look at Martin.

"You know Marina Gorelov?" he says.

"Yes," says Martin, surprised that Julian noted Martin's activity amidst the tumult of the sale yesterday.

"I saw you talking to her last night," says Julian.

"Yes. Right. She was the girlfriend of my housemate," says Martin.

"Your housemate?"

"Yes." Is it too odd to have a housemate still at thirty-one? "Rent is expensive," says Martin.

"What?"

"Never mind. Sorry. They went to school together. We all went to the same university."

"Great," says Julian. There are four mugs on the table. He picks up one, sniffs at it, drinks. "I suppose you can guess why I'm interested?"

"Her husband?"

Julian nods. "Certainly. You know of his collection?"

"Some of it," says Martin. When he first heard of Marina's marriage to Oleg Gorelov, he read about the man. "You were speaking with him yesterday, I think."

"Indeed." Julian nods again. "He owns some amazing contemporary pieces."

"So I understand."

"And now it seems you have a link to him."

"So does the house, no? You invited him, right? You were talking to him."

"Of course. But, hard to believe as it is, he seems immune to my charm." Julian makes a clownish face of disappointment. "He is suspicious. Maybe *correctly* suspicious of auction folks."

"Right," says Martin.

"He doesn't want a close relationship, it seems. But perhaps my junior specialist might have a natural way to approach." He points to Martin as if he is back conducting a sale.

"I can try," says Martin.

"If we could have a connection," says Julian, "it would put us ahead of the other place. We could alert him to items he might like. And, well, if he were to sell . . . These Russians are always . . ." Julian searches for the word. "Unstable."

"Yes," says Martin.

"Let me just say that it would be a collection that would generate interest, I think."

"I can imagine."

Julian sits back in his chair now, done with the thrust of what he wants to say. "It's about the Russians these days."

"Yes."

"The good times won't last forever. Low rates. Super-high-net individuals."

"I understand."

"The operating officer, he says to me, 'Julian, the future is about the BRICs. Our commitment to the BRICs is total.'"

"Right."

"Perhaps, if I wasn't a modern auctioneer, I'd have thought that he was talking about the sculpture of Carl Andre." He grins broadly, nods at Martin.

Martin smiles.

"Whose most famous sculpture . . ."

". . . is a pile of bricks. Yes."

"How very sharp you are today."

"I'm back in 'Introduction to Western Art'?"

"You'd be surprised by how many people in this building could benefit from such a course." Julian laughs to himself. "Anyway. I *am* a modern auctioneer."

"Indeed."

"Brazil. Russia. India. China."

"Yes."

"Is there a K? Is there Korea?"

"I don't think so."

"Well, I'm committed to the BRICs. And I'm committed to Korea too, for that matter. That is what you see today." He laughs again. "This could work out for you, I think."

JAMES IS watching a Spanish football game when Martin gets home. He's in his tuxedo. He has his feet on the coffee table. He holds a half-empty mug of tea against his chest.

"Good day?" Martin says. James nods noncommittally. Martin thinks of Marina, of the fact he is going to contact her. He takes a moment to observe his friend. James's lips shape soundless commands to the footballers on the screen. James is absorbed in the match, happy maybe. What does James own of Marina anyway, that he should be owed knowledge of her? Martin wonders. She is her own person, is she not?

Martin goes into the kitchen. There are six beers in the fridge. He takes two, opens both. There is a rising sound of cheering from the TV broadcast in the other room. "Offside," says James. "Surely."

In the living room, Martin places one of the beers in front of James, who nods in acknowledgment. Martin takes his place on the sofa. The football plays on an illegal feed, breaking occasionally into pixilation. He glances at his friend, who sits forward as an attack builds. James's top buttons are undone, and Martin can see that behind James's neck the collar of his shirt is yellowed. The more Martin puts off mentioning Marina, the harder it will be, he thinks. But one can know that, and still . . . James slumps back as a player shoots wide. He sighs. "Not the best game ever," he says.

"No."

James turns to look at Martin. "Good day?"

"Fine," Martin says. "Nothing special."

6

MARINA MOVES through the house disordering the soft furnishings. Martin and his colleague are due in an hour, and though she is certain that they won't notice the work she currently does, she can't help herself.

The issue is the cleaner, Nadja, who is so ruthlessly efficient. Even in magazines the designers think to leave some sign of human life in their interior tableaux: an open book or a couple of petals shed onto the table from a vase of flowers. And yet this aesthetic note is alien to Nadja, who cleans the house as she would a hospital. She comes on Tuesdays and Thursdays and Sunday afternoon, and walking through the rooms afterward, Marina thinks of a charity party she once attended at Versailles: of those endless, sterile rooms of gilded mirrors and a kind of order that speaks not so much of plenty as of the limitedness of any life, the sheer absurdity that anyone could need this. She recalls the beds of the king and queen made to seem tiny by the tall ceilings and acres of parquet floors, the sense that she had fallen into a repeating loop, an Escher image of a palace. Nadja is Polish and displays a surliness that Oleg diagnoses as a product of historical memory. "She comes to England," he says, "and finds herself working not for the English but for those old enemies to the east." He is unworried by the possibility that the staff might not like him. "What use," he once said, "is being liked by the person who changes your sheets?"

It's Marina who can't help herself in seeking Nadja's approval. For a time, she gave Nadja bags of her old clothes. Yet this seemed an affront to the cleaner's pride. Nadja would come to work wearing those castoffs. Marina would be wandering around the house on a Sunday and enter the drawing room to the confronting sight of Nadja dusting the skirting boards while wearing a pair of four-inch heels and a red Balenciaga cocktail dress.

They squabble about candles. Nadja replaces any candle that has been lit even once. "They're not used up," Marina has told her.

"But they don't look nice," Nadja replied, pointing to a seam of wax dried to the side of a candle. In Nadja's mind, Marina supposes, Marina and Oleg should be living in a pristine, markless environment, a place of such plenty as to preclude entropy of any sort.

Being wealthy is like packing a suitcase, of course: no one can watch another doing it and feel they couldn't perform the act better themselves. Marina is conscious of this as she prepares for Martin's arrival. She readjusts some flowers at the window in the second-floor corridor. The last they knew each other, she was pretending to be normal, trying to have the average student experience. Now, this house, this husband.

Yet maybe Martin will be unsurprised to witness her living in a place like this. A certain kind of Russian spend their lives in English mansions, and in many respects this is exactly Marina's profile. Her family left St. Petersburg when she was nine and moved to England, to a townhouse in Chelsea and a small estate out to the southwest of the city. She went to prep school in London and then off to a girls' boarding school, situated in a Georgian manor in South Gloucestershire.

When she thinks of birdsong, she thinks of the calls of birds of the home counties. The climate by which she judges places she visits is that of England. She has visceral memories of the gardens of their Sussex country house: the smells of wild garlic in spring and lavender in summer; a slow worm she found under a rock one August, which curled into a question mark on being revealed. Her memories of Petr are in comparison half-formed, impressionistic: the odors of the kitchen in their first apartment, the crystal northern sunlight, the tang of exhaust on cold days, the press of crowds in the station, babushkas looming around corners in their grubby winter coats.

Oleg says often that she is hardly Russian, sometimes impressed, sometimes reproving. When she is uncynical, he says this in awe; when she expresses indifference toward some delicacy or cultural touchstone, he shakes his head and says the same. "You do not want kvass?" He spits air and sighs.

Some impulse of her parents' caused them to try to make her an English girl. Still, the others at boarding school weren't having that. Russians were common enough to be a stereotype then, too uncommon to form a clique. Sasha, the other Russian in Marina's class at the school, read children's picture books and gnawed her fingernails. Marina laughed too late at everything. English words gummed up in her mouth. She didn't know the Latinate school slang. They called her "the robot," because of how she spoke and because the work of being in this new place flattened her responses.

IN THE library, she takes a couple of books from the shelves and leaves them on the side table. The fruit in the fruit bowl is stacked into a neat pyramid, which she topples and rearranges.

IN THE introductory video to the school that her parents had been sent before Marina's enrollment, a group of girls did aerobics to a workout video. It was the midnineties. "Are you dancing in front of the TV with the other girls?" her mother asked when they first spoke on the phone after her arrival.

No, was the answer. Mostly the girls were trying to be subversive. In Marina's first term, Jane Fuller Booth sneaked into the kitchen of the seniors' dormitory and melted a load of biros in a baking tray. Alice Tomkins ate a block of butter. Virginia Tzjakinsky skipped meals and consumed only baby food that her older sister posted to her in multipack boxes. Poppy Beaufontaine went walking in a summer storm to see if she would be struck by lightning. Cynthia Isadore, it was rumored, accepted the marriage proposal of an imprisoned murderer from Arizona with whom she had been corresponding by mail.

Yet Marina knew of these acts only from what she overheard. She sat on a bench and watched a group of girls plotting together on the lawns in front of the dormitories. She had fantasies of some gesture that would make things work for her, make those girls see her as more than mechanical. She stole some matches from the science lab and then sneaked out of bed and walked around the grounds of the school looking for something to burn. She wondered about trying to set fire to the old pavilion by the seniors' garden or the gardener's shed. There was no story that she could fit these ideas into, she thought, no progression that led her where she wanted to go. She jimmied the small lock off the shed. She took out a petrol can and poured a circle of petrol onto the lawn near the boundary gate. She threw a match onto this damp circle, and it flamed and sputtered and smoldered until it gave out. In the morning Alice Tomkins, smoking, found the patch before the gardener did. She came back into the dormitory bathroom and told Poppy. Poppy rolled her eyes. "Just a circle?" she said, and sighed in exasperation.

The other girls had a reaction to this place Marina couldn't counterfeit. It was their destiny to be confined to these grand rooms, these neat gardens, these ugly pine-green school uniforms. They had some idea of the lives of their illustrious ancestors, and how those lives had led to their own existence in the most boring of all environments. Their desperation had a vintage.

There was some link between this and the way the school music teacher spoke of Marina's piano playing. "You're technically very good," he said.

There was a further clause, beginning with a *but*, that he didn't articulate. These people valued naturalness above all else. It was the shared ideology of the school and the girls' insurgency.

"We want to nurture the right *instincts*," said the headmistress in the first assembly. "We want to produce girls whose actions are true."

"That top is so tacky," said Cynthia when she was browsing through Marina's closet.

"It's the new Dior collection."

"So it's tacky *and* expensive," said Cynthia. She sighed and tugged off a sequin.

How had these girls gained such affirmative taste? They hated things that were cheap and crude, but what they hated even more was the guileless use of wealth.

At the start of her first half-term at the school, Marina's dad arrived in a brand-new helicopter to collect her. The girls assembled at the dormitory window to see it come down. They watched Marina's father jogging out of the craft, hunching from the downdraft of the rotors in a way that Marina herself could see was ridiculous. "You're only going to London, right?" said Jane Fuller Booth. "Does he not have a car?"

Still, while becoming only marginally more popular, Marina was learning parts of her schoolmates' code. She realized this with each return home from boarding school. *Who are these people?* she asked herself when her parents made such a loud entrance to a restaurant, when they clicked their fingers at staff. She wasn't sure whether she'd gained a new sensibility or merely a vocabulary for what she'd already felt, but her parents' way of living seemed gross. She disliked the overdone decoration of the two houses. She despised her father's table manners. He liked to eat and he liked to talk, and because he was rich he now performed both acts at once.

During that first Christmas break from school, her family went on a ski holiday. She, her little brother, and her parents had brand-new, top-of-the-line equipment, though none of them had downhill-skied before. They tumbled down the pristine slopes in this gear, their professional attire exacerbating the appearance of their incompetence. Their ski guides helped them back to their feet with neutral expressions (which hid, Marina guessed, the scathing anecdotes they would tell about the family when the day was done). Marina's father spent the evenings berating staff at the chalet for what he perceived to be mistakes in the service they provided. He complained that the water from the taps was too hot. He sent back steaks for being undercooked. He suggested that the sommelier was pouring his wine badly. "Don't do it so splashy," he said loudly in a packed restaurant. Marina sensed the other guests looking at them whenever they came into the lobby, her father having inevitably stopped at the front desk to raise an issue. She wanted the broad floorboards to part and the floor to swallow her. *We're doing this all wrong,* she thought.

SHE STOPS in the second-floor living room to leave open one of Oleg's car magazines. She sits on the sofa for a while. The clouds shift and the light in the room changes, suddenly bright, sun catching the mirror in a way that draws her eye to it, to her own reflection. She looks anxious. The sleeves of her sweatshirt are rolled up, and she drags them down again. The cloud shifts once more, and the brightness in the room diminishes.

SHE JUST about managed to fit into the school eventually. She shed her accent and learned to choose the right clothes. She despised her parents in the most detailed possible way: for how they held their knives and forks, for the sort of perfume her mother wore, the manner in which her father knotted his tie. When they addressed her in Russian, she answered in English, and they accepted this (though she sensed they didn't always fully grasp the nuances of what she said). She was a tool for their despising of themselves, she thinks now. They had no sense of who they were, and so they had raised a daughter with only the instinct that she should be a completely different person from themselves. They had both been party members in the USSR.

Marina's father had made his money not through seeing the ultimate defects of the system, but through a totally Soviet capacity for improvisation. In this new country, they had no ideology, no fixed picture of the world. For want of a greater understanding of their situation, they spent money and complained.

The thing that helped Marina in the end was music, though not the form of music she would have assumed would assist her. At fourteen, Jane Fuller Booth put up a poster of the Ramones on the wall beside her lower bunk. One late-spring Saturday, Marina entered the dormitory and found Jane trying on a ragged linen blazer.

"Do I look like Debbie Harry?" said Jane.

"Harry who?" said Marina.

Jane sighed and passed Marina a magazine, pointing to a photograph. There was a woman in it, standing between five men wearing leather jackets. The woman's hair was dyed inconsistently. She looked outraged at being photographed. The men around her had haircuts that reminded Marina of old pictures of her father. They were standing in some filthy hallway. "Um. Yes, I think you do," she said. She wasn't sure whether this was the correct answer, but Jane seemed pleased to hear it. It was all surprising, hard to understand. Marina's father liked American rock, but a different kind: peacocky men in shiny outfits with long hair and oddly shaped guitars. Marina held the magazine and said, "Can I borrow this."

Jane shrugged. "Sure."

Marina went out to the lawn with the magazine. It was an issue of *Mojo* dedicated to punk music, filled with references to bands and records she'd never heard of. She read about the Clash, the Sex Pistols, the Ramones, the Slits. She looked at the photos, studied the ragged style, the hostile poses of the subjects. It was like some strong flavor she'd never tasted before. She didn't *like* these pictures exactly, but she couldn't stop herself from looking.

Marina returned the magazine to Jane later that evening. Jane gestured at a box of other magazines by the bed. The rest of the girls were in the lounge watching *Pop Idol*. "There are others if you want," she said.

Marina read about punk for two weeks before she heard a record. One day, when they were again in the dormitory room alone, Jane came over with her minidisc player and offered an earbud. "Television," she said. "*Marquee Moon*." It was not what Marina expected: ghostlier and more unsure than she had imagined this music would be. Jane liked the New York scene. "The Sex Pistols were posers," she said. "There was more originality and invention in America." What compelled Marina, beyond the shocking possibility of Jane's acceptance of her company, was the focus of the study of this music: lines of influence, band breakups and formations, relationships between artists. The fandom was about excavating an old social network, and this wasn't dissimilar to the work of interpretation Marina had been doing at the periphery of the school's cliques. There was a pattern to it all she could apprehend.

The other girls were unwilling to follow Jane in her obsession. They liked contemporary pop or dance music. Jane cut her own hair in front of the mirror, dyed it black. She was given a detention for this. "What can I do?" she asked their housemistress. "Grow it back?" She'd seek out Marina when she came into the common room. The two of them went to Bristol on Wednesday afternoons to visit a record shop run by a man prone to lecturing them about great gigs played years before they were born. Marina bought *Marquee Moon* on vinyl before she owned a record player. She pinned the cover to the wall above her bed. Jane cut Marina's hair into a voluminous kind of mullet. Marina didn't wear it with as much hairspray as Jane suggested. They smoked menthol cigarettes behind the tennis courts. They exchanged glances when someone used the lounge hi-fi to play Justin Timberlake.

That summer when she went home for the holidays, Marina could answer her mother's questions about friends honestly: Yes, she had friends (or a friend, at least). No, she wasn't just sitting alone always.

"And all this heavy metal?" said her mother when they were being driven to lunch one day. She was looking at Marina's New York Dolls T-shirt.

"It's not heavy metal."

"Whatever it is."

"Punk."

"You're such a talented musician."

"Thank you."

"Don't be dumb."

"What?"

"It is not just a compliment. Don't make me say this. This heavy-rock stuff is trash. Why waste your time with this shit? You want to be an idiot like your father?" Her mother was speaking with a neutral expression and at a volume honed with practice, loud enough to be heard clearly, quiet enough that the driver wouldn't pick up what was said. She smiled all the while.

"Punk," hissed Marina. "*Punk.*"

"Maybe we try a different school, I have been thinking."

"I'm fine."

"Before you didn't like your school. Why don't we try another?"

And with that, Marina was on to a new start: another sprawl of old buildings between rolling hills. There was a stable in this one, a giant sports complex, a whole separate music block. And boys. There was a skinny, sick-looking boy who played the piano like she did. He looked like Tom Verlaine from Television, she thought. His hands were long, thin, and creepy like those of a racoon. She said this to him and he laughed at it, which put her off for a moment because she hadn't previously been thought funny, or thought herself funny.

He took her to his home one summer. He also lived in a manor, but a different kind of place: full of food odors and mess and other kids. She recalls digging her hands into the earth, rich with worms and rotten leaves turned in. It wasn't the private home that she and her parents didn't know how to live in, nor like the houses of her school friends, with their instinctive reverence for old things and their peculiar

English worship of their ancestors. James's parents talked to him as a grown-up in a way that her own parents never could have managed, and he had a freckled, hesitant friend. The two boys were gentle and caring toward each other in a way she hadn't ever imagined teenage boys could be. There was a sincere and uncomplicated intimacy in the way James looked at his friend that she found she envied a little.

7

HE PLACES his temple against the car window and watches the tops of the hedges rise and fall. The sky is gray, heavy. Martin can hear the tires tearing through the standing water on the small lane. Julian is playing a nineties Dylan album, tapping his finger against the steering wheel of the Mercedes.

Martin wrote to Marina on Facebook. It was nice to see her at the auction, he said. He'd mentioned that he was curious about Oleg Gorelov's collection, because he was aware that Marina valued directness, and also because the simple fact of meeting her—his pleasure in her company and in reminiscing—seemed too plain a motivation to draw them back together.

This is your work, right? she wrote back. Come and see him. Come and see the pictures. Bring a colleague if you want.

This is Martin's part of the country. Huntley Hall, his parents' home, is only half an hour's drive away. Julian breaks sharply as a dilapidated VW van emerges at speed around a blind bend ahead of them. Foliage caresses the side of the car as the two vehicles inch past each other, sodden cow parsley and tendrils of bramble reaching down as if trying to force open a window.

Julian tuts. "These locals have no fear."

"The people around here could drive the roads with their eyes closed," says Martin.

"You're right," says Julian, clearly glad to be set up for an obvious joke. "In fact, I think they do."

• • •

THEY MAKE a left, to be faced with large wrought iron gates, a guardhouse. A broad red-haired man in a dark suit comes out and inspects their driver's licenses.

He gestures them past. The gates begin to roll apart.

Julian presses the accelerator. The Mercedes crunches up the curving gravel drive, a lake to their left, a willow leaning over it. The house comes into view between oaks and limes. A big building. A neat but unlovely face. Gray stone. Bay windows of small rectangular panes. It looks down the hillside over stepped gardens.

Julian stops the car on the semicircle of gravel in front of the house. The place is large, uneven, one wing a slightly different style from the rest of the house. There's nostalgia in this visit for Martin. This place is so much better maintained than the house in which he grew up, but it bears its history in a similar way. The house was constructed century by century, reworked and revised by so many owners long dead. This is an attraction to the kind of people interested in such property, of course: all the stunted plans of men and women who have come before, and the challenge to impose oneself successfully on the place.

AS THEY approach the door, Marina emerges. She's wearing jeans and a baggy sweater. She looks like any other woman of Martin's age on a weekend morning, not the lady of the estate. Julian and Martin approach her through sideways-sleeting rain.

She beckons them straight into the hall. She closes the heavy door behind them. They're in a paneled entranceway as large as an average living room. Marina embraces Martin, stands back, smiles, an uncharacteristic apprehension in her look. "Welcome to the house," she says. She shakes Julian's hand. He introduces himself carefully.

"Yes," she says. "I've seen you at the block."

"You make me sound like an executioner," says Julian, and flashes his teeth.

Martin studies the suit of armor that faces the door.

"Please don't look at that," Marina says. "It's a monstrous piece of shit. Every piece from a different era. It's the first thing he bought for this house." She waves her hands around. "It goes to a man's head to buy a place like this."

"A little excess is always forgivable," says Julian. "It's a charming property."

"If you like excess," says Marina, "this is the place for you." She directs a rueful smile in Martin's direction.

They move out of the entranceway, past the foot of a broad staircase, down a corridor into the body of the house. The décor is modern: drapes of a simmering orange, a chandelier at the foot of the stairs composed of a spiral of gold, hanging like cut peel. Still, a chill to the air Martin remembers from childhood. There are always hints of cold stone and mildew in houses like these. Marina is wearing thick socks on her feet, scuffed down. Martin notes Julian behind him, looking around frantically as he follows, a native need to inventory the place.

They come into a library then. Dark wood shelving. Leather-bound books. Two new sofas upholstered in a straw-colored suede. "Please wait here," says Marina. "I'll go and find him." She's nervous, Martin thinks. He recalls what Julian said about Oleg's suspicion of auction people. This is a gesture of friendship. This costs her effort.

Julian and Martin take seats on the sofas, facing each other. There is a low table between them, a bowl full of small orange fruits. Martin frowns at the bowl. "Tamarillos? Kumquats?"

Julian shakes his head. "Persimmons."

The ring of a telephone reaches them faintly from somewhere else in the house. Martin stands and walks around the library. The books are Victorian classics: Dickens, Eliot, Thackeray, Austen. He takes down a volume of *Bleak House*, and the door opens as he does so. Oleg comes in. He is shorter than Martin recalls. He has heavy, somewhat

sensuous lips. Close up, his blue eyes betray the kind of serious tiredness that a decade's sleep wouldn't rectify.

Martin holds the book in his left hand, puts out his right to meet
Oleg's handshake. The oligarch's fingers are stumpy and thick like
those of a toddler. "Oleg," he says. "You are a great friend of my wife,
I am hearing."

"Yes," says Martin. He introduces himself.

Julian does the same. "We were examining your bookshelves," Julian says. "Such an impressive collection."

Oleg shrugs. "I have not read them," he says. "They were selected
by the brothers."

"Oh?" says Julian.

"The designers. They were chosen for me." Oleg smiles. "I suppose they are correct for who I am."

The heavy door opens again and Marina reenters. The four of
them stand in silence for a moment. "You'd like a drink?" says Marina.

"Of course they want to see my paintings," says Oleg. He lifts one
heavy hand to shoo away his wife's suggestion.

"He's direct," says Marina, "my husband."

"Rude, she means," says Oleg. "I do not eat shit."

"That's fine by us," says Julian.

"I'm serious," says Oleg. "Probably you must be serious to get a
house like this."

Marina tuts and rolls her eyes.

"Although it seems my wife is thinking that houses like this are
falling out of the sky."

OLEG LEADS them off. They pass a small office, in which an empty
chair faces an array of CCTV screens. They walk past a dining room,
down a corridor at the rear of the house with large windows offering a
view of damp lawns, an overcast sky. They arrive at the threshold of a
Victorian conservatory, a pristine swimming pool in the middle of this

space, rain drumming down on the glass. Oleg turns away from this, however, toward a set of stairs leading down below the house. The other three follow him as he descends.

"This house is very old," says Oleg.

"Indeed," says Julian. "Totally charming."

"Yes, yes," says the oligarch. "But you need permissions to build. You cannot make an extension as you would wish." He stops at a heavy red door, inputs a code. "Fortunately, I can build underground. Many structural engineers." He looks at Martin. "And do not worry for the pictures. A war against the damp. Specialist technology to reduce the humidity."

The corridor is white, evenly lit like a medical space. The door closes firmly behind Marina, who brings up the rear of the group. Oleg is walking ahead. "Very secure down here," he says, turning. He is warming up, enjoying himself. He points to the ceiling. "Maybe they have dropped a bomb up there and we do not know."

They walk to the end of the corridor, past identical doors. Marina is beside Martin. "Not as interesting as you might think," she says, as if reading Martin's mind. "A gym. A storage room. A private cinema. Luxuries you seldom actually use."

"Is that so?" says Martin.

"Things have changed a little in my life since university, I suppose."

"Yes." Martin laughs.

"Or I've returned to this kind of life."

At the end of the corridor, Oleg has stopped and is waiting for Martin and Marina to catch up. He shrugs off a question from Julian.

WHEN OLEG pushes open the door, the space is a surprise. The corridor hasn't prepared Martin for a room so large. Though perhaps this struggle to recontextualize is the very point of the modest approach.

The space is the size of a basketball court. The walls are the color of baked clay, the room dim but for the pictures, lit by spotlights recessed into the ceiling. By the entrance, a small machine churns, paper moving between two rolls, a stylus against it recording the humidity. Oleg is standing a few yards into the room, looking eager, even anxious. "Incredible," says Julian. Oleg returns a guarded look.

Martin sees a Hockney, a Richter, a Twombly. There's a Hirst spot painting, and an Emin neon work. There are some small Bacon paintings on the far wall. Good works. Museum-quality. Familiar gestures, colors, lines. Pictures known to the eye as it alights. Martin thinks of something Julian says often: "*Iconic* is a very expensive word."

He moves properly into the room. He looks at the Richter. Paint squeezed across the canvas. A titanium shimmer to the color. The Twombly is very good, early sixties. The spot painting is a spot painting (and there is something in that harmonious anonymity). There is a bad, but likely valuable, Warhol. The Emin is neon tube text, reading *Trust Yourself*. The Hockney is a portrait. Eighties, Martin estimates. Rougher than his seventies work. Charming. The Bacon is another thing: three paintings, in fact. Study for a head. They have a charisma, a way of drawing the eye toward them.

Martin turns to see Marina beside him, looking ahead at the Richter. Julian moves around carefully, his right hand clasping his chin, a finger extended over his lips. Part of the wonder of the space is the reaction of those who enter it, Martin thinks: the recourse to the mannerisms of the gallery.

Oleg still waits, watching them with an expression more open than Martin would expect. Martin thinks of people who keep wild animals and painstakingly make habitats, simulacra of natural environments.

"This is in your home," Martin says to Marina.

"Yes," she says. "I know this isn't normal."

He didn't mean to underline her privilege, merely to marvel for a moment with her. She turns, looks at him, perhaps sees this.

He says, "You come down here alone?"

"Sometimes," she says. "I come down at strange times. That's the magic of this room. To be here at two a.m. To find this waiting underground."

There is something in that, Martin thinks: the fairy-tale nature of the space. If the rich must be so rich, then this is not the worst thing they could be making.

Oleg and Julian now stand in front of the three Bacon pictures. Martin approaches them.

"These are truly spectacular," says Julian. "You had assistance in these purchases?"

"No," says Oleg. His manner has hardened again. "Perhaps a little."

"I'm impressed," says Julian.

"Of course."

The three men look at the heads for a moment. Martin listens to Marina's tread on the carpet as she moves between other pictures.

"They are valuable, are they?" says Oleg.

"Most certainly," says Julian slowly, trying to fathom how much naïveté there is in the question. "An extremely robust market for Bacon at the moment."

"Yes?"

"A limited catalogue raisonné," says Julian.

"Not so much supply?"

"Right."

"Because he is dead."

"I suppose."

"I too have found that it can be useful for business when certain people are dead." Oleg turns and laughs then, an eye on his guests. He's playing with them, Martin thinks. Martin laughs before Julian does.

"I joke," says Oleg. "Because you think I am a gangster. Really you would be shocked by my business, though." He pauses, looks at both men intently. "By how boring it is."

Martin beats his boss to the laugh again.

• • •

AT THE end of the gallery space, there's another door. Oleg gestures toward it, leads the group through. The room is smaller but has the same red walls, the same hum of climate control. "The Russians," says Oleg. "But sorry. No Kandinsky."

There are a couple of nineteenth-century landscapes, some Soviet realist pictures, a faux-naïve oil. There is a small sketch of a reclining nude, toward which Martin moves in examination.

"Larionov," says Oleg.

Julian moves over to study a portrait of a bald man leaning his head against his open palm, looking forward, out of the frame.

"It's Shevchenko," says Oleg. "The poet. Not the Shevchenko you were thinking of."

Julian smiles, his eyes confused.

"The footballer," explains Martin. "There's a footballer called Shevchenko."

"You see," says Oleg. "He gets it." He winks at Martin.

Behind them, beside the door, are two pictures. One is a white canvas divided by thin blue and black lines, a cluster of triangles and rhomboids in red and yellow and black in the upper middle of the image; the other is a larger work in which a yellow band bisects a gray background, over that a thick arcing white line, and thin black lines drawn radially from the edge of a red sphere at the bottom of the canvas, with a cluster of other shapes in the bottom right of the plane. These pictures are drink to Martin. He loves this kind of abstraction: shapes and spaces and a keening toward some other, precise ordering of life. Both images have their logic. Harmonies are drawn to mind by the interaction of the bodies. The first image is sparer, enlivened oddly not by what is on the canvas, but by a sense that the organization of the shapes is just part of a pattern not fully elucidated. "Malevich?" says Julian.

"One of them," says Oleg. "Can you see which?"

"One is perhaps by El Lissitzky," says Martin. He points at the second, gray image. Oleg looks at him, waits. Martin indicates a rhomboid in the corner, where it overlaps the corner of a cuboid shape. "There's a three-dimensional effect here, which Malevich usually resisted."

Oleg winks. "Ten points to the boy."

Martin spends a moment more looking, enjoying the balance, the conjured space. "And the colors, I think," he says. "Malevich usually favored a more limited palette in these kinds of images."

"A man with a code," says Oleg. "I like it."

IN THE blank corridor, they walk two by two. Oleg next to Julian, Martin next to Marina. Julian's hands are in constant motion as he speaks. Oleg walks with his hands clasped together at the small of his back.

"What are you doing these days for work?" says Martin to Marina.

"Financial marketing and communications," Marina says. "Lodestone Capital."

"I think a couple of your colleagues are clients of ours."

"I'm sure."

"You like it?"

"I suppose."

"You were the cleverest person I met at university, you know."

She halts momentarily, so he is half a step ahead of her now. "And why do you say that?" she says.

He meant only to indulge in nostalgia. They did many things that were naïve and grandiose, but there were blessings that they had then but didn't see. These are things he wants to linger on. He must turn his head back to look at her now that she walks slightly behind him. "It was just a compliment. I'm sure you're good at your job."

"Right," she says.

At the red basement door, Oleg stops. "The temperature is controlled to point-nought-one of a degree," he says.

"Amazing," says Julian.

"You see," Marina says to her husband. "This isn't so bad."

Oleg shrugs.

"He's always skeptical about visitors," she says.

"Sometimes people are not serious," Oleg says.

ON THE stairs, once the basement door has closed behind the group, Oleg and Julian pause to examine a gap in the stonework. Martin strains over their shoulders to see a hole, three feet by two, that leads through to a small chamber. Oleg points inside.

"I think, perhaps, it is for dogs," says Oleg.

"I think it's a priest hole," says Martin.

"Yes?" says Oleg.

"For hiding a Catholic priest, during the reign of Elizabeth the first." There was such a space in Huntley Hall.

"The priests want to hide?"

"Because Catholicism was outlawed," says Julian.

"I understand," says Oleg.

"The entrance to this place would be covered by something. Either wood or tapestry," Martin explains. "The priest would slip in if the house was searched. It would mean that this section of the building is older than the face, which is Jacobean. But that isn't unusual."

"This friend of yours is clever," says Oleg to Marina. He turns to Julian. "An employee who is good for your company, I think."

Martin looks at Marina and she smiles.

IN THE conservatory, they take seats in wicker chairs next to the swimming pool. It's warm and humid. Rain drums on the glass above, streams down the windows. The glass is fogged on the inside. At the other end of the room two bodyguards sit together, scanning around, backs straight, a theater of vigilance.

"They are army," says Oleg, noting Martin looking at the men. "Used to be special forces. More gentlemen than me, even though I am the owner."

A woman brings cups of tea on a tray. Oleg sniffs his, drinks. Martin looks at the pool. The tiles are china blue. There is a tiny bulge in the surface above the clean water intake: a translucent boil.

"Marina was clever at university?" says Oleg.

"Of course," says Martin.

"You were all clever?" says Oleg.

"Most of us were second-rate," says Martin. "Marina was clever."

"That's not true," says Marina.

"Clever is overrated," says Oleg. He taps his chest as if to suggest some other, deeper quality is dear to him. His phone rings in his jacket pocket. He takes it out, looks at the screen, rejects the call. "But there are many very stupid people in the world."

"We're keeping you from your business?" says Julian.

"Business?" says Oleg. "Always everything is keeping me from my business."

They drink their tea. The conversation slows. "We should get on our way," says Julian.

Martin and Julian rise. Oleg stands, offers his heavy hand again to shake.

"Thank you," says Julian. "The collection is amazing."

"Not bad for a man rich from potash," says Oleg. "Not all of us Russians just want to buy football teams."

"Of course not," says Julian.

"Though perhaps I should," says Oleg.

"The good ones are taken," says Martin.

"Aston Villa?" says Oleg.

"I think the Bacon pictures are horrifying enough," says Martin.

Oleg laughs and winks at Martin. He sits again and takes out his phone.

"I'll show you out," says Marina. She leads the way. At the door of the conservatory, they turn in a different direction from that by which they arrived. They pass rooms decorated in a similar style to the rest of the house: oranges and golds, drapes and dark woods.

"I want to show you something," says Marina. She opens a door into a room: green wallpaper, a fireplace, dark-stained floorboards. In the middle of the space, sucking up light, is a giant black piano.

Marina steps across the threshold and indicates that Martin and Julian should follow her. Martin goes over to the piano, places a careful hand on the top.

"James would be thrilled," says Martin.

Marina hesitates. There is an expectation in her look, an uncharacteristic sense that she seeks his approval, and he is glad to see this room, to feel her sincerity. "That's why I'm showing it to you," she says.

"You play?" says Julian.

"A little," says Marina.

"That's not true," says Martin. "She was a childhood prodigy."

She frowns. "Now I play only occasionally." She stands by the piano and presses a key. A note rings out crisply. "This is too much of a piano to play occasionally," she says.

"It's a pleasure, though?" Martin says.

"I suppose so," says Marina. She seems slightly lost, Martin thinks, so much less sure than she always was before.

THE RAIN is still coming down when they reach the car. Julian turns on the heaters, clicks the windscreen wipers on. He swings the Mercedes around the turning circle. They descend the meandering drive.

"You were a hit," says Julian.

"With Gorelov?" says Martin.

"Of course, with Gorelov. Good spiel about that hole." Julian sighs. "Though football talk. Christ! Fucking football!"

8

OLEG HAS to fly to Malta on business, so Marina eats dinner in the kitchen alone. Midway through her meal, Tim, the security guard, comes in to fetch a glass from one of the cupboards and is surprised, turning with that glass in hand, to find her eating at the breakfast bar.

"I'm sorry," he says.

"You want some?" she says. "Marcus made plenty."

He smiles apologetically, tells her that his wife will have saved his dinner for him, that he'd be slaughtered if he didn't save his appetite for that. "Home is where I really need to be vigilant," he says. "Home is where the real danger is."

She laughs. She likes Tim. There's a shyness hidden beneath the stern mannerisms that the army endowed him with. She suspects that he is a man who has had to work against tendencies, to shape himself for his role.

"Is that so?" she says.

"I suppose," he says. "She's intense. She's from Brazil."

"Brazil. Gosh. How did you meet her?"

"I used to work in São Paulo. They have a lot of security contracts. It's good money."

"And she followed you here?"

"Yes."

"But now she wants to go home?"

"You know how it is," he says. "The language. The weather. The manners people have."

"I do know," she says. "Though if you come from Russia, England is preferable in each of these respects."

Tim gives a little laugh. The joke is too wordy, Marina thinks, and anyway she is more from Britain than Russia. "Maybe she'll find some close friends here," she says.

He returns a cautious nod. This is making him uneasy, this small talk beyond the plain duties of his job. He would prefer for her to act like her husband and look right through him. She says, "I'm sure you have things to do. Don't let me distract you."

"Certainly." He puts the unused glass in the dishwasher. He goes to the window and looks out of it intently, as if to reset himself to his professional mode. He checks his watch and leaves the room.

Marina presses down on the salmon with her fork. Pieces of flesh slide apart. After Martin's visit, she still has a residual sense of being watched, of her present life being reappraised in contrast to her time at university. She thinks of those menthol cigarettes she used to smoke. She tried hard at being ordinary, or being cool in an ordinary way. She recalls times at boarding school when she would sneak out of the dormitory with a mirror and a flashlight and sit behind a wall and look at her reflection as she lit up, practicing holding her cigarette.

Martin has changed since she last saw him, worked so hard at this transformation. Though unlike Marina, he seems assured of his capacity to transform. Her time smoking into the mirror would never end satisfyingly. She'd stare into her own reflection and feel herself breaking down before her own gaze, her face falling into a sort of incoherence, an inhuman randomness, no longer features but strange shapes.

She finishes her dinner and clears the plate to the side. In the corridor, she notices that the lights of the music room are still on. She wonders at the masochistic impulse that led her to show the piano to Martin and his boss. She goes into the room to turn off the lights and close the curtains, but finds herself lingering. The piano *is* a magnificent thing. Black like wet tar. The point of bringing the men in here was confirmation, she supposes. At times, she feels those years of university a dream, and needs to be reminded that the sense of possibility of the time was real. Martin called her a childhood prodigy, spoke the silly words reverently. Julian assented in his too-smooth way. She thinks of her music teacher at the first boarding school: that odd little man who always wore a waistcoat, and sat at his desk and listened with his eyes closed, moving his full lips in approval or disapproval at what he heard.

She never had talent, really. She had capability instead. She never quite understood the game. She didn't live her expertise, didn't lean into it. She thought it was enough to practice, to produce what was asked of her. And yet there was some way of carrying her skill that men like her music teacher sought but didn't ask for: an easiness that looks like modesty, but actually rests on the firm assurance that one will get one's due.

She sits at the piano now and starts to play from memory: pieces she could not have known she recalls before feeling her fingers playing them. She plays a snatch of Chopin. She looks at the dark window, catches a reflection of herself. She *was* good, she thinks. She loses the thread then, however, and her playing stutters, breaks down, suddenly ugly in the too-harsh acoustics of the room.

What did Martin say again? *You were the cleverest person I knew at university.* As if to say, what? That the work she was telling him about doesn't befit her? He lets things run on too much, Martin. She should have told him that her work is no worse than his. There's an easy case to be made that there is something more honest about financial services. She talks money, thinks money. She's not dealing in crusts of oil paint, bashful that they are really just another asset class. She engages with the world on its real terms. She never managed to be quite as oblique, quite as modest as the English girls she went to school with, and yet she has found herself in a world where it's necessary to talk straightforwardly about wealth, where English discretion is of limited use. She's good at her work. "Clever is nothing until clever makes you money," Oleg said not long after she met him. It sounded like an odd

Chinese proverb, but it felt true, like so many of the unabashed things he said then.

She stands from the piano stool. She goes over to the wall and presses the button that pulls closed the curtains. The point of money is that it means everything and nothing, and the key to having money happily is to work out how to believe both of these things at once. Her husband was a man who seemed, when she met him, to have mastered the art of being rich. He enjoyed the accumulation of cash unapologetically, and he spent it as he wished. Her regret is that by the time she met someone who offered another perspective on her parents, her father was dead. Oleg had better table manners than her father, but he also didn't try, as Marina did, to match the English in their affect. He understood that he could have eaten as primly as the queen and yet been perceived only as a curiosity: a great bear that could use a knife and fork. His part was that of the Russian billionaire—bigger, madder, crasser than those around him—and he played that part with a verve that served his own purposes.

She hadn't considered the possibility that her parents had glimpsed the futility of trying to be accepted. After Marina's father died, Jane's parents, whom Marina knew very well, excused themselves from the funeral. Though Jane's father's firm had even done some accountancy work for Marina's dad, the couple didn't want to be drawn into the drama of Marina's father's passing. "We'd be a distraction," Jane's father said. "We wouldn't understand the service."

There is some invisible threshold these people won't let you across. And though such a refusal is their right, so should a reaction against it be hers: a turning away from their manners and whispers and unspoken rules.

Marina leaves the music room, closing the door carefully behind her. She showed Martin the piano to prove that she didn't quit playing without consideration, she thinks, and to show that this life of hers is one she chose.

9

THE FRONT door is swollen with moisture, and Martin must barge his shoulder into it to force it open. James is on the sofa watching German football.

"Work?" says James. "On a Saturday?"

"Visiting a client," says Martin. He takes off his shoes, puts down his satchel.

"You made a deal?"

Martin shakes his head. "It's not all deals. Sometimes it's just getting to know them, letting them know us."

"I see. So, you're their friend?"

"Not exactly, but they have to like us." Martin takes a seat on the sofa next to James.

"Right. And do you like them?" James is watching the screen, a neutral expression. Are they just chatting? Or, Martin wonders, does he have suspicions?

"The couple I saw today?" says Martin. "They're interesting."

"Right," says James, his eyes on the screen.

"Ultimately, of course, we'd love to get our hands on their collection. We're like vampires. We're well-dressed. We're polite. But in the end, we'll need to feed."

Martin waits, and James laughs politely, continues to stare at the match with an intensity that seems put-on. He knows something is up, Martin thinks. On some level or other he knows and doesn't really want to know for sure.

The feed breaks up for a second. James sighs. There's some tobacco on the table, a couple of dirty mugs. Martin stands up and goes into the kitchen. There's a pile of dishes next to the sink, a slick of water over the countertop. The kitchen smells of wet chipboard. Water has been leaking around the collar of the kitchen tap for four days. The landlord has requested that James or Martin organize for a plumber to come, and James said he had time off to make the call on Friday. Martin goes back to the living room. "I meant to ask," he says. "Did you call the plumber?"

"It's Saturday," says James. "He doesn't work Saturday."

"But yesterday," Martin says. "Did you not call then?"

James shrugs. "Well, no. Obviously not."

Martin stands in the doorway waiting.

"I'm sorry," says James. "Things came up."

Martin goes back into the kitchen. He fills the kettle and waits for it to boil. It's so exhausting finding oneself angered by little things like this. There is just a dribble of milk left in the bottle, so Martin's tea is chocolate brown. He goes back into the living room, settles on the sofa. James is rolling a cigarette. He stands and goes outside to smoke, yanking the door closed behind him. The game is ongoing. The Bundesliga. Frankfurt versus Hoffenheim. It is 2-1 to Hoffenheim. Martin looks around the room. The Ikea Billy bookcase is overloaded on the top shelf, which sags a little under the weight of Martin's art books. Martin can see a ball of hair and dust near the skirting board, beside the mess of cables that lies to the rear of the TV. There is a bit of paint peeling from the wall by the door. The tone of the German commentary changes. Hoffenheim has scored again. James comes back in. He retakes his place on the sofa. He carries the odor of his cigarette with him.

"Do you ever feel like we should be living aboveground by now?" says Martin.

"You want to move?" says James.

"In a general way. Wouldn't you have thought we'd have moved somewhere better?"

"Maybe." James shrugs. "The rent is affordable here, though."

Martin thinks of Oleg. The subterranean gallery. The war against the damp, as Oleg described it. Interacting with these rich people, there is always the issue of just-a-little-bit: the hunger for only a crumb of what they have, the knowledge that what they would not miss would change one's own life.

"The point is not to be too impressed," Julian has said to Martin previously. "It's embarrassing for them to see you salivating."

James licks a finger and rubs at a white spot on the lapel of his tuxedo. Martin reclines back on the sofa. He looks up at the window. He watches the legs of a family group make their way past. Trainers. Leather boots. Trailing laces from a child's shoe. A terrier stopping to take a sniff of something.

"We don't have anything for dinner," says Martin.

"Let's go for a curry, then," says James.

"Okay. Sure."

Martin retreats to his room and lies on his bed and reads a book. Eventually, the sound of football commentary cuts off. Martin can hear James moving around, throwing open cupboards, shifting dishes. He dozes and is woken by a rapping on his door.

"Ready to go?" James calls. He's cleaned the kitchen, Martin finds on entering. Though Martin knows the sight should mollify him, it actually irritates him more. If it is so simple to do this, why must James wait until Martin has had to drag the issue to him?

It is drizzling when they go outside. Dark now, though there is some light left at the horizon. "Nautical twilight," says James.

THE WAITER at the curry house recognizes them. The place is quiet, and he seats them by the window. He brings poppadums and chutneys. The window is steamed up, the world outside broken into smudges of light: shop displays, car headlights, bus interiors. An ambulance shimmers past.

"You have gigs this week?" says Martin.

"A couple of evenings at a hotel," says James. "Two weddings next weekend." James cracks a poppadum, picks up a shard. "I'm readying myself for the coming of Christmas. I'll be up to my waist in it before I know it, playing all the worst hits."

"Well, don't do it," says Martin. "Do something else."

The waiter arrives. They order Cobra beers and the same dishes they always have. "I make triple what you do per hour," says James when the waiter has departed.

"But I like my job," says Martin. "I'm making a career I enjoy." They're just jostling now, not yet resolved to bare their teeth.

"I value my freedom," says James. "There's nothing I absolutely need to do ever."

Yes, thinks Martin. *But don't you want to be tied to something?* He realizes that he can't really be bothered to press his point, though, to agitate, as he is so often forced to with James, for received wisdoms. He says, "This isn't their usual mango chutney."

They eat the rest of the meal silently. Martin is holding off telling his friend about Marina out of concern for James's fragility, and for what? For this foul atmosphere? When they're done, they split the bill, though counting the cash Martin realizes that James has paid none of the tip. He can't be bothered to chase his friend for it, though. Why is it always him, he wonders, keeping a tally? He's thought often this evening of Marina in the piano room, and this reflection has provoked a sense of guilt. And yet why should this guilt fall to him? This guilt born of the fact that his friend can't get over his old girlfriend? Why this allowance for all the drama James makes of things?

Outside, the drizzle has stopped. The roads and pavements are damp and dark. The traffic has died away, shops are shut up. James lights a cigarette. They turn down the back street that leads home. James crosses the road on a diagonal. Martin follows. "I'm moving out," Martin says to the back of his friend's head. Has he decided this?

He supposes that saying it is his decision. "I'm going to get a place on my own."

James stops in the road, turns and looks at Martin for a long while. He is surprised, to Martin's satisfaction. "Because I didn't call the plumber?" he says.

"Of course not," says Martin.

James smokes in silence the rest of the way home.

10

A BRIGHT autumn morning in the park. Marina chooses a table facing out of the plate-glass window from which she can see the Serpentine. She can just make out the Saturday swimmers up at the lido: figures on the swimming jetty, preparing to lower themselves into the flat, frigid water. She suggested the meeting place. She came to Hyde Park with her parents and brother on the first morning that they moved to the city, when everything was new. They'd watched people feeding the swans, and felt proudly that they had arrived fully in London, in the middle of the place. Though, of course, real Londoners don't come here often, but for the wizened swimmers, but for Marina's mother who still lives in the city like a tourist herself.

Martin arrives in the café looking well-scrubbed and nervous. She stands to greet him. "The bus," he says, in explanation. She gestures to the view to show him that her state of waiting was not unpleasant. She feels less exposed here, not so open to his assessment as she was when hosting Martin and his boss at home. She watches him fumbling off his gloves and coat and feels the urge to tease him a little. A waitress comes and takes Martin's order, and when the girl has departed, Marina says, "I suppose you don't have a girlfriend."

He laughs, unsure, put off as she hoped. "No," he says. "Not at the moment. How do you know?"

"Well, it's Saturday at eight a.m., and you're here."

"You're married, and you're here."

"Marriage is a different thing," she says, and he laughs properly then.

• • •

THEY WALK, and she feels closely observed by him, though this observation isn't unpleasant. He lets her lead their meandering way around the park. They are reactive, each of them. They're similar in this respect: not people who act first of all, but those who watch others act, who try to understand. And that, in fact, is what she senses from him today: a will to understand her life now (as she herself sometimes tries to do), an urge to see how she got here from where she was when he last knew her.

She says, "You live near here?"

"In Shepherd's Bush."

"I haven't spent much time there."

He smiles at her.

"I go no farther west than Notting Hill," she says, making it a joke.

They emerge into a space of open grass. It's the hour of people with dogs: old ladies with terriers, kids with puppies, exasperated men in waxed jackets bellowing at Labradors.

"These days," she says, "I'm no longer trying to hide the fact that I'm rich."

Martin nods at her. "I never felt that you were, to be honest. We all knew you were rich. You were fitting in. That's all."

"Right."

"After your breakup with James . . ."

"Yes?"

"I was always surprised I didn't bump into you going to lectures or at the library."

"I switched my degree to only English literature, stopped the music. I worked very hard, but I didn't go to many lectures."

"I see."

She finds herself inclined to give him the full, true version: "And my dad died in the last year, so I was home for most of the time. I finished, but I wasn't really around." She drifted from a lot of friends back then. Either they knew about her father and were weird, or they didn't and she felt bad dropping the news on them.

"I'm sorry to hear."

"It happens," she says. They turn onto another path between trees. A group of men come past in running gear, each man more tired than the one before. The final participant staggers down the path swimming his arms through the air and gasping. They both watch his loping progress away from them without comment. Marina says, "I spent a lot of time trying to fit in at university. And now, I guess, I'm doing something different."

"What's that?"

She shrugs. "Accepting it, I suppose. I inherited a lot of money after my dad died. I'd always had access to wealth, but that made it more tangible. It's okay to want to reject being rich, but then you shouldn't take the money, and I wasn't ready to do that."

"I would have taken it," says Martin. "Everyone would take it."

He assumes she is seeking absolution, Marina thinks, but that isn't what she wants, exactly. "I went to school with lots of English girls who'd learned to deny that money means a thing." She shrugs. "But it does, doesn't it?"

He smiles at her. She felt she was saying something more consequential until she spoke the words and watched him listen to them. "Of course," he says.

"Perhaps it looks like I'm complaining, but I don't mean to be pitying myself," she says. "It's just that some of your people are out of control."

"My people?" He raises an eyebrow.

"Your compatriots."

"Right."

They rejoin a paved path. They pass a street musician playing a violin to general indifference. She says, "You like your job, I see."

"I do." He nods shyly. "I like the art, and I like the game of it."

"The game?"

"Judging the value of things on the market."

"Right."

"We're a bit like the English girls from your school. We don't talk about money, but we're always thinking about it."

"This is my work too," she says. "Knowing the price of something. Seeing the trends. Seeing value before others do."

"Exactly," he says. "Andy Warhol said good business is the best art."

"That elevates my work, does it?" She smiles. "Mr. Warhol's approval?"

THEY FIND themselves at the edge of the grass, Park Lane ahead of them. She suggests another coffee, and Martin agrees. They're finding a dynamic, a new way with each other. They cross the road. They walk toward Grosvenor Square. "What are you doing today?" he says.

A leaden feeling to consider the day ahead, after this. She says, "Chairing a board meeting for my husband's foundation."

"That sounds worthy."

"Not particularly," she says. "I run it now, pretty much. He doesn't care. It's a PR exercise."

"What does it do?"

"We teach teens in depressed Russian towns to refurbish electronics. My husband used to work with computers. This was supposed to be his legacy."

"But?"

"It's been badly run. There's corruption. Mostly the kids arrive to steal the glue. We're one of the biggest users of solvent adhesive in the country, but not much gets done."

"What do they do with it?"

"Sniff it!"

"People still do that?"

"Of course."

"Well, it was a nice idea, I suppose."

He is being too kind, too agreeable. He seems to think this life
of hers needs his modest flattery. "It was a terrible idea." She laughs.
"And now I have to chair meetings full of people who can't admit this."

They walk past an Aston Martin showroom, past other high-end
businesses marked out only by brass plaques next to Georgian porticos.

"There's a good commercial gallery on this street," says Martin.

"Show me," she says. "Why not?"

A YOUNG woman is opening the place when they arrive. She opens
the door, and then retreats to the desk to lay out sheets of information
about the show. Martin goes to take one of these sheets, and he and the
girl share some small talk, moving into industry chat as Marina, giving
them space and resenting just slightly his brief desertion, drifts into
the first room. The show is of figurative paintings by an artist, Peter
Doig, whose work Marina doesn't recognize. There are paintings of
strange figures, many in twilight. Scenes of beaches, of jungle. There
are lots of dark blues and greens and purples. Night pictures. Quiet
scenes of half-suspended life. Marina reads the information about the
artist on the wall. The pictures are ominous, she thinks, spare and yet
complex. She likes the owned dissonance, feels the unease of the Scottish man who has chosen to live in Trinidad, to reside in a land shaped
by the colonial brutalities of his forbears. The paintings are all wrong,
perfectly so, shadowed by something grand and terrible. She hears
Martin's steps behind her, moving through the rooms more quickly
to catch up. They arrive together in front of a large image of a man
playing Ping-Pong against a gridded background.

"This is the best piece, right?" she says.

"You think so?" There is something glad in the tone.

"Do you?"

Martin smiles. "I do. But tell me why." He's on home turf now,
relaxed, and she likes this new sense of him.

"You first."

"The grid. The tension. The color. It's a picture that understands itself."

"Right," she says. "What about the man's face, though?"

"The face is good."

"Certain men play games like this. He's trying to not try and failing. He's leaning too far into that table. He's giving himself away."

Martin nods. "There's something sort of grotesque. The inversion of the colors. His odd gray skin. His belly. He's not in control. And the picture itself is also out of control. Look at the jungle grass encroaching at the edge of the frame, the trees behind the tiles. It's all almost too much. It's all pushing us too far."

"I feel for him, and yet I think, 'This man is not a good man.'"

"I like that," says Martin. "That's true."

"This is a kind of man I know. They're very impressive, always on it. They have total confidence. You feel when you first meet them that they can make the world as they wish it. They don't suffer bullshit or the self-defeating doubts the rest of us have. You meet them and you think that they're utterly serious and maybe you want to be near this determination." Martin nods silently, watches her, pleased as she is by the easy rhythm of their talk. "And yet, this is the other side." She points at the picture. "This is the shadow of this kind of man. You can't believe so truly in yourself without being a little petty, I think, without a little ignorance of your own foolishness. These men don't doubt what they want. These men are relentless, so tiring eventually. These men can't let a single thing rest."

"Is that so?"

"Believe me."

Martin grins, and Marina feels a flush of pleasure at their playful chatter, at finding herself understood.

11

ON WEDNESDAY morning, Martin is passing through the public rooms of the house when Julian beckons across the gallery space to him. Julian stands in front of a colorful Diebenkorn abstract. He's with an Asian couple. The man is in an indigo-blue cotton suit, the woman wears a navy cocktail dress. They appear to be in their late thirties. The man holds his arms behind his back, one hand clasping an elbow, stooping forward a little. Martin thinks of footage of Prince Charles visiting hospitals: the posture of a man being shown a thing and attending politely.

"It's in the color, the unlikely way that the shapes fit together," Julian is saying. "There's a form you feel you know somehow, like impressions recalled from childhood, a language you used to speak."

"Yes," says the man. "Very simple. But interesting."

"This is my colleague," says Julian. "Martin. He's a great fan of this picture. He'd buy it himself if we paid him a little better."

"Or sneak it out in my briefcase," says Martin.

The couple titter. Julian's look is approving.

"Big briefcase," says the man. They all laugh again.

"I think it's not the kind of color we're looking for," says the woman. "The space where we will hang it needs to be warm. We want something with strong, warm colors."

Julian looks at her for a long moment. "Of course," he says. "I'm not going to tell you that you can't leave this house and go to a bookshop in Soho where you can buy a warm red poster of a Rothko." He keeps the firm expression before he breaks into a smile, draws on the couple's uneasy laughter. "Everyone has their own conditions when buying a picture. They're the ones paying. I'm not in a position to tell anyone that their reasons for buying a thing are incorrect." He waits. He scratches his scalp. He is more boyish suddenly. He doesn't need to vocalize the *but*. "Maybe it's too much of a stretch, yet I think buying a picture is like having a child. Do you have children?" he says.

"Yes," says the woman.

"Well, you know. The child doesn't fit into your life. The child changes your life. That's the point of having one, isn't it?"

WHEN THE couple leave, Julian pats Martin on the back.

Martin shakes his head. "Go and buy a poster in Soho?"

Julian is enjoying Martin's surprise, his mock-scandalization.

Martin leans into it. "And he probably owns a quarter of Guangzhou."

"Chengdu, actually."

"And you tell her to go and buy a Rothko poster?"

"You don't need these lessons. You know these lessons. Coffee?" Julian points the way to the restaurant.

Martin nods. "I understand the psychology. The need to encourage them to impress you. But you really push it."

"These people respect assertiveness. There are many billionaires in the world," Julian says. "*Someone* will buy the fucking picture."

In the café, Julian leans against the short bar area, taps a long guitar-playing fingernail on the marble. "Acquiring money is just the first part of being rich."

"Yes?"

"The actual materiality of being rich, the confirmation of it, we sell here."

They order flat whites from Pierre, who runs the bar, and the man goes to work on the coffee machine, which gurgles and hisses and spits out a jet of steam. "There's a way to be properly rich," Julian says, re-suming. "That's our business."

"Yes."

"Do you know the quote from Chekhov, about how every happy man should have an unhappy man with a hammer in his closet?"

"No."

"Reminding the happy man with his tapping that there are un-happy people in the world." Julian smiles. "I too, in this job, have a hammer, and I with my tapping remind the rich that they are not truly rich, that they are just impostors, that *real* wealth belongs to other men: those with the proper tastes and manners of the truly wealthy."

"Right."

"And there are a lot of them. Don't forget that."

Julian spots someone he recognizes near the front door. He rises and moves off to greet the woman. The coffees arrive. Martin sips his, enjoys the muted clamor of the dining room. Cutlery against plates. Glasses being moved in the kitchen. Julian comes back, smiles. "Sorry."

"It's fine."

"Her husband's cancer is in remission."

"That's good."

"I've always wanted to build a sale around a damn fine Ben Nich-olson he has." He sighs. "I suppose it can wait."

LATER IN the day, Martin is at his computer composing an e-mail to a client. A bubble rises through the watercooler, breaks the surface with a rumble. Henry drums lightly on his desk. His Instagram ac-count is open on the screen in front of him. He's typing a caption to an image of a Henry Moore sculpture. "Fucking Wednesday," he says. Julian comes through, points to Martin, points to his office. Martin stands. "Hump day," says Henry. "Let's keep things positive."

In the office, Julian beckons Martin to close the door. "You have plans this weekend?" he says.

"Why?"

"I told you that you'd made a good impression."

"With whom?"

"Mr. Gorelov."

"Yes?"

"He wants you to deliver the Basquiat."

"Really?"

"You've been to Geneva before? He keeps part of his collection there, in the Freeport."

"Tax considerations?"

"Naturally."

Julian leans back in his seat. Behind him, a pile of papers collapses sideways, splaying out onto the carpet. Julian doesn't react to this. "I have to say that you've done well."

"Thanks."

"You're likable."

Martin shrugs to dismiss the compliment.

"Not everyone is. You've got something about you that he appreciates."

Martin laughs. Julian stays solemn, however. "Let's see how far this can take you, shall we?"

12

MARTIN STANDS in front of the mirror. It's two-thirty, and he's unsure how much he slept or whether he actually slept at all. He went to bed just before nine but didn't drift off for what felt like hours. He recalls a sense of shifting, of time passing unaccountably, and then the alarm. Outside, it's dark but clear. If he crouches down in front of the window at the back of the room, as he did when he got out of bed, he can get an uninterrupted view of the sky.

Now he wears his trousers and shirt, holds a couple of ties in his hand. The shirt is clean, well-ironed, though there is a little blue mark on the top of the yoke. He steps toward the glass. It's just a piece of lint. He picks it off with a fingernail and flicks it away. The shirt has a straight point collar, French cuffs. He didn't ask for these features, just bought the shirt off the shelf, and yet he has learned to identify them. He is not one of those bores who rattle on about what kind of tie to wear to a garden party, but something has driven him to distinguish the cuts of cloth. He checks he has his passport one last time. He puts on his coat. He goes up to the street and sees the taxi approaching.

AT THE auction house, the picture is in the storeroom, packed up in a wooden crate of the auction house's signature blue, amongst other crated works. Clive, who handles the logistics of these transfers, stalks around, looking aged under this fluorescent light. He places his hand against the plywood. "This is it," he says.

"Yes," says Martin. "Funny to think that you could buy a country estate with—"

"Please," Clive cuts in. "Let's think about that when it's delivered."

AT THE airport there are checkpoints, forms to be filled in. Clive, Martin, and the security man keep an eye on the painting as it is unloaded from the van. "The forklift guys are the ones you have to watch," says Clive. "For them there are only two types of people in the world. Those who have forklifts and the idiots who don't."

They follow the painting out onto the runway, special passes hung around their necks, helmets and fluorescent jackets on. All this for a painting, Martin thinks, for this object Basquiat made one day in a run-down warehouse loft. There's a hint of sun on the horizon now, a smell of jet fuel in the air, a little moisture on the wind. When the forklift arrives to bear the picture from the truck bed into the hold, Clive advances. "Slowly," he shouts at the driver. "No prizes for speed."

IT'S A passenger flight, and Martin boards via the gangway with the other travelers. He thinks of the picture beneath him in the hold. It's not long after dawn when the plane rises over a landscape that has yet to gain its color: gray-green grass at the side of the runway, oily tarmac, wire fences, half-molted trees. He looks down at houses, gardens, streets with vehicles moving slowly on them, and then they pass through cloud, and then the details are lost to pattern: the camouflage of fields, the branches of highways, the flat shimmer of rivers and ponds. Martin sleeps and only wakes again to the plane's descent into Geneva.

He disembarks. Another access pass. Another runway. The air is warmer here, the sun is out. He stands next to the plane and watches the Swiss forklift man's pink hands on the controls. The Freeport people come to pick up the picture after it has been unloaded. He sees it into their care. Martin himself must clear customs; then the ride to the location. He waits outside the airport for his cab. His mouth tastes of sleep. He sucks a breath mint. The car pulls up. They drive down a four-lane highway. Car showrooms. Shopping malls. Overpasses. Blocks of flats clad in colorful materials. The sky is blue and clear.

The Freeport is a large, blocky building, calculatedly anonymous. At the first security checkpoint, Martin hands over his passport. The man behind the desk studies it, types sightlessly into a computer. He is a mousy, neat man. He gives a neutral smile. A sign says ENHANCED SECURITY PROTOCOL. The man points Martin toward the main building. An automatic door opens. "You will wait there," he says.

In the main building, Martin checks in at another desk, hands over his documents again. He is directed to take a place on a large sofa, is brought a coffee. Two men in thigh-length, sky-blue caretaker's coats come out of an office and head down a corridor. He drinks the coffee. He feels a wave of tiredness wash over him. Hushed voices, the sound of shoes squeaking against a painted floor. He loses himself in sluggish thought, then looks up to see Oleg coming through the front doors.

The oligarch looks smart. He wears a tie, a suit of mottled gray wool. He looks like he's caught some sun since Martin last saw him. He smiles tightly and reaches out a hand. He goes to the desk, where a couple of men in dark business suits have appeared. Marina arrives in Oleg's wake. Martin feels a wave of gladness to see her. She wears high-waisted, juniper-green trousers and her hair is up. She kisses Martin on both cheeks. She blows air through her mouth in mock exhaustion. "He rushed in," she says. "He's ecstatic about getting this painting of yours."

"His painting," Martin corrects.

MARTIN FOLLOWS two men in blue coats toward the viewing room, where they will extract the painting from the plywood box,

ready for Oleg's inspection. The director of the Freeport is now brief-
ing the oligarch about a new section of the storage facility that will
soon be opening. As Martin departs, he hears the start of the pitch,
which begins with the glee of military excess: so many tons of rein-
forced concrete, so many hundreds of millimeters of steel.

"They could drop five nuclear bombs on Switzerland," the director says, letting the oligarch finish the thought.

"That seems excessive," Oleg says, and laughs. "Even one is probably too many."

IN THE viewing room, the porters move with a performative care
as they lift the painting clear of its crate. They watch Martin watching
them. They mount the picture on an easel. It appears to be as it was
when it was placed into packaging in London. Martin consults notes,
walks around the picture studying it, ticking off numbered points. He
hasn't had such a responsibility before, and hopes self-consciously that
he is acting as the Freeport men expect. Eventually he nods, and the
men move off.

Oleg enters, pushing the door back forcefully. "There it is!" he says.

Marina comes in behind him, carrying a bottle of carbonated water.

Oleg moves close to the painting, lowers into a heavy squat. He
clasps his own knees, pants a little. He is studying a point at the bottom of the canvas. He stands again. He looks at Martin. "That is quite
a picture," he says. He laughs breathlessly.

"I think you're right," says Martin.

"You like it, Marinka?" says Oleg.

Marina shrugs. "Yes," she says.

"Marina is not naturally enthusiastic," says Oleg. "This is her de-
fect and her charm."

"It's a good painting," she says, "but did you have to buy it?"

"I spend about ten percent of my yearly income on art," he says.
"This is healthy, I think." He looks to Martin, who feels compelled to

nod back. Oleg gestures at the picture. "This particular work was interest on a few investments. That's all."

"You're very clever," says Marina flatly. She takes a long pull from the carbonated water.

The three of them stand, studying the picture. After some time, Oleg turns to Martin. "I have something to show you."

Outside the room is one of the porters. He points down the corridor. "Please," he says, indicating the way. They pace past identical steel doors. The floors are blue-painted concrete, a tone off from that of the porters' coats. Oleg is walking next to Martin. Marina lingers behind.

They pass a storage room with its door ajar. It's stacked with boxes and there are a couple of Louis XVI chairs standing in the middle of the room, a man in a suit looking at them intently, a porter waiting patiently next to the man.

"They say this building houses one of the greatest art collections in the world," says Oleg. "All these rooms, all these works. A dark collection."

"I see."

"I have pressure from the insurers," he says. "Too much art in here. Their exposure is great. They want us to spread things to different facilities. This concentration makes them nervous. They have fantasies. Heists. Terrorists." Oleg laughs. "I tell them, though, I want to be part of a world where evil people still care so much about art."

The porter stops at a door. He taps a code onto a pad. He inserts a small key into a lock. There is a click. He slides the roller door back to admit himself to the room. It's an anonymous space, fluorescent-lit, a single easel next to plywood boxes.

Oleg points to a box. "Could you get that one out?" he says. They stand out in the corridor as the man works. Oleg hums tunefully, though Martin can't identify the melody. From somewhere else in the huge building echoes the basketball-court squeak of a person walking quickly on the gloss-painted floor.

When the man has set up the picture, he comes out of the room. He nods to Oleg, who in turn gestures Martin into the small space.

Inside, Martin stands in front of the easel, examines the painting placed on it. The picture is, to Martin's eye, about seventy centimeters square. An arshin, he thinks, an archaic measurement, because the painting, he knows on sight, is nearly a century old.

"Malevich?" he says, just to say it, to let Oleg respond. It's a bigger work than the other Malevich abstract at Oleg's country house. It's a picture of greater complexity, also.

The oligarch nods. "Because you admired my other one."

On the canvas, a single tapering line of dark red, set on a white background, is overset with perpendicularly oriented shapes: rhomboids in black and blue and lighter red and a black sphere overlapping a dark-navy rectangle. Near the top of the canvas an eye-shaped block of brownish yellow is offset across this central red line.

If Martin squints, this single line, cross-strutted with other lines of varying lengths, is like a cartoon image of a fish skeleton without the head. He lets his eyes focus, lets his gaze slacken again. He can hear Oleg breathing heavily behind him. It takes some time to take in. That is the pleasure of this kind of picture, Martin thinks: the apparent simplicity that yet gives rise to the complicated interaction of the few elements, like a haiku. The line made and broken. The particular angles chosen, certain shapes and colors alternated. There is a sense of movement in the image, a weight born of the tones contrasted. Angles echo. Diagonals repeat. There is an inevitability about where each part is placed, and yet it does not feel programmatic. He wants to spend more time with the picture, to stand and consider it, yet Oleg is looking at him expectantly. "You like it?"

He knows Martin likes it, Martin thinks. He nods. "Of course."

"*Supremus Number Fifty-One*," says Oleg. "People think it's lost."

"Really?"

The oligarch shrugs. "But as you can see, it isn't."

"How did you acquire it?"

"From a man who acquired it from one of the artist's students. The lineage is very clear, I can assure you."

"But you didn't publicize it?"

"It was a discreet sale, I should say."

"It hasn't been studied?"

"The student kept the picture a secret, and the man I bought it from, because he got a bargain, wasn't shouting about it either."

This news, the shock of the rareness, the privilege of the sight, causes a knot in Martin's chest, a pleasure hardly distinguishable from panic. It's too much, he feels. This new context draws the moment fearfully close to a dream that reveals itself as such in hyperbole and incoherence. "Can I take a photograph on my phone?" Martin asks.

"It's just for you? Of course." Martin raises his phone, double-checks that the flash won't go off, takes three photographs in quick succession.

Oleg says, "The painter wrote about this picture. It was a major advance for him."

"It's amazing," says Martin. His breathing is shallow. He realizes that this must be the most valuable picture he has ever seen outside a museum. He pushes away the thought. He turns back to Oleg, who still watches him carefully, pleased to see the effect of the work on Martin. "What a thing to own!" says Martin.

"A privilege," says Oleg. "Yes. Indeed."

WHEN THEY emerge from the Freeport, a black Range Rover is waiting outside. "You will come to the restaurant with us?" Oleg says to Martin.

Martin looks at Marina, who smiles neutrally. "I'd love to," he says.

MARTIN RIDES in the front passenger seat, next to the driver, a bodyguard, who drives straight-backed, manipulating the gearstick and indicators with firm, definitive movements.

When they arrive at the restaurant, they enter through the back of the building, the bodyguard preceding them. They emerge onto a private mezzanine. A view of the lake through large windows, the clamor of the restaurant rising up from below. "This is my favorite place in the city," says Oleg.

"It's amazing," says Martin.

"It is a place to make deals, Switzerland. A straightforward country. I was trained as an engineer. I like things to be logical. I do not like uncertainty."

"Yes," says Martin.

"These days, Russia has much uncertainty."

"I can imagine."

"I am no longer a young man. Now when I have breakfast, already I would like to know what is for dinner."

"Yes."

"As an example."

There is a silence then. Martin wonders what to say, wonders what it would take for a man like Oleg to like him. Is such a thing possible? The oligarch is staring out of the window at the lake. Marina asks Martin whether he has been to Geneva before, asks about how much he travels for work. She speaks formally. In front of her husband she is dialing back from the familiarity with which she talked when they met in the park. The new reserve gratifies him, he finds. They have something worth keeping between themselves.

A waiter comes and greets Oleg warmly. Oleg orders the tasting menu for each of them, a bottle of red wine.

"The chef here is very good," Oleg says.

"I'm sure," says Martin.

"I like food. The greatest pleasures of this life are food and art."

The sommelier arrives to pour the wine. "How long have you been collecting art?" says Martin.

Oleg thinks. "When does buying art become collecting?" he says. He smiles. "I have been buying good pictures since the nineties."

"You have an incredible collection," says Martin.

Oleg inclines his head to the side, looks at Martin slantwise. "I am not one of those Russians who is collecting for show."

"Certainly not."

"Art opens a window to you. It reminds you that there are things beyond your own life."

"Yes," says Martin. "It is like that thing Chekhov says about having an unhappy man in your closet, tapping with a hammer to remind you that there are unhappy people in the world."

"Perhaps," Oleg says. He frowns. "But as I remember it, the man is tapping to remind you that one day the world will take you in its jaws."

A PÂTÉ arrives, warm bread to accompany it. The wine is incredible: a flavor that comes in waves, changes in the mouth. The pâté is rich, piquant.

"So, you like the Malevich picture?" Marina says, looking at Martin.

"It's amazing," says Martin.

"That simple picture?" says Marina. She smiles.

She wants to tease, he senses. Martin says, "Of course it's simple, but the simplicity is what's so amazing about it. He does so much with so little. At the time he made this work, the idea of painting in this way was totally new. He was trying a new approach. His aim was a method of composition that is only about itself, *nonobjective*, as he called it."

"How so?"

"Not based on objects. Not representational. He wanted to make a type of art that was free, guided only by its own logic. Not the game of pictorial painting, not *portraying* something. Not a picture of a tree, say, that gets judged primarily on how much it looks like a real tree."

"I get that," Marina says. "But what *is* he painting?"

"*How*, I think, is the question. His canvases are about geometrical and spatial relationships. He did weird mathematical calculations.

He was interested in the fourth dimension. You sense the harmony in them, right?"

Oleg observes Martin and Marina talking with equanimity. He sniffs at his glass of wine. He sips and gazes at his wife.

"So he's making his own laws of painting?" Marina says.

"*Discovering* them, he would say," says Martin.

She laughs. "Of course."

"What's funny?"

"I get the theory, but does it work? These pure forms? This pure art? He decides these new rules, and then says—what?—that they're absolute, natural?"

"Not natural, exactly. It's complicated. They're invented, he says, but they're not dependent."

"Isn't that just, well, marketing? How's he proving this? He's casting around blind, alighting on these shapes, and then he says this is the hidden thing, this is the world as it really is underneath."

"I think he believed this."

"Of course." She smiles. "But is this the true account of things? These nearly holy influences? These pure motives? It's good history, but it's never so simple. What about the broader trends, the aesthetics of the time, the other people doing similar things?"

"I'm sure you need an ego for such radical work."

"Right, but part of his importance to you is not the work at all, but the pose, the claim to truth. Don't you see there's something megalomaniacal in the story you're buying? Gauguin to Malevich to Pollock. One man, one maniac after the other, turning over the board game, shouting out his own genius." She is grinning, playing her exasperation as comic. There is some real irritation behind that, though, Martin thinks, some anger she is uncomfortable plainly unleashing.

He pauses. He says, "Malevich didn't mean to put himself at the center. He said, 'Art doesn't need us and it never has.'"

"He's speaking for art like a ventriloquist with a dummy." Marina laughs. "He has his hand up art's ass."

Two waiters mount the stairs to the mezzanine to remove plates and replace cutlery.

"It's hard work, with my wife," says Oleg. "It's difficult selling her anything."

AT THE end of the meal, Oleg looks at his phone. "Business," he says. "I must go. Thank you for delivering my painting." He waves his hand at Marina. "My wife will look after you. You fly when?"

"Tomorrow," says Martin.

The oligarch stands. He puts out his hand for Martin to shake. At the back of the room, the chair of the bodyguard scrapes the wooden floor. The two of them go out.

"You'll look after me?" says Martin to Marina.

She smiles. "Sure."

13

OUTSIDE, THE people on the street are a surprise after the quiet restaurant. Crowds go about their ordinary afternoon errands, and Marina and Martin drift amongst them, numbed by wine and fine food. They walk without discussing their direction, along shopping streets, pedestrian alleys, downhill, toward the lakefront. Marina looks at Martin moving carefully between the shoppers, past people queuing for a bus, skirting a man who is walking quickly while typing into his mobile phone. Martin plays with the button of his blazer with his left hand as he walks. He's nervous, she thinks. She wonders now whether she was too forceful in voicing her skepticism regarding this picture of her husband's.

She says, "You're okay?"

"Very much," says Martin. "It's a very interesting day. I'm grateful."

"Thank my husband."

"But you put in a good word for me, I think. He asked specifically for me to transport the piece."

She smiles. "I made a suggestion. You're a puppy. You're a puppy and it's hard not to want to give you a treat."

"When you put it that way," he says, "it sounds, well . . ."

"I'm joking. I'm glad of you. You're an old friend. Living with him is an overwhelming experience. I forget I had a life before. You're part of that life, I suppose." She recalls visiting James and Martin's childhood house when she was a teenager: the shabby kitchen gardens; the dilapidated chicken coop, painted a fading blue; the shed filled with rusting tools and an odor of old metal that brought back trips to Marina's grandparents' tiny dacha that she didn't even know she recalled until then. It was something she needed, a route to a part of herself that had been dormant.

She senses he feels the same pull she does toward nostalgia, the same wariness too. He turns the conversation back to the purpose of his visit. "Your husband's collection is remarkable," he says.

"He's proud of his paintings. Those pictures in that building are among the only things he actually owns."

"Really?"

"Strictly, in a legal sense, the houses are owned by offshore trusts, the planes and cars by a shell company. He has the only stake in these enterprises, of course. He leases these things back to himself. You know these kinds of deals."

"For tax? I try not to pay attention, to be honest."

They are on a narrow, quiet lane now. Martin walks at Marina's side, on the road. With him stepped down off the curb, their eyes are at the same level.

"Tax and security, and protecting his assets," she says. "It's a complicated game. It's not my work, but I know some of the people who do this stuff. It's a system that forgets itself as it works. It's clever. Men and women around the world who do a single thing and don't ask questions. Safe deposit boxes full of documents. Small offices in Caribbean countries. That kind of stuff."

"Yes," Martin says.

"You deal with these people too, I suppose."

"Sometimes. The Chinese clients often pay from many different accounts, I'm told. It's not specifically my business, the way they pay."

"Of course," she says. "It's part of the plan, this separation."

"You mean?"

"Between the work and the source of the funds. Your Chinese clients will be getting around currency controls."

He laughs. "Our Chinese clients love art and have excellent taste. I can't speculate on anything else."

She cuffs him on the arm, feels a quick charge in the contact, notes a change in his look. "You see. You're perfect. You're good at this."

THEY GO to a café. They order coffees. "You don't have to work?" Martin asks.

"Of course," she says. "Always. I can take the afternoon, though. You?"

"This is a part of my work."

"Spending time with me is your work?"

"Well, no . . ."

"You're easy to fuck with, you know."

"I do."

The café looks out at the junction of a quiet street. A couple come past on bicycles. A bus stops to discharge a passenger. Martin is sitting back in his seat, more relaxed than he was earlier. He notes her studying him, seems to flinch at it. "Why are you staying here tonight?" he says.

"I have an appointment tomorrow."

"Work?"

"No," she says.

"Money things?"

She playacts a grimace. "My dentist is here." She exhales. "I know, I know. Going all the way to Switzerland to visit the dentist is fucking ridiculous."

Martin laughs. "What's special about him?"

"Everyone goes. His clinic is very clean. It doesn't have that dentist smell. He doesn't ask you questions while he has his hands inside your mouth."

"I hate it when they do that. You have to come all the way to Switzerland to avoid that?"

She smiles. "That's what it takes, I guess." With Martin, she thinks, this light chatter is natural. This is not work, where they view her with suspicion, and she is thus exasperated and laconic if she jokes at all, nor home, where it is all lost on Oleg.

THE AFTERNOON drifts into evening. An autumn cool rises on the breeze up from the lake. Neither of them wants to eat. They take window seats in a bar on a back street, and drink wine and watch people parallel-parking in front of the flats across the road. The sight of these people returning to the lit kitchens above the street makes Marina feel a long way from London. She finishes her glass of wine and says, "Why didn't we share a bottle?"

Martin smiles. He says, "We still can. It's not too late."

They call the waiter over. She chooses a light, fruity red. "Not good for the dentist tomorrow, I suppose," she says. She and Martin reminisce about university. They talk about their hopes for their jobs, the realities of their jobs. They talk about why neither of them wants children, and the talk and the bottle push them smoothly past a threshold beyond which, she senses, they would otherwise have felt nervous to pass. They are doing nothing, yet this easy intimacy already has the nature of a secret between them, and she would quail were she to find her husband watching them. She goes to the bathroom and puts her hand on his shoulder as she passes him, and he seems surprised by this contact, and she finds herself surprised and gladdened by his surprise in turn. You make choices, sometimes, before you know you have made them.

They finish the bottle of wine, and then decide to go for a cocktail, but they find nowhere suitable as they walk. She could look on her phone for a place, but this isn't the game. The logic tonight is doing what is in front of them. They round a corner and there, ahead, is Marina's hotel. She says, "Let's just have a cocktail here."

14

OLEG SITS in the library and watches the video. The penis goes in. The penis comes out. The woman groans and clutches the bedding. Oleg sits in the padded leather chair in his dressing gown, the laptop on the desk in front of him. He's in the London house and it's around midnight. He should go to bed. He got back from the airfield in the evening. Victor chauffeured him through the drizzle into town. Oleg ate a steak alone in the dining room. On the screen, the woman cries out in theatrical ecstasy and the man grunts and thrusts. Oleg doesn't touch himself. He isn't aroused. He just sits and watches. The couple are in a sun-filled apartment: a bed in the middle of the room, an ugly tripod floor lamp in the corner. There is a hideous sculpture of a nude woman on the dresser. It is a cheap idea of a luxury flat. Watching the video, he can almost smell the chipboard, the plastic odor of things made in bulk in China. These kinds of locations are rented, doubtless. Though perhaps the production crews of these videos have to furnish the rooms themselves. That would make sense, he supposes, for hygiene and stains. Or maybe they have a cleaner like Nadja. She did very well when he spilled tawny port onto a white sofa recently. Why is he thinking about stains and furniture, though? The couple shift into a new position. Some hope springs within Oleg that this should lead to something. He sits and watches and waits for his old desire to return. The woman is being fucked from behind. She presses her forehead into the bed and moans. The man is blank-faced, hard-bodied, and robotic. Oleg still feels nothing. He turns off the video, shuts down the computer. Just a black screen in which his reflection is suddenly visible. He looks very tired. He looks not good, he thinks.

IN THE morning, Galib arrives by taxi. They travel together in the back of Oleg's car to Jacob's offices on Park Lane. It is a journey of barely five minutes. "How was your picture?" says Galib.

"My picture?"

"The painting you bought."

"Oh. Fine."

"Good."

He looks at Hyde Park to his left: the trees stuttering by, the crowds of tourists. Galib is silently appraising Oleg's mood. The two of them have been in business together for nearly three decades.

"How's your back?" says Galib.

"Ach. Bad. I don't do the exercises."

"They work. They work for me. The man is good. His advice is good."

"Of course. But the drudgery . . . the routine . . ."

"We're getting old," says Galib. "Learn to cope with drudgery."

Victor parks in front of Jacob's building. They get out and are waved through reception. They ride up to the office in a glass elevator. This is the great feature of Jacob's building: the way one can look out at the park as one rises, the trees partly in leaf, the Serpentine, Kensington Palace, the city stretching to the west where on a day like today it peters out in a haze of cool autumnal sunlight.

Jacob is waiting by the elevator when they emerge. He is tall, so much so that this characteristic strikes Oleg afresh each time they meet. They are often tall, these well-bred Englishmen. Though actually, as Oleg recalls, Jacob is self-made, from somewhere unpromising. Birmingham, maybe? He went to an ordinary school and an average university, Oleg seems to remember. He has the flintiness of someone who has fought his way to this office, this view, this role managing the assets of men like Oleg. He offers his hand and Oleg takes it. "It's good to see you," Jacob says.

"I would like to say the same," says Oleg, "yet always you have bad news for me."

Jacob grins. He has a shaven head, wears blocky, black glasses. He is spry, slightly ageless. Probably, he is a man who *does* do his physio exercises.

Jacob says, "That means you can trust me, right? The people to worry about are those who feed you only good news."

"You have a point," says Oleg. He nods at Galib. "You and him are my two closest associates because you spoon me shit all day."

"Always happy to help," says Galib.

THEY SIT in Jacob's large office and drink tea, and Jacob says, "The mine is an inconvenience to me."

"You say this before," says Oleg.

"The structures, the scale, the cash flow out of it. This is all hard to manage. Even more so when they put pressure on you."

"I know these people. I deal with this pressure. I accommodate. How do you think I acquired the mine in the first place?"

"Well, it's a vulnerability, at least."

Oleg pauses. He waits to make his point with the requisite force. Outside, behind Jacob, a pigeon flaps up past the window, making for the roof above them. "The mine was the great achievement of my career."

"It's hugely impressive, of course."

"You could drop central London right into it."

"I can imagine."

"*Thunk.*" Oleg presses a fist into a palm.

"The thing is, the scale is one of the issues. It's hard to manage with the subtlety we apply to your other assets."

"You know what potash is used for?"

"Fertilizer?"

"Mostly, yes, but you have to guess and you want me to sell?"

"I know the numbers. Four hundred dollars a ton. There has been some price instability recently, but demand is fundamentally inelastic. What else do I need to know?"

"Your food is fertilized with potash."

"It's very impressive, the grace of the system, the way it serves me. Really. But you're not agile, and from my perspective you should be agile."

Oleg likes Jacob. He likes the doggedness, the challenge. "Agile?" he says. "Help me with the language. Agile is a way to say, run away?"

"Consolidate. Prepare. You're exposed in Russia. You want a rerun of 2008? You want a crash? Or you want the government to start going after your property?"

"And then I own what, if I do your suggestion?"

"We reinvest. We diversify."

"A stock portfolio?" says Oleg. He flutters his hands to indicate flimsiness. "This mine is solid. This mine is a whole city in itself."

"I think we agree on this, to be honest. That's my concern."

"Suppose I sell. I won't get what it's worth?"

"Did you pay what it's worth?" Jacob can be sharp when he wants to. He grins.

"I put a lot of work into it. *Everything* needed to be modernized."

"I understand, but let's not get sentimental."

The word sets Oleg back for a moment. *Sentimental.* He heard that right. Yes. Understood it. The word has a Russian cognate. "I'm anything but sentimental," he says.

"Good," says Jacob. "You'll put some thought into this sale, then?"

Oleg stands. "That was the subject of this meeting?"

"That and some contracts to be signed off. I'll get Katy to give them to you on your way out."

Oleg nods. There is a photo on Jacob's desk of Jacob riding a bicycle in a tomato-red skinsuit. Funny hobbies these people have. Funny decorations they choose for their rooms.

They shake hands. Oleg steps toward the door and turns around. "Look at me," he says. "Look at me and tell me, am I so suited to all this running away?"

VICTOR IS waiting with the engine running when they leave reception. They pull out and merge with slow-moving traffic. Two policemen are riding horses along the edge of the park. These meetings, Oleg thinks, wear him out. Always a cascade of so many fine words with which people speak of retreat. What is his business now but *consolidation*? Is he sentimental to wish things different? Perhaps he is.

He worked hard to try to get his son, Alexi, interested in the business. He's put assets in Alexi's name, after all, as a way of finessing tax issues. The boy doesn't feel the real pleasure of money, though. He knows just the quick flush of spending it, not the more durable satisfaction of its accumulation. And yet what of that pleasure is there in Oleg's work presently? He exercises only the resolve of an old dog guarding its scraps.

Galib breaks the silence. "You'll consider his suggestion?"

"Certainly. He was persistent." They move haltingly through the traffic at the roundabout.

Oleg once plotted huge deals, built his holdings like a jigsaw. He has technical knowledge, foresight. He bought the mine because it was undervalued and because people will need ever more potash as the population of the earth increases. His was an understanding of the drift of history, but he's now in the same pattern of consolidation as all the thugs who merely levered their fortunes out of the state with force. "We need to do something big," he says.

Galib looks at him with sympathy. "Now isn't the time to do something big. You know that."

"I heard that Vanya has increased his factory holdings."

Galib nods. "I heard that too."

"That guy was a toady. That guy was a nobody."

"Yes."

"I remember him waving his finger at me in 1990. 'The party will survive this, and you will be forgotten.' What a little shit. And yet he's ridden in the President's slipstream to this."

"It amazes me that a man like you can still believe in fairness," says Galib. "You're very impressive in this respect."

"This man is a fucking beetle. This man is an insult to the world."

"Maybe. But does that concern you?"

"I have another move in me, I think. This is not quite my final position. I feel the tilt of the universe readying to right itself." He is exaggerating, speaking in a humorous tone, but he knows Galib well enough to know that Galib will understand the seriousness under all of this.

"You're a man of history," says Galib. He winks.

It's silly, and yet it's true. When it all drops away. When the pleasures of wealth diminish, this is what remains: his feeling of being situated, of knowing the truth of power.

They stop outside the London house. "I'll sort out those contracts," says Galib. Oleg flicks his hand to acknowledge this.

"It'll be okay," says Galib.

"Yes. Yes."

"Do your exercises."

15

AT MARINA'S hotel, they go to the bar, which is largely empty. The space, just off the hotel atrium, is dim and filled with excessively loud R&B, which reverberates through the structure of the booth at which they take seats. "What do you want?" says Martin.

She gestures at the bar. "I don't know. I'll go. I want to read their cocktail menu. You?"

He grins. "I want what you want."

She walks to the bar, conscious in that particular drunken way of how she places her feet, conscious as she talks to the barman of how she forms her words. She orders pisco sours, for some reason. *Swiss pisco sours,* she thinks. The logic of the night, now that it is night, is illogic. The barman takes his time making the drinks, and when she has them, finally, she turns and walks carefully again across the wide expanse of floor between the bar and the booth. A few couples huddle at tables, leaning together to be heard over the music, and at the table she moves toward, Martin sits back and watches her approach and grins. It strikes her that he is happy. It is that gladness of his that has been attractive about him today. He was so pleased by the picture he was shown, by the meal they ate, seems pleased—she flatters herself—by her company. Oleg is not like this, and she is not like this, and though it is easy to be condescending to someone so plainly satisfied, that is not the impulse she has. She feels that he has a freshness that she lacks and needs. She is taking great care not to spill the drinks as she approaches the table, which she reaches eventually, like a weary swimmer making land. She puts the drinks down. Martin's smile is encouraging, full in a way that makes her think of the young men who accost passersby on the streets outside her office sometimes: suited, square-jawed boys, proselytizing for the Church of Jesus Christ of Latter-day Saints, grinning, vibrating in fact, with the power of something greater than themselves.

She shouts against the music: "Pisco sours."

He says, "Excellent," firmly, as if congratulating her. He moves along the bench seat on which she sits, perhaps responding to her movement toward him or perhaps prompting it. She feels their impulses are tumbling together at this point. He smiles up at her shyly, shy in response to her look or shy in response to his own pleasure. She lowers herself down next to him, feels his shoulder warm against hers.

16

IT'S PAST 1 a.m., and they are both drunk, and they have both been waiting for this situation, he feels, for this point at which a certain amount of recklessness is just a given. The bar is now totally empty. People are still drinking in this city somewhere, Martin thinks, but not here. The barman has been keeping an eye on them all night, and now that Marina and Martin are the only customers, he sits on a stool next to the till and plainly stares them down. "They want us to go," Martin says.

Marina says, "Shall we, then?"

She stands and beckons him. The day has progressed in ever more ridiculous degrees, and at some point, Martin just felt he must surrender to it. He is like a gambler on a streak, he feels. Either that, or he is Wile E. Coyote, run off a cliff and yet to see that there is nothing but air beneath his feet. He follows Marina out of the bar to the escalator that runs up through the tall atrium of the hotel and to banks of elevators and rooms beyond. He is going up to her room, of course, yet he is not the kind of person who does this. He never would have thought himself possessed of the confidence to really step toward an old friend he has admired for such a long time, his best friend's ex, a client's wife. . . . Marina looks back at him as they rise past elaborate, tacky chandeliers: hanging bursts of plastic and metal and sculpted glass. A phone rings down at the circular reception desk beneath them. He thinks of Julian's injunction, to be bold with these people, to make things real with confidence and belief.

When Marina first went to the bar to buy drinks, Martin googled *Supremus No. 51*, and there was a black-and-white photograph of six pictures from an art show in Moscow in 1920, and the painting on the top right of the arrangement was unmistakably the canvas Martin had seen in the storage locker earlier that day. He flicked back on the phone to the photograph he had taken. The same work, yes. But alive here, colored so that the logic of the composition was actually percept-ible, the weight of the shapes and all the motion and lightness of the arrangement plain. He toggled between the two pictures: the proof of the painting in the past, next to Malevich's other works; and then his own photograph of its real existence, the proper truth of it. The feeling was linked, he felt, to the rest of the day with Marina and with Oleg. He was seeing something usually hidden from the likes of him. His colleagues back in London didn't know of this picture. The experts in the field, presumably, knew only that it had been lost. Yet Oleg has owned it for years, and now Martin has stood and examined it. The real work. The full idea of it, ushered through time unscathed. If that is possible, then what else?

There will be a time to doubt, to check the details and caveat the joy he feels to consider the picture, but that moment is not now, Mar-tin thinks. He feels happy to the point of anguish, a happiness he wants to test with pressure, like a loose tooth. At the top of the escalator, Ma-rina leads him off down a broad corridor. She is walking quickly. She puts out a hand and brushes the gold-painted molding on the wall as she walks. Then they reach the door, and she swipes her keycard, and fiddles and swipes her card again and they are in: a big suite, armchairs and sofa and dining table, and floor-to-ceiling windows offering a view of the lighted city giving way to the dark lake, and the floodlit plume of the fountain out in the water. This is ordinary for them, he tells himself, for people like her. He walks to the glass, looks out, puts his hand on the cool pane. He feels a little unsteady. Marina has kicked off her shoes and moved through the double doors to the bedroom. He waits. An empty bus rumbles past on the street before the hotel. He hears the sound of water running. He has drunk so much, but he feels oddly sober, present. The bedroom doors—French panel doors with imitation gold-leaf detailing—swing open to admit Marina with an easiness that belies their presentation as antique. A skillful illusion, he thinks. She is in her stocking feet, walking across the carpet. Her hair is down. As she approaches, Martin turns from the window to fully face her, pushing back his impulse to hesitation, disbelief. Her loose hair frames her long face, her alien, inconstant prettiness. She reaches out and grips his elbow, and stands very close, their torsos separated by an achingly short distance that he readies himself to close as she looks at him in happy expectation.

II

Autumn/Winter 2013/2014

17

OLEG GETS the call when he's walking the dogs in the garden. It's a drizzly day, the wind whipping in from the east. The grass is boggy. He wears an old pair of running shoes, wet around the toes.

It's Evgenia, the carer, and she takes some time to get to the point. He can hear that she's in the hallway of his mother's apartment from the distinctive chime of the elevator in the background. One of the dogs, Gena, returns to pant at his feet. He shoos Gena away. He senses that Evgenia is trying to ascertain his state, his readiness for what he is about to be told. His mother is ninety-three. He says, "Has something happened?"

"A stroke," says the girl, after a pause. "But she hasn't yet left us."

HE TAKES the jet out of Farnborough in the early evening. He drinks a glass of red as the plane gains altitude. There's cloud cover over London. The wing lights blink into fog. He catches only occasional glimpses of the illumination of the city below. A stroke, Oleg thinks. He thinks of the cells in his own brain, the flickering of nodes, switches. He considers the dimming, the shorting of her mind. He sloshes the wine around his tongue, tastes it: earth, acid, a long mouth. He can't think of it coolly. She was born in 1920. She once related to him a story of her own mother bringing home the news of Lenin's death. Oleg has urged her to leave Russia in recent years, but she hasn't wanted to. "I've moved around too much already," she said when he last proposed the idea. His father died twenty years ago. There has been nothing keeping her in the country since then. He wanted her to migrate to somewhere warm, told her she would be more comfortable there, happier. "Who am I to think that I should be happier?" she said. Yet why didn't he push? Would this have happened out of the city? In a cool villa with a view of the sea? The shock is not that she should be dying but that she should be alive at all, but he still feels the need for reasons. He cannot renounce the idea that he had the power to prevent this. She could have had better treatment, lived somewhere more conducive to health. Even now, something has incited this.

THEY TOUCH down at Ostafyevo Airport at 2 a.m. It's wet. The cold hasn't really come in. It's a transitional time of year. November. Dates will be significant now.

There is a car on the runway waiting to take him to the hospital. The ring road is quiet at this hour. The city glows silently to his right. They drive into Kuntsevo. There are trees around the road: bare branches reaching up against the deep blue of the night sky. They come to the hospital. He gets out and smells pine on the air. He is taken to her room by a woman in a medical uniform.

Then he's with her. She's lying on a bed, looking so small, an oxygen mask over her face. She's tucked so neatly in, her hands placed together on the covers. They're wrinkled, angular hands: blue and yellow and purple and pink. Hands, he thinks, from an expressionist picture.

She was an older woman—thirty-eight—when she had her first and only child, and he has always felt that this fact is noteworthy, important, that these years she waited for him made her different from other boys' mothers. She had grown up in the east, exotic even to her own son.

Her hands are a little cold, but soft, still living. Her face doesn't move. The respirator continues its work. The nurses are there, attentive but out of the way. This is what one pays for in a place like this: discretion.

This is the hospital were Yeltsin died. Where the others before him did. Perhaps it will be the hospital in which Putin will die. This is a thought that he tells himself to push away.

They lodge Oleg in a room in another wing: clean, quiet, a window facing the dark forest. He sleeps, and when he wakes a rhombus of sunlight is falling through the window onto his white sheets and a nurse arrives to tell him that the specialist would like to talk.

HER BRAIN is shutting down, the doctor says. He shakes his head. "We can't know what she feels at the moment, but the possibility of a recovery is extremely remote."

Oleg nods. He knows that it is hard for the doctor to say these things, that he should agree, but he can't.

"She's ninety-three," says the doctor, as if in explanation.

"Yes."

The doctor gives a little bow of his head: a strange gesture, performed, Oleg senses, when he really wishes to shrug.

"She was a doctor also," says Oleg.

"Right," says the doctor. The man plainly can't link that idea to the frail old body. He nods affirmatively, as if he must pantomime his agreement, as if what Oleg is telling him is so utterly mad that it must be humored.

OLEG SITS at her bedside. There is still a smudge of dirt across his sock from walking the dogs the day before. He wears the suit he put on when he came in from the garden. His shirt smells of sweat. He's normally a clean freak, but without his notice he has gained a half-animal odor that makes him think of his father returned from work at the university. He looks at his mother's hands on the covers again.

When he was much younger—when he had hair, when she was still a middle-aged woman—she would rub his scalp: combing her fingers between the follicles, digging her nails ever so slightly into the skin. It's strange, already, to recall the electric feeling of it.

It's the machines that alert him when she dies: monotone bleeps sounding as the systems track failures. The doctors and nurses talk in serious, hushed voices. It arrives for her in a moment: a little drawing back of the lips against the gums; an animal gesture. And then her face slackens and the life is out of her.

THEY TAKE her away when he finally gives them the signal. An attendant covers her and wheels the hospital bed to the elevator, careful not to knock against the doorframes. She is taken down to the morgue. A car comes for him and he goes not to his apartment but to hers. It's the same as he last saw it in late summer.

There are cushions on the floor, an upturned glass. He remembers being told that she'd been in the living room when she collapsed. He puts the cushions back on the sofa. The carpet is dry under the glass. It must have been empty, or whatever it held has evaporated already. He places the glass on the coffee table. The room is perfectly neat now. A room she could just walk back into.

The apartment smells of geraniums. She grew geraniums everywhere. There's a picture of her parents above the fireplace, a picture of Putin. She loved Putin. "Olezhka," she said once. "Look at his posture, study his posture. He doesn't slump like you do." Oleg couldn't argue with her on this subject. Once, when Putin criticized the oligarchs, she took the President's side, rejected the Harrods basket Oleg sent to her apartment. She loved all kinds of fruit. He made sure these hampers were full of mangoes and papayas and persimmons. She went fruit-mad in the nineties when she could get everything she wanted at any time. He inherited this from her. Still, she hadn't wanted that basket. She'd sent it back with a haughty note in her wonky handwriting.

Above the glass-fronted bookcase there's a picture of the town she grew up in: an eastern city built to a plan, streets that had only ever been named after Communist heroes. She moved there with her parents when she was a child. Oleg's father went to the city for his first university job, met her, brought her back west eventually.

OLEG FALLS asleep on the sofa. He sleeps amongst her things, amidst the smell of her. She didn't smell like an old lady, he thinks, though maybe he only believes that because she was his mother. He wakes in the middle of the night. He walks home to his own apartment, his security man following in the car. His father died in '94, and Oleg barely paused. He thinks of the fat man his father became, with that bloated red face, falling to the ground holding his chest. Oleg wasn't there when this happened. Later, his mother wouldn't talk about the moment. Oleg paid for the funeral, for the plot in the cemetery, but he didn't really feel the departure of the man. Those were fatherless years, in which he felt that he was creating himself.

He showers but doesn't shave. He sleeps again and then wakes and has no clue what time it is.

OVER THE next few days, he tidies her apartment. He works through cupboards and drawers, sorting photographs, letters, bills and receipts. She was young during the great patriotic war. She lost a sweetheart somewhere in Ukraine. He learned this from her only after his father had died. He finds a drawer full of orange-and-black Victory Day ribbons.

He gets caught in the groove of old things, suddenly attentive, say, to the aesthetics of a sixties tin-opener, an eighties ashtray. He establishes a routine of going to her apartment each morning. His beard gets thicker. When he leaves the apartment, he notices the Soviet-era buildings around which life in the city continues. He feels like he's seen an old world excavated, and yet not a gram of soil has been moved.

HER FUNERAL is on the Friday. There's a scattering of snow over the frozen ground, and the dim light gives everybody in attendance a gray pallor. The workers here must have used machines to break the frozen soil, he thinks. That is the engineer in him. Men from the undertaker's carry the coffin. Though their load is light, their slow movements try to conceal this.

The nurses have come, as have Evgenia and a couple of the neighbors. Marina arrived from England in the morning. The small turnout pains him, but who else could be expected? Her friends and relatives have died. There is no close family: cousins—yes—far in the east, but nothing more. It is shocking how quickly the traces of a person disperse. Who in this city could be counted upon to come to his own funeral? he wonders. Plenty to gawp, doubtless, but who to close their eyes and fondly recall him? German. Galib. The others have moved away from him or died. His mother was his strongest link to the city.

HE SMOKES in the graveyard afterward. On impulse he bought himself a packet of cigarettes at a street stall yesterday, and now he tears open the plastic wrap with his nail and smokes one and then another. He hasn't smoked for years.

Eventually he turns from the grave, from the tug of her in the dirt, the loneliness of it. They drive to his mother's apartment through drizzly twilight. Marina will fly back to London tonight. He hasn't yet made his plans. He senses that his wife observes him with concern.

•   •   •

THEY RIDE up to his mother's apartment in the too-small elevator. The building was the home of important people in former times: party organizers, ministers. It is old-fashioned now, though. The lifts are slow. The plumbing is bad. His mother felt the building the acme of privilege, though, refusing offers of anything better.

Mourners from the funeral are in the apartment when Oleg and Marina arrive, along with a couple of neighbors and the girl from the restaurant downstairs who used to bring up plates of pork cutlet and potatoes. He's approached by the old woman who lives next door and who wears a ragged cardigan tainted with a faint smell of fried meat. "She was a tough woman," says the neighbor. "I'm fifteen years younger. I worried she was going to outlast me." The guests pick at the food. The girl from the restaurant is getting through quite a bit of wine, trying to surreptitiously take photos of the view of the river through the window.

The carers accept the gifts and cards Oleg hands out. They smile and try to say kind things, though they are the general sorts of observations that could be made about any old lady. She was already very elderly when they met her. "She had integrity," says Evgenia, and he murmurs his thanks for her efforts. They thought that his mother held herself too aloof from their care. She *did* think she was special—yes—and yet she *was*. That is what they can't see. They witness only the shadow of her specialness, what was left of the entitlement her abilities allowed her. She was smarter than anyone. When he was small, she would answer his childish questions for hours. You could build a world from what she told him. Asking about how metro trains ran, for instance, taught him about electricity, about tunnel digging, about the history of the city and the ingenuity of great men.

AFTER THE funeral guests have departed, the caterers clean up. He and Marina drink tea in the kitchen. Marina looks at her watch. She wants to say something sincere to him, he senses, but he must make space for it, open himself to her care. The river rolls away morosely outside, the city light reflected in its oily surface. Marina puts her hand on his, and yet it is too much. He shakes off her grip and walks the apartment.

When Marina departs for the airport, he looks through his mother's books. He grazes on the food the caterers have left in the refrigerator. He chose his mother's favorite dishes—*syrniki*, *pirozhki*, and *golubtsi*—and the guests have hardly eaten anything. The potted plants look wrong where they've been placed back on the coffee table. He rearranges them, but can't seem to locate them as they were. He sleeps on the sofa.

WHEN HE wakes the next day, he thinks that he should attend to the mail that has arrived since his mother's death. He sorts through catalogues and bills. He throws all of it into the bin apart from the last letter, which, to his surprise, is addressed to him. The envelope is rough and blue, his name written out in neat script. He sits on his mother's flower-patterned sofa. He opens the envelope to find a handwritten letter.

Cousin—

I am writing because your mother died. I used to write to your mother once or twice a year, and her carer called me on the telephone on the day on which your mother passed. Perhaps I should have spoken to you, Cousin, but forgive me: I see you on my TV screen sometimes, but I don't know you well. I don't have a number to reach you.

I mean to offer my prayers for your mother. She died on the day of Saint Alexander Nevsky, who ruled Russia as an instrument of God. I don't think that your mother practiced religion, but she believed, I think, in the strength of our country. I didn't believe in God for a long time. I couldn't find God in my life. Yet now I do. Our church has made mistakes in the past, certainly, but one thing it has known is how to wait. It waited for me, and perhaps it waits for you also.

Here in our city, they say that you sold Russia with the Jews, but I know that the story is not so simple. People are not only good or bad, though it seems possible to live a whole lifetime without realizing this.

Your mother and my mother had their disagreements. My mother said that it was because they were too similar, but I don't believe that. Your mother has just died, and my mother died many years ago now. My mother couldn't leave our town, as your mother could. She always worried about other people. She was an old-fashioned woman. She didn't seek out what she wanted as your mother did. My mother said that when they were children your mother got good results at school and she didn't. My mother was a poet. She used to read and write poetry, as I did and as I still do.

I remember that when we were children we saw each other at our grandmother's. Later, I remember hearing for the first time—"Nika's boy is a rich man now." Before that we only heard that you were interested in computers. What were computers to us then? We didn't have a need for computers at all. We didn't understand what your wealth could mean.

We used to laugh at you at that time when we saw you long ago. You were the boy who would sit in the corner with his screwdriver and his little bits of metal. You didn't like our games. You were used to being alone. Your mother treated you like her little prince. Your table manners were good, while ours were poor. You were a small adult already, while we were all still children. Everybody thought well of you in that respect, though now, as an adult, I have met other children like that

and realize that likely the other adults must have found such
composure eerie, as I have done when encountering it in a child.
    Your mother was very glamorous to me then. She wasn't
like my mother. She wasn't so tired. I remember that her
fingernails were so very well cared for. They weren't painted, but
they were so neat and so clean. I asked her about it, and she said
that she took care of her hands because she worked in a hospital.
She let me massage her hands. They were so smooth, unlike my
mother's.
    I live in my mother's apartment. One of my brothers moved
away. Dima, my brother, your cousin, died five years ago.
Maybe you know this. I live with my son. In our flat there are
many things that used to be my mother's. We have a rug that
came from Thailand. The place is probably small to you, but it
is enough.
    Am I sick for the past? Maybe. A little. I know that it was
bad at times, but also that it was simpler. People were closer
together. Some people worked themselves down to nothing, like
my mother, but we were working for the same thing. As I get
older, the past seems better and better. I understand this is an
illusion, but why do I need the illusion? Our church has long
understood the need of people to believe that we have fallen.
    Anyway, I intended to write only to say that I have
memories of your mother and of you. I have a memory of
touching your mother's hands, of rubbing the soft, white skin
of her palms.
    I will light a candle for her.

                                        Your cousin,
                                        Yelena

He folds the letter and slides it into the envelope. He puts the
envelope on the coffee table and looks at it. He thinks of his mother

cleaning her hands before she started to cook. He can imagine the smell of her skin: the mineral, sour odor of old-fashioned soap. She is there in the letter, in that image and yet also in other ways: in the sense of tension that runs through the letter. She had a hardness in her that this cousin understands, that the woman exhibits herself.

At lunchtime, he eats in the restaurant on the bottom floor of his mother's apartment building. The girl who came to the wake takes his order. It's a Russian restaurant, consciously retro now, decorated with Soviet posters. All this is for the young, for the tourists. His mother ate here because it served the kind of food she liked. The tabletop is glass, and pressed beneath it are old banknotes: the kind of Soviet rubles in which he first made his fortune.

When his pork cutlet comes, it's dry. Did he come here because of the letter? To show that he knows the past his cousin spoke of?

He has heard the kind of thing she said before, of course: the buried implication that her benighted backwater is somehow more authentically Russian than his own part of the country, the idea that his success should have taken him out of the life of his compatriots. It's all a familiar kind of small-mindedness, lamentably adjacent to bigotry—he thinks of that mention of "the Jews." He shouldn't even entertain it. His mother had softer hands, maybe. She didn't work in a factory like her sister, but she worked every day in her dilapidated hospital. He grew up in that same kind of *krushchoyovka* as his cousins, in small rooms with hideous furnishings. Those are days he fought to leave behind, breaking from them so cleanly that the memory of them remains crisp.

He eats the whole cutlet, and when the waitress comes he tells her that he hasn't had such a dish for some time. He says, smiling, that it was just as he remembered it.

HE GOES outside then. He walks onto the street. He doesn't call his security. He turns up his collar against the wind cutting in from the east.

He walks along the embankment, the river to his left. The day is dull, the encroachment of dusk perceptible already. A boat is moving by on the water, a crowd on deck with phones pointed to photograph the Kremlin buildings on the opposite bank. He used to walk through those halls as if they were the corridors of his home, he thinks. The nineties, when he was ascendant.

Before then, he had stood in great crowds outside these buildings, amidst great masses of humanity clamoring for a change they didn't even understand. Prior to that, he lived in a block of flats like any other. He went to his job at the railway offices. He made his business deals.

He hears voices raised. He follows the sound and then rounds a corner and there is a compact group standing on the edge of a car park and holding signs. A man is shouting through a bullhorn. The signs are about the President. Through the bullhorn, the man says, "The time has come! Enough is enough!" The people around him echo the call. Across the street is a counterprotest: tranquilized-looking young men who stare at the crowd in the car park, lobbing insults and threats over the traffic that moves between the two groups.

These are Navalny's people, the dregs of the protests that happened two years before when Putin moved to take back the presidency. Oleg's mother was dismayed by these protests. Oleg himself kept track of them from London. People he wouldn't expect came out onto the streets, even some people he did business with, people who didn't usually take such risks. He got up early to read the news from Moscow. It wasn't going to work, but still, they were crazy days. From his exile, Oleg watched the dissent die away. It was only in this failure that he came to understand what he felt. Part of him had wanted them to succeed. It might have complicated business for him, but there was an impulse in him to disregard that, to dream of turning things upside down. That longing was what was behind the eagerness with which he read the news each morning, his urge to wake and reach for his phone and see how his old country had moved. He was envious of those men and women out on those cold streets and of the wonder they must have felt to be amidst the crowds.

He stands now and looks at the group of protesters. They're getting ready to leave. The counterprotestors are swearing and waving their fists around. The people in the car park begin packing up their signs, tying them together, folding them and pushing them into backpacks. They look calm, like people shutting up a market stall after the end of trading. This calmness, Oleg thinks, is a kind of response to the thugs who holler and hiss like a football crowd. It *is* a kind of routine work doing this every day. A cluster of protestors gathers to smoke and watch the aggressive men across the road. They talk inexpressively from the sides of their mouths and keep their gazes fixed on the hooligans.

Oleg feels a degree of admiration. No one is listening to these men and women, but they are enduring the abuse of the thugs and the cold late-autumn weather. He considers moving to join the group, but doesn't. They would know him, of course. They would be no fans of his. Perhaps the facial hair he is growing protects him somewhat, separates his face from the one people might have seen on the news. Farther into the car park he thinks he sees a flash of somebody moving in a parked BMW. The security services will be watching this little performance, of course.

He starts off again, and walks along the river and feels oddly energized. He feels present to this city. He was once so hopeful for this country, as hopeful as anyone. He had his business interests, yes, but he felt then their success was tied to freedom. Everything happened so fast here—he lived whole days as if they were lifetimes. His cousin implied that he missed things, and yet he feels quite the opposite. He was everywhere, he felt. He sensed the tremor of every footfall in the city.

He gets back to his own apartment just before midnight. He calls Victor and asks that Victor book him a flight to his cousin's town. "You don't want to take the jet?" says Victor.

"I want to be inconspicuous," Oleg says. "It's a little personal visit."

· · ·

IN THE morning, he reads his cousin's letter three times. Even the implied criticism in the letter—the idea that his mother was somehow more selfish than her sister—isn't unpleasant to him. This is the real stuff, the accounting of a life, not the platitudes about an old lady he heard at her funeral. He didn't think that she was selfish, but that's an interpretation of something that she *was*. She was self-possessed, not just an old lady in a chair with a sharp tongue and a love of grapefruit.

Oleg's phone goes, and it's German, who expresses his condolences. Oleg doesn't care to know how German has learned of his bereavement.

The message on the back of these commiserations—the real reason for German's call—is that it will be necessary for Oleg to give up a portion of his shares in his timber concern. Oleg listens and pictures his old friend speaking stuffed behind that giant mahogany desk of his. A couple of people important to the President want an interest in the firm, German says. It would be severely inadvisable to block them. "We will get market rate for the shares?" Oleg asks. He knows the response, of course. He just wants to make German say it.

Where formerly German would have made a joke, he declines to answer. "Also," he says, "there is some factory that it has been suggested you might be interested in."

"Right," says Oleg. "What does it make, this factory?"

"I don't recall," says German.

"It's that kind of deal."

"Yes."

He puts the phone down. He has foreign partners in the timber concern, and it will cause him some embarrassment to explain this new arrangement. This is no doubt part of the plan.

He sits for a while at his mother's kitchen table. He looks out at the river, at the stretch of the city all around. He calls his foreign investors, and eats the requisite quantity of shit.

He has lunch in the restaurant downstairs. There's a birthday party in progress in the main room, but the waitress lets him sit alone at a table at the back. A man is playing the accordion badly as people clap and sing along—one can only assume that to be allowed such a performance, it must be the man's own birthday he is celebrating. Oleg slips out as the revelers make their first toast.

ON HIS flight, the other three men at the front of the plane have small eyes. Their expressions are pinched as if they've been drinking for too long before their evening takeoff and now must concentrate to talk.

They speak haltingly. They're involved in building some kind of shopping mall. One of them is getting a divorce, Oleg overhears. They're pleased with the drinks the flight attendant brings them. "First class," they say. It sickens Oleg, somehow—this low-grade luxury and the men's satisfaction with it—despite, or perhaps because of, the fact he once spoke in a similar way himself. He shuts his eyes and their conversation washes over him, niggling him until he falls asleep.

18

MARTIN GOES to the local library on his way home from work and reads about the painting, *Supremus No. 51*, that Oleg holds in storage. The library doesn't have the books about Malevich, but Martin brings them from the auction house, loping from the Tube like a hiker, flagstone-sized art volumes weighing down his rucksack.

He sits at a desk in a quiet corner near the third-floor storage cupboard. He's been coming to the library for two weeks, taking the same place each time. The air of the building smells institutional: of carpet tile and cheap cleaning products applied liberally. In the evening, when Martin arrives, there are schoolkids in the library using the computers near the entrance to watch YouTube videos. They spin around on the computer chairs and squabble, provoking tuts and sighs from the old men reading books about military history.

Martin has paid the last month of his rent. He's paid the deposit on a new place. James has found a flatmate online to take Martin's room, and Martin has recently noticed himself staying out of the way of his friend. James, who has organized more gigs than usual, seems to be doing the same. Martin often weighs the paranoid thought that James knows—though how could he possibly know?—about Martin getting together with Marina. They still play football together in a five-a-side game with mutual friends on Thursday nights, and when Martin finds James dribbling toward him, he overthinks his defense. James favors his right foot, and yet James knows Martin knows this. Will he fake, or double-fake, or triple-fake, or simply act, realizing the endlessness of this refraction? Sometimes their knowledge of each other seems so close, so lacking in perspective, as to be no kind of knowledge at all.

The work that Martin does in the library is a distraction, and maybe also a justification. This is his new project, and signals a new stage in his career and life, in which a break with James is maybe natural. This acquaintance with this painting of a value that makes Martin feel queasy—£60 million? more?—is the kind of thing he has longed for. He has seen a picture in color that experts only know as a black-and-white photograph, that people thought lost altogether.

It's a thrill to open an anthology of Malevich's correspondence and find letters about the canvas. The work is hugely significant, Martin comes to realize, thought so by the artist himself. For Malevich, it was a turning point, the next stage in his quest to establish nonobjective painting, independent of the need to represent. He wrote to a friend, "I'm finding something new in the picture, a law on the birth of forms dependent on their distance from each other." He was seeking a new ordering of shapes and color, a new painterly logic. Martin reads this and thinks, with a certain charged pleasure, of Marina bristling at the megalomania of the painter. The artist felt himself to be working with absolutes, with facts of existence. Malevich writes of the gravity of his forms, of the relationship of their scale. Martin studies the old photograph of Oleg's picture in a 1920s exhibition, studies reproductions of other paintings. The colors and the way the shapes carve the white space beneath them make something leap in Martin. On his return from Geneva, Martin told Julian about Oleg's picture, showed the photograph on his phone to the house's specialists in Russian art. They are researching the work assiduously now, yet Martin wants to do his own reading because he feels a sense of possession over the picture. After all, he has seen it—felt the full shock of its revelation—and they have not.

"Through me passes the force, the general harmony of creative laws that guides everything," wrote Malevich. It is mad, of course. Martin thinks of Marina, of her smiling across the table at the Swiss restaurant and saying, "He has his hand up art's ass like a ventriloquist with a dummy." Yet Martin finds himself arguing with this absent, imagined Marina. Can't it be a benign self-centeredness? The fuel the artist needs to make these beautiful, simple pictures? She's in Moscow, traveling to the funeral of Oleg's mother. When he imagines her, with him in the library at the tucked-away table at which he sits, her voice, rising above the ambient fizz of the fluorescent lights and the hum of air vents, tells him that Malevich's megalomania isn't just some detail, but a crucial quality in why people value the paintings. "They want a shouting man," she says in his mind. "They want the show. They are taken in by his carnival barking."

Martin reads accounts of the artist written by contemporaries. Malevich was a broad man, his face marked by smallpox. He had an odd accent, inflected by his Polish and Ukrainian background. He spoke quietly, but with force and authority. In photographs he is stout, an unlikely possessor of such a fleet, inventive mind. One of his friends thought he looked more like a country prelate than an artist. Yet this strength was also necessary in his assertion of ideas, his theoretical battles. Sergei Eisenstein wrote in recollection of his "huge, hairy, cubic fist." And this resolute strength is what fascinates Martin. Yes, maybe Marina is right that he was a zealot and even an egotist, yet he was also, always, seeking to articulate ideas that seemed beyond articulation. A contemporary complained that "Malevich was always drawn toward some kind of mysticism that was incomprehensible to him." Malevich himself wrote of a lecture to ordinary citizens: "The fact that I spoke precisely and answered their questions was my downfall. An uproar of indignation, disappointment. They shouted that I shouldn't speak of things that weren't comprehensible, we came to get to know Cubism, we came to find out the truth. . . . And the women said, what a haircut he has!" The haircut, Martin thinks, *is* strange: a thick covering of helmetlike black hair, beneath which the artist peers out suspiciously. After the lecture, Malevich wrote that he "came to the conclusion that the more clearly you understand the question at hand, the narrower the circle of those who understand it. . . . My understanding is completely obscure to those around me: the more precise it is, the more obscure."

Is this, Martin says to the imaginary Marina, *not a sign that the artist didn't think he had all the answers? This stunted yearning to communicate something beyond articulation?* If his grand visions were so false, he was the biggest victim of this fraud. Malevich believed in his work in a way that no one today could believe in their art without suspicion of insanity. It was supposed to take him somewhere else. He complained of a friend's paintings that they were "completely within the earth's gravity."

Martin underlines and reads, and drinks water from his flask and feels himself a little dizzy with the bright light of the library and with a yawning evening hunger, but he keeps reading a little longer.

There is a letter about the Neva flooding in which Martin feels that the artist is partly speaking about himself, about his work. Malevich writes of being alerted to the flood by rats and mice fleeing past him as he walked the streets of Leningrad. The artist describes the river overflowing the "channel that civilization had created for her," and this image seems to recall the man's own thoughts about his practice, of the objectlessness of art, counterpoised against the attempts of humankind to vainly circumscribe the phenomenon. "Everything in nature has the objectless source, but man wants to objectify it," writes Malevich elsewhere. His art is a reaction against the human tendency to control, against "the idea of using everything for one's own personal or social benefit." His only aim, he avers, is "a completely new creative fact, a new reality, a new truth." The painter should have "no dependency other than his painterly attitude toward the world, none of the content of a political attitude to the state of social conditions. . . ." Malevich's art is not political, like the flood, which to him is a horror yet also a "magnificent spectacle of matter in movement." At the time of the rising waters, it is 1924. He will go to Berlin in three years, organize a show there, leave many of his works behind.

He will be called home early by his government, before he can realize his dream of visiting Paris. The year after his return he will be arrested and questioned by the secret police. He will stop painting for years, give up trying to explain his discoveries, and concentrate instead on teaching and making strange architectural models. In the thirties he will be arrested and held for much longer than before, questioned again, and then a couple of years later he will be dead from cancer, little more than a decade after the rising of the Neva. His work is not political in the way that the flood is not political, Martin thinks: that is, a manifestation of a force generated by causes beyond politics perhaps, but still a thing that will be reckoned with on political terms. Either he is naïve, or he is supremely dedicated. In the late twenties, Malevich's art will fall distinctly out of favor in comparison to painting that directly depicts and glorifies the workers of the state. Malevich, committed to his own kind of realism—the realism of painting as the act of creation itself—will suffer disfavor and suspicion. Yet to paint in service to another cause was not the man's desire. Speaking to his friend Nikolay Punin, he renounced even the inspiration of the natural world: "To reproduce choice objects and little corners of nature is just like a thief in raptures over his fettered feet." Of the flood, he writes, "At six thirty the water began to flood my floor too. The phone stopped working, light, darkness, the splash of water, and the noise of the wind, at times Mars could be glimpsed through the gaps in the storm clouds. We came out onto the balconies, and dragged up people who were still walking through the water; the wind knocked the more daring of them over like a wave. The water was higher than the floods of 1724 and 1824. Then, for an even greater spectacle, a fire broke out somewhere—how interconnected it all is—water, fire, a thief, each one holds on to the other or one generates the other; a huge mass of people hid and awaited their fate." His story was always that his art was bigger than him, that his only duty was to this art itself. You cannot reason with the flood. You must just observe, describe it if you wish. The only folly in facing a force like that is to think that it can be constrained, used to one's own ends; to think that one can master and outlast it.

This sense of destiny and sacrifice is probably why men like Oleg treasure the artist's pictures in their airless, temperature-controlled vaults. Malevich believed with a fervency with which now, for some reason, we cannot rouse ourselves to believe. And for that reason, maybe, we need him. For that reason, his work is invaluable. Yet the real wonder of the man's work is not his stubbornness in response to the callous idiocy of the state. The real glory of Malevich's stance, Martin thinks, is the idea that the artist sought to protect: the notion of an art insulated from use, not in the sense of being a vapid or decorative art, held off genteelly from life, but in the sense of being utterly *other*. "Where it is possible to retell painting in words, then it wouldn't exist," said one of Malevich's students, "because then painting wouldn't be necessary."

Martin wants to believe, as the artist did, that creativity can speak of the real ordering of the world, can express relations between objects in a manner distinct from logic, beyond mere straight resemblance. He wants that sense of interconnectedness that Malevich had, the ecstasy born of his belief in plane without earthly gravity. When the librarian comes to tell Martin that the building is closing, Martin packs his art books, and descends to the street and begins his journey back to the underground flat. The traffic on the Westway is roaring to the north. A train screeches and clatters into the Overground station two roads over. Some teenagers are fighting in a bus stop. Several men are doing road work around a flashing construction truck, from which comes the foul smell of hot tar. After hours of reading, Martin experiences it all with a yearning for Malevich's eye, with a wish to make something singular of the jumbled stimuli. Cloud is packed very low overhead, uplit white by the shifting glow of the city beneath it. There are no gaps through which the sky might be seen. Though were there, Martin thinks, he wouldn't know where to look to pick out Mars.

19

IT'S DARK when Marina wakes, still so when she gets into the car to travel to the airfield. She boards the plane in the predawn. A mist lingers around the hedges and hollows of fields beyond the fence that encircles the runway.

She's served a croissant and a cup of dark coffee. She has only a garment bag and a small holdall. She'll return that same evening, citing work. Russia for her will only be a graveyard.

This is what she wanted, Oleg's mother, Veronika. The old woman had a fixation on being buried in the mud of Russia: a sentimentality surprising in an old doctor who so often complained of the irrationality of others.

Marina's father had always asked to be buried back at home. It was the kind of silly request he made when he had had a few drinks. He would put his hand on his own chest when he did so, regarding her with a heavy alcoholic candor. What is it about people wanting to plan what happens to them after they have gone? Some illusion of control? She is thankful that her husband, at least, doesn't make requests like these.

Of course, her family was powerless to give her father his wish when the time came. "This is the risk you run," her mother declared, "when you play around on boats." It was an anger Marina recognized in herself. She was twenty-one then. She didn't know what to do. She told herself she was an adult and tried to act accordingly.

Her father and his assistant had disappeared. Her father's boat was half-sunk, fifty miles off the south coast of France. It was typical of her father to have gone beyond his limits: he who never met an activity he didn't believe he had a natural aptitude for. Still, that confidence had carried him places, carried them all along with him.

KAREN, THE plane hostess, brings Marina another cup of coffee. She knows there's no limit to how much coffee Marina can drink. "We're over Germany," Karen says.

Marina thinks of her husband. She'll see him soon, changed, no doubt. Veronika adored him beyond anything, with a love that sustained them both. Marina has never fully fathomed such love, never been able to give it.

When they touch down it is midmorning, flatly gray. Marina has changed into her funeral clothes. A car comes onto the runway to collect her. The Russian driver opens the rear passenger door of the vehicle.

It's colder here, a chill in the air, trees bare.

HER MOTHER called her at university. She was in the shared house with Kathy, Kathy who was very tidy but could also be a tyrant about, say, how coats were arranged on the rack by the door. Her mother called and said, "They've found his boat, empty." Her mother was always launching into stories without the appropriate context, yet here Marina found that she knew exactly what her mother meant. She hadn't known that her father was on a sailing trip, but it made an ominous sense.

Her father and his assistant, Vilis, were lost at sea. It was odd to lose a father at twenty-one. She didn't know what to expect of herself. She made many of the necessary phone calls. It was easier than her mother doing so with her odd English. Her brother was eighteen and lacked the practicality for such tasks. Talking on the phone to the coast guard, Marina heard someone in the background of the call refer to her as "the daughter," and that clarified things somehow. There must always be family in these cases, and she was that family, dragged into this story that she hadn't chosen.

She shouted at her mother for the way her mother had scorned her husband: this from a daughter who could hardly bear to be seen in public with the man. She spent £40,000 on a single afternoon's shopping trip. She bought clothes that she would never otherwise have bought or worn, clothes for someone else.

She learned from the coast guard that they had sophisticated maps of where bodies washed up from incidents in that part of the Mediterranean. It was a typical migrant route. The man she spoke to on the phone had been glad to learn of her father's tattoo: an ugly little bird on his shoulder. Her father had gotten it when he first started to make money, had resisted her mother's pleas for its removal. The coast guard kept records of these identifying marks. Many of the corpses that were recovered from the sea were unmarked, however, or arrived with marks that were not among those that the coast guard were looking out for. There were cemeteries in Sicily populated with unidentified bodies.

Marina could have used a provision in the university regulations to get reprieves from her exams. She didn't, however. Maybe this was a lingering guilt regarding her privilege, but at the time it didn't feel like such a thing. Rather, it felt that her father's disappearance, or death, was too strange a thing to be compensated for by such plain logic. The boat, floating out there in the sea, and the exams were part of different worlds, their connection somehow obscene.

She went into her exams and did well. She got the top marks in her class in a Modernist poetry module. It nauseated her, such success as would have so pleased her father, all in the wake of his disappearance.

There were four things that could have happened, though she couldn't balance the possibilities in her mind. Likely, there was an accident and the two men were washed overboard. The weather had not been perfect, though her father had sailed through worse. Warnings, he felt, were for other people.

Maybe it was suicide. She didn't think her father was that kind of man, but it was possible, likely that if he were to do it he would do it so grandly as to provoke speculation. His wife didn't like him. His daughter didn't like him. His son never turned his face from the Xbox. He drank too much and did nothing of consequence in the daytimes. Perhaps he'd paid Vilis off, asked the man to disappear and leave him to himself. He had covert sources of funds. Vilis could be living somewhere in South America. He was the type who could live well in exile: a small town, a sparse cinder-block hut, an evening trip to the bar in which he'd sit gripping a bottle of beer.

Or perhaps her father himself had emigrated and was living elsewhere, a new man. There is a childish part of her that wishes for this to be true. Sometimes in public spaces she finds herself moving with a care born of the idea that perhaps she is being watched, and realizes that somewhere deep within her she still believes that the man could emerge, just like that, from a crowd.

The last possibility was foul play. For a long time, she used that phraseology—*foul play*—in the way she considered this possibility. The British ambassador had said the words when she had talked to him (her father had taken British nationality a couple of years before). It was a very English way to think about things, as if it were part of a game, as if murder were most of all ill-mannered. Her father had enemies. He'd worked, he asserted, in a time when making enemies was unavoidable. In the last year there had been a share-ownership dispute he wouldn't speak about; but then again, there had been many such problems, mysterious to Marina and her mother, and he had always negotiated his way out of them.

Marina doesn't believe in ghosts as Oleg professes to do, though in her father's absence she found more of him within herself: a new kind of determination, an ability to emotionally disengage if needed. He endured the complaints of his family and the downturns of business in a stolid way, and she could endure too, she found. She looked in the mirror and caught glimpses of him frowning back at her.

SHE ARRIVES at the apartment and Oleg is standing there, ready to leave for the cemetery. There's a rawness to him that Marina has never seen. He's grown a beard, and lost weight, and he looks younger but less healthy than he did two weeks before. There's an intensity to his expression that unsettles her. He is stripped back to a man she has not encountered before. He is holding a dried purple geranium. "Hers," he says. "She grew this."

Marina embraces him and senses his new energy. He's tense. She thinks for a moment she can feel him shaking. "You're here, finally," he says, and the gratitude with which he says this takes her back to a better time.

They don't speak on the drive to the cemetery. She watches him looking out of the window—the buildings, the cranes, the white sky— with a gaze that seems to take nothing in.

Afterward, she leaves him in the gray churchyard and sits in the warmth of the car. He smokes—a one-off, she supposes. As the night is coming in, he lopes down the path to the car park.

THEY HELD the funeral of Marina's father two months after her mother called her at university. In an English graveyard they stood and watched an empty coffin lowered into the ground. "None of this was what he wanted," Marina said to her mother.

Her mother cast her hand around the graveyard. "You could carve that on any of the stones here," she said. "Don't you think?"

20

THE CAR is waiting for Marina at the front of Veronika's building. Oleg's Moscow driver holds open the rear door. She gets in. She lays her satchel beside her. She shuffles down in her seat so she can look up and back at the apartment block as they pull away. The building looms: the columns in front, the expanses of smallish windows, thick flat slabs of pink stone. It is a building for people who—for better or worse— still believe in the power of this state, still want to feel the scale of this country. She is not sad to think that she won't visit the building again.

The traffic is poor, of course. They lurch forward through a press of other vehicles. The driver is finding space in the traffic, changing lanes with a certainty that causes the cars around them to yield. He is silent, calm. He dares the other vehicles not to make way for the cus- tomized black Land Rover. You need a very expensive or a very cheap car to drive like this. The idea one needs to project is that a collision is worse for others than it is for oneself. Invulnerability is largely the appearance of such.

WHEN THEY reach the airport, they drive through successive check- points and out onto the runway. It's nearly midnight, and it'll be early morning by the time Marina arrives back in the UK. There's a wind cutting in from the north. Her garment bag is nearly snatched from her grip by a gust as she mounts the fold-down stairs of the plane. A jet roars down from the sky at the other end of the airfield. The door is closed up behind her, the sound of the landing jet cut to a rumble. She takes her seat and hears the engines of her own plane starting to turn over. Karen arrives with a glass of red wine.

As the plane ascends, Marina looks out of the window, regards the Moscow suburbs picked out in lights: the pulsing ring roads; small knotted towns around the airport; cars moving on unlit roads between these settlements, seeming to create the lumpy asphalt ahead of them as they bear down on it; the center of the city in the far distance, glowing like a hot coal. Then the aircraft is above the clouds and Marina can see only wing lights, blinking to themselves.

Karen comes and asks whether Marina wants her to prepare the bed in the cabin. Marina shakes her head. She thinks of Oleg. Her husband will doubtless be awake in the middle of the smoldering city. She recalls his eyes as she saw them when she arrived in the morning, made so much more intense by the beard he has grown. She finishes her first glass of wine, and Karen brings her another, along with a small bowl of almonds.

Veronika's adoration was constant, pervasive enough that Marina senses it must have been hard to know for itself. She did the motherly things. She fed her son when he visited. She told him he was handsome. Yet more crucially, she initiated a story that he came to know as his own: he is unique, he is good, he is able to do things others are not. Marina thinks of the woman's tales of her son as a child. He corrected the teachers at his school. He fixed his uncle's motorbike while he was still too short to reach up and touch the handlebars. He always shared chocolate with other children. Mothers tell such stories, but there was an extra quality of belief in the woman. She created a hunger in him that was almost impossible to sate.

Marina sips her wine, and thinks of a time just after she'd first moved into Oleg's house. They'd had their quiet wedding. They were beginning their grown-up marriage, refitting the house to suit this adult life. She'd suggested putting in a little wet room by the back door in which the dogs could be washed when they came in muddy. He scowled and shook his head. "It will create a big plumbing problem," he said. Yet later, when work was being done, he called her to the rear of the house to show her a little dog shower he'd designed. "What do you think?" he said, and she looked at him, incredulous that he shouldn't remember that two weeks before this idea had been hers. "It's unusual," he said, misreading her silent confusion, "but it will be useful when the weather is bad."

"That's my idea," she said eventually.

He waved his hands. "No. No," he said. "I wanted to do this years ago, but Katya disagreed."

She felt briefly and intensely insane. She'd claimed the idea again later and he denied it. Her perturbation was increased by the fact that the idea was so silly. What did she care about this dog shower? And yet the issue was more than that. The issue was her sense of reality. He couldn't act on an idea until he felt it coming from him, and he had become an efficient machine for producing that impression. He *really* believed what he said. He warped his own accounting of the world to flatter himself. He had been allowed to become such a thing.

After that, she'd listen to his mother's stories and note that the great moments of their lives together were recalled as authored by him. Did Veronika know that she was giving him all of this, or did she have a complementary madness: a drive to reattribute all that was great to her boy?

He was frustrated that his mother urged him to get closer to the President. He felt that she favored Putin before him. Marina thought this the wrong interpretation. His mother liked the President, yes, but she grumbled only because she felt the President needed help, felt the best help available to be that of her son.

She finishes her second glass of wine. She closes her eyes and enjoys the muted hum of the plane. She sleeps in the seat. She wakes later, surprised to have slept, to the sudden rush of air that accompanies wheels of the plane folding down in preparation for landing.

Victor is waiting. The air is cool and damp. They drive to the

London house. She sleeps again in the back of the car, is woken on a section of poor road. They move swiftly around roundabouts, past empty shopping plazas, dark parks.

She was impressed when she first met Oleg by all his certainty. And yet she should have known that such self-belief requires fuel. She can't believe as faithfully in him as he does himself. On meeting him, she marveled at his confidence not because it rang true, but because it made him unstoppable. Of course, he doesn't act in such a way because it is effective but because that is simply him: a man of such firm certainty that his own limits are invisible.

THE NEXT day, a Saturday, Marina wakes later than usual, and works distractedly in her office at the London house. At noon, she texts Martin: Are you busy tonight?

They meet in a cocktail bar she has suggested. She arrives early, as her time with Oleg has conditioned her to do, and finds a table at the back. She watches Martin enter and seek her out. He takes a seat opposite her, looks around. The tingle of chatter, and the clink of glasses and the whispery percussion of the barmen shaking cocktails and scooping ice. She says, "The drinks are mediocre, and the prices are terrible. But there's always a bit of space."

He laughs. "Good to see you."

She is struck, this evening, by the fact he still looks so young. He doesn't occupy his space. "I was very sorry to hear about your bereavement," he says.

"Thanks."

A girl comes to take his order. When she has departed, Marina says, "To be honest, it is my husband's bereavement."

"You didn't get on?"

"She was fine. She was old. For my husband it's just so much more."

"How's he taking it?"

"Going a little mad."

Martin listens well, she thinks. She thinks this when she has already started telling him more than she intended to, speaking of her sense that her husband will need from her some adoration she can't provide. Rueful, she catches herself. She says, "His mother died, and I'm only thinking about myself."

He smiles and says, "You only are yourself."

It feels like this is all happening out of order, from the night of falling into bed, back to this: fathoming each other, stumbling occasionally to say welcome things. Martin says, "I'm in a new flat now. You should come and visit sometime."

21

THEY TOUCH down early in the morning. It's still not light. The passengers descend to dark tarmac, biting wind. They ride to the shiny glass terminal in a bus, while the hold luggage is loaded into the trailer of a tractor.

Oleg carries a plastic bag with a bottle of champagne. He wanted to get his cousin a gift, and the champagne—a vintage Krug—seemed the best option in the gift shop next to his departure gate. It came in a presentation box, and now as he walks out of the terminal doors, the bag dangles beside him and the corner of the box strikes his shin painfully.

He takes a taxi into town driven by a man in a military jacket. "Are you a veteran?" Oleg asks.

"Yes." The man smiles and shows his few crooked teeth. "I've survived everything." The car smells of dogs. There's a thick layer of snow at the side of the road.

The taxi driver stops in the central square. That was all the direction Oleg had given when he got in. "Here?" the man says. His breath smells yeasty and foul.

Oleg gets out. He looks at the administrative center, the dry fountains, a statue of Nevelskoy staring out toward the river.

The air is totally frigid. The taxi drives off, leaving an odor of half-combusted petrol. He pulls up his collar, wraps his scarf more securely around him. He pulls his hat right down. The sky is lightening to a bruised blue.

•   •   •

THERE IS a park in the administrative center. From its entrance, a winding, stepped path leads uphill through trees. It is still early, and Oleg has a need to move. He decides to ascend this path. He crunches up the snow-covered steps, his thighs beginning to burn as he ascends.

At the top, he doubles over to recover himself. The sun is rising at the horizon now. He can see his breath. He can see the city stretching out. This is where the photo in his mother's living room was taken, he realizes. He watches cars moving on the streets below, buses and trams inching down boulevards.

Somewhere out there his grandparents lived, his mother grew up. Someone beeps a horn down in the center. He feels as if he is claiming the day before others. He's of the place. His mother and father walked these streets, lived their lives here. Here, they wore down carpets with their footfalls, compressed mattresses into their shapes, left fingerprints on latches and taps. It all seems so crucial as he thinks about it.

HE DESCENDS into the city with the new light. Old cars rattle past, choking out dark smoke, ghosted with lines of salt. He walks until he sees a sign for a hotel. He crosses the road, goes in. A stout woman sits behind the desk eating an apple. She chews and looks at him with a bovine vacancy. She doesn't seem to recognize him. His new beard is doing its work, he supposes. "I'd like a room," he says.

"How many nights?"

He looks at the clock above her, plucks a figure from the air. "Four," he says.

THE ROOM has white and gold wallpaper, embossed with flower patterns. It smells of cigarettes. He runs a finger over the bedside table and finds it to be tolerably free of dust. He lies on the bed.

He sleeps and wakes and thinks in his waking of his mother. Here. In this city. Bustling home in the winter. Amidst crowds in the town square on holidays. Walking to school along new streets. His thoughts tumble to an image of her in the hospital: the baring of her teeth in the moment when she died.

He goes to the window. He can see bare trees, the bases of their trunks whitewashed against disease, the weather-beaten concrete apartment blocks across the street, traffic moving on the road between. She had so many memories of this place, and he didn't ask her about them. They could have come here. They could have taken a trip, he thinks. He has to stop, to work logically back against the flow of his thoughts: that wouldn't change things, he tells himself, wouldn't have prevented her death.

In Moscow, he'd been frustrated by the carers who knew his mother only as an old lady. But he only knew her as his mother, as a Moscow doctor. He didn't work back to the factors that had shaped her into these things.

He opens his bag. He takes out the envelope and pulls out the letter: his cousin's address is there in a neat script. He takes out his phone and types her address into his maps application. He studies the image that comes up: her place, and across town the pulsing point that represents him.

At dusk, he goes down to reception and asks for a taxi. Outside, the temperature has risen above freezing. Waiting at the curb, he can smell this in the air, the loosened aromas: mud and dirt, the smell of bleach rising from an open window next to the hotel door. He carries the bottle of champagne in the plastic bag.

The taxi drops him at his cousin's building. He stands under a streetlight and looks at his watch. He feels very visible, standing there on the street. He is too early, he thinks. She'll be at work. He can see what looks like a café down the road. He trudges toward it, through the grayish slush at the verge. A couple of dogs are sniffing around in a pile of torn plastic bags, pausing to bark at cars as they pass.

In the café, which is empty but for two women working at the cash register, he has a bowl of soup and some fried fish. He's very hungry in a way he seldom is these days. The place is permeated by the smell of nail varnish, wafting from a beauty salon in the room next door. Opposite the café is a large derelict building, its roof caved in. A factory, he thinks. It made what? He dimly recalls that agricultural machinery was once associated with the city. And yet these buildings have been abandoned how long? Since the nineties? It seems inconceivable that dereliction should have happened in such a short time. But is it so short? Twenty years, he thinks. Yes. Twenty years.

He leaves the café and walks across the road to the block of flats. In the time since he got out of the taxi, someone has run over a cat. The corpse lies mashed into a patch of mud.

He feels nervous. He imagines himself to be the string of an instrument: liable to be set quivering by the smallest impulse. He studies the cat, thinks that if he has to explain himself, the cat can be his excuse for lingering in this strange part of the city. He is a distressed owner, seeking his pet.

Someone starts a car near another block of flats. Oleg looks at the car and looks at the cat, preparing to get into character, but then he looks back toward the road and is struck by the sudden certainty that he has seen *her*.

A woman has just disembarked a *marshrutka*. She crosses the road toward the flats. She has short hair, dyed an unnatural reddish color. She wears a black ski jacket with lime-green and purple detailing. She lights a cigarette as she advances, unbothered by the Kamaz truck that rumbles toward her. The driver slows a little as he approaches and sounds the horn. The woman looks back at the driver without concern and carries on walking. There is something in her bearing—in the firmness—that Oleg knows. Has he moved this way? Has his mother? He didn't think that he would know her, but he does. His heart leaps. She doesn't look at him, but moves into the courtyard. He follows her. Another cat chases its shadow into the darkness. He sees his cousin at the door of one of the buildings. She pulls the heavy steel door open. He jogs forward. He finds his voice. He says, "Sorry! Sorry!" The woman turns and sees him lumbering across the grass toward her. Her expression is totally calm. She watches him come to a stop in front of her without alarm.

"Hello," he says. He needs to catch his breath. He bends at his waist and puts his hands on his knees, his belly hanging down, straining at his shirt.

He pants and looks up and says, "Sorry."

She studies him. She sucks on her cigarette. She says, in the familiar form, "I know who you are."

HER APARTMENT is on the sixth and top floor. When she reaches the heavy door, she taps it forcefully with the knuckle of her forefinger. "My son is in," she says. She looks Oleg up and down. "Your second cousin."

The boy who comes to the door is very skinny. He has a wispy trace of a mustache on his upper lip. His hair is very fine and saturated with gel so that it lies in combed lines between which Oleg can see the boy's white scalp. He must weigh half of what Oleg does, though he is only a few centimeters shorter. He keeps his gaze down, as if examining the floor of the hallway behind Oleg.

"Nickolai, this is your second cousin," she says. The boy nods cautiously.

"Hello," says Oleg. He is moving past Yelena to hold out a hand, but already Nickolai has said a curt hello and retreated into the flat. Oleg hears a door close.

"He seems nice," says Oleg.

"Come on," says Yelena. "Let's be honest. He's difficult and bad with strangers." She takes off her jacket and hangs it. She takes Oleg's from him and puts it carefully on a hook next to hers. She is watching him remove his shoes. She says, "Your feet are very wet."

"Yes," he agrees.

She goes into the body of the flat and then returns with a pair of thin blue socks. "These are Nickolai's," she says. "Put these on. I'll make us some tea."

He bends to put on the clean socks, which are huge. It's a long time, he thinks, since he has been to an apartment like this. The amber wallpaper is familiar. There are new laminate floors down, but other than that the place is a museum, colored with a palette one doesn't see these days: ochers and beiges, dirty greens and browns. He feels gladdened to be in the space, gladdened by his recognition.

He enters the living room, holding the plastic bag. He puts it on the low table beside the window. He moves around the small room: a strategy of his that has hardened to habit. He learned early doing business never to enter another person's environment and merely to sit, making oneself an object to be judged or used. When his cousin comes back in, he is looking at a photograph of her and Nickolai: summer somewhere, the two of them standing next to a body of water, squinting toward the camera.

She says, "Please sit," gesturing to the sofa.

She takes her place opposite him in an armchair. Now they are inside he can see her better. She has high cheekbones and thin lips, lines around the edges of her eyes. She has, he fancies, a broad nose similar to his own.

"Thank you for inviting me into your home."

"We're family," she says. And he is glad to hear this, although he feels the words are spoken without warmth, merely in explanation.

"Thank you for your letter."

"I was sorry to hear about your mother."

"Thank you." She offers him just a hint of a smile then.

She is a serious woman, he thinks. Guarded. He senses that her trust will have to be earned. From the next room, he can hear the artificial clattering sounds of a film or computer game. His cousin looks at him and seems to wait. She is comfortable with the silence. Is she like him in her patience? Is he like her? He watches her watch him, and he has a realization. He has turned up without a sense of what he wants. An old mantra of his early business life: go into every interaction knowing your aim. It is amazing how many people will request a meeting only to sit in front of his broad desk and wait as if needing clues from him as to their own desires. Yet this evening he feels utterly ignorant as to why he is in this living room looking at this woman. He is like one of those petitioners he has so often found contemptible. He is here for his mother, he thinks. But how?

He picks up the plastic bag. He takes out the box and gives it to her. "I brought a little present."

His cousin puts on reading glasses to study the box. She opens it and slides out the bottle. "This is very impressive," she says. "Though I don't drink."

"Oh."

"My old husband. Nickolai's father. It was a problem for him. I'm not in the habit now. It's expensive also to drink wine and suchlike."

"Right."

She goes to the kitchen. She comes back with a tumbler that she puts down on the table next to him. "But you must drink," she says.

"You're making tea."

"Of course. But this is special. You can please open it?"

"Really?" he says.

She nods. "You must." He takes the bottle out of the box. He peels off the foil. He begins to work out the cork.

"This bottle was expensive?"

"Yes," he says.

She nods.

"Nikolai doesn't want some?" he says.

She shakes her head. The cork comes out into his cupped hand with a pop. The bottle is already overflowing. He fills the tumbler, which spills over. She's watching him. "I'm making a mess of this," he says.

"Yes," she says.

She goes out and comes back with a plate: some pieces of salmon, fried bread, some dried squid. She holds a cup of tea for herself. "Eat," she says.

He drinks his champagne, feels it fizzing around his tongue. He eats and swallows.

"You remember visiting as a child."

"Yes."

"You were an odd boy."

"You said so in your letter."

"We thought that you felt yourself better than us. Perhaps you did."

"Maybe I did. I was a spoiled child. I don't deny it."

"Yes," she says.

A minute passes. The ugly yellow clock next to the TV ticks. "Well, I'm here," he says.

"Yes." He can hear someone parking in the courtyard. "Well," she says. "What do you have to tell me?"

He drinks some more champagne. It tastes sour: not what his body wants. "Thank you for your words about my mother," he says.

"I have a good memory."

"Thank you." He finishes the glass of champagne. She watches him do so, gestures that he should refill the tumbler, which he does. "I was glad to hear that you corresponded with my mother."

"She wrote to me first. She missed her sister once her sister was gone. Too late, of course. But I was still here. She was nostalgic for her old home. They were pioneers here. The first children in a new city."

"She had a photo of the city on her wall. I didn't know how much she thought of this place."

"She didn't talk about this with you, no? She wrote to me that you were very busy with your business. Clearly, you didn't have time to realize all her wishes."

He senses that she likes speaking bluntly. "I regret it," he says. "I'd have brought her here. The three of us, together. A happier meeting."

"Why not?" she says. "And I'd bring my mother, your aunt, back to join us. And why not Peter the Great as well?"

"Yes. I'm going too far. I just didn't credit that she missed places like this."

"I see."

"I wanted to move her to London, or France or Italy. Even Sochi." He looks at her. She is watching him carefully, waiting. He says. "I don't mean to say that there's anything wrong with this city. I just didn't *see* that she missed it."

"There's plenty wrong with this city."

He takes his own turn to be blunt. He says, "Why live here, then?"

"I'm from here. We're from here."

"I moved in my life more than once," he says. "I haven't regretted it."

"You're your mother's son. Some people move. Some stay. This city was nice once. Your mother remembered that."

"I know it must have been tough in the recession, and the collapse in the nineties. I should have helped you."

"That's not what I'm saying."

"I'm not talking about giving you money. I could have helped in other ways. Can help. Maybe Nickolai wants to go to a good university. Abroad, even?"

"Nickolai is too much of an idiot for university."

"Ah," he says. "I've had similar problems with my son."

"We don't need to be helped, the two of us."

"Well, what, then?"

She sighs. She laughs at him mirthlessly.

"It's not an issue for me, to do things for people. For family. I have more money than I could ever need."

"You're going to change this whole city, take it back to what it was? It wasn't all good before, but they closed the factories. They sold things. They took the money. I'm sure you did well out of it."

"I didn't do business here."

"Your type of people."

He doesn't know what to say to stop her. He realizes that she has been ready for this, that in her imagination she has said these words to him many times.

"Nickolai's father worked in the tool factory. One month they paid him in shovels. He brought shovels home. 'What are we supposed to do with these?' I said. Every man in the factory had been sent home with shovels. Who wanted these shovels?"

He nods. She's angry, he thinks. It was in her letter: an anger modulated not by uncertainty—as he thought when reading it—but by decorum. She's been telling him, and he hasn't listened, really. It's true that in the years of privatization, he once flew out to a town not unlike this to buy a factory. It made paper, the factory, but what was special about it was the machinery, which had been imported from Germany not so long before. He'd worked out a deal with the owners whereby they would hold the auction for the factory on the grounds, rather than in Moscow, and at short notice. He flew out only for the auction, came to the factory, placed his bid. When the hammer went down, any other potential buyers were thousands of miles away. He made an agreement, almost immediately, to sell the machines to a factory in China. He flogged the land and closed the place down. He never went to the town again. He was not better or worse than anyone. People all around him were doing similar things. He was simply following economic logic. He was the personification of the market in a good coat and Italian shoes.

"Some of my business was regrettable," he says. "The choices then weren't so easy. We were taking these factories from crooks, from a broken system. There was something that was meant to come after. That didn't happen. We didn't realize the mess of it."

"You didn't know?" she says. "Of course you knew."

He slaps the table next to his tumbler harder than he intended. "The actual quality of it," he says. "The physicality. The widespread effects. I'm one man."

"Is that so?"

He is sweating. He feels his shirt clinging against his belly.

She says, "Shall we go out to the balcony? I smoke out there some-times."

"Yes," he says. "Absolutely. Yes."

THE SMALL balcony is packed with detritus: an old clothes rack, a bicycle, a shovel. He points at the shovel. "Yes," she says with a slight smile of complicity.

She gives him a cigarette, lights it. He exhales. She says, "I can think out here."

"Right," he says. She looks down at something in the courtyard beneath them.

Now that they are out on the balcony in the half-light, he feels he is more able to study her. She exhales. She taps her cigarette on the concrete railing. There are some cloths on the plastic line above them, dried hard like curls of bark. The air is very cold now.

"It'll snow tonight," she says.

Do they have things in common? What would Marina say on meeting this woman? "Why did our mothers fall out?" he says.

His cousin inhales again, holds the breath, then blows smoke through her nostrils and half-closed lips. "They were different," she says.

"That's all?"

"Isn't that enough? They talked less, wrote less. My mother bri-dled at this, raised the issue. Your mother called even less then. 'She doesn't think about us out here,' my mother used to say." The voice she puts on to speak her mother's words is brittle, sad.

"She left for good reasons."

"Yes. My mother stayed for good reasons, also. Who was here for Grandmother in the end?"

"Right," he says.

"She was a sour old bitch, our grandmother." She laughs to herself. "She took her share of the inheritance, your mother, when Grandmother died. My mother didn't like it. You were already a rich man then."

"Maybe it wasn't about the money," he says.

"When is money not about the money?"

"It was her share of the history."

She frowns. "My mother didn't need that money as a symbol."

He wants to explain his mother's side better, but he doesn't know how. The sweaty shirt is clammy against his torso. It all takes so much energy, he thinks. This business, these memories, his mother gone, and these things he didn't think of. He draws on the cigarette, concentrates on his feelings for a moment: the taste of the smoke, the cold air in his lungs. His cousin reaches out her hand again, and his mother is there in a momentary movement, so sharp and vivid it almost pains him: the way she flicks cigarette ash over the balcony, the arc of the fingers and the quick tapping of her thumb against the butt. Watching her makes him want to cry, to let himself go, but she looks up to see him studying her and frowns again.

INSIDE, SHE offers him more champagne. He shakes his head. She takes his glass to the sink. He notices an improvised ladle hanging on the wall. It's an old cup with a broken handle, tied with wire to a wooden dowel. It takes his breath away for a moment, because he improvised something just like it when he was a young man. He is taken back to his old room in Moscow. His cousin sees him looking at it. "Whatever it looks like, it works," she says.

"No," he says. "You don't understand. I made the same thing years ago."

"Right," she says. "Nickolai's father made it. I keep it to remind myself that he could be useful sometimes."

Oleg is smiling widely, though his cousin doesn't return this grin.

He taps his pockets. Takes out his phone and puts it away again. He wants to show her a picture, some proof of the uncanniness of the similarity. But his own ladle is where? Thrown away thirty years ago without a thought, buried in some refuse heap outside Moscow with all the other detritus of the eighties. "Don't you think that's odd?" he tries.

"Perhaps," she says. Her tone suggests she is unconvinced. Can't she see that they are alike, he thinks, tied by odd echoes, chords of resemblance and memory? That movement of his mother's that she made outside, even the frown she now directs toward him? He looks around the kitchen. The pots and pans. The calendar decorated with a sentimental painting of a snowy forest.

"I should start making Nikolai some food."

"Oh," he says. "Yes."

"You should stay to eat."

"I have a flight," he lies. He has the sense that he must not stay, that he isn't up to it.

"It was nice of you to come." She calls Nickolai from his room to say good-bye. The boy seems to look through him, until he moves forward quite suddenly to shake Oleg's hand with a gaze held down. Oleg thinks that he will find a way to remedy this. He feels clumsy, embarrassed. The boy's hand is clammy. Oleg hasn't made a connection.

He tramps back to the café and drinks a beer and awaits a taxi. On the ride back through the dark city, he thinks of tying that fishing line around that broken mug at the small table in the room he shared with his young wife, Katya. The way she walked around that room: the loose, frustrated pacing of a creature caged. His pack of cigarettes. Belomorkanal. Those blue and yellow packets. The little map. The crescent of writing. The rough flavor. Later, he smoked better cigarettes, but he realizes that he never enjoyed smoking so much as he did then. They had a slightly foul aftertaste, like fish skin. He sat at the table and worked to make that ladle, and Katya, his wife, was on the bed reading. He would wake and go to the railway offices. He was doing computers for the railways then. It was all ahead of him. The mess of actually having something he would need to protect. His pleasure then was getting by. His pleasure then was the sense that everything was falling apart, and that he was ready for whatever was being born.

He gets back to the hotel and treks up the stairs and sits for a long time on the edge of the bed. He realizes that he is still wearing Nickolai's blue socks.

He calls Victor, and asks for a seat on the overnight flight out of the city. He packs, takes a taxi to the airport. This time, he's alone in first class, a little curtain between him and the others. He looks out of the window as the plane ascends. This town has always been waiting for him, he thinks. His brain is churning, turning over in a way it hasn't for years. Those factories dark and cracked apart. His cousin is right in her outrage. There should be lights stretching out beneath him. He didn't attend to them before. Others didn't attend to them. They could have, he thinks. Still could. He thinks again of the ladle, the memory of making the thing. He was improvising then. Waiting. He was at the center of this great thing that no one else could see, not even Katya, rising from the bed to come and place her hands around him as he worked. Yet he felt it. He was right. He could do it again, he thinks. Why not?

He sleeps in his seat and dreams of his mother as a girl. He recognizes her, even as a child. She laughs. Her open mouth. Her white teeth. Sun slanting from behind her. She seems glad.

22

MARTIN'S NEW flat has a view of the river, as long as one stands at a particular place next to the bedroom window and looks back and down to the end of a perpendicular alley and through a small garden to the water beyond. Between his viewing of the place and his moving in, the trees in the garden have lost the last of their leaves, and he can see more of the slow, brownish water, the silt slopped up on the banks by the inflow and outflow of the tides. It's in Fulham. The pavements taken up with prams. The old men doddering toward their allotments. The rent on the place is three-quarters of his paycheck. He's taken it in anticipation of advancing in his career. The agent knew Martin's salary, assented to the deal. People manage, Martin tells himself, this is normal.

Marina comes on a Saturday, while Oleg is still away. She drapes her coat over the pile of boxes in the hallway. She walks down the hall, studying the place, pausing to examine the calendar he has pinned above the shoe rack. He shows her the rooms with a fake estate agent manner. "Superbly equipped," he says. "Endowed with a breathtaking view." She laughs.

"You're proud," she says.

He doesn't know what to say. What is this small top floor to her? "Well, yes," he says in the end, more serious than he'd like to be.

She laughs. "It's fine," she says. "I like it."

He shrugs. He feels himself the awkward boy he was at university.

"Just don't be embarrassed by your pleasure," she says. She laughs again.

"I'm English," he says. "I'm an Englishman. Of course I'm embarrassed by my pleasure."

"Ah," she says. "Right. This isn't so much the case for a Russian man. The Russian man very much enjoys his pleasure. It's just that he knows his pleasure is only an interlude."

Oleg is brought back into the room with these words. The Russian man she knows best, lives with. The man, in many ways, who has brought the two of them to this little apartment. Martin remembers a Sartre quote that James once recited: "Absence is a fundamental presence."

SHE LOOKS in the fridge. "All these single portions!" she says. "You poor bachelor!" She comes over and puts a hand against his chest. His awareness rushes toward that hand: her fingerprints, the cotton of his shirt, his skin.

"I suppose I have been lonely," he says. It is a game, of course, played over a dynamic he can't fully fathom.

They make love in the bedroom. The bedroom is finished enough: a new bed in there, crisp sheets, a mirror, a chair on which he usually places his folded clothes.

He went to many different flats with the letting agent. He imagined sleeping with Marina in different rooms, all over London. He viewed places he couldn't afford and places he couldn't bear to live. It was an act of fiction-making, building up stories in these flats, drawing scenes from the layouts, from the way sun falls across a room. He only wanted a place that was not grubby and mean, that was not sad, that had some daylight. Marina goes to the bathroom. The fan runs with a slightly sickening, high-pitched moan. She comes back and sits up in bed, checking her phone. He rubs her shoulders and she smiles.

Her husband is still in Moscow. Martin wants to know when Oleg will be back in Britain, but doesn't want to ask. He looks at her and feels a dread that is almost delicious, a roller-coaster plunge in his stomach. Such danger is reifying. This means something, he tells himself.

He makes coffee in the kitchen. Marina sits at the breakfast bar, and he thinks that the room is too bare. He had to get her into the place to be able to see it with her eyes. It's the kind of apartment a middle-class father would get after his divorce. He fills a cafetière. After a couple of minutes, Marina plunges it with a steady resolution. She pours the coffee. He bought croissants in preparation for her arrival, but she declines when he offers them. They've done none of this playing house yet, this ordinary couplehood. "I should be on my way," she says. There is a skylight in the kitchen, above the breakfast bar. He looks up to see a plane passing overhead, heading toward Heathrow, the hum of the engines arriving after a slight delay.

When she goes, neither of them seems to know what to do at the door. They negotiate their way, silently, awkwardly, to a kiss on the cheek. He is more nervous about that moment than the sex, he realizes. The door closes behind her. He goes to the window and watches her cross the road. She is calling someone on her phone, walking quite quickly. There is a shower coming in. Flecks of rain on the windowpane. A van makes a U-turn. She dropped a hairpin on the floor of the bedroom. He opens an empty bedside drawer and places it inside.

23

"THE WORLD wants to move," he says when he arrives back from Russia to the country house.

It's late on Friday night. Oleg speaks like a sleep-talker. He's lost more weight. Marina marches him upstairs and instructs him into his pajamas.

When he was away, she worried about him. She spoke to him on the phone and sensed that he was tipping over into something. There is a characteristic control that is gone from Oleg, the man who has always landed catlike on his feet. He's finished clearing out his mother's apartment: the plants, the endless bookshelves, the pictures of him as a boy, his childhood room, re-created by his mother when he—aged forty-five—bought that place for her.

He falls asleep the moment he hits the bed, and yet in the middle of the night Marina wakes to find him sitting in a chair at the window. He looks at her. She is bleary-eyed and without contacts or glasses and he can see her more clearly than she can see him. "I'm fine," the blurred outline of him says.

She falls asleep again. When she wakes the sun is up and he is gone and there are five pages of his illegible handwriting on a pad on the chair.

SHE MET Oleg at an event organized by her company. It was a panel discussion on the theme of "The Work of Tomorrow." People listened to a talk by a Dutch intellectual in a bow tie who spoke with a mix of dread and rapture of the coming of a robot workforce. People drank wine and drifted around the firm's grand meeting room. Oleg stood looking at the view of St. Paul's. Marina introduced herself. He had some investments with the firm, but most of what anyone knew of him was hearsay. It was a coup to have him at the event, and she thanked him for coming. "I needed a reason to leave the house," he said. He shrugged. "I'm getting divorced."

"I'm sorry to hear," she said.

"Maybe it's better," he said. "I'm a hard man to be married to."

There was something true about him, she thought. He was a person acting as he would ideally wish to. She stayed close to him that night. The two of them moved between groups of other people, joining conversations and drawing off. She studied his way of answering questions, meeting people. She sensed he was studying her also.

"Did you like the talk?" she asked him.

"Of course," he said.

"Really?"

He sighed. He looked at her for a moment. She felt herself to be judged worthy of frankness. He said, "Do you really think that anyone who knows what will happen in the future is traveling around giving talks?"

She smiled. "His fee was quite big."

Oleg spat air. "The fee is not it. The interesting thing isn't talking. What is important is to do."

He spoke sparingly. He had a reticence she hadn't observed in other successful businesspeople, who tended to dominate conversation. Later, when she knew him better, he'd tell her that impatience was a sign of weakness. It was not that he wasn't as hungry as others, but rather that he was sure of satisfying that hunger.

That night, he asked her to go for a drink with him after the event. It should've been awkward to be asked something like that by a client. She wanted to go, though.

They went to a cocktail bar near the old Smithfield meat market. He spent a lot of time chatting with the waitress about the composition of the drinks. *This man is diligent,* Marina thought. He had a heavy face, a striking solidity, as if he were some grand bronze statue of himself. Yet when she studied him, she noticed that he had faint freckles around his nose. His eyes were strikingly blue. His English was good, but he talked very slowly. In Russian he was more expansive. His Manhattan came and he sipped it and said, "Seven out of ten." She felt a compelling ambivalence.

He knew of her father, he said. He hadn't met him. She waited for him to give her more, but he didn't. They talked about Russia, about the diaspora in London. He seemed concerned that Russians were not regarded well, torn between joining criticism of his countrymen and frustration with the prejudices of the British.

She knew that he collected art, so she asked about his collection. He talked about it at length—too much, really, though she credited his genuine enthusiasm. She found herself telling him about her piano playing. He asked interesting questions. She asked whether he played an instrument. "I never had a vocation like that," he said. "If I was truly good at something like that when I was young, I would still be doing it in some dingy Moscow room."

"You think?" she said.

"I don't have talents," he said. "I have obsessions." He winked, and she wondered whether she could love someone who did such a thing.

Outside the bar, he called a taxi for her, waited for it to arrive. When she got in, he walked to a car that was waiting for him across the street. He walked slowly, with a total assurance. She wondered whether she could do a thing to dent that confidence. The thought of sleeping with him did not disgust her.

THEY ORGANIZED another date at a restaurant to which she was late. She apologized fulsomely when she arrived. "It's okay," he said.

"People think it is a humiliation to wait for others, but I'm always glad to wait. My life is organized. This is a source of power." She thought he was making a tacit criticism of her personal disorderliness, but she would later come to see that this was not his point. He was only talking about himself, as ever, about how he was different from others.

She was aware that he might have done objectionable things. She asked him once about his first million. "I wasn't Gandhi," he said. "But then, even Gandhi wasn't Gandhi." There were a lot of mad and contradictory rumors about him. There had been such rumors about her father, especially after his death. Marina's impulse was to distrust such rumors. She understood that men like Oleg drove people to speculation.

He didn't want children. That was one concrete, simple thing that gladdened her. He already had one son, Alexi. He treated Alexi terribly, but then, Alexi was terrible. The first time she met Alexi, he called her a "sour, skinny bitch." The relationship seemed validated by such opposition.

Sometimes it felt like she was trying on different reasons for loving him, as if it were a theoretical exercise, and in that perhaps was some hint of what was really true: it was about freedom, loving him. She surprised others and herself. The sheer excess of him gave her license.

AS SHE descends the stairs, he comes through the back door with the dogs. Gena jumps up at her. Oleg wipes his boots on the mat, grinning.

"You were up early," she says.

"Yes! I have so many ideas. I can't believe I couldn't see this all before."

They have breakfast by the pool, as is their Saturday morning tradition, but he doesn't attend to the pastries or yogurt or berries, and instead looks at her with an expression of anticipation, waiting for her to draw his ideas out of him.

She doesn't want to give in immediately. She points up to the leaves stuck to the glass above them. She says, "We should get the roof of the conservatory cleaned."

Oleg simply says, "I have a cousin I didn't really know I had." He doesn't look up at the leaves, flattened and damp against the panes overhead. He pushes his coffee cup aside. It squeals against the glass top of the table.

"Didn't know you had?"

"Didn't attend to. I went to visit as a child. Our mothers didn't get on. But she wrote to me."

"Where is she?"

"In the far east. I visited last week. It changed me deeply. There are some things I haven't been able to see until now."

It's so grand, so pompous, that she should laugh, but she can't. "What would they be?" she says eventually.

"The lives of ordinary people."

"In Russia?"

"Yes," he says. "Of course."

He's waiting for her to ask a question. She looks at him. She looks at the light dappling the surface of the pool. She looks back at him. He says, "There are people with nothing. With the tiniest, ugly little lives."

"Do you think they think of it like that?"

". . . and I am here and they are there."

"Yes?"

"Maybe this is obvious for you, but now I see that my cousin is there. It means something, blood. It makes me feel I could still be in a town like that, where life is not so good."

"You're going to give away some money?"

"No." He shakes his head. "This is bigger than that. I feel it."

"Oh?"

"The government has failed these people."

•   •   •

WHEN THEY were first together, Marina asked Oleg what he saw in her. "You challenge me," he said, and she believed that for a while, suspects that he himself still believes it. And yet she came to think that he misunderstood himself. He only meant that her confirmation was more hard-won, more rewarding. He still wanted assent. That first year with him was a tour of what he felt most impressive about himself, her role to be the witness to all of it. He lived so easily. He was not discomfited as she was so often discomfited. She was sent circling back to teenage years, to innumerable hours of shame regarding her father's overexuberance. She had spent too much time in self-loathing, in loathing of her family. There was a redemption in loving this man that she didn't truly want to examine. "You know what is truly tasteless?" he said. "Wealth without pleasure." He lived by formulas that had the dull banality of all that is true. Yet she ran out of energy for all his earnestness after a while. She came to realize that he needed her gaze, her engagement with what he was doing. She'd thought she was not the doting, encouraging wife. But perhaps she was merely the premium version: a serious woman whose distrust and eloquence made her eventual approval all the more valuable.

He has always been in recovery from the best years of his life. Often, in those first years, they'd dine with Galib, and the men would talk about the glory days of the nineties. Theirs was the narrative of addicts. They knew their old actions were regrettable, yet those actions had coincided with their greatest successes. "We used to run the country," Oleg once said. He shook his head and laughed. "There was nothing you couldn't do with a big enough bag of dollars."

"Nothing," Galib confirmed.

He'd tried to hold off the nostalgia for those days. She was supposed to be some part of that effort, she sensed. "Have you ever read about the men who made it into space?" he asked her once. "When they come back?"

She said she hadn't.

"They struggle. What is there to do after that?"

It was well put, she thought. It laid out his problem: in what he intended to say, and in the revelation that he thought his past as grand as having walked on the moon.

HE'D MADE a commitment to the President not to go into politics. Everyone knows this. He and other businessmen codified the agreement at a meeting at Stalin's dacha. She thinks of a photograph she has seen of the event: the meaty heads of the billionaires and in the midst of them the President, new to his role then, each man smiling a smile that is firm and false and held in the expectation that it should be he who will triumph from this situation.

Oleg gets up from the small table and walks around the pool, his hands behind his back. His posture seems to her a caricature of thoughtfulness. He peers out of the fogged glass of the conservatory.

"You want—what?—to be president?" she says.

"Maybe," he says. "Perhaps that is the best way."

"Our lives will change if you do this."

He stops walking. The sole of his slipper scuffs on the tile with a gasping sound. He looks at the water, and then at her. "Yes," he says.

"My life," she says.

"Of course."

"You've considered this?"

He shrugs. "Life is always changing."

"You're a Greek philosopher now?"

He thinks about this.

"This is going to be dangerous."

He looks at her. "I don't choose to do this," he says. She wonders if he has rehearsed these words, the better to bear the melodramatic silliness of them. He touches his chest. He looks at her. He waits a beat. She knows what is coming. "I feel that I *must* do this," he says.

When he has departed, Marina sits in the conservatory. This was coming, she thinks. He was restless. He has never, despite himself, stopped looking for his next triumph, never reconciled the need within him. She thinks of finance terminology. An endogenous shock: a crisis born of factors inside the system, of inherent contradictions.

Oleg retreats to the upstairs lounge and clicks through the TV news: the Russian channels, BBC, CNN. Passing the room, Marina hears the flaring, jabbing jingles. Later, she goes in to retrieve a book from the shelves. "How can you take so much of this crap?" she says.

"I'm steeping myself in it," he says. "I'm gaining my immunity."

He is watching footage of men fighting in the Turkish parliament. He sits there, unblinking.

She isn't able to locate the book. The organization of this house is impossible, beyond her. She stands to leave.

The broadcast has switched to a segment about the price of oil, footage of traffic rolling slowly down European roads.

"The world wants to move," Oleg says. "The world wants to move."

24

WATERFORTH STAMPS across the gravel from his oxblood-colored Bentley. He pumps Oleg's hand and looks him in the eye. "Good to see you, old chap," he says. He inhales. "The country!" He takes off his blazer and hangs his jacket over his arm. His shirt is the yellowish white of old paper, his tie pinkish purple. The suit itself is a shiny dark green. If Oleg wore such a thing, people would think him a ridiculous and gaudy figure. On Waterforth, however, this suit signifies an iconoclasm, a resolve to do things that others would not. This is authentic, insofar as Waterforth would do anything. This quality is why one calls such a man. Waterforth licks his lips and says, "This place is exquisite. It wows me every time I arrive." His eyebrows are thick, black, shot through with wiry curls of white.

"Thank you," says Oleg.

"It is so good to see you, old chap." Waterforth exercises charm the way a Russian policeman initially denies a bribe: the gesture is not serious. The point of the earnest performance is to underline the essential naïveté of performing such an act sincerely.

In the living room, they sit separated by a small table in two Hepplewhite mahogany elbow chairs. Oleg pours the tea.

"So, we're thinking of a new approach to your PR?" says Waterforth.

"Yes." Oleg stirs the lemon in his tea, plays with a cube of sugar. "I want to change everything."

"Only that?" says Waterforth. He flashes a smile that shows his over-white teeth.

"Yes. I know it's a lot."

"I understand completely."

"I want to change things. I saw my cousin back in Russia. I haven't seen her for years. I sensed a fury in her."

Waterforth chuckles. "Do you remember when we met? Jesus, people fucking hated you."

"It was hard for people to understand the situation. There were many, many problems."

"Oh yes. And you guys were doing okay for yourselves."

"Yes."

"It didn't help that a fair number of you were Jews. I say this as a quarter of a Jew myself."

"People have their prejudices."

"You were all taking your cut, also."

"We were protecting our investments. We were using our own money to prevent the country sliding back. People didn't see this."

"Of course. Of course."

Waterforth was the man they brought in when things got serious in 1996. They were a group of businessmen working together—former enemies, bound by a realization of the fate they faced if Yeltsin were to lose the election. Yuri, one of the other businessmen, said: "They're going to string us from the lampposts if the Communists get back into power." He wasn't wrong in this.

They all agreed to work together. They funded a campaign. They used their television and radio networks. They were trying to reelect a half-dead drunk. That was the truth of it. And yet, it felt noble. It was either the drunk or those angry old generals who had tried to take the government back in 1991. The Russian people had suffered the change to the free market, certainly, but there was still so much hope in those days. They were just fighting to survive, to preserve freedom. The public was not really aware of what the other side wanted. There were those with designs on power who looked at Tiananmen Square with envy.

Oleg and the others were carrying Yeltsin into the Kremlin on their backs. They did things a little dirtily, sure. They ensured they were rewarded for their work. Yet with such men as they were, self-interest was important. That was the world they were heading toward. Oleg would have done it for less, yes, but not the others. And if that is the case, why pass up one's portion? It was that deal or no deal at all.

Lord Waterforth arrived in the middle of all this. He was the public relations expert from London, the guy who had worked with Margaret Thatcher. He was a lord. The businessmen were like schoolgirls around Waterforth. His was the kind of assurance they all wanted. He didn't bother with the gangster swagger they cultivated. He simply deployed a toxic quantity of scorn to everything. He acted as if the earth itself should be grateful to have him drawing breath upon its surface.

"We were young then," says Waterforth. He sips his tea and looks toward the window.

"Younger," says Oleg.

"We slept with young women," says Waterforth. "How about that?"

Oleg's English was not so good when he first met Waterforth. He didn't understand everything Waterforth said. Yet perhaps he understood the man as well as he ever would. He watched the way that Waterforth spoke and moved and saw that he was not to be trusted, though also that such a man could be of value to Oleg if used in the right way.

The thing he remembers most is the man's shoes: monk shoes in a light-brown leather that blended to woody orange toward the toe. They were shoes of a beauty he had not seen before. He was mesmerized to see Waterforth walking down the halls of the Kremlin: a heavy man who trod so lightly in such elegant footwear. Now such a style is cheap, copied, but then it was a revelation. Oleg already had lasts of his feet stored in a shoemaker's studio in Milan, and yet the Englishman's shoes were something else. Later, when Oleg moved to London, one of the first things he did was get himself five pairs of shoes made by this cobbler of Waterforth's. What was classy was not having a new pair, but an old one. Durability was the point. The real concern was not merely having nice things, but understanding how those nice things might be made to last. The Prince of Wales had worn the same pair of oxfords for a quarter of a century. Oleg has on a pair of dark-blue V-front brogues now. He crosses his legs, sees a shapely toe poking out from beneath the table, and feels momentarily calmed by the sight. He looks up at Waterforth, who says, "Anyway. You're becoming a democrat."

"I was always a democrat."

"Already in character. I like it."

"We did some things that were regrettable, but the plan was that this was temporary. . . ."

"And yet everything is still, as you say, regrettable." Waterforth bares his teeth again in a rueful grin.

"Yes."

"So . . . More money for the foundation? A few speeches?"

"I'm serious this time."

"So am I, my friend."

"I want to really change things."

"Yes. Your cousin had it hard. You could do something in her town. A hospital. A factory. A new university with your name on it."

"I don't want to buy her off. The problem is not that she hates me."

"No?"

"The problem is that she is right."

He thinks then of his mother. In the election of 1996, she didn't want to vote for Yeltsin. She talked about her pension, which wasn't being paid. "I make your pension in a moment," said Oleg to his mother. He clicked his fingers. She didn't need the pension. He gave her plenty of money. Of course, her concern was the work she had done, the recognition of it, the earning of it over so many years. She was driven by the same stubbornness and pride that drove him. It was more than money, and though other rich men like him would be happy to pay off their own consciences with a hospital, Oleg is not like that. He sees things through.

"Things went wrong," Oleg says. "We fucked things up."

Waterforth makes a tent of his hands. "Talking politically, *we fucked up the country* is a hard sell."

"Yes."

He smiles. "I think we can do something though."

"We can."

"You want, what? To run for the presidency eventually?"

"Why not?"

Waterforth winces. Oleg knows the man. This wince hints not at impossibility but at what it will cost Oleg to initiate such a scheme.

"We have four years until the next election," Oleg says.

"Oh, good. Yes. Four years to remake the world's fifth-largest democracy."

"You won't do it?"

"Of course I'll do it. You just have to be patient. You just have to give me the right resources."

"We make space for alternatives first."

"Yes, yes. The squishy civil-society stuff. And we stop people hating you, show you're trying."

"And change things."

"Sure. Sure. It'll take a lot of work. My bills won't be small, but you're good for that, naturally?" He raises an eyebrow, and Oleg nods. Waterforth stands and goes to the window. He turns back with a new face, a grin. "I can see it now, actually," he says. "Yes. You look good. You're older and wiser. You will look quite stylish on a poster, I think."

25

IT SHOULDN'T be this easy, she thinks. Yet her husband is so pre-occupied that it is. Marina has booked a guesthouse in Oxfordshire for a long weekend. She told Oleg that she's spending the time with Jane. She and Martin meet at Paddington and catch the train together.

The air in the station is tainted with diesel exhaust, the hollow body of the giant space filled with echoed talk and the grumble of idling engines. Marina spies Martin through the crowds. He's still wearing his work clothes. He hugs her in a chaste embrace. He smells of a sickly brand of deodorant, and beneath that the cumin odor of perspiration. He carries a leather weekend bag and looks nervous as they walk together to their platform. She says, "How was work?" and this feels odd as she says it. Couplehood, temporarily. Going out to the world and returning to each other.

Martin has brought cans of gin and tonic with him. Their seats face each other across a small table. "When did you last get a train?" says Martin. He rocks the ring pull of his open can backward and forward with his finger.

"I don't know," she says. "University? School? Do ski-resort funiculars count?" Martin laughs. *This is easier each time,* she thinks. She says, "I fucking needed this. He's losing it."

Martin cringes slightly, however. He says, "Remember we're in public." Though she isn't sure whether this is to do with the swearing or her glancing mention of her husband.

•   •   •

THE STATION at which they disembark reminds her of the station near her first boarding school, from which she and Jane would set off for Bristol on their record-buying trips. She and Martin walk off the short platform and past the small stone ticket office. There is only a single taxi outside, which they take. The driver has thick gray sideburns and chews menthol gum.

Their guesthouse is attached to an upmarket pub, where they eat dinner. Crooked stone walls. Horse tack nailed up as decoration. A cast-iron stove in the corner. She drinks a glass of wine and then another, and realizes that she would very much like to get drunk. She does so, Martin loyally accompanying her.

Sleeping together drunkenly takes her back to that night in Switzerland and the feeling she had then of wanting to find in his presence something she had lost of herself.

In the morning she wakes to him dressing and going out. He's trying so assiduously not to disturb her. He walks to the door with a care that is cartoonish, and she closes her eyes so that he won't look back and see her watching him. She wakes again when he returns to the room. She looks at her watch: 11 a.m. Martin has a tote bag. He must have brought it with him. He plans too much, she thinks. He takes out the *Guardian* and an orange bottle. "Lucozade," he says. "Good for a hangover. One thing I did learn as a student."

"Lucozade?"

"What? Billionaire Russians don't drink Lucozade? They didn't drink Lucozade at your fancy girls' school?"

"It's a sports drink?"

"Sort of. Fizzy."

"Billionaire Russians drink something like it, actually, in my experience." She opens the bottle.

"It's nice?"

"It's fizzy orange."

"This is the original, before your Red Bulls, your Monster Energys."

"You art people with your originals," she says. She rolls over in the bed so she can reach her bag on the floor. She takes out a joint. "This works for a hangover," she says, lifting it.

"You're going to smoke that here?" he says. He looks up at the smoke alarm.

"Of course," she says. He nods, and she feels a twinge of irritation seeing him trying to swallow his apprehension. When the joint is going, though, he takes a few puffs, careful to blow the smoke out of the open window through which the warm air of the bedroom flees into the cool morning.

AS THEY'VE missed breakfast, they eat an early lunch in the pub instead. Martin orders a beef sandwich. Marina has a sad-looking salad. Martin eyes it when it arrives. "I always remember you eating peanut butter sandwiches at university."

"I didn't know how to make anything else, and I felt embarrassed about ordering stuff. Someone told me that you could get all the nutrients you need from peanut butter, bananas, blueberries and milk, so that was all I ate."

"Ha."

"We loved those things. Little tricks. Did we call them life hacks then?"

"I learned to get the creases out of a shirt by leaving it in the bathroom near the shower. I felt very grown-up."

"Exactly."

"You've broadened your diet these days, I take it."

"These days I have a chef."

"Right."

"Or two, in fact. One in London and one at the estate."

Martin shakes his head and smiles.

"This thing is bigger than me," she says. "Oleg wants these

luxuries. We have guests for his business. Sometimes we might as well be running a hotel. The situation necessitates these things."

"Don't think I'm judging. It's just the scale. It's all so amazing."

"You're impressed?"

"I guess."

"That's worse. Don't be impressed. My life is easy. My life isn't good."

"It seems full. I'm jealous of the fullness."

"Don't be impressed," she says again.

"And yet you live it."

She says, "I'm a coward. If I gave it up, what would I do?"

"Go back to eating peanut butter sandwiches?"

"Exactly."

He laughs. "That's not so bad."

"I'm a coward."

"You're not."

"Loss aversion. That's the most prevalent psychological fallacy. I work in finance. This is fundamental to the species."

Martin bites his sandwich and it begins to fall apart in his hands. He puts it on his plate and picks at it with his fork. "You'd be fine, you know," he says. "But anyway, I understand. I'd do the same in your position."

Of course, she thinks. She doesn't want to hear this, though. She wants his judgment, his censure. She could give so much more of her wealth away. She knows this, but she suffers a jealousy she can't forsake. What if she gives it to those who waste it? If some grand humanitarian plan backfires? Does anyone truly trust others to spend their money as well as they themselves would do? There's perhaps more honesty in the explicitness of her husband's position: that relinquishing a single thing is folly.

She says, "I'd like to get laser eye surgery."

"Right."

"But there's no day I wake up and think, *Today I'd like my cornea burned away.* I accept the risks in an abstract sense, but there's no particular instant when I can face them. You see?"

"I suppose."

"I'm a coward," she says again.

THEY GO for a walk in a botanical garden on the edge of town, and then rain comes in, so they retreat to the guesthouse, and smoke again and each read a little. In the evening, they pace through drizzle to a half-timbered pub next to the church at the top of the village. They find a seat in a back room with whitewashed walls and twisted beams holding up the ceiling.

The rest of the people in the back room are locals, having a bit of a session, but going about it cheerfully and joking with Martin about being a giant when he hits his head on a low beam while carrying drinks from the bar. Marina feels very far from Oleg and from the country house, and free and glad of it. She drinks sour wine, and Martin drinks local bitter.

They go back to the guesthouse and have more-sober sex, and Marina looks at Martin and thinks that he flickers, that he can't quite hold in character in this role, that there is part of him still unsure of all of this.

She wakes in the night, and looks at him in the glow that comes through the curtain from the streetlight across the road. She can smell the faint odor of a half-smoked joint on the bedside table. To watch someone sleeping is, of course, to feel one knows something that the sleeper does not, and Marina feels exactly this: that Martin isn't quite ready, isn't aware that this can't hold, that at some point he will have to choose between her and her husband. She wants him to choose her, she realizes. Not forever. Not definitively. Not even for her sake, but just ahead of her husband's business. Because he is good, Martin. Better than some of the other groveling men and women who work for Oleg. Better than what he will have to become to stay in orbit of her husband. She can see him more clearly in the low light as her eyes adjust—his open face—and she feels a little melancholy, excessively sentimental. Martin won't make such a choice, won't understand the urgency, and this passivity itself is the odd reason that she would never tell him such a thing, would never want much more than whatever they are doing now. He is not a man who acts first, but a man who is acted upon, who will let the world roll over him and not even realize it is doing so.

THE NEXT afternoon, as they're preparing to go for a walk, Marina gets a call from Oleg. She gestures at Martin to stay quiet. "Hello," she says. Oleg wants to know when she's coming back on Sunday, as he has a meeting with Waterforth. "After Waterforth has gone, preferably," she says. She grins. Martin, watching her from across the bed, is pale with fear. She says she'll be back in the late afternoon. She says she's having a relaxing weekend with Jane.

They smoke again and then go for a stroll in a woodland on the hill behind the village. She likes the mild stonedness, the cool air on her face. The forest is bare and open and carpeted with fallen leaves in a way she suddenly finds to be beautiful.

Martin wears boots, but they're fashion boots, city boots, and he advances gingerly where the route is muddy and waterlogged.

At the top of the forest they come to a stile over a fence and they clamber over that and walk up a path through a field, turning back at the top to look down on the towns scattered across the valley beneath them: spires and slate roofs, sunken roads and the railway tracks leading east to west, curving very slightly. They sit on a fallen tree trunk at the top of the field. There's an airplane moving in the far distance. A smudge, slowly resolving as it descends to the plain.

"You and me here," she says. She wants to linger, to precipitate something.

"Yes."

"The old gang."

"Part of the old gang."

"Right. How is James?" It is a relief to speak of him, she supposes. The wounded ex. Another boy prince.

"He's okay. He hasn't changed."

"Work?"

"He teaches a few piano lessons, turns pages for concert pianists, plays gigs for hire."

"Where?"

"The Royal Sussex Hotel is one regular place."

"You've been?"

"I've only met him afterward there. He doesn't want to be watched. This was never where he expected to be."

"I know the feeling."

She wants to walk farther up the hill, though Martin objects. "It'll be dark in an hour," he says, and he is right, though she doesn't want to worry about this.

"It's not dark now," she says. He nods, and they stand and walk. They cross another stile. They follow a weaving path up through another section of woodland.

At the crest of the hill, they emerge onto a narrow road. On the other side are fields, the path continuing through them. There is a brown signpost pointing across the fields to a fenced area around a hump of grass. The sign reads LONG BARROW. She looks at Martin and smiles. She feels vindicated in her desire to continue the walk. "A burial mound," she says. "You want to see?"

"You knew this was here?" he says.

She shakes her head.

An information board stands next to the mound. The finish has weathered and cracked, leaving only a corner of the image left: a drawing of two Neolithic people, staring in brutish awe at nothing. The long mound points toward the head of the scarp, a stooped entrance into the middle of the thing. The entrance opens to a low chamber that extends a couple of meters. She squats and turns on her phone flashlight, advances in a crouch. The walls are built with thin stacked stones. She puts her hand against them and feels the coolness. She's acutely conscious of the earth over her head. Turning to the entrance, she can see Martin's lower legs. She closes her eyes, and when she opens them again the legs are gone. She crawls from the mound and stands. Martin is at the end of the scarp, looking over the valley, beyond which the smallest sliver of sun is visible above the horizon. She goes to him. He says, "It's all in line."

"What?"

"The mound. Sunrise. Sunset."

"Right," she says. "Tell me about it."

"I know nothing."

"They're your people."

He smiles. "Weren't these people displaced by others? Who knows where the people who made this went."

She looks back. "What a place to bury their dead, though."

"Not all their dead, I don't think," says Martin. "Just their kings and queens."

There is a cold breeze rising up the scarp, blowing in their faces. She says, "You know what we could do?"

"What?"

She moves to kiss him. He accepts her into his embrace. She pushes a hand up his sweatshirt, against his skin, and he gasps at the coldness. She says, "In there."

"What?"

She points to the entrance of the low chamber.

He says, "You're not serious?" He is watching her, trying to read something on her face.

"Come," she says, and steps a pace back from him, but the gesture doesn't play as she expects. He doesn't follow her.

"Are you serious?" he says again. "What if someone comes?"

"Christ!" It's her turn to look at him now, to study his expression.

She wants to do something reckless here. She wants to feel the power of the location. Yet he is snagged in practicalities.

They walk back to the village down the narrow road. There's no pavement, so they press themselves to the hedges at the side of the road when they hear vehicles. They stand, lights raking past them. The village is streetlit when they reach it.

At the guesthouse, they take it in turns to shower. Marina goes first and then, while Martin is showering, sits on the bed reading about long barrows on her phone. Martin was correct that not everyone was buried in these places. The remains account for less than a single percent of the populations. Some forgotten logic, strong enough to sustain the ceremony and the years of backbreaking work with crude tools, informed who was put inside and who was not.

AT DINNER, she picks at some chicken, pushes overcooked vegetables across her plate. Martin has ordered sea bass, which he says is very nice.

The waitress comes to ask how the food is, and Martin, chewing, moves to respond with a gesture and spills Marina's wine onto her lap. Then he makes a show of trying to clean it up, apologizes too often. She is irritated with him, and he takes this as a cue to apologize more earnestly. She shakes it off and feels mean as she does so. There is something about Martin that makes her want to be cruel at times. He is like a puppy. He is eager and guileless in a way that precipitates the urge to violate that vulnerability, to assert the natural indifference of the world. He eventually understands that the jeans are not the issue. They continue the meal quietly. Though in the room, afterward, they recover something. They are both getting ready for bed, and he looks at her reflection in the mirror he stands in front of and says, "You know, once, at university, you and I and James were out, and someone we met asked me whether you were my sister."

"Really?"

"I was flattered." He laughs. "To think I was similar to you. To have such a pretty sister."

She smiles. "And now what?" she says. "You're sleeping with that sexy sister."

He blushes. "I suppose so," he says. "That's messed up."

She holds her grin. "Maybe this isn't natural."

26

THE BATTERY life of Oleg's laptop has gone to shit. Although he has plenty else he should be doing, he finds himself turning the laptop over, readying himself to dismantle it.

He has barely slept for days, though this altered state offers flashes of insight, he feels. He goes to the cupboard in the corner of the room, takes out his electronics toolbox, extracts from it his multimeter, his mini screwdrivers. It is vanity that he keeps these tools, yet this was his trade years ago. This is something he can do.

The base plate of the computer comes off easily. The speakers in the room are playing Schubert. His attention catches to the music, holds a second, drifts away. It's a little dusty in the body of the machine. He uses a can of compressed CO_2 to clear the space. The fine dust rises around him, visible in the rays of his desk lights.

The smell of the circuit board isn't the same as the old ones, yet there's a faint odor there: wires, housings, solder, plastic that has been warmed. People don't understand the physicality of these machines. His son is supposed to be working with computers—investing in apps, apparently. But for Alexi, a computer is as impenetrable as a rock. And yet, they are *things*, networks of electrics, logic manifest. They had to be built from metals dug from the earth. It is a nostalgic act to pry the panels off the laptop, to look down at the wires and chips laid out like a little city.

. . .

WHEN OLEG was a child, it was said that he had magic hands. His fingers knew what they were doing before his mind did. His father was a frustrated professor of mathematics, yet Oleg had no talent for numbers himself. What was easy, however, was taking things apart and fitting them back together. Oleg picked apart toys, cleaned them, re-assembled them. There was a logic to these projects that raced ahead of him, that he could chase but couldn't articulate. He fixed the telephone when it broke. He found the failing connection within his father's Elektronika calculator and soldered it. He liked to take things fully to pieces, to risk irrevocability. His father would bring home the broken possessions of colleagues for his son to fix.

In time, Oleg learned to use that understanding he had of things to understand systems. He studied in the Faculty of Computer Science at the Moscow State Forest University, and did well. He didn't quite understand the approbation of his teachers. He was just interested, methodical, but that was enough. On graduation, he won a transfer to the Institute of Computer Sciences in Kiev.

They knew so little then, but the future was also more open. They weren't just thinking of boxes in people's homes, but of nationwide networks, new social configurations. The institute sprawled over a block to the south of the city center. There were rooms of immaculate parquet floors. Oleg walked across these floors in a pair of imported Japanese shoes he'd acquired from a friend in advance of his move. The computers were colors you don't see now: muted blues, synthetic greens, beiges. He liked to listen to the spools of tape whirring through them.

The other workers were more enamored with the well-provisioned café than with the machines. And perhaps there should have been a warning for Oleg in their satisfaction with liver cakes and cutlets. "If you'd only been here ten years before," people said. It was the motto of those days. The great Viktor Glushkov had died a year before Oleg arrived, his dream of a grand Soviet network having expired in the decade before that. There were maps of the proposed network in the institute

archives: perfect worlds that had never been, landscapes so painstakingly worked out that you wanted to go to the window to check that
they hadn't been realized in actuality while you were working at your
desk. Yet the military men in the Soviet hierarchy hadn't liked the network. At the time, Oleg assumed that the generals hadn't understood
it. Yet later he came to think the opposite: that they foresaw the way
their portions of power would have been lost to the thrumming of the
machinery. In this lurked a fact Oleg would learn and use later: the
state is not a single monster, but a pack of dogs that fight as readily with
each other as with outsiders.

Still, the institute had its pleasures. There were so many intelligent
men and women. There was a large park half a kilometer away. In the
winter, they'd skate. In the summer, they'd grill shashlik. On Sundays,
Oleg took off his top and went fishing. He played volleyball with others from the institute. On Mondays, his sunburned skin sloughed off
beneath his shirt. The equipment he had access to was unlike anything
he'd known before. This was where they made the Mir and Dnepr.
This was where they designed the machines that flew the space rockets.

The programming was done in Latin script by coders who were
mostly female. He went to watch the programming being done, so he
might talk to the girls who did it. Oleg knew the letters. He said the letters to himself. He knew some English words then: *chair, table, station.* He
didn't know at the time, of course, that one day he would live in England,
speak English daily. The institute had abandoned Cyrillic programming
as they moved from their own projects toward replicating the Western
machines. Yet reverse engineering was, in many ways, harder than creating from scratch. The elders of the institute bridled at the copying and
the consequent abandonment of the institute's own schemes. Engineers
now studied the hardware of the Americans, West Germans, and Japanese not as something that could be beaten, or even built upon, but as
the ultimate aim. They had leeway only to make mistakes.

On one machine Oleg worked on, he wanted to increase the
DRAM; 32KiB hobbled the machine needlessly. It was a clear oversight

on the part of the Americans. He took the idea to his superior, Pavel, but Pavel batted it back. "They won't like it," he said.

"I've done the calculations," said Oleg. He proffered the pile of notes that he had written.

Pavel nodded gravely. He had a way of looking, a way that many people at the institute had. His expression said, *This opinion I am articulating is not my own.* He said, "But then we have to rework things in other respects. The project changes."

"The project is better."

"The people who I answer to, they want the American machine."

"The Americans are already building a better machine."

Pavel shrugged. "Well, God help us."

YOU LOST your faith after a time, drifted and caught to other things. The older men and women drank, but Oleg didn't take to that then. He found love instead, for the first time in his life.

Anna was one of the programming girls. She was a real Ukrainian. She had hair so blond as to be almost translucent.

Thinking of Anna, he thinks of something his mother said not long before she died: "People don't love now like they used to. People don't spend the time. Now it's all about money." He didn't agree with many of his mother's complaints about the new Russia, but this notion had seemed true. He and Anna had so much time. They talked about everything. Despite her job, computers didn't interest her a bit. She spent her evenings reading philosophy. She wanted to discuss morality and free will. Her interest in philosophy was not just the ordinary stuff: the progression of Hegel and Marx and Lenin. She was snagged on Kant. She hurried home to arguments people had been having for hundreds of years. He didn't think she liked him at all, but she turned up. His little room was filled with the smell of her.

What he didn't realize then is that people don't need to be solved. He couldn't understand her entirely, and she couldn't fully understand him, and perhaps they could have lived with some productive space between them. He was intoxicated by the idea that the state held secrets. He wanted nothing more than the truths hidden by his government. She too believed in truth, but the truths she cared about were grander. She wanted life to have some pungent meaning. She was worried about free will. "How does it get into us?" she wanted to know. "If we work like machines, where do our choices come from?"

This didn't bother him at all. "We are the machines," he said. "So what? We work away."

"But then you're not doing anything," she said. "It's just your mechanism running."

He thought of a game he had played as a child. He'd throw a stick into the brook that ran past the tower blocks in which he lived. He'd walk along the bank, watching it, borne on the flow of the water. It'd tumble down rapids, slide along concrete channels. He rooted for it, credited its success as his own. Was his life not like this stick: something he was invested in, whatever the real causes that made it move? He cared about what happened to him. He didn't understand her panic. It seemed so easy. He was a fan of himself, of that great grinding machine that she said composed himself.

It was only many years later that he really pondered freedom: how people want it, how they can actually realize it. Yet he had long lost touch with Anna by then. In the late nineties, he'd had someone try to locate her. She had emigrated. The man tracked her to Canada, and then the trail went cold.

REALLY, IT'S risky to handle batteries ungrounded. But though Oleg's fingers are chubbier than they once were, he has as delicate a touch as ever. He breathes evenly as he works. He fiddles the battery case free. He pries open the case. There are six cylinders inside: the 18650 cells. He lays them out on the green leather top of the desk. He uses the multimeter on them one by one. They are all good.

The batteries aren't the issue. Which means an efficiency failure: a problem, likely, with the software. This isn't so much his thing. His pulse has quickened. He didn't want to jump to conclusions, and yet if the batteries are intact, that fact invites other considerations. Is malware a factor? If it is, then there are questions behind that. Are they already mounting a serious surveillance effort? He has a computer security guy. He takes precautions. But they are able to do things you wouldn't imagine.

He picks up his phone and calls Jerry. Jerry answers, breathless. Jerry is a heavy guy, a cliché of an IT manager. Oleg should let him catch himself, and yet he feels the prickling attraction of a bit of drama. "I think we have a breach," he says. "I think someone might have access to my machine."

"Really?" says Jerry. "You've followed the protocols?"

"Of course."

"Why do you think this?"

"The computer's slow. It's not a battery issue. I've checked the batteries."

"There could be many explanations," says Jerry.

"A breach could be an explanation."

"Yes. I suppose."

"I'm going to scrap it."

"Is that rash?"

"I think I can afford it."

"Well, off you go, I suppose."

Oleg ends the call. He puts the batteries aside. Though he can figure no use for them, the thought of discarding them right away displeases him. He undoes a few more screws, pulls the hard drive from the carcass of the open laptop. He turns it over, and a little dust spills from it. It is still warm, as if he has extracted it from a living body.

· · ·

THOSE FEW years at the institute shaped him, he feels, so much more than the several decades he's lived since. The frustration of what they could have done back then still smolders. He thinks of the time he was reverse-engineering an American circuit board. He sat at his bench and turned it over, examined the soldering. Pavel came over and said, "Have you seen it yet?" He smiled ruefully, departing without an explanation.

Oleg looked for a moment longer before he realized that the board had Cyrillic writing on it: poor Russian that read, "You copy that which is the best."

He felt as if he would look up from the bench to see someone watching him. It was a joke intended for him by the makers of this hardware, a bold acknowledgment that they knew their work was being copied. Somewhere in America were men with an image of Oleg: a Russian engineer, hunched studying this board.

Later, he'd think so often of this moment that it has now become dreamlike, an unreal crystallization of all his feelings of those years. Oleg stood at the lab bench and barely breathed. The Americans had realized their products were being replicated, and yet this was a *joke* to them. The sense he'd had before, that he and the others were chasing toward something (behind—yes—but in pursuit), was mistaken. He felt a blistering kind of shame. They were being played with as if they were nothing. He thought of midnight fishing trips, when he'd shine a flashlight into the river, and the trout would swim in the direction of the light, thinking it to be the moon.

Oleg moved back to Moscow to take a different job. Someone was needed to work on the new railway computer system. The computers were giant things, mocked by the workers. He looked at them and felt the melancholy one feels to see a sad zoo animal. These machines were meant to be tied to others, gridded into a system; instead they sat idle, waiting to be fed data as a captive creature is brought its grain.

In Moscow, Oleg went to parties where he drank and had long and pointless conversations. He was drifting. He heard about cooperatives from an old friend he had known in his Komsomol chapter when he was young. This friend knew a man who had started making dachas. Oleg sought out this man, Vasyli, and introduced himself. Vasyli was scraping together materials to make rustic sheds beyond the outskirts of town, and it was legal, condoned. Oleg had expected to meet some visionary, but Vasyli was quite the opposite. He was a tall, skinny man with a thin mustache. He seemed to have arrived at his scheme without thought, like a bird that had made a nest somewhere ingenious. When he mentioned that they worked with very old machines, Oleg said that he could fix them up. "Please do," said Vasyli.

Oleg would leave his job at the railways in the afternoon and then trek across town to a warehouse where he would service ancient cement mixers and drills and saws, covered in oil and metal shavings. He'd moved backward—from computers to these rusty tools—yet he loved the work. He made a shovel from an old road sign. That little project gave him more satisfaction than anything he had done in years.

It was in this period that he met German. German ran the cooperative program. German didn't look like he worked in the mayor's office. He wore a light-brown jacket, shoes unlike any Oleg had seen before: black and slightly pointy with a shapely leather sole. "They're from Sweden," he said, when he saw Oleg looking.

German had ended up in his role by accident. The suggestion of a cooperative program had come down to the office from above. There was just the assertion that businesses organized as cooperatives were now acceptable. Yet all this seemed to fall to precisely the right man, Oleg thought. In the whole city, there were only a handful of men and women who had any ideas whatsoever for how the years ahead might be shaped. It was German's talent that he found these people.

ONE DAY Oleg went to get some paperwork from German because Vasyli was working on a site. German seemed satisfied that Oleg had come. He said, "You men are making a fair amount of money. You're doing well. This is your area of expertise?"

Oleg explained that he worked with computers. He sensed that German already knew the things he was telling him.

"You have a head for figures?" said German. "I think Vasyli needs that. He's good at what he does, but there are other possibilities now that you have cash reserves."

"Yes," said Oleg. "I have some ideas."

"Do tell me," said German. "I can help you."

Oleg told him about the computers the institute imported. "Their basic machines are better than ours. If we can get machines from West Germany or Japan, there will be demand."

German nodded. "I'll talk to some people," he said.

German was as good as his word. He had contacts who could make things work. Oleg drew on those he knew from his work to source and sell on the machines they imported; he contacted old Komsomol friends for help with the importation. He filled half the warehouse with electronic hardware. Vasyli grumbled about the lack of space. "I don't know why people want these ugly things in their homes," he said.

"It's the future," said Oleg.

"Ha!" said Vasyli.

VASYLI TENDED to stay on-site, while Oleg went to the offices. One day, German spoke of Vasyli: "He's a reliable man, isn't he?"

Here was Oleg's first encounter with a trend he would come to recognize in later life: often in business when people assert your goodness, they are preparing to fuck you. Appreciation is easiest when the object of that appreciation is at their weakest. "Vasyli is very good at building these cheap sheds," said German. "Remarkable, really."

Oleg nodded.

"I'm not in this office only to help men build sheds, however," said German. He laughed dryly.

"Yes," said Oleg.

"But he's not really a man of vision in this respect. You, though, I can help."

And he did. He showed Oleg how to use the cooperative law to start a bank, as others were doing then. Oleg had offices by then, employed clever young men and women.

After that, it became necessary to push Vasyli aside. The business was no longer primarily construction. "You keep building your dachas," Oleg told him. Yet Vasyli wasn't satisfied. He screwed up his face. It was the first sign, to Oleg, of how ingratitude comes most naturally to those who owe the most. Vasyli knew so little that he was unaware of all that had been done for him. German backed Oleg, of course. They managed to maneuver Vasyli out of the way without incident. They agreed to German's stake in everything. It was only years later, in the wild years, when Vasyli came back at Oleg and the act became one of self-defense, that Oleg had to resort to violence.

In those years Oleg thought often of the failures of Glushkov's network. The idea of the network was to allow the state to regulate itself. Yet in those years, Oleg's greatest asset was disorganization, the blind spots and irregularities that the network was supposed to eradicate. A certain branch of government would have some product it had no use for. There'd be price discrepancies in materials between two cities. One company would have access to cash reserves and nothing to spend that cash on. Oleg took these opportunities, made his profits, waited for the system to recognize itself. He didn't feel guilty. He had gone to the computer institute to work for the state, he had been sincere, and it hadn't succeeded.

HE STANDS from his desk holding the hard drive. He puts on his Barbour jacket and drops the hard drive into the pocket. He descends the stairs at the back of the house. He goes to the dogs' room, where Gena rises and looks at him with wet eyes, pads over to greet him.

There was a storm last night, and there are leaves blown down onto the driveway, a branch fallen onto the gravel, which Gena runs over to sniff. Some rooks call from the woodland behind the house.

Oleg walks around the house to the place where the gardener makes his bonfires. There is a circle of ash, half a blackened log within it. He goes into the gardener's shed and fetches a can of petrol. He stacks up twigs, throws on logs from the pile beside the shed. He used to take great care making fires on fishing trips, but now he just splashes some petrol onto the wood, throws on a match. Flame jumps up immediately. He shoos Gena away. The twigs crackle, and after a time the wet wood starts to hiss.

MOST PEOPLE don't have such a memory as he has of that chip inscribed with its little message. They don't really recall what life was like before. They remember chaos. They remember Yeltsin standing on the tank. They think back to that moment, and ask, *What happened to all that?* They remember the failures of the reforms, not their necessity.

Through German, Oleg met some of the young men who would later put into practice the marketization of the country. They were types Oleg would not normally have noticed: overgrown students with ill-fitting clothes. They talked of everything as if it were a kind of game; looking back, this should have been alarming. Yet how else was one to face that era other than without a certain measure of incredulity?

These men, of course, made a mess. But then, these men were left a mess. The party had created the ruble overhang that later resulted in so much inflation. Oleg didn't like it necessarily, but you had to be a fool in these conditions to not make money hand over fist.

Maybe it wasn't right for the country to just start selling factories and oil companies. These firms belonged to the people. Yet they'd been of no benefit to the people, mismanaged as they were. And things were urgent too. The Communist state was not fully broken; it could have reassembled itself. Forces were readying to effect this. The system needed to be destroyed, to be cracked up and shuffled until its dismantling became inevitable. Who could have known better than Oleg the attraction to rebuilding a thing as it was designed?

And, yes, this dismantling made Oleg richer. He bought factories and utilities so fast he struggled to recall what he owned.

He had access to extra cash by then. He had been observed in those first years, his successes noted. One of Oleg's acquaintances from Komsomol came to the warehouse one day with another, older man whom German knew. They were both KGB, of course. The younger man sat straight-backed. He had a splattering of acne across the top of his thin cheeks. The older man had short-cropped gray hair and thick eyebrows. He was handsome in a totally conventional way.

What the men wanted to talk about was their "shared interest." Their organization had money that they said they needed to protect. "This is a time of great chaos," said the younger man, Oleg's acquaintance. "We want to be sure of our holdings." Men like them talked in starchy language, so different from the ambiguity of the young democrats. There was no uncertainty. They were not playing at having power; they knew what it was like to wield it.

Oleg had heard the rumors about dollar and gold reserves, money squirreled away by the KGB as the federation began to fall apart. "You invest our money. And, well, we look out for you," said the older man. "It's simple."

"I see," said Oleg.

When the men had departed, German said, "Things are just beginning. It'll pay to have such men on our side. We need this."

"I am already a rich man," said Oleg.

"You're a millionaire," said German. "Soon everyone and their uncle will be a millionaire."

"From now on they will own us."

"They've always owned us." German smiled. "We're just making it official."

•   •   •

OLEG DID gain from his new partners. He learned how to shift money around, how to protect it offshore. He set up complex systems of exchanges, nested trusts. He employed ex-KGB men in his own firm, created a security apparatus worthy of a small state. He felt magnanimous. He had seen the new world, and they'd merely clung on. They were good workers, serious to a fault. Perhaps they maintained certain connections, certain loyalties, but he was the one giving them their money, and they were happy to put their strength to his service.

He shouts at Gena to keep back from the flames. The rooks are taking off from the tree en masse again. They fly over him crying out. He takes the hard drive from his pocket. The warmth has gone from the thing. He's wiped the information on it, but he knows that some trace of the data will remain as a charge in the circuits. There is something satisfying in this base, inescapable physicality.

Things have changed, of course, and now the state security men do not need him as they used to. He used to be keyed into fluctuations of power at the center of things, but these days he is adrift. German does still call, but to convey the instructions of others. Oleg has a suspicion that one day in the future German will sit down with another and recite a tribute to Oleg as a counterpoint to the initiating of some great act of betrayal.

Perhaps this was already building, even before Oleg made his new plans. The hunger of such men is insatiable. They are not the kind to stop at what is fair. They needed him once, and maybe they will never forgive him for that. He has lost supporters, lost influence. These past few years—these diminished years—there has been a knowing deep within him that the time will come when he must turn around and fight back.

He steps forward, tosses the drive underarm into the center of the fire. It lands between two logs. It looks unharmed for a moment, until it flares very suddenly, sending up a plume of smoke darker than that which rises from the wood around it.

27

SHE FINDS the bar on the second basement level of the hotel. It's tucked between the hotel's laundry room and a small gym from which emerges the plaintive moaning of treadmills running.

She enters the bar cautiously. She can hear that James is playing. She's glad to realize that he's facing away from the door. Though she can only see his back, she feels that she can surmise his mood just by studying his posture. He is playing "Für Elise." His head is inclined forward, cocked to the right. His playing is characteristic only in its perfect anonymity. She pictures his face: the slightly open lips, the glazed eyes, the cowlick tuft that springs up from where he parts his hair. He has always been able to take himself out of the process when he wishes to, to give without giving. She takes a seat at a table in the corner. The room is bordered with thick red drapes. The small round table has a tea light in the center. There are drops of wax on the red tablecloth. A waiter takes Marina's order. James finishes, and tepid applause rises from the occupied tables. He takes a drink from a battered bottle of mineral water. He begins again abruptly. Liszt. Marina's glass of white wine arrives with a small dish of peanuts. The bar is ornate: dark wood, gold mirrors behind it. The floor is tiled with an Arabic pattern that matches nothing. She looks at the others in the room: the family seated in front of the piano, the men with a cluster of empty pint glasses on the table between them, the old woman who films James on her phone. A chalkboard propped against the bar bears the message LIVE MUSIC EVERY NIGHT. People like live music because they feel like something is happening, Marina supposes: the promise of uniqueness, of minute variation, exquisite difference. The irony is that there is nothing less unique than the way that James plays for these people. She watches his hands moving on the keys. If you want uniqueness, get a recording: Glenn Gould laying it down like he never will again. Not this. James finishes the Liszt piece, and takes another drink, starts again abruptly. Pachelbel's Canon. He seems committed to playing in a certain way, to a clipped limitedness. He has always had an element of petulance in him, a performative sort of martyrdom.

At university, she thought herself more serious than James. He barely played. She got up to practice and he stayed in bed. And yet now in this room she sees what she should perhaps have seen years before: music is crucial for him, something he can't fully commit to and can't escape.

There are other, easier ways to make money, she thinks. And yet he does this.

When he takes a break, she hunches and studies her phone. She watches him from the corner of her eye, and realizes that she doesn't need to hide at all. He moves utterly inattentively. He goes to the bathroom. He rubs his hands together as he walks.

She knows him so well, she realizes. She can recall the feeling of his scapulae beneath her hands.

He is playing Schumann when the waiter drops a tray of glasses: half a dozen tumblers smash on the tile. The pieces skitter across the hard floor.

James doesn't stop playing for a moment. A woman at the table nearest the bar is looking at the fragments of glass showered over her plimsolls. The bar staff begin to work at the mess with dustpans and brushes, muttering and apologizing, and James plays on faultlessly. When he finishes, it takes a moment longer than usual for the pattering of applause to fill the silence.

•   •   •

AFTERWARD, SHE goes to him because she feels she must. She's drunk three glasses of wine while waiting. He packs his things—his battered bottle of water, his sheet music—into a supermarket tote bag. The broken glass has been swept away. The bar is emptying.

She touches his shoulder as he moves away from the piano. He turns, looks at her as if she has struck him. He says, "What are you doing here?"

THEY GO to a bar he knows: a small place above a shop, the windows open, cool air so welcome after the stuffiness of the basement. They drink whiskies. The blond girl behind the bar has a tattoo of some word running up the side of her neck in an Asian script. It makes Marina think of the radio earpieces the security men at the house wear, specifically the coiled cables that extend from these devices to their collars. "What do you want?" James says.

"Do I have to want something?" says Marina.

"I haven't seen you for a decade," he says. "Honestly, I'd have preferred if you'd made contact beforehand. It's my job, that stuff."

"You're very serious about this job."

"Yes. You seem surprised."

"I suppose I am."

"Why so?"

"I wouldn't have thought it was the kind of job you'd like."

"It's fine."

"Really?"

"It's a job. I need the money. I suppose that situation is hard to imagine for a woman like you."

"I work."

"But you know you don't have to, right? There's a difference in that."

"You fucking hate it. I watch you and I see that you fucking hate it. There's some sick compulsion in doing it, like picking at a wound."

"Perhaps."

She says, "You had such a talent. You played so well without really practicing. You could have been so good."

He looks at her intently. He waves a hand. "No."

"That's not true. You had such potential."

"No," he says more forcefully, irritated now. "My talent was making you believe things like that." He dusts his hands together. "You were always better. Would have been better even if you didn't practice. You just didn't make a show of things. You doubt yourself."

She says, "It never felt like that."

"Well . . ." He pantomimes a shrug.

This is him, she thinks. She loves it and hates it. Serious about himself, yes, but about others too. He is pompous, but sometimes his sincerity also lets him speak perceptively. She rises and goes to the bar. She buys two more whiskies and returns to the table. "Thanks," he says. "I think it was my round."

"I'm filthy rich," she says. "So it doesn't matter."

He laughs at that, takes his drink from her, sips it. "How did you know where I was playing?"

"Martin told me."

"Martin?" he says. He nods as if trying to understand something.

"He told you he's been visiting? He's interested in my husband's paintings."

There is discomfort on James's face. "Martin thinks I need protection from the world."

"He hasn't mentioned me?"

"No."

She nods. "Right. That's nice of him."

"Is it?"

"I don't know. He feels for you, I suppose."

"You've talked about me?"

"I don't mean that."

"Uh-huh?"

"I mean you're just part of our history. We can't not talk about you."

His expression is hard. "You're having a thing, the two of you?" he says.

She considers the words, the acute way he is looking at her. She nods. The least she owes him is a confirmation of this suspicion. Yet the way his face reacts to this confirmation—the shock in his expression—makes her think that he must actually have been merely trying on a knowingness.

"I'm sorry," she says.

"What grounds do I have to complain?"

"It's not a serious thing," she says.

"He's a good guy," says James. "My best friend. I hope it's serious, actually."

She pauses and drinks. Feels the warmth of the spirit on her tongue. The woman behind the bar is cutting limes now, the click of the knife coming rhythmically down on the hard board. This, Marina thinks, is what she couldn't take before: the polite woundedness, the apparent incorruptibility that is actually a resolution to see the world as only spoiled. He suffers, yes, but always on the terms of his story of himself. James closes his left eye, rubs at the tear duct with his index finger. He opens his eyes to stare at her again, waiting apparently.

"We're all adults," she says. She sighs. "It's always a surprise, isn't it?"

28

THE LONDON house on a Tuesday, lunchtime. Outside, the postman lopes between front doors looking miserable and bedraggled. Oleg stands at the living room window and watches the man digging in his postbag for the letters for the next property. An old family owns that one. English aristocrats, holding on, just about. The man comes down the front steps and then paces toward the next address through the slanting rain. What makes these people wear shorts every day? Professional pride, Oleg thinks. A particular sense of who they are.

It's only when Oleg has given up expecting Malcolm that the man's arrival is announced over the house intercom. Oleg looks at his watch. Eleven fifty-two. He descends the stairs, and there is Malcolm in the hallway talking animatedly about the jacket he's handing to Damian. The member of parliament for . . . Oleg forgets. Some leafy southern place: a location with much history yet no notable present beyond the stately perpetuation of a certain kind of well-fed Englishness. "Fantastic," says Malcolm, gripping Oleg's hand firmly, spluttering the words out. "How fantastic to see you."

"Yes," says Oleg. "Thanks for coming."

"Don't say it," says Malcolm. "I'm late. I know. Excruciating."

"I didn't notice."

"Traffic," says Malcolm, pushing into those *f*s so hard that a tiny speck of saliva is shot from his mouth onto Oleg's lapel.

"Of course," says Oleg. "How terrible."

Malcolm was the defense minister before he was ousted in a scandal relating to military procurement. Now he's a backbencher with connections. He has curly brown hair that Oleg imagines to have been cut in the same style since he was a boy. There's something purposefully chaotic about him. He arrives as if rushing away from somewhere else.

They sit in armchairs in the upstairs living room. Oleg has had a fire lit. Malcolm touches his rubbery nose as if it is a costume he must check is still attached. His eyes are light green with full lashes: strikingly feminine, Oleg thinks. Malcolm says, "My goodness. This is such a wonderful house."

"Thank you."

"Jonathan tells me you have some interesting ideas." Jonathan is Waterforth. The men went to university together. Only Malcolm, of anyone Oleg knows, uses Waterforth's first name.

"I suppose so."

"Well, I'm all ears."

"Lunch is all ready to go. We could go through to the dining room." Oleg gestures at his watch. "If it isn't too early."

Malcolm's eyes widen. "Well, as it happens, I didn't have so much breakfast. I think eating now would be just the ticket."

WATERFORTH INTRODUCED Malcolm to Oleg. It was part of Oleg's arrival in the country. Oleg funded a committee on British economic cooperation with the states of the former Soviet Union, and Malcolm was the chair. Oleg has hosted the man many times, made a few donations. Malcolm helped with Oleg's visa and with a bit of trouble Alexi got into once. It is all gray. That's the thing here: not big bags of cash, but little treats, favors, sweeteners; a childish kind of corruption, as Oleg sometimes thinks of it.

In the dining room, the two men take their places, and Carla comes through with a decanter of red wine, then returns with two plates bearing perfect quenelles of game and port pâté. "You're spoiling me so wonderfully," Malcolm says.

"Of course," says Oleg.

The relish with which Malcolm eats is unpleasant, yet having food in his mouth mostly prevents him from speaking. Malcolm wipes fresh bread through the remains of his pâté and chews. Oleg says, "Waterforth has explained my plans to you?"

Malcolm swallows and says, "I think I got the gist from Jonathan. You're going to take down the President."

"I prefer to say 'create a legitimate opposition.'"

Malcolm moves his lips as he thinks. "The issue is, my friend, that this is all very *delicate.*"

"I know. It's my country. I grew up in this country. I made a fortune in this country."

"But now you live here," says Malcolm.

Carla comes back through to retrieve the plates. Oleg's is hardly touched. Malcolm's looks like it's been through a dishwasher. "Be straight with me," says Oleg.

"I always am."

"Okay?"

"I've been very discreetly sounding people out. Foreign Office people." Malcolm touches his red nose. "Intelligence people."

"Yes?"

"There are issues—of course. Serious, nay, *grave* issues with governance in your country."

"Yes."

"Hmm. But can we be seen to be harboring someone who is working so directly against the government of Russia?"

"I am not planning an armed uprising."

"I know. I know. But they are touchy. The government doesn't like that we give dissidents residency, even at the best of times. But also, they have their own assets here. They rely on our rule of law. It's a balance."

"Am I a dissident?"

"Oh. I don't know."

"This is a weak country if you don't let me say things that are true."

"Come on," says Malcolm. "Let's not play it so naïve. Aren't you a little old for games of Scout's honor?"

"I wasn't in the Scouts. I was in Komsomol."

Malcolm frowns. He doesn't want to joust today. "The point with a balance is that you don't want to upset it. You have a nice life here. Secure. Safe. Do you have to push it?"

"I want only accountability. I'm talking about funding some independent press, some civil-society networks."

"Certainly."

"Democratic institutions." The door opens behind Oleg, and he can see that Malcolm is already looking past him at Carla bringing in the steaks and potatoes. "These are the same things you prize here. Do you not believe in democracy?"

Carla reaches around Malcolm to place his plate in front of him. The man beams at it for a moment, then looks up at Oleg. "My friend," he says. "It's as if you forget that I am a parliamentarian."

THE DESSERT is a cheesecake covered in delicate purple flowers. Oleg watches Malcolm dig greedily into his portion. Important people like Malcolm. They tell him things. His information is always reliable. Such a fact sometimes makes Oleg still feel like a total outsider to this nation. Perhaps people tell Malcolm momentous things because it is the best way to shut him up. The cake arrived as Malcolm was recounting an anecdote about his time as defense secretary, when he was organizing joint military maneuvers with the French army. Now he swallows, and finally reaches the punch line: "Zis is very unzatisfactory, monsieur!" he says. He laughs and hits the table. Oleg smiles as much as politeness demands.

Oleg says, "Russia is a mess. You know this. The law means

nothing." Malcolm looks weary. He is readying to say something, but Oleg pushes on. "All I want is to make Russia like Britain: safe, predictable, with rights and laws and property protections."

Malcolm frowns. "You want a realist answer, old chap?"

Oleg nods.

"Our comparative stability is a useful distinction, as I see it. Your people trust us. Your people invest here. Perhaps it would be good if they didn't have to, but would it be beneficial for *us*?"

"You like the chaos?"

"I wouldn't say that." Malcolm sets down his fork and holds up his hands. "I just point out that you can't assume that our interests are served by your project."

"I see."

Malcolm returns to his dessert. "I'm being straight with you," he says.

"Thanks."

"You're welcome."

"What if I am totally sure that I do my plan?"

Malcolm pauses with the fork on its way to his mouth. "Old chap," he says, "I can't stop you doing anything. Do what you wish. It's just that I'm led to believe that our people won't tolerate too much antagonism of the Russian government. There might be issues with your residency here, if you go too far. Also, it might not be possible to guarantee your safety. You know these people. These people are ruthless." He puts the bite in his mouth and chews, frowning.

IN THE late afternoon, Oleg goes downstairs to the swimming pool. When he bought the house, he had two floors dug beneath the existing basement. It scandalized the neighbors in a way he rather enjoyed.

It was a complicated process: a conveyer belt installed into the center of the house carrying all that dirt from beneath the foundations. Polish and Bulgarian builders caked with soil tramped through his grand hallway. He was intrigued by the work, came often to check on its progress. The little trivialities. This was enough to absorb him, then.

Still, he feels that since they've had the basement dug out a persistent smell has lingered in the place: the filth of this old city, the old plague dead, perhaps. He has used flowers, candles, air purifiers, and yet it hangs at the edge of things.

He swims and feels himself in a flooded catacomb. In the low light, the off-white tiles on the walls are bonelike. Foolish thinking. He performs a very slow breaststroke, and the water around him stays flat.

He thinks of Malcolm's question: *why.* Of course, it's just the thing such a man would ask. Malcolm wouldn't do anything that didn't promise the possibility of a wine or steak or piece of cake. Yet it's a valid question.

His cousin. Yes. But also, a feeling that has been gnawing at him for too long. He has been asleep. This money, this comfort, this acceptance of his place has not befitted him. He has drifted. Things have been slipping from him. Power is like a muscle that must be exercised.

OLEG FIRST encountered the President in the midnineties, long before the man ascended to his current role. Oleg thought, along with everyone else, that Putin wasn't important. It was the lowest point for the intelligence men, then. Oleg had fifty KGB guys like him on his payroll.

The future President was based in St. Petersburg when Oleg first met him at a party. Later, when organizing a party of his own, Oleg was advised by German to invite the man along. At the time, Oleg had just bought himself a Gauguin, accepting the applause of the London auction hall when he doubled the high estimate. Those were good years, years of such possibility. Every time he looked at the picture, he felt a little taller. Yet at the party, Putin looked at it and said, "How do you know that it's real? How are you sure that they didn't cheat you?"

Others around tittered. Here was a man who couldn't see beyond the borders of his own venal state, who thought the whole world as wild and ungoverned as Russia.

"That's not how they do things in London," Oleg explained to him. "They have a whole system of experts, of verification."

Putin wasn't convinced. Oleg recalls that he pronounced Gauguin wrong—Galkin, as if he had taken the painter to have been a Russian. The group dispersed to recount the story in other corners of the room.

Yet Oleg did lose money on the picture. He sold it on in two years. It was a poor painting, and he had overpaid. He even came to harbor doubts as to its authenticity. And as for Putin's lack of trust, Oleg would have done well to display as much himself in those years. He and his friends thought their credulity was worldliness, were too sure things were improving. He even wonders these days if the future President hadn't mispronounced Gauguin on purpose.

29

MARTIN'S PHONE buzzes in his pocket. He looks at the screen and sees that it's James. Martin is standing in the kitchen of his flat in Fulham. There's a frozen pizza on the countertop. The oven is heating.

"You didn't tell me you were meeting Marina," says James.

Martin has expected this, he realizes in the moment. There is some relief in finally hearing James's assertion. He walks to the window, looks out at the street, at an old lady lumbering down the road pulling a wheeled shopping bag. "It was random," Martin says. He tries to sound calm, light. "She was at one of the auctions."

"Well, yes. But you hid it from me."

"I evaded. I didn't mention it."

"Can we try not to talk like fucking lawyers?"

"Do you want me to answer you, or do you just want to be angry?"

"You didn't tell me."

"No."

James sighs. "Well, I know. I'm calling to say that now I know."

"Okay," says Martin. "I'm sorry. I should have told you."

"I don't mind."

"You sound like you mind."

"I wouldn't have minded, if you'd been straight."

"Very well. I'm sorry. Next time."

"Well. Okay."

"It's just business," says Martin. "I see her now and again. I'm only doing my job."

"Less than a minute," says James.

"What?"

"I know you're fucking! You just said you'd be straight, and then . . ." James scoffs. The call is gone. Martin tries to call back, but gets only James's voice mail. The oven beeps to signify that it is warm.

Martin opens the door of the oven, and tosses in the pizza. The rush of escaping hot air makes his eyes sting and stream. He goes to the window and calls Marina, who picks up straightaway. "How are you?" she says.

"James just called," Martin says. "He was furious. You met up?"

"Yes."

"Why didn't you tell me?"

"Why didn't you tell him you'd been meeting me?"

"I was getting around to it."

"You have to choose," she says. "You have to make your choices and own them."

"I know, but you could have warned me."

Marina laughs. "I'm the one who is married, and yet you're the one who needs your secrets kept?"

"It's more complicated than that."

"Sure. Well, I'm sorry, anyway."

"Thanks."

"No problem. You want to get a coffee tomorrow? Do you want to try to make up?"

THE NEXT day, he leaves the office just before dark. It's an oddly warm winter afternoon, and the smokers who normally congregate near the loading dock sit together on the steps of a fire exit, observing the sunset glow diffusing through the tight streets. Clive, the storeroom manager, raises his mug of tea to acknowledge Martin. Martin returns the greeting and then moves up an alley, and out into the press of shoppers and early commuters.

Marina occupies a table in the rear of the coffee shop. Martin would rather sit at the window, in the last of the light, but, of course, discretion is wise.

He orders a flat white and a slice of cake. He sits opposite Marina.

"Good to see you," she says. She grins, she puts out her left hand and touches his knuckles where his fist rests on the tabletop.

"Good week?" he says.

She rolls her eyes. "Let's not talk about it. I'm sorry about James, by the way. I just wanted to see him."

"I understand. He's the same, right?"

She smiles. "He's exactly the same as he was at university. Down to maybe even some of his clothes. But isn't that a bit remarkable?"

"Indeed," Martin says, though even this plain agreement feels a little treacherous.

Marina nods. She sips her coffee, regards Martin as he eats a mouthful of cake. She says, "I need a favor."

"A favor?"

"You have a new catalogue out for the spring sale," she says.

"We do."

"I've been thinking we could organize for you to show it to my husband."

"That'd be good, but what's the favor?"

"He's going mad alone. He's obsessed with the idea that he can change Russia. He needs some other distraction. He needs someone who won't just encourage his mad political plans."

"I'm that person?"

"I mean, I don't have a clue. I just thought, it might be a little thing that's worth a try."

"What do you want me to do?"

"Sell him a picture. Calm him down."

"Just that?"

"It's a break from all the scheming. It's something else."

"I'm not sure I have much influence to really push if he's not interested."

"He likes you. He'll be open to a meeting."

Martin nods.

"There are some good things in this new catalogue of yours. He could be interested in them. I'll set something up very soon. Tomorrow maybe. He needs to see people. He needs other things in his life."

"Okay."

"Please don't swallow any of his savior-of-democracy nonsense."

MIDMORNING THE next day, Martin walks from the auction house to the square in which Oleg and Marina's London home is located. He enters from the south corner, walks an L around the private gardens in the center of the square. He arrives in front of a porticoed doorway. The door is dark green, almost black. He rings the bell and waits. A man of about twenty in a navy suit answers. Martin introduces himself, and the man gestures him in. Seated by the door is another older, bulkier man. Martin smiles and nods at this man silently, though the man's expression—a flat, serious neutrality—doesn't alter.

Martin is shown upstairs to a library by the skinny man. It's a small, square room, some architectural leftover, Martin thinks. The books, as in Oleg's other house, are leather-bound. Half of them are Russian, half in English. The English books are reference works: dictionaries, encyclopedias, style guides. On the wall is a large-format image that appears from a distance to be an abstract composition of beiges and burnt reds, yet on closer inspection reveals itself to be a photograph, a giant aerial picture of some kind of mine. Martin studies the image: the sculpted tiers of smashed rock and slag, the vehicle tracks leading between these tiers, a couple of tiny trucks with dust rising behind them.

Oleg comes into the room. "Martin," he says. He holds out one of his heavy hands to shake.

"I like the picture," Martin says. "It's a Burtynsky?"

Oleg smiles, shakes his head.

"A Gursky?"

The oligarch laughs now. "My director of marketing," he says. "This is my mine. Siberia. Potash."

"Right. Yes."

"I'm sure he is influenced by these artists you've mentioned," says Oleg. "Art influencing business. Business is a kind of art, I have always said."

The office that Oleg leads Martin into is large, classical in decoration. A huge desk sits in the middle of the room, a couple of windows behind, a view of the tops of trees in the square. Oleg sits behind the desk, gestures for Martin to take his place in one of the two chairs facing him. Martin is struck viscerally for a moment by the thought that he spent a covert weekend with this man's wife. He feels so easily readable. He looks at the grain of the desk, tries to collect himself. He looks up again and takes in the room.

Against the back wall is a case of sculptures: a bronze of a child's head, which Martin suspects to be an Epstein; a couple of female figures that could be Archipenkos.

"Quite an impressive office," says Martin lamely.

Oleg nods. "Yes."

There are a couple of photographs on the desk turned toward Oleg. There's a wooden letter opener, and a tiny screwdriver of the kind one might use to adjust the hinges on a pair of glasses. Martin opens his satchel and takes out a catalogue. He puts it down carefully on the green leather of the desk and slides it toward Oleg. The cover is an image of Lucio Fontana's *Concetto Spaziale*: a red canvas with five crisp vertical slices in the middle of it. Julian lobbied for this particular cover, and it is fantastic. So stark are the slashes that one wants to run one's finger against the catalogue just to see whether they can be felt.

Fontana wanted to break out of the flat plane of ordinary pictures, attempting to do so with cuts to canvases.

Oleg opens the catalogue and flicks, stopping apparently randomly.

"I'm really proud of the sale," says Martin.

The oligarch looks at him, and then, delayed, nods. He says, "Yes. I see." He closes the catalogue.

Martin points at the image of the Fontana. "Another foundational piece. It reminds me of Malevich's work, though it's less significant, of course."

Oleg nods, says, "Yes. Less significant."

Does the man see through him? Is that what causes this vacancy? Martin waits.

Oleg says, "Forgive me, I am not talking about art so much these days."

"Of course. No need to apologize."

Oleg studies the front of the catalogue. "You look at this work and you think of what is missing. What am I not seeing?"

"Yes?"

"The knife. Or—what is the word?"

"A scalpel?"

"Yes. You think, *Who did this?*" Oleg flashes his eyes.

They sit for a moment, the catalogue on the desk between them. The climate control system clicks into a different mode. A vacuum cleaner is being run in an adjacent room. Martin gestures at the catalogue. "We'd really like to have you at the sale."

"Art is not my preoccupation at the moment," says Oleg.

"Right."

"I want to change my country."

"Right. Wow."

"Marina has told you about this plan, perhaps."

Martin says, "No," and regrets saying this as he does so. He feels the lie so plainly obvious.

Oleg seems not to notice. "Marina thinks it's too dangerous and difficult," he says.

"Is it dangerous?"

"Of course."

"You're doing it, though?"

"Yes." Oleg smiles. "I must."

Martin points to the catalogue. "Well, if you want a break from it all."

Oleg opens his hands, shrugs. "The cost is an issue. I am not utilizing my funds in this way."

"I see."

"Maybe I will even be disposing of my collection." He nods. "I require liquidity."

Martin feels giddy, as if he has stood up too quickly. His left hand in his lap, he realizes, is clasped tight. He anticipated this moment in Switzerland somehow. He saw the *Supremus*, felt that one day he would acquire it for the house. He says, "All of it?" and Oleg nods slowly. This is happening. This could be happening. *Will be happening,* if he can just bring it down to earth, *secure it*. Oleg is watching him and waiting. "Well, your collection is certainly valuable," Martin says.

"You're thinking, of course, that I am very rich, so why do I need money from some pictures?" Oleg smiles. "My money is tied up in many ways. I can access it—yes—but with a lot of shifting about. This is neat. I like things to be neat."

"I see."

"Marina wants me to buy more paintings. Before, she asks why I buy so many. Now she says, 'Buy some more pictures, Olezhka.' She wants that I have a hobby." He snorts through his nose. "Like I am some kind of fucking dentist."

"You have more of an eye than a hobbyist. Maybe she sees that talent."

"No, no. She wants only to stop my political plans."

"I see."

"She says I don't understand politics." He grunts. "But I understand power."

"Yes."

"What do you think?"

"Sorry?"

"Am I deluded?"

"I can't imagine you are."

"Is it foolish to dream as I do? To want to change a whole country?" He taps his chest. "When your country is sick, you feel it inside. It makes you sick. Also, because perhaps I helped make it sick." He opens his hands. "I want to try."

"Right. Yes. It's very bold, I suppose."

"Yes. Yes."

Oleg still waits for more. Martin thinks of Marina, of the hope that caused her to organize this meeting, her idea that this man could be put off all this. Her husband is slumped slightly sideways in his chair, one elbow resting on the desk. He looks comfortable, a great pile of a man. His blue eyes are alive now. He breathes evenly and deeply through his broad nose. What is Martin supposed to do? What does Marina want of him in this situation? She is treating him like staff, like her errand boy, he thinks. He sits in this antique chair in this office, which occupies greater floor space than his entire flat. Oleg breathes heavily, taps one forefinger against the green leather of his desktop. He waits for something from Martin. Gray cloud has come in over the square, and the room has darkened by degrees. What does Martin know of anything the oligarch seeks to do? He has tried to interest the man in the catalogue, and he can do no more. He thinks of the storage room in Switzerland, the picture people don't even know exists. There are some things that are just bigger than any one person. Martin's mother would hate this man, hate all he is and all he represents. And probably she'd be right. He isn't good. He is greedy. He is full of himself. He doubtless can be cruel. And yet what if he has chosen to do one good thing—this gesture toward reforming his country? Martin looks at the man glowering at him and thinks that this is what power looks like. Immense. Immovable. What if for once power is working in the correct direction? You can only hope, Martin thinks. You can only look at the man and hope that he is right about himself, about his project. And who is Marina to say that Martin should leave this room with a bad conscience for doing so? Martin says, "I think you're a brave man."

The oligarch smiles and turns his face toward the window, trying to hide the extent to which this pleases him.

30

OLEG IS driven to the country house in the afternoon. The sunken lanes around the house are grimy and dark, layered with a mush of dead leaves, and the shrubs and trees that make up the hedgerows are mostly bare, slightly menacing in the jagged silhouettes they make beneath the dull sky.

He sits in the kitchen as the dark comes in. Marina won't be back for a while. He should work, but he can't summon the resolve. He goes to the wine cabinet. He takes out a bottle of Pauillac. The temperature of the bottle—neither cool nor warm—is a pleasure to him. Will he pour a glass? He retrieves a corkscrew and pushes its point down into the cork. Yes. He is opening the bottle. Yes. He will have some wine.

He thinks of the boy telling him he is brave. He wanted the words, rather pathetically. What else would the boy say, prompted that way? Likely, Martin was informed of Oleg's plans by Marina, who paints a very partial picture of Oleg's activities. Yet Martin *did* assent. And the boy is bad at lying. Oleg has always sensed this, valued it. The boy said Oleg was brave, plainly and without hesitation, and so that was the truth.

He sniffs and sips. A richness. Fruit and wood. A strong, clear odor that is almost foul.

OLEG DESCENDS to the basement rooms carrying his glass. It's quiet when he closes the heavy door to the upstairs. He walks along the corridor, hearing only his own breathing and the scuff of his footsteps on the carpet.

In the gallery space, the lights blink on. The pictures are waiting for him. His pictures. They were like air in those first days of collecting. He needed them then, when his work was like an ongoing siege. He required that proof of life beyond his own.

He knew nothing. Yet shapes on a canvas could make him feel a yearning, a pleasurable incomprehension. Also, he must admit, he wanted to separate himself from the other men who only sought to be rich so they could eat steak for three meals a day, whose skin consequently turned blotchy red, whose farts smelled like the foulest dog shit.

He sits on the floor and drinks his wine and looks at the small Malevich canvas: the blocks, the matte colors, fine lines and divisions of space. Or maybe not space, exactly, because Malevich felt that he had moved beyond normal dimensions, into absolutes, fundamental essences. Some days such a painting makes Oleg feel very small. On others, he feels he understands it totally, and gains from that understanding a sensation of great power.

The man knew how small he himself was, but knew how big his own ideas were: beyond his own life, beyond the uses others wanted to put them to.

There is something under this, or beyond this. More real. Possessed of a truer energy.

Yes.

THERE'S A sound outside the room—the long, low beep of the basement door permitting entry—and Oleg goes out to the long corridor and sees his wife walking toward him. He says, "You're back early."

It is an odd walk she has: a little frantic, always, as if she can't abide the time it takes to cover ground. "I am," she says.

There is something in that walk that speaks of the way he once thought she would undo him, the way he still hopes she will. When she reaches him, she looks at his empty glass and says, "You opened some wine?"

"Yes."

"Good idea."

They go back into the galleries to shut off the lights, and before the glow goes down she looks at the Bacon studies, keeps facing them as the spotlights die. He feels that he knows momentarily what she is considering: that crazy dualist keening of Bacon's. The tortured body: its limits and its desire to be limitless. The violence of separation. The violence of consubstantiality. One can still see the silhouettes of the heads when only the floor lights remain. Suggestive dark shapes. He thinks of something she quoted to him once. The Irish poet, if he can get the words right. A soul trapped in a dying animal. Perhaps. Yes. Good enough. He says, "You like those pictures?" but he realizes as he speaks that that isn't the right thing to say, because liking isn't quite the right measure, and she won't give him everything so easily.

She says, "I've never said they're not great."

"Right." They turn and he closes the door, sets the alarm with the keypad. She is preoccupied with something that she won't share. How did they get here? He walks ahead. He says, "I'm going to sell. I'm going to sell them all."

He turns and she looks at him full in the face, and he realizes with pleasure that he has managed to surprise her. "Oh," she says. "That's a fast decision."

"Yes."

UPSTAIRS, HE pours her wine, pours more for himself. "You're selling the pictures for the political campaign?" she says. She sits on a stool across from him at the high kitchen island. It's made of polished marble from an ancient quarry outside Florence. No one prepares food on this island, however. Marcus has his own kitchen in which most of their meals are cooked. If they give him the day off, it is to order a takeaway, or to go out. This counter is only for pretending to themselves that they are ordinary.

"Naturally," he says. "I met your friend Martin today, and he showed me a lot of pictures and I thought, *This doesn't interest me.*"

"I see."

"Just like that."

"But you want to get rid of the ones you've got?"

"The public image is good if I give things up."

"Waterforth suggested this?"

"I'm not an idiot, you know. I know that people don't think I'm a saint. Also, the money from the pictures would be perfectly accounted for. There won't be issues with the source of the funds."

She inclines her wineglass to the side, straightens it up and examines the legs of the wine. She sips, nods. "So, you're pushing ahead?"

"I'm putting everything into it."

"I see."

It angers him now, this affect: as if she perceives something about him that he doesn't see himself, as if he has a speck of salad on his teeth. He lets something ratchet up in him. He speaks a little loudly. "You didn't know me before," he says. "You don't know what I have done." He waves his hand around to encompass the house, his holdings beyond that.

"Of course I do. But maybe you should quit while you're ahead. Maybe you should reflect on your luck in getting where you are."

He can't believe this. He says, "It didn't just happen. I barely slept for five years. I was risking my life. Other men couldn't do this. I was making huge deals in cash."

"Yes. Of course," she says. "But you were lucky too. Effort and luck are not exclusive."

"You were born into a life like this," he says. He slaps the cool countertop. "You were born like this, and you say that I'm lucky."

She shakes her head and sighs as if it is he who is being unreasonable. "I'm not saying I haven't been lucky," she says. "I'm saying you might have been too."

"Fine," he says. "Fine. Now and then. And so what?" There were times, she is right, when things turned on fine margins. And yet luck, he feels, is simply not the word. The outcomes that came to pass were just more—he thinks—more *necessary*. They had a greater weight than the other possibilities. Marina is still talking, however. Oleg thinks for some reason of Vasyli's old workshop, the rusty tools, the piles of materials to make the dachas with. There was a particular smell he will never forget, of sweat and metal and grease and wood.

She says, "Imagine you flip a coin ten times. What are the chances of ten heads in a row?"

He begins to visualize the problem, to turn it over in his head. His father could have done this in a snap.

She says, "It's about one in a million."

"That sounds right."

"It's not likely, but it can happen."

"Yes."

"Imagine everyone in Russia is asked to flip a coin ten times. There's a competition to get ten heads. How many people will succeed?"

"We're excluding children and the very old?"

"Sure."

"One hundred and twenty, maybe?"

"Do you see where I'm going?"

"A lucky few. I get it."

"But do those people who get ten heads understand the statistics? You imagine they'd have stories, right? Lucky charms, things they did or didn't do, prayers that were answered. They'd write books and give lectures on how they did it."

"I can imagine that," he says.

"They'd all have stories," she says again.

"Yes."

She looks at him.

HE DOESN'T sleep for a long time, and when he does his rest is fractured. Yet when he wakes to the morning light, Marina is gone from the bed.

What she doesn't understand about the events that fell his way was the momentum of them. It was as if they were written. In those years he was so *sure*. He was a person who was certain, and he felt that this certainty made things happen. He thinks of the Malevich picture in the basement gallery. A structure underneath things. A logic that others couldn't apprehend. It sounds mad, of course, but didn't it all work out?

And also—yes—the other side. The cost of it. The cost of knowing. They put Malevich in prison. Oleg knew his destiny, and sacrificed too. If he is the beneficiary of luck, then why does his knee hurt on rainy days?

His office was bombed once: a security guard killed, a secretary lame afterward. Oleg was thrown across the room, but got up again, realized only later that something bad had happened to the cartilage in his knee. That was business then. He had to react to that, to make choices that years before he would never have imagined being faced with. It is not luck to choose such things, such dark decisions as can never really be explained to others, as must be buried deep within oneself. He is here because he did one thing after another, unwavering. Necessary things. If he is lucky, well, his is the kind of luck in which one discards again and again notions of what one would not do. He is here, missing parts of himself. That is what Marina cannot understand, riding her chauffeured car to work. He is here because he chipped bits off himself, and fed them into the furnace.

He gets up from the bed. He dresses slowly. He touches a small shrapnel scar on his forearm as he pulls on his shirt. He goes to the window, looks at the hills, the risen sun.

He is here because others are not, and maybe that is luck, but maybe it is just everything. He was the right man for the time. Without his good fortune, without his perseverance—well—there wouldn't be a bit of him left.

31

IT'S OLEG'S birthday soon and Marina feels that she should organize something. "Nothing big," he says when she mentions it. Previously, he's always gone to see his mother in Russia, hosted a grand dinner of about a hundred people on his return. This year is, of course, different.

She's in the bathroom, using a cotton round to work off the last residue of mascara from the thin skin between her nose and tear duct. She got home from London an hour before. Her back aches from sitting at the computer all day. She ate a salad in the kitchen as he drank a cognac and talked in great detail about his plans to "pivot the mission" of his charity foundation. Now she comes back into the bedroom. She says, "What is big?"

He's propped up in bed. He's been trying to read Tony Blair's autobiography, which he places on the bed beside him. He's trimmed his beard finally. "I said *not* big," he says.

"I need to know what I'm avoiding."

"I'm sure you're organizing something appropriate. It's nice for me to have a little surprise."

He is a fifty-five-year-old man who wants a surprise party. She's half exasperated, half admiring of the gall. With his last wife, Katya, he had parties so lavish that people talked about them for months afterward. Katya once paid Elton John to play a private concert. His life with Marina was supposed to be different, formed in contrast to that existence he had before.

He picks up the book, has a thought, puts it down again. "You need to invite Waterforth," he says.

"Really?"

"I'm seeing him often now."

It's true. Her husband is meeting with the PR man weekly. She says, "We'll need to have some scented candles to mask the smell of sulfur."

"Sorry?"

"Like the devil."

"Oh, yes." Oleg nods. "Very funny. Perhaps he is the devil. If so, aren't I lucky to have the devil working for me?"

"You want music?" she says.

"Please," he says. "Choose. You want me to wrap my own presents too?"

"I don't want you to be disappointed."

He picks the book up again, definitively now.

"I have a busy job, you know," she says.

He stares at the book for a time, then gives in to the temptation to reply. "Marcus does the cooking. People come and do the rest. People do it for you."

She goes back into the bathroom and runs the hot tap. She washes her face carefully: lathering behind her ears, rubbing at the scalp line, taking care to wash the declivity between her jawline and neck. He is blind to the work of living with him, she thinks. She splashes her face, and water drops into the broad basin with a clapping sound. He wants attention lavished on him, like a child. She thinks, *Oh, yes—like a child who has lost his mother.*

She dries her face, wills herself to calm. He's not the man for self-awareness, so it's merely martyrdom to expect it from him. This party is the kind of thing they have done well previously, she tells herself. This could be a route back to a bearable equilibrium.

•　•　•

SHE CLEARS an evening to make calls. She speaks to Marcus about the menu. She talks to a friend of a friend about a piano quartet. She even consults with Alexi and makes a point of humoring his suggestions. She resolves that she will give Oleg a sober party of fifty-six people: one for each year her husband has lived. He is considering his public reputation now, after all. He affects sobriety and restraint, so why not give him a muted, serious party? She and Marcus settle on a main course of Iberico pork. Marcus picks wines and spirits. The cake will be a honey cake delivered from a bakery in Moscow.

She makes a guest list and revises. The objective is keeping him from worse influences—from the Waterforths of this world (though that particular battle is lost).

She puts Martin on her list, crosses him out, and then adds him again. Why place the three of them in the room together? Yet Martin is a positive influence, his work a useful diversion of her husband's energies.

She works from home for two days before the party. A marquee springs up at the back of the mansion to house the extra hands Marcus is drafting in to prepare the food. Men in red overalls roll circular fold-up tables into the main hall, like a low-key circus act.

ON OLEG'S birthday, which falls on a Saturday, she wakes before him, and when he opens his eyes she says, "Happy birthday." She feels generous, ready for the day.

He says, "Thank you." He closes his eyes and sleeps.

She showers and dresses. He's still in bed when she is ready to go down for breakfast. Normally, he'd be in Russia with his mother right now. Marina thinks of those visits, of the old woman sitting and looking at her son with the concentration of a lizard watching a fly.

LATER, THEY eat lunch in the conservatory, from where they can hear the hum of the floor polisher running in the big hall. Oleg opens his club sandwich, peers at the chicken, reassembles it, and takes a bite.

When they've eaten, Marina fetches Oleg's present, which is a bottle of wine Martin helped her acquire at auction. Oleg studies the label, whistles through his teeth. "Nineteen forty-three," he says.

"People kept enjoying life," she says, "even in the dark times."

He nods. "Yes. A lesson."

The bottle is clean but not pristine. The label is yellowed, printed in an antique, crowded font. He holds it up to the light, studies the liquid through the glass. He's not displeased. "I'll save it for a celebration," he says.

GALIB IS the first to arrive. He lands in Oleg's helicopter and trots across the lawn. His suit is badly cut, and he has hair of such a dark sheen that it always causes Marina to ponder whether he wears a toupee. The hand he holds to his head as he paces from the aircraft supports her intuition. He is as rich a man as any of the other guests, and so his lack of style is a quirk to be fruitfully considered. She wonders whether some deference to his senior partner keeps him dressed in broad-shouldered, nineties tailoring, or if persistence with an outdated style is merely a sign of the same constancy he expresses in his loyalty to her husband. He has a present under his arm. Marina meets him at the edge of the grass. It's an hour before the party is due to start. "Thanks for coming," she says.

He has the wide-eyed look of someone coping with exhaustion. "I wouldn't miss it, of course. It will be a wonderful evening."

"You came from London?"

"Moscow, this morning. Your husband is in his office?"

"I believe so," she says.

"This party will be a nice break for him tonight, I think."

"Yes." She has the sense talking with Galib, as with other of Oleg's old business contacts, that there is often an intimacy being tacitly asserted. He knew her husband long before she did, is aware of things about Oleg that will never be known to her. It has outlasted Oleg's last marriage, Galib and Oleg's association, and perhaps Galib is not wrong in assuming that it will outlast this present one. "He will be glad to see you, Galib," she says.

"I hope so. Your dress is very nice, by the way. You're doing a new thing with your hair?"

"Yes."

They walk across the gravel in front of the house. The sky is red. The late winter light creeps over the hills. They go through the front door, and he trots upstairs toward Oleg's office as if the house is his own. The quartet is setting up on a little stage at one end of the hall. There are some stabs of violin. A caterer arrives to ask Marina about glasses for sparkling wine.

THE HALL fills before Oleg emerges. Alexi lingers with his new girlfriend at the edge of things. She, Sarah—the name comes to Marina miraculously as she turns to welcome the girl—is wearing a silver dress with sheer panels beneath the arms, her hair uncombed. The girl is the daughter of someone or other, if Marina remembers correctly. She greets Marina languidly, the affect familiar from Marina's classmates at school. She is stoned or superior or both. "The old man isn't here yet?" asks Alexi.

"He's in his office with Galib," says Marina.

"Well"—Alexi frowns—"we didn't need to get here for seven thirty, then, did we?" He has his father's heavy forehead, thick brows. Unlike his father, he cannot control this heaviness. He tends to glower.

"You think I can determine where he is?"

Alexi adjusts his cuffs, strokes down the arms of his green blazer. "Mum was always good at managing around him."

He looks up then, aware belatedly of his mistake. He's given too much of himself away in that complaint, she thinks, and there is regret in his expression. "Well," Marina says, "I suppose that's another matter."

She greets a couple of Oleg's lawyers: diligent public-school boys, dressed in double-breasted suits. Most of the guests are people with whom Oleg does business. Even Raina, calling back a caterer for another sous-vide quail egg, came to know them doing work as an architect. Marina arrives in front of Raina as she is still swallowing the egg. She thanks her for coming.

"A long time since I've seen you," says Raina after she has wiped her mouth.

"We've been less social, I'm afraid."

Raina studies her. "You're pregnant?"

"No! He's just getting old and misanthropic."

"That's much better." Raina is wearing a dark tartan suit. It's odd to have their old architect here, perhaps, but they are fond of her. She's funny, able to needle Oleg in a way he seems to find amusing. "You're not missing much, anyway. Those other parties are usually full of twats," Raina says. "The present circumstance excluded, of course."

"I did the guest list," says Marina. "There are plenty of twats here."

"You're a good wife," says Raina.

"Tell my husband that, if you see him."

"I will do."

"You need to design him something new. He needs a new project to supervise."

A caterer comes to refill Raina's glass of wine. Marina waves him away from her own glass.

"Sure. I'd love to. What does he want?"

"I don't have a clue."

"A boathouse? Some land on the coast somewhere. Portugal. Morocco. Scandinavia. Simplicity. Rough-knit sweaters. Painted wood and cast-iron stoves."

Marina smiles. "Get him alone and sell him this."

•   •   •

AS MARINA moves back into the middle of the room, she sees Lord Waterforth making his way into the hall in a rust-colored suit. A blond lady in an apple-green cocktail dress holds his arm. They clash horribly. Marina goes over to them. "My current wife," Waterforth says, indicating his partner, "Theresa."

Marina offers a hint of the laugh he seems to be expecting, and greets Theresa.

"How nice to be invited," says Waterforth.

"It was natural, given you've been seeing a lot of my husband."

"Renewing an old friendship, yes." Waterforth licks his lips. "We did some things together back in the olden days. We share our war stories."

"So I've heard."

"There were really no rules back then." He winks.

"Still, you got what you wanted, I suppose."

"My dear, I'll do anything to make sure of that." He winks again. "I mean *anything.*"

Marina smiles. "Don't say it too loudly. They'll take away that peerage of yours."

"Darling!" he says. He flashes his eyes, glad of Marina offering him such a setup. "Why on earth do you think they gave it to me?"

OLEG SHOULD be here, Marina thinks. She leaves the hall intending to fetch her husband, and there outside the room, returning from the bathrooms, is Martin. He is a tonic after Waterforth, and she can't resist detaining him for a moment, enjoying a tiny respite from the work of the party. He looks good in his suit, she thinks, handsome in the low light. The piano room is to her left. She beckons him in. "I missed you," she says. She touches the lapel of his jacket.

"Right," he says. He's nervous. He's looking at her fingers, though this nervousness, she finds, causes an opposite reaction in her, helps dissipate her own concerns. She rubs her hand over his shirt behind his tie, feels his chest. She thinks of their meeting weeks before. "I'm sorry I pestered you to show him the catalogue. I guess it was inevitable he wouldn't bite." He shouldn't need the apology, she thinks, but she gives it.

"It's fine," he says. "Obviously, I can't do much to change his mind."

"I didn't expect you to," she says. "I just suggested you shouldn't kiss his backside."

He frowns. "Kissing his backside is my job. You can't order me not to do my job."

"I wasn't ordering you. I just wanted a little help."

"I have my own objectives," he says.

"I know. I just wanted someone on my side, as a friend." She was looking out for him too, she thinks. She was trying to protect qualities of his that he cannot fully see.

His left eye twitches with irritation. "Right," he says. "But this is my job, my career. Understand what I'm trying to balance."

He feels that she has some expectation of him, some claim to control. She was just asking freely for a favor. She has stopped moving her hand against his chest, and merely holds it there, feeling his heart thumping. "I wasn't thinking that way," she says. His face changes quite suddenly again, and she wonders what exactly he has taken from her words, what further mistake she has made. But then she turns and sees that her husband is standing on the threshold of the room. She steps away from Martin instinctively. She feels this motion implies guilt, steps back. Oleg is watching her with his slow, steady gaze, like a Komodo dragon. She says, "We're just having an old argument."

"The old ones are the best," says Oleg. Martin is white.

"Yes," she says.

"Tonight is a very special occasion," says Oleg. Galib is behind him. Marina merely nods.

"We just sold the mine, you know. We didn't get what we deserved, but we didn't do badly."

"Your mine?"

"Yes. More money to fund my campaign."

SHE THINKS of her feet as she walks into the hall with her husband, her body flushed with adrenaline. The hall is overwarm, and she feels the heat on her forearms and shoulders. She thought she had been found out, but no. The terrible glare was occasioned by something else. He was looking past her to his project.

He has sold the mine. He once took her there: a crater in the landscape that she felt could not possibly be made by humans. The buildings in the town were all subsiding because the permafrost was melting, and because they'd been built badly in the first place. There were sinkholes in the road, uprooted saplings tossed into them to warn approaching motorists. You drove down the main road and saw small trees sticking out of the asphalt. They flew to the town airport and then took a car the last few kilometers. They could have taken a helicopter, but Oleg wanted them to approach by vehicle, to feel the history of the place. Later they did fly over it in a helicopter. It's the only thing she has encountered that allowed her to understand the scale of her husband's wealth. It validated something for him. The mine was the logical endpoint of all his dealing: the dachas, the computers, the utility companies, and finally all this land of the home country, carried out ceaselessly as if in a military convoy. Those trucks were covered in every part with dust inches thick, driven by grimy, rough men in overalls with faces from another century. On that first trip, Oleg climbed from the car and went and greeted a group of workers. She was surprised by the way they seemed pleased to meet him. These men who earned in a month what her husband spent on an ordinary meal crowded around him and laughed at his jokes. He slapped backs, and shook hands, and clasped shoulders. He was the boss. There was some energy to him they respected. He moved among them with a confidence they couldn't doubt. Marina watched him from the idling car: the big man in the fine suit in the middle of these piles of slag. He squatted and picked up a handful of the dirt and crumbled it in his hands, saying something to the men and worrying not for a moment about the china whiteness of his shirt. He threw the dirt up into the wind, and the men all laughed. He was alien to the place, and yet this otherness was necessary. The man who owned this piece of inconceivable land was acceptable only if he was inconceivable himself. The man was beyond logic. The mine was supposed to be the end of things.

OLEG STOPS just beyond the doorway into the hall, and his heavy steadiness draws eyes toward him. "Welcome, all of you," he says. Someone gives him a champagne glass. People begin to sing "Happy Birthday." The quartet play along. He raises the glass aloft.

He is a public person in a way that Marina is not. He draws energy from a room.

People find their places at the tables. The food arrives. Oleg pronounces the pork the most delicious thing he has eaten in years. He stands afterward and gives a speech in which he tells a story of his youth, one she has heard very often, though always recounted differently. It's a piece of personal folklore that he reworks depending on his audience and aims. The story is about a car he used to own that had a broken reverse gear, a Zaporozhets. "The main idea," he says, "was not to enter a situation without a plan of how you were going to get out again." He leans into his accent as he tells the story. "Honestly, it was not a problem on two conditions: you never stop, and you never make a mistake. From this came my life philosophy." He mugs and milks the line for laughs. The story develops with him driving down a narrow road on his way to stay at a friend's dacha for the weekend, and coming up behind a walking funeral procession. "No reverse, of course, so I must go as they go," he says. "So I say to the man at the back: 'Excuse me, I am here to give a ride because I hear some of the family are infirm.' The man lets me by, and before long I am driving behind the coffin with the widow beside me in the passenger seat." He ends up telling the widow he was a great friend of her husband, and so he is compelled to go to the funeral service and from there to a reception at her home. At the home, it gets late and a neighbor invites him to stay. Who knows what of this is true, though the story is so familiar that Marina herself feels she has lived it. The next morning, he returns to the city without ever seeing his friend at all. "The friend was very cross with me. He wanted to know where I had been. The people I had stayed with were the most friendly people, though. Lovely people. The next year, when I go back to the region again"—he pauses—"I stay with my new friends." He laughs. Others laugh. He begins to raise his glass. "I have done some foolish things, but I have always been lucky." He catches Marina's eye, something defiant in his expression. He scans his assembled guests. "I see you all here, and I think again that I am still lucky. Thank you."

The cake is brought in, and Oleg cuts it and hands out slices himself. "My childhood love," he says. "When I was small, I would do anything for this cake." The whiskies and brandies and liquors come out. Martin is sitting at the other end of the room, next to Waterforth, looking drunk and anxious. Marina and Martin's recent times together, in hotel rooms, in that sterile Fulham flat, seem suddenly very far away. Waterforth makes a joke, and she sees Martin laugh without enthusiasm.

Oleg is explaining to Galib the difference between a single malt and an independently bottled whiskey. "One *maltings*," he says. "Not one barrel."

"What is a maltings?" says Galib.

Oleg sighs theatrically. "You are a rich man too, Galib."

Waterforth stands and taps his glass with a dessert spoon. "If you would all permit me just one more toast," he says.

There is a murmur of assent.

"I want to speak for other guests for a moment. We've only so far heard the humble words of our host. That won't do, because it is this wonderful man's birthday, and so an opportunity to say what cannot be said enough. This man is remarkable. Like him, I am very lucky. I've worked with many fantastic people over the course of my career: men and women who will be the major figures in the history books of tomorrow. I've worked with prime ministers and presidents and heads of the largest industrial corporations in the world, and few of them, in my opinion, could hold a candle to this man." Waterforth puts a hand on the breast pocket of his blazer, turns to look at Oleg. "What judgment, what charm, what generosity! Honestly, I am perpetually impressed. I'm very grateful to have met you." He turns from Oleg and surveys the room again. "There are rumors of this man beginning a political career. Well, we don't yet know whether this is true, but we must be forgiven for hoping that it is. The world needs more men like this." He picks up his glass. "Permit me, in hope," he says. He raises the glass to his eye level. "To the next president of Russia."

People are standing and clinking glasses all around Marina. Oleg, next to her, is on his feet. She hurries to rise with the others. She tries to set her face. She turns to her husband, who is raising his whiskey glass. He drinks. He puts the glass down, empty. He wipes his mouth. His blue eyes are shining and he is smiling. He looks toward Waterforth with a glance of pure, unshaded pleasure. This is what he really wants, she thinks. This is what he really loves. He wants to be told that his time is not at its end.

These plans of his roll on against all sense. But still these people around him, with their poisonous tinkling chatter, are happy to clap and commend her husband, glad to look past his faults, and not dwell for a moment on his vulnerabilities. She feels the need for air, has an impulse to run out of the room, but instead she holds her expression, watches her husband as he rises to speak again.

"Thank you so much, Your Lordship." Oleg claps his hands together. "You flatter me, but I am very grateful. I cannot confirm your rumor, but I hope that one day I will live up to your expectations."

III

Spring/Summer 2014

III

32

MARINA IS working from her office in the London house, because the security consultant is due. He arrives on time, as such men must. He stands in the hallway looking befittingly suspicious. His name is Douglas Stillman. He is a compact, wiry man, suited but tieless. He speaks in a Scottish accent with a burry, clipped precision. He says, "Can I take it that I experienced your standard visitor protocol?"

"Protocol?" she says.

He speaks wearily. "Is this the normal way you greet your guests?"

"Yes."

He nods gravely. He has the tight energy of someone with a purpose. "Could you give me a tour?" he says.

Marina guides him through the house. Stillman raps on the walls and opens cupboards that Marina herself has never looked into. He picks up a piece of sculpture and holds it as if considering throwing it down the hallway. He slides up windows and leans out to study drainpipes as routes of ingress. It's like childhood play: the hypotheticals, the threats, the story-making. "You can't imagine what people try," he says.

"Yes?"

"There are some nasty bastards out there, you know."

"Right."

"Nasty bastards with extremely vivid imaginations."

Occasionally he whistles under his breath. He asks her to fetch him the house plans, and when she returns she finds him studying a second-floor window, slightly ajar. "This," he says. He raises his arms in amused exasperation. "This. Well . . ."

They drink coffee in the upstairs living room as he studies the plans. "Tell me about your security staff?" he says.

"They're nice," she says. "I like them."

He frowns. "You know that isn't an indication of how good they are, right?"

"What do you think of them?"

"They're sloppy," he says.

He mixes three sugars into his espresso and drinks it quickly. "What precautions do you take outside the house?" he says.

"I don't get into cars with strangers."

"This is serious."

"Okay?"

"I want to put a man on you."

"A man?"

"Figuratively speaking. This man might be a woman. What I mean to say is that you need eyes on you twenty-four-seven."

"Really?"

"I'm not sure you quite understand the seriousness of your husband's position."

"I didn't ask for this. I'm not doing anything to do with Russian politics."

"Well, it doesn't work like that, and you know it."

The way he says certain things reminds her of the way colleagues talk of financial instruments: the pull of jargon, the world-making abilities of technical language.

He says, "Given your husband's project, we're dealing with nation-state actors here."

"Yes," she says.

"They will utilize intelligence networks, vulnerabilities in electronic systems, cutting-edge technologies."

The words fit together, create their own logic. It is a waking dream, a situation born of its own prophecy. *Listen to yourself,* she wants to say to him. He senses her skepticism, she thinks.

He says, "These people are ruthless, and they are going to want to do something about your husband. Do you want to be a widow?"

It's that final word that triggers a moment of concern. The archaic feel of the term makes her think of her mother standing in front of the mirror applying lotion to her face. She thinks of the near-endless fights the two of them had after her father's death. Marina imagines all the conflict that would happen around her husband's estate. Katya is not so bad, but Katya knows how to fight, does so on instinct. And Alexi, of course.

"No," she says.

"Excuse my language," Stillman says, "but this is really fucking serious. I'm going to make some proposals to your husband. I'm going to suggest some serious changes. You have concerns, we can deal with them. We can be discreet. It is not our business what you do. It is not our job to report on your behavior if it doesn't impact the safety of our client."

"Right," she says. What does he know? she wonders.

"I want to be clear. We do not exist to keep tabs on you." He is looking at her very intently.

Under this gaze, she feels vulnerable, panicked. "Yes," she says, trying to hold her composure, trying to keep things together. He will have done his homework for this new project, and she feels suddenly, sinkingly sure now that he knows of her time with Martin. She tries to breathe evenly. Stillman looks at her with an open expression, almost a smile. Or does he need to *know*? Perhaps he can just predict. Her crisis is commonplace. The younger wife sneaking off with a young man. She nods, and he smiles more widely. She feels an upwelling of desperation, a childish impulse to surrender. She is losing too often these days. She listens to him begin to talk, incanting his sacred phrases. He speaks of planning for different contingencies, a graded assessment of threats. He gestures, grins. She watches him. She chips in words of assent, and when he has finished, she says, "Do whatever you think is necessary."

33

AT THE rental car location, Martin now knows the line manager, Jason, a slick, friendly man who looks about fourteen in his ill-fitting pinstripe suit. "We've given you an upgrade," Jason says to Martin, winking. The car is a giant Audi 4x4. The interior smells of leather and air freshener. At the center of the dashboard is a touchscreen. Martin works out how to play digital radio, sets off from the lot to the sound of "Young Americans." The weekend is mild. He runs the climate control because he can, because he feels a car like this needs to be separated in atmosphere from its surroundings.

HE GETS to the house in the afternoon. "They finally unchained you from your desk," his mother says when she greets him at the door.

She goes back to working at the kitchen table, sorting old packets of seeds from a battered apple crate. His dad is out walking through the woods with his metal detector. Martin pours himself a glass of water. An odd facet of his parents' home life is that they have one glass each, their names scrawled on with permanent marker. Guests are encouraged to get a cup and tumbler from a box in the cupboard marked GUEST GLASSES. The idea is to save washing too many things. "Dirty glasses multiply around the house like rabbits, otherwise," Martin's mother explained when they initiated the scheme a few years after he'd left home. He goes to the cupboard and selects a pint glass with a handle. He fills it from the tap and drinks. Martin's parents are eccentrics. His understanding of this has deepened as he has aged, as he's come to see the little ways this state has announced itself, the ways such a thing can just happen to someone. One has ideas about how to shape one's life to one's comfort, one becomes too satisfied with one's own difference and cleverness. One drifts to this.

"These are from 1996," says his mother.

"What?"

She's holding up a packet of tomato seeds. "John Major was still the prime minister." She chuckles to herself at the unlikeliness.

The window of the kitchen is open. Brian, one of the neighbors, is using a chainsaw to cut up a fallen tree. Martin's mother begins piling seed packets into a bin bag. "Such a waste," she says.

He feels very tired. He says, "I'm just going to go and put my bag upstairs."

He tramps up to his old room. The bed is made, a folded towel placed on it. The towel is scratchy and ancient, decorated with faded images of seashells. He turns it over, finds a tag bearing his own name stitched onto it. He used this towel for school swimming lessons two decades ago. He opens the window, flicks a couple of dead flies off the sill and out into the winter air.

HE HAS wondered about bringing Marina to the house, wondered about what she would make of the place these days. Years before, when she came with James, she was enamored with it all. Martin's mother, he remembers, was irritated by Marina's zeal, feeling that it wasn't quite genuine. Marina helped weed around the cabbages and exclaimed over the dirt, and perhaps her enthusiasm was strange, excessive. She is odd, maybe, to people unfamiliar with her, though this thought is a source of pleasure to Martin, a reification of an intimacy that wavers, that he can't altogether trust.

The old friction with his mother is no reason to not bring Marina here. The problem is the need to keep everything discreet. Still, he imagines walking in the gardens. Time and space together. Fresh air.

When he comes downstairs, his dad is in the kitchen. The metal detector is propped against the table. "Did you find anything?" Martin says.

His dad shakes his head. "It's not about finding things every time," he says.

MARTIN'S PARENTS suggest walking to the village pub for dinner. Though it's dark, the moon is full and the sky clear. Martin borrows a pair of his father's boots.

They ascend the hill away from the house, making their way across the sloping east lawn. The moon hasn't fully risen yet, so they use flashlights. They pass into the woods between raggedly shorn box bushes. It's difficult not to compare the place to Oleg and Marina's pristine house. At the back gate of the property, his mother tuts at the broken latch. "Another thing for the to-do list," she says. The air is cold and still. They come out into fields. They turn off their flashlights and let their eyes adjust as they pick their way down a path beside a field. They come down into the village: the hunched stone buildings, the steep streets, the smell of woodsmoke rising from chimneys.

THE PUB is busy. It's a Saturday night. At the bar, Martin nods at a couple of men he went to school with. He locates a table in the back room.

His dad is insistent on paying tonight, so Martin stays with his mum at the table as his father goes to order drinks and food. They talk idly about the house, the neighbors, the winter weather. Martin's dad comes back with drinks. "Well, we have news, as it happens," he says to Martin.

"Yes?"

"We're selling the house," says Martin's mother.

"The unit?"

"The whole house. Everyone together at once. Selling it to a single buyer."

"What?"

"We're winding up the whole project."

"Really?"

"The price is crazy," says Martin's mother. "We had a valuation for insurance purposes. Well, it was a surprise!"

"We were the last to vote in favor," says Martin's dad. "We thought long and hard about it."

"You love this place."

"Well, yes. But that doesn't mean we expect it to stay the same forever."

"It's difficult to find people with the right skills," says Martin's dad.

"With the time to contribute," says his mum. "People think communities like this fall apart because of sex scandals, but actually they fall apart because of difficulties fixing the roof."

"Yes."

"Like the church."

"I think churches do fall apart because of sex scandals, actually," says Martin's dad. "But the point stands."

"We're tired," says Martin's mum.

"And potentially rich, also," says his dad. "This means we could actually live where we want. Buy a decent-sized place nearer to you."

"How much is your share?" says Martin.

"Two," says his mother.

"Million?"

"Yes. We've put the years into that house, and if it has to end, I'm glad we made it to the finish."

"Closer to London?" says Martin.

"You're there," says his mum, "and a lot of my protests are in London."

"You know they say the queen thinks the world smells of wet paint? Well, Tony Blair thinks the world is populated by women who look like your mother holding signs."

"Right."

A man emerges from the barroom holding three glasses of lager between splayed fingers. He takes a step and lets slip a glass, which smashes on the flagstones, showering his trouser legs with beer. People turn to look at him. From a table in the corner, his friends berate him jovially.

"I didn't see this coming," says Martin.

"It just felt like the right time," says his dad.

THEY WALK home with the moon up, the landscape bleached in the clear white light. They make their way through the dark woods and come out above the house, which stands out arrestingly in the moonlight. They must have been protecting this secret of theirs for months now, talking to him on the phone and holding this information back. They didn't tell him until now, and they didn't tell him because they know it contrasts badly with the puritanical way they judge the world (and have judged Martin's work, in fact). Martin gains his voice at the sight of the place. They'll expect him to say they have no right to sell this way—and that is what he feels—but that would be too refutable. Of course, they have the *right* in a technical sense. Martin says, "I'm just surprised."

"About what?" says his mum, though he is sure she knows.

"The house. Selling up. Because of all that money."

"The money is incidental," says Martin's mum.

"But not unwelcome," says his dad.

"It goes against everything you've stood for," Martin says.

His mother stops, speaks harshly now. "Oh, does it? Thank you for telling me what I stand for."

34

THOUGH IT'S a Saturday, Marina has a work commitment and won't be back until the afternoon, so Oleg takes his midmorning coffee in the upstairs living room. He has the TV on, playing the news in Russian. He turns it off. He can hear the gardener running the wood chipper. He wishes his wife were in the house. He'd like to ask her about Navalny, who is organizing another demonstration, the latest in a line of protests that have run on through the autumn and winter. He thinks of the protestors he encountered in the days after his mother died. He imagines standing on the slush-covered streets amongst his compatriots. Breath visible in the air, amidst the heaving of a crowd moving together and apart with a logic beyond any one of them. Yet it's not the time for Oleg to be involving himself with such things, apparently.

For now, they are concentrating on the question of whether he should work with Navalny. There has been contact. The message relayed is that Navalny appreciates Oleg's opposition but is keen to push on with his own campaigns. Their brands, he says, are different. "We are both defined by our histories," he said on the telephone. The man wants to run for president himself, of course, and is therefore wary of anyone who might have their own ambitions. Navalny is perhaps even wary of the possibility that Oleg might be working on behalf of the President, standing as a false opposition candidate to split the vote against Putin. They have used this technique before, the government, though Oleg, of course, is a man with too much integrity and gravitas to play a part in this kind of theater. He hopes that people understand this.

Waterforth himself has no time for Navalny, made this clear on the phone earlier in the day: "He was what—a teenager?—when you and I were last working together. The system will fucking run him over."

They are in what Waterforth and his associates have described to Oleg as the foundational phase. They're establishing Oleg's credentials as a source of opposition to the President. Oleg wants to be touring Russia already, to be showing his resistance. "Forgive me," Waterforth told Oleg on the phone when he stated this desire. "What my analysts have found is that you're seen—how shall I say it?—as a bit of a crook. If you go back home and start agitating, then it's not much of a problem for the government to lock you up, or worse. When we can establish you as an *activist,* a moral force, then it becomes a risk for them to deal with you. Internationally, it becomes an issue. You have a sort of halo. An invisible protection to move into the country and speak with freedom."

For now, the work is establishing the foundation: the linking of activists, the creation of an infrastructure. Galib is doing this work, spending longer in the jet than he does on the ground. There is evidence that the government is pushing back already: issues with building regulations, legal problems for those Galib is liaising with. "They're running scared!" said Waterforth when Oleg mentioned this.

"Let's tell the people what they're doing," said Oleg. "This shit. Let's start to actually speak."

"Patience," said Waterforth. "Build your evidence first of all. The next elections are years away still. Your man Galib is doing great work. Stay here. Prepare. Work on your political philosophy. Do some blue-sky thinking."

Now Oleg sits on the sofa and tries to do this blue-sky thinking. He thinks of his cousin out east. It's nighttime at the moment there. The barren dark. The end of the long winter there. He thinks of Yelena on the balcony, watching the courtyard, thinking what? He has no ideas.

Kids are a good place to start, he supposes. The future. The schools. He sits again and takes up his paper and writes "TABLETS" in large letters. He underlines the word. Do they have iPads in the schools? At least generic equivalents? When Alexi was young, Oleg recalls him having trouble with his spelling and the teachers always talking about how computers could be of use to the boy. Though actually, Alexi seemed to play only some kind of battle game on his computer. The boy was perpetually invading Gaul with the Roman army. Oleg writes "No games!" He looks around the room, trying to force some other thought. The gilded mirror. The ornate plasterwork cornicing on the ceiling. He has an impulse toward the telephone—to do what?—to call his mother, he thinks. Oh. Yes. The wood chipper cuts off, and the silence that follows it is eerie.

WHEN MARINA arrives home, she and Oleg eat a late lunch together in the kitchen: grilled salmon and salad and some new potatoes cooked just the way he likes.

He says, "Waterforth says I shouldn't coordinate with Navalny."

Marina takes her time to swallow. She has taken her contacts out and is wearing her glasses. "You know what I think of Waterforth."

"I do," he says. "But what about his idea?"

"You should give all your money to Navalny."

"Ha!"

She finishes another mouthful. "I'm serious."

"He's not so popular. Not enough to be president."

"Neither are you."

"But I have a campaign to do. I'll show the country the true me over the next few years. And then . . ." Marina is smiling in a way he doesn't like. Can she not resist the urge to snipe? He checks himself, breathes.

"You could do the same campaign for Navalny, though."

"But why him?"

"He has integrity. Maybe people don't think him a leader yet, but they trust him."

"Marinka," he says. "Integrity is like a white suit. Very nice when the weather is fine, but too easy to spoil. The world will have its way with him. You don't get to power without choosing between bad and worse choices." He's talking about himself, of course, and he can see in her face that's she's registered this, is tired of it already. This is what he knows, however, this is important. Russia is not her home. She doesn't understand the different mind-set, the way people can betray you. She simply watches him with her lips pressed together.

"Tell me why you're doing this," she says.

"My cousin. I explained."

"Did you?"

"These people," he says. "I didn't think of them. It was all going wrong in the nineties. I just thought they were shortsighted or slow, but they weren't as ready as I was. They lost out."

"You're guilty about making your money. Well, give it back. Give it to a cause that helps them. Walk away."

"No," he says. "No." She has laid down her knife and fork on her plate, and Calum comes in to refill their water glasses. Oleg wants to explain, but he lacks the power to do so. He thinks of his cousin again. The tap of the cigarette on the rail. It's not about the money, as Yelena said, though he's not sure what it is about.

"Don't you see?" she says. "This is what they want."

"Sorry?"

"A man like you, in opposition. A man who is so . . . objectionable."

"I'm sincere, my dearest."

"They can cope perfectly well with you," she says, "and meanwhile you ruin both our lives." She stands from the table and lays her napkin down beside her plate. She leaves the room. He has another serving of potatoes as he sits at the table alone. He chews slowly, and a thought resolves itself: his great prize was not the money, as she seems to think.

The prize was his *foresight*. The feeling of it. The sheer power. That vision that allowed him to do anything. And it is now his foresight that he wants to recover, to put to the service of others.

OLEG WALKS upstairs, hears Calum coming in and taking the plates as he departs. In the living room, the lowering sun comes in full from the west windows. He picks up the landline telephone and calls Waterforth, who answers eventually.

"You're busy?" says Oleg.

"Never too busy, though I'm billing you from now."

"Understood."

"Well, what is it, my friend?"

Oleg explains that he talked to Marina about Navalny, explains her point of view. He just needs Waterforth's scorn for the idea, which is immediately forthcoming. "He is not a *robust* candidate, like yourself," Waterforth says. "You start from a low base, but you will build. We have time and resources."

"Yes."

"He is—what?—a blogger?"

"A lawyer too."

"Everyone's a lawyer," says Waterforth.

"Yes," says Oleg. "True. He's just a kid. I bet his mother still does his washing."

Waterforth laughs at this weak joke with such enthusiasm as to make Oleg regret it. "That's a good one."

Oleg goes to the window and looks out at the garden. Waterforth is still speaking reassuring words, talking of paradigm shifts, halo effects. Oleg feels very suddenly sad, very much not himself. The sky is turning a wonderful orange. He can see a car moving very far off, on a road at the brow of the hill in the distance. Other than that, just fields, woods, walls, and hedges. For some reason the view makes him feel very small today. "Look out of this window," the estate agent said when Oleg bought the place, "and you'd barely know that it isn't the seventeenth century."

That is this country, Oleg thinks, where they think that history is a thing to be sold, rather than something to be lived through.

Oleg sits heavily on the sofa. Waterforth's talk still patters on. "I have to go," he says.

"I'm not that expensive," says Waterforth.

"Sorry?"

"Oh. It was a joke about my billing. Never mind."

"Okay. Good-bye."

AFTER DINNER, he turns in early, and lies awake until Marina makes her way to bed. He listens to her in the bathroom: the water, the electric toothbrush. She slips under the covers and lies on her side, facing away from him. She falls asleep with irritating ease, while he broods and fidgets and can't turn off his mind.

Can she not see what he sees? What he can do? Of course, he knows her resistance to his plans has a history, a logic. Her father, of course.

She sighs and turns onto her back. Her lips move. She doesn't wake.

A secret that he has kept from her is that he knew her father. The man was dead before Oleg met Marina, and yet Oleg had met him many years before. He hasn't told her this, though without real calculation behind the choice. The omission is so inexplicable as to be shaming. He feels it inside him, rotten almost. He met her father and he thought, *I know how a man like this works.* The man was not special: neither so good, nor so bad. Oleg had met many like him before, has met many like him since.

Oleg had his guys look back into the death a couple of years ago and they found nothing suspicious, though such findings can never be definitive. The engineer in him wanted to know the practicalities, though the practicalities might well be unknowable. An ordinary man. An accident. What more should there be to it?

Yet why didn't he tell her he knew the man? Why hide this at all? He didn't want to consider her connected with that plain, uninteresting guy, he supposes, this woman who seemed anything but ordinary. He didn't let himself see her, he thinks. He took that liberty. Was that too much? There are things he must still make good with her.

Her breaths are long and even. He thinks of Anna in Ukraine. All that talk. So much talk. And yet, he now knows, he didn't understand a thing. He doesn't want this again. Anna lost to him. Canada. Katya hating him. He climbs from the bed slowly, puts on slippers.

He goes to his office and opens his laptop. He watches footage of protests in Kiev. The squares, the fountains. He knows these streets, knows this place. He thinks of Anna again. He was once young on those streets, in what now seems a different lifetime.

35

"I'M AFRAID I have bad news," says the woman in the uniform. "Mr. Gorelov is delayed." Martin looks at her and then at the land behind her: the jumbled, colorful houses of Positano, the scrubby hillside above them. The sea is calm, but he still feels nauseated. A ferry comes past on their seaward side, and then behind it the wake, spreading its fingers until it reaches the yacht and causes it to sway and pitch just enough to make Martin's insides quiver.

"How delayed?" says the other man, Thomas. Thomas is the assistant of Oleg's PR man, Lord Waterforth.

"I'm afraid we're talking hours," says the girl in the uniform.

"He's a busy man," says Thomas. "No need to apologize." Thomas has arrived better prepared than Martin has. Thomas wears a light turquoise suit. He has a hat and sunglasses. Martin wears his ordinary suit and left his sunglasses in the seat pocket on his flight from Heathrow to Naples.

"Would you like another drink?" asks the woman.

"Sparkling water would be fine for me," says Thomas.

"Nothing," says Martin, squinting at her, then looking back at the land. "Thank you."

Martin feels himself studied. "Not a boat person?" says Thomas.

"I could get travel-sick in a golf cart," says Martin.

"Look at the horizon."

"I'm trying."

"There are medications for this kind of thing."

"I thought a big boat, good weather, a glassy sea . . ."

Thomas laughs, mouth open to reveal a set of very straight white teeth. "All true . . . and yet?"

"I wasn't made for boats."

"With clients like these, you've got to deal with boats."

"I know."

The woman in the uniform returns with a glass of sparkling water for Thomas. Thomas takes off his sunglasses and says, "I'm wondering whether it might be possible to put us ashore while we're waiting."

"Of course," says the woman.

Thomas sips the water, winks at Martin.

"THANKS," SAYS Martin, when they're in the speedboat, the town growing larger ahead of them. They cut in past the smaller, moored boats, past the buoy-demarked swimming area, empty in the off-season. When they approach the dock, a man in uniform jumps from the speedboat with a rope and hauls the boat close enough that Martin and Thomas can step off easily. "We'll call you when his arrival is imminent," says the man.

"Thank you," says Thomas.

Martin stands on the dock and breathes evenly and tries to settle his insides.

Many of the shopfronts are shuttered for the winter. Martin and Thomas ascend into the old town, where they find an open café and order Aperol Spritzes. They sit at a table on the terrace in front of the café. "You have to ask for things," says Thomas. "These people serve their bosses and their bosses want to host you well. To hold back what you need is unsporting."

"Of course," says Martin.

"This your first trip of this nature?"

"It is."

"I guess his art collection is a big deal?"

"Yep."

"You're the guy helming the deal?"

"I suppose. It's not a deal yet, officially. This fell to me. I went to university with his wife. I was lucky. I knew the right person."

"Knowing the right person is everything." Thomas winks again. He's a handsome man, Thomas. His cheekbones are high, his nose thin and straight. At their shaded table he has taken off his hat. His black hair is cropped short, receding a little in a widow's peak.

"Where?"

"Sorry?"

"University."

"York."

"Right."

"You know people who went there?"

"No. Or maybe." Thomas flaps a hand. "Perhaps some people from my school went there. Anyway, this is a fun project. The art sale. The political rebranding. Have you met my boss?"

"Lord Waterforth?" says Martin. "I sat next to him at a party."

"Oh yes?" Thomas grins. "What was he like?"

"He was, um, nice."

Thomas laughs in a new brittle way that makes Martin feel he has said something ridiculous, which, of course, he has. "*Nice* is a new one to me, in regard to him," says Thomas.

"I didn't want to say—"

"Why not? He's a total bastard," says Thomas. "He just happens to be very good at what he does." Thomas beams. "An utter cunt," he mutters. Martin has the sense that Thomas is the kind of person who takes pleasure in the starkness of his own opinions. Martin thinks of art history tutorials at university, and of the well-spoken men who arrived late, having done none of the reading but armed instead with unflagging confidence and a tendency to challenge the assumptions behind the simplest questions posed in the seminar with a well-practiced line of contrarian logic.

They order more Aperols. A sour kind of sewer smell hangs in the air. A teenager is coaxing a choking scooter up the steep road that runs past the café.

"I'll need coffee after this," says Martin. He points to his drink. "I'll be asleep otherwise."

Thomas nods. "Lots of waiting for these kinds of meetings. When your clients make millions of pounds an hour, can you blame them?"

"Where else do you work?"

"Everywhere. Europe. Africa. I do a lot in South America."

"A nice place to go."

"Not exactly a jolly holiday destination, given my work. We work for right-wingers there, usually. People who were in power in the eighties and are trying to mount comebacks, guys who've done some terrible things and now want a new reputation. They know the buzz-words. They know social media. They just don't seem to understand that it might be problematic if they worked twenty years with a police officer who likes clipping car batteries to people's scrotums." Thomas laughs ruefully. "The thing that always surprises me is how much these people still want to be *liked*. It's like, *Mate, did you not see you have to choose?*"

"Is that not depressing?" says Martin.

"Depressing? I wouldn't say. No. Morally dubious, maybe."

"Yes. I guess that's what I mean."

Thomas clucks his tongue. "I suppose my job is harder, and so more interesting, the worse that they are."

Martin laughs, dislikes himself a little for laughing. Is he agreeing? Is he humoring Thomas? He says, "You'd have done a good job with Stalin, I suppose."

"You joke, but . . ." Thomas opens his hands and grins.

Martin laughs, tries to speak lightly. "Is that the best use of your skills?"

"I'm a cynic, and I'd like, one day, to buy a decent-sized London house."

"Sure."

"You're not uncompromised yourself, surely?" Thomas gestures down the hill, toward the dock and the sea and the yacht. "Our guy, for instance. Our guy rinses money out of the state for years, helps fix an election. Now he wants to be a democrat."

Martin returns Thomas's firm gaze, says, "Wasn't your firm helping him fix the election?"

"The official line is that we were assisting his legitimate political operations, and we had no knowledge of any bribery or vote-rigging." Thomas chuckles. "We can be very naïve when we need to be."

"He thinks that he did the right thing."

"It's my job to argue that. It wasn't his fault the regulation was absent, after all. He was a rational man, making the most of his resources."

"That's the story you'll tell?"

"Sure," says Thomas. "We'll say something like that. Get him some votes in a few years. You'll get your paintings to sell."

"That's one way to look at it."

"How else?"

Martin thinks of Marina. "It's a risk for him, politics. The oligarchs were warned off, as I understand it."

"I suppose."

"You've reckoned with that?"

Thomas's expression is grave; there is some professional pride at stake, Martin supposes. "We weren't born yesterday."

"Uh-huh."

"He's not going to win, is he? One of our guys has contacts in the Russian government. It's broadly understood that he's not a genuine threat. If anything, he might help the President by taking votes away from other opposition parties. They'll keep an eye on him, I think, but they feel that they can live with him."

"Really?"

"Speaking strictly confidentially . . ."

Martin nods to assent.

"We don't intend to challenge that assessment. He's not going to be able to endanger them or, in that case, himself."

"Wait. You're not trying to win?"

Thomas sighs. "Well, *trying* isn't really the issue, is it? We'll take him closer than he would have been without us. I'm not going to win Wimbledon. But does it matter if I believe I might? If my tennis coach doesn't tell me that I can't?"

"I see."

Thomas slumps back in his chair. He looks tired now, perhaps even, Martin thinks, a little regretful for what he has given away in his justifications.

THE DAY lengthens in increments set by calls from Oleg's PA, putting back his arrival by hours each time. They eat lunch in their café. They have more drinks. They walk around the empty town. The shadows cross the beach as the afternoon stretches on. The sun is almost down when the speedboat finally comes for them. The sky is darkening, and the sea has turned a dark greenish hue. The yacht is lit up, all the more impressive for the way the illumination makes clear its size. The speedboat slaps over small waves, and Martin's stomach twists again. The nausea isn't just seasickness, but the perpetual fear he experiences encountering Oleg these days: that the man will have found out about Martin and Marina.

On board, Martin hears the helicopter before he sees it. Then a speck appears in the sky. He and Thomas stand in the dining room and look out at the lighted aircraft and its faint shadow on the dark sea. Martin can see the illumination of southern cities far off, in a haze at the horizon. The helicopter approaches and disappears over their heads, then comes back into view, descending. The boat rocks slowly. The helicopter wobbles as it nears the helipad on the back of the boat, then lurches lower in a series of minute adjustments. The skis touch

the deck. The engine cuts off. The rotors slow from a blur into vis-
ibility. The resolution feels anticlimactic, Martin thinks. The delicacy
of the maneuver made part of him wish for complication.

The door opens and Oleg steps out. He stands on the deck and
adjust the cuffs of his blazer. He looks up to the cabin of the boat. He
waves at Martin and Thomas.

"I'm sorry," Oleg says when he enters the cabin.

"We've had a perfectly pleasant time," says Thomas.

The oligarch nods and smiles. "I'm glad to hear," he says. He seems
happy. He surveys the two men in front of him for a moment. He says,
"You've been following this Ukraine news?" He leans his head back
and looks at them with a slight squint.

"Naturally," says Thomas.

"I have confirmation that Russian special forces are being deployed
in Ukraine." Oleg nods at what he says, as if receiving the news himself. "This is a real war," he says. "A new war. I never thought they
would do something like this so quickly." He rubs his large hands
against each other.

Thomas looks shocked. "Really?" he says.

"My contacts have good sources."

"It certainly changes things." Thomas takes out his phone, looks at
the screen for a moment, puts it away again. These developments don't
lend themselves to the compartmentalized plan Thomas explained on-
shore, Martin thinks.

Oleg nods solemnly, turns to look around the cabin. He's playing
a role, Martin thinks. He is playing a statesman. "Indeed, it does. This
is an opening for us. Our work becomes even more important."

"Yes."

"I didn't know I was waiting for this. Maybe I was."

"Yes," Thomas says. "Perhaps you were."

"Events rising up," says Oleg. "Events rising up to meet me."

• • •

MARTIN IS allocated a cabin. He calls the office and rebooks his flight. He becomes used to being on the water, to the slight sickness that lingers at the edge of things. He eats dinner with Oleg and Thomas, though the oligarch gets so many calls that he's in the room for less than half the meal. In Oleg's absence, Thomas and Martin look at each other uneasily.

Martin's cabin is beneath the lounge, and when he retires to sleep he hears activity above him. From beneath him comes the humming of the boat's engines, and from the lounge the play of Oleg's voice.

He thinks of Oleg's Malevich picture. Above deck, Oleg speaks of a nascent war, of political dynamics Martin cannot fathom, and yet Martin is still snagged on the picture in the Swiss storage room. He has felt a sense of fate in regard to this picture, felt somehow that it was the painting's time. Malevich's ideas have survived; the notion of a pure, necessary painting is still compelling.

The man painted not the world as we see it, but what he felt operated beneath everything, the potential that lurked beyond. Yet in reminiscences he also talked of his childhood in Ukraine. His father worked in a factory that made sugar from beets, and the young artist played in the fields where those beets were grown. He recalled dreams of flying over those fields, over the uneven grids, the rhomboids of colored crops, and diagonal slashes of road. These were Ukrainian fields over which, Martin thinks, troops will be fighting. You think a picture can be just itself, yet the material comes from somewhere, always. You dream of flight and the dream soaks into your work. The work is supposed to be pure, essential. But there, suddenly, is the world again. For better, for worse.

WHEN MARTIN wakes in the morning, he ascends to the sun-flooded deck. Oleg is seated at the breakfast table wearing sunglasses and a crisp white shirt. "You slept well?" he says.

"Yes. Thank you. Yourself?"

"Not at all." Oleg flashes a broad smile. "Not a single minute."

"I suppose that makes sense."

The oligarch nods proudly.

Thomas comes in, looking tired. Like Martin, he is wearing yesterday's suit. Oleg greets him warmly, and he rouses himself to respond in kind, some effort detectable to Martin in the way he does so.

Oleg sips his coffees, says, "And so what now?"

Martin says, "I suppose we'll consider the sale of your works at another time?"

"Why?" says Oleg. "Now is the perfect time. An event to tie with the other events. The Gorelov Collection. In aid of my foundation, which, by the way, we are pivoting toward my democratic mission and opposition of this conflict."

"Really?"

"Of course. Why would we not? The same stakes, but just a little more heat." He winks. "Malevich's story—his struggle against oppression—perhaps it even sheds light on my own."

Martin nods. "Yes," he says eventually. "I think I see what you mean."

"His last works were made as Stalin starved the peasants in Ukraine, and now . . . history comes around. History lays itself out for us," Oleg says. "We need to attack this opportunity."

Looking across the table, Martin can see that Thomas is now the one looking out of sorts, bereft of the easy grasp of this project he boasted of on land. Though perhaps it should not gladden Martin, this wrong-footing of Thomas is satisfying. He himself grins at what the oligarch says, nods with each pronouncement.

Oleg claps his hands together. "You both want eggs? We must all keep our strength up, no?"

36

MARINA MEETS Martin at the station. It's a while since she's seen him. Since they went away months before, they've had a couple of dinners, a couple of afternoon liaisons at his flat. Now he awaits her on a street west of Gare du Nord with his satchel in his hand. He sees the Land Rover and steps to the curb. Everything feels heavy, too much. She doesn't want to be doing this now, but she is.

Martin looks to the driver's seat as he gets in.

"This is Chris, my bodyguard," she says, managing a neutral tone. "Don't be weird."

They start off, moving south toward the river, inching through traffic-packed roundabouts, passing crowds in the plazas. Their tires buzz on cobbles. They cross the Seine. It's a blustery day, and flags are drawn taut above the museums and government buildings on the banks. The sky is the bluish gray of fish scales. Spring will properly arrive soon. Marina says, "Shall we go straight to the restaurant?"

Martin turns from the window and agrees. He is made cautious by their having company in Chris. She is glad he is experiencing this, though: the claustrophobia of her present life, these new security concerns necessitated by her husband's plans.

She is here for her annual medical checkup, which she completed an hour before. The plan was that they would use this as an excuse for Martin to come through for twenty-four hours and they would spend an afternoon and evening together, but the plan was made before this new phase of her life, when they'd imagined they could walk the Paris streets together alone, when they might have blended into the city crowds. Instead, they have only staggered onto this.

He says, "How's work?"

"Okay."

She could tell him that work has been bad, that she has been distracted and ineffective. What would seeking his commiseration achieve, though?

He smiles nervously, shakes his head slowly. He is at a loss. They wait at traffic lights. "Oleg?"

She recalls a scene from a couple of weeks before: her husband doing a chaotic video call with activists from all over Russia. All this hope rising from these people on grainy feeds in small rooms—this cacophony of the forgotten and the damned—and directed toward her husband, who only nodded his heavy head cluelessly, and repeated that things were very serious like some strange, glitching android. "He's the same," she says. "He's pushing on."

Martin nods. Martin is part of that story too, drawn in like those flickering faces on the conference call. Her husband's story is Martin's work now: a narrative that tightens around her from all sides.

They park outside the restaurant. They go in. They're seated, and Chris is given another table, not far from their own. They order. Martin says, "How was the checkup?"

She shrugs. "Fine. He thinks I work too hard, but then he's a French doctor."

Martin laughs more than the small joke merits. She pushes into it then. She says, "I don't want to do this anymore."

"This?"

"Yes. This." She waits. She feels light-headed. She tells herself that she can do this, play the role for the time it takes to close things off neatly. For a time, it all felt different with Martin. She felt a sense of escape. But this is not escape, she thinks. She thinks of Douglas Stillman eyeing her, speaking of discretion.

"Right," says Martin. He looks at Chris at the other table. He looks back at her. He is confounded. He is all but asking why, so she speaks before he does.

"It was fun, right? But it was just that, no?"

"Was it?" He shakes his head. She can see he is seeking to form a fuller response.

"You got your deal with his pictures."

"Well, yes . . ."

The sommelier comes and pours their wine. Marina wants to release Martin from her with anger, to give him that, at least, to go away with.

He says, "Is this because I didn't confront your husband?"

"Sure," she says. "Why not?"

"You're not taking this seriously."

"Does it have to be about anything?"

"It was about something." He sips his wine, studies his plate. He can't fully look at her.

"Yes," she says. "I liked the reminiscing. I liked spending time with you."

"But?" he says.

"What if there isn't a but?" she says.

37

HE WALKS out of the restaurant. It rained while they were eating and now the air feels cleared, fresh. At the end of the street, he turns randomly, seeking a metro.

He had what he felt to be good news for Marina, but they didn't reach that. He wanted to tell her about Thomas's admission that his company didn't expect Oleg to really contest the election. *Just wait,* he'd imagined telling her. *Waterforth is terrible, but like you he only wants an easy life. Trust him, or trust at least that he is betraying your husband. Be patient and it will all flare out.* But he hadn't said that. He'd merely gulped air like an expiring fish. His poise with her has come and gone, and deserted him when he needed it. There was a life for them beyond this, he wanted to say: Oleg's pictures sold, and Martin's reliance on him done.

And then? Just Martin and Marina, whatever that would be like.

He books into a hotel not far from the Gare du Nord. He showers, dresses in the same clothes. He eats dinner at the first bistro he comes to on leaving the hotel. He has a poor salad, a dry leg of duck, half a carafe of white wine. A couple of Australians, a man and woman, are seated at the table next to him. They're trying to savor the food. The man consults the menu. "*Boeuf,*" he says. "*Boeuf.*"

"Weird, eh?" says the woman.

Martin hates these people, hates himself even more for hating them. No one here is doing what they should be doing. He wonders where Marina is. Martin has a sudden sense of being shut out of the real city, pushing into this eerie simulacrum. The Australian man says, "*Boeuf, boeuf, boeuf.* I just can't pronounce it." The waiter shows Martin a trolley of sad-looking desserts, and Martin chooses a tiramisu.

The bill comes and the mineral water is three times the price of the wine. The Australians are mispronouncing Camus now. "They all drank in these kinds of places," says the woman, "and they fought like cats too."

Martin returns to the hotel and sleeps in his small room in which he can hear rain rattling off the roof above him.

He lies asleep and twists and turns and thinks of returning to his empty flat, thinks that he will go home and change everything. He is losing people, and for what? The art? The value of the art? He could give it up.

Yet he wakes, and the light is different and he has none of the bravery for those resolutions, merely a heavy regret and a sense of self-loathing that he nurses as he drinks a gritty coffee in a café across the road from the hotel.

MARTIN'S TRAIN back to London is due to depart after lunch, and though he could transfer his booking to an earlier train, he doesn't. He leaves his bag at the hotel reception. He walks south to the Musée National d'Art Moderne, the Pompidou Centre. He thinks of a joke Marina once made about his similarity to the building, his inability to withhold: everything with him is visible on the outside.

He hasn't been to the museum before, and takes some time to find the picture. He consults a map, asks a docent in his poor French. The man nods and points, and Martin follows the direction of the finger. He turns a corner and comes into a small room and there it is, a little larger than he thought it would be, that blue behind the figure deeper, more arresting, than he expected: *The Running Man*, one of Malevich's last works.

The man isn't quite there, drawn from another place, another state.

Inconstant. Perceptible in traces. The common idea of the picture is that it is about the artist's persecution at the hands of Soviet authorities or about the starvation of peasants in Malevich's homeland of Ukraine. The dread. The bare ground.

In the last years of his life, Malevich painted figuratively. For all his theories of nonobjectivity, for all his yearning to advance his craft beyond representation, he depicted things in the end. When he returned to painting after an eight-year hiatus, he painted stylized images of peasants. Perhaps this was to save himself. Maybe he was accommodating his work to what the authorities wanted, or filling the hole in his history created by the paintings he had left behind when he visited Germany. Or maybe he'd just reconciled with a different type of working. Maybe there are still relationships of shape and space in these pictures, absolutes that he could have believed in on his same old terms. The man seemed always to have a story of his work, after all: reshaping, self-mythologizing, holding to just enough truth to survive.

The figure runs forward on his thin legs, his beard like a fire around his absent face. In the background are two crosses. The fields behind the man are beige and purple, raw: paint reapplied and scraped off again so that the bareness yawns. A woman comes into the room behind Martin, walks around, goes out again. One of the man's hands has been blotted out into the background. He's half-there. There is a resonance to it, a note that reverberates, that builds as one looks. Was this a defeat, or a small victory for the painter? Maybe the man didn't know himself. One of Malevich's old friends, visiting Malevich's apartment after the artist had died, looked at the canvases and said, "I never knew how lonely he was at the end."

Martin looks at the painting for a long time, until his back aches from standing still. He circles the small room. He returns to his spot in front of the picture. To have given up so much could be a defeat, he thinks, or else a gesture of dedication, a defiant tribute to a surviving vision, to the resolve to carry on. This far along the journey, Martin wonders, would the artist even have known the difference?

38

OLEG LANDS in Malta just before sunset. The air when he emerges from the jet is the temperature of blood. Victor is waiting for him in a hired Land Rover. Oleg and his new security man, Marc, get into the rear of the vehicle. They drive away from the airport on a divided highway. They circle a roundabout on which a palm tree leans over groggily. Everything seems so dry after the country house.

The restaurant is on the port, and he lowers his window a little as they approach. He can smell the sea, he can smell the sweet-sour exhaust of the scooters that weave through the traffic.

Victor stops the car outside the restaurant. Oleg and Marc leave the vehicle and walk through the main dining area to the elevator. They ride up to the terrace. Oleg studies his reflection in the mirrored cabin. He looks tired. He'd be doing things wrong if he didn't look tired.

The elevator doors open, and Oleg steps out onto the terrace and sees his old friend immediately. German occupies the prime table at the railing, the view of the dark harbor behind him. He has taken the better seat, which offers clear sightlines of the routes of ingress. He stands and comes around the table to greet Oleg.

He is the same old German. He is a little heavier perhaps (though weight gain, if anything, is a sign of changelessness: German packs on bulk like a rolling snowball). He embraces Oleg. He smells good. His hair, Oleg notes, is as irritatingly thick as ever, though the color is too dark brown, too obviously artificial.

"It's been too long this time," says German.

"Yes."

"I miss you. In the old days we met all the time, like lovers, and now . . ." German spreads his hands.

"You should call," says Oleg.

"*You* should call."

They sit down. Marc takes a place at an adjacent table at which German's man already sits. There are a couple of big yachts moored out to sea, their windows lit. A small dinghy is heading out into the harbor, the sound of its outboard motor rising to the terrace as an insect buzz.

"I was sorry about your mother." German holds eye contact.

There can still be something real between them, even now, Oleg thinks. "Thank you."

A waitress arrives and German chooses the wine and they order food.

"How long since we've been in Malta together?" German says, when the waitress has left.

"A while."

"You remember being here for the first time?"

"Of course."

German speaks in English, a purposefully thick, bumpkinish Russian accent: "International businessmen."

They both laugh.

They talk of the logistics of their travel. Their starters come. Oleg has a seafood consommé with langoustine. "This place is still wonderful," says German.

"A little old-fashioned, maybe. But good, yes."

"I don't have such time to follow all the trends," says German. "Quality is quality to me."

"Certainly," says Oleg. "I don't have much time either. I just try to stay informed, to keep up."

"Or you are changing yourself?" German winks.

"Surely it would be foolish to not move with the times?"

"Perhaps more foolish to think you can predict the way the times are moving?"

Oleg sips his wine. The waitress collects his and German's plates. The hum of music from the restaurant rises for a moment as the waitress opens the terrace doors.

"I've been informed about your activities," says German.

"I expected so," says Oleg.

"I think, *What is my old friend doing?*"

"I'm doing something you don't dare."

"No, you're not," says German. He shakes his head. There are flecks of gray in his eyebrows, which contrast badly with the flat hue of his hair.

They're silent until the main course comes. The waitress refills their glasses. German cuts into his steak, waits for the waitress to retreat before he speaks. "Things are not perfect, of course. Some of the men around the President have let him down. The President himself has made mistakes. He understands this. It's good you're alert to these things. He's grateful. But to approach the situation as you do? This is reckless and destructive. At this time in particular."

"That's the official line?" says Oleg.

"It's my line. I want to help you."

"Really?"

"Some dissent. Fine. They can tolerate this. Even a campaign of yours, perhaps. If you weren't so *forceful.* Maybe there could even be a helpful discussion of things that might be changed."

"My issue isn't something the President will fix. My issue is the whole system. The man needs to go."

"Oh yes? I thought your main concern was the continuation of the Oleg Gorelov show."

"This isn't about me. It's a shift, this war. They have a new hunger."

"This is Russian territory, historically." German scoffs. "Come on! You don't think we have some claim on these places?"

"I object to the manner of the war, most of all," says Oleg.

"It's posturing, mostly," German says. "You don't like it, sure. There are ways to moderate things. Don't turn the table over."

Oleg glares at German, waits until the other man meets his eyes. "We fucked things up. Do you not wake up in the night and think of this?"

"I wake up in the night because of my prostate. We're old, my friend. We had our time. It's necessary for us to step back."

"We made a mess of our time."

"We negotiated. We made choices. We made deals, some of which you're now reneging on."

"Don't you want to live in a normal country?"

"It's not that simple."

"You remember when we met? Your tiny office? You were taking risks. You didn't care you were annoying the old men. Now the President asks you to squeeze my balls and you say, 'How hard?'"

German slices and swallows some meat. He says, "Those times were those times."

Oleg grunts.

German leans forward in his chair. He speaks with the same soft clarity with which he spoke of Oleg's mother. "My friend," he says, "they will crush you."

Oleg looks at him for a long time. German is sad, or making a very good impression of looking sad. Oleg says, "I agree, it is a risk."

THEY SKIP dessert. German insists on paying. There is some urgency behind this insistence. It strikes Oleg that his old friend is thinking of this as their last meal together. German will distance himself, will have to distance himself. German waves his credit card around, and eventually Oleg says, "If you insist."

They go one after the other. German leaves first. He walks toward the elevator. His face is different now: blank and unreadable. He stands in the elevator looking heavy and menacing. Oleg raises his hand very slightly and the doors close. Marc comes over to tell Oleg that Victor is ready for them, waiting in the Land Rover down on the street.

39

HE IS Julian's guy now, rising through the house with his boss. This will be Julian's sale, but in the offices, people know the credit is due to Martin.

He arrived back from Switzerland with word of a great painting that was previously presumed lost, and in less than a year he has secured the sale of the thing. People who previously didn't notice him make a point of speaking to him in the hallways.

Moving around the building, he feels at home. The fluency, the easiness he couldn't counterfeit on arriving is suddenly more attainable. He tries to live his new role. He wakes and irons his shirts carefully in the long summer dawns. He buys more ties. He walks from the Tube along quiet streets, past the rumbling street-cleaning vehicles as they brush and scrub and leave their mollusc trails through the gutters. He lets himself into the building. He's memorized all the codes. He is gaining a sense of possession over the place. He knows the names of all the cleaners.

Martin manages the work on the catalogue, promoted over the senior Russian specialist, Galina, who takes little care to hide her displeasure. "I suppose there are some advantages," she said, when Julian called her and Martin into his offices to explain their roles in organizing the sale. She looked sideways at Martin, "I suppose he offers a nonexpert perspective."

It stung at the time, but Martin understands Galina's position. He isn't, as she'd have it, totally ignorant about the Russian works they will be selling, but he doesn't speak the language as she does, doesn't have the grounding in the histories of the works she has. He is where he is because of luck, because of knowing the right people. (Though, he tells himself, he still negotiated his way to acquire the paintings, still made hard choices in his pursuit of them.)

Galina is a petite, dark-haired woman, a decade older than Martin. Her manner is firm, but there is a degree of play in this firmness. She fixes her gray eyes on him when making her objections, when ranting about his ignorance. Now he has started embracing her criticisms, trying to make a game of them. She reads a draft of text about Malevich, in which Martin writes about the painter's arrest by the secret police and discusses the leveraging of artistic truth against authority. "It's overdone," she says. She takes off her glasses and looks at him. "The same old story of Russian tyranny and resistance, right?"

"Is that so totally wrong?" he asks.

"For you, Russia is just an imaginary romantic place. A place of madness and intensity."

"And what is it?"

She smiles. "A place like any other, of course."

GALINA IS doing the work of chasing down the details of Oleg's Russian paintings. She flies to Moscow, to seek out confirmation of Oleg's acquisition of the Malevich picture, and to consult a couple of experts about the picture's history. Oleg bought it from the estate of a man who acquired the picture from a student of the artist. Galina works to verify this.

She returns with binders of documents, triumphant.

"You got the confirmations?" Martin says.

He has been moved to a desk next to the door of Julian's office. Galina sits facing him from the next row in the open-plan layout. Now she leans sideways to look past her computer monitor. "I did indeed," she says. She rises from her seat and approaches. She pulls out a vacant chair to sit close to him. "It all checks out. I got confirmation of the Malevich sale from the businessman's widow."

"Yeah?"

"And also the confirmation that the man bought the picture from a student of Malevich's."

"Right."

"An absolute bargain, of course. Back in the early nineties, when people needed money, when the market hadn't developed. Now the man's thirty-five heirs have lawyers, and are seeking their inheritance, but this was different. The old woman, Malevich's student, had hidden the painting away. She was protecting his legacy, she felt. She thought he wasn't fairly appreciated. Until one day, someone found her and asked to buy this picture. I'm sure this woman didn't get what the work merited."

"Sad," says Martin.

Galina nods. "This student was very old. A painter herself. Not bad, actually. Also, the man who bought the painting was quite famous." Martin notices that she speaks quietly. This is why she has moved close to him, he supposes. "Or maybe *notorious*," she says. "He was very flamboyant and very rich."

"Yes."

"He made his money in mining. They say he made some enemies. That was a wild industry in the nineties."

"I've heard."

"Anyway, he had a car accident driving back from his dacha. It was a winter day, a deserted road."

"An accident?"

"Ice, the police said. It could have happened."

"But you're saying . . ."

"I'm not saying anything."

"Okay."

"Our client, Mr. Gorelov, acquired a great deal of the man's property after this event. Not just the painting, but the mining interests. He bought it all from the widow."

"I see."

"People have suspicions."

"Yes. I think I understand."

"Do you? I don't." She closes her eyes for a moment and then straightens up and looks at Martin.

"What do I do with that?" he says.

"I just thought you should know." Galina smiles. "You're the boss on this. I thought you should know that people talk about these things."

"Did the widow say anything about our client?"

"She signed some documents. She confirmed the sale. Maybe she's not a big fan of Mr. Gorelov, but it seems they reached an agreement."

"Right," says Martin. He thinks of sitting outside the café with Thomas in Italy. The nausea of the boat and then the nausea of Thomas bragging about the crooked men he worked on behalf of. *You're no better,* Thomas had suggested to Martin, more or less, and yet Martin had thought of Oleg and thought, *He's not perfect, but . . .*

"You look like you've seen a ghost."

Oleg could have done it, Martin thinks. He has known this. The man's manner, the man's firmness tells him this. He has not wanted to contemplate this. Galina is looking at Martin wonderingly. He looks at the papers on his desk, tries to collect himself. "It's just that I didn't know that this is the kind of man we're dealing with."

"This is speculation," she says.

"Right."

"There is always this kind of gossip. Perhaps he did nothing."

"Right. But perhaps not. I mean, if he did that, doesn't that mean he's dangerous?"

She smiles at him. "This was a long time ago." She winks. "In a country far, far away, as you would have it."

He smiles as best he can. "Yes. Of course."

"And anyway, we're not his enemies. What have we done to antagonize him? We're on his side. We're helping him make a lot of money, are we not?"

40

MARINA COMES back to the country house after a week working in London to find the bedroom filthy. Her husband has stopped letting staff into the room. There is a mound of dirty clothes by the window. There are eight glasses on the bedside table.

"What's the plan?" she asks her husband.

"Security," he says. "You can't understand how sensitive this moment is."

"Who'll clean our bathroom?" she says.

"I will."

"You'll run for president of a superpower and clean your own toilet?"

He nods solemnly. He is gaining weight again, she thinks.

"This isn't a joke, Marinka."

"Believe me," she says, "I find it distinctly unfunny."

SHE GOES to the bathroom to brush her teeth and wash her face. When she returns to the bedroom, he is sitting in bed, staring at nothing. She closes the curtains, she gets into bed next to him. He smells sweaty. He has the fusty odor of an old man.

He says, "There's a TV crew coming next week."

"What?"

"American TV. For publicity. It helps my campaign."

"You're not campaigning to be president of America."

He winces. "We discussed this. My reputation abroad will protect me in Russia."

Marina lies back in bed, looks at the details of the ceiling rose: the little fruits and flowers carved in plaster.

"One idea of Waterforth's is that maybe we can involve you a little."

"Sorry?"

"You work. You are articulate. You are a modern woman. It's all very relatable."

She doesn't say anything.

He says, "Perhaps they could even go to your office? Film you there?"

What blindness does he suffer in order to suggest this idea? At how many points could he have stopped and considered her possible objections? He is looking at her, lying propped on his elbow, waiting for her answer. She didn't want him to begin this project for all its impact on her life, and yet now he thinks she will do his PR? She feels ill.

He doesn't see her. He doesn't see her even a little bit. The first she knew him, she felt so closely seen, and yet he was attending only to his own reflection in her eyes.

She says, "I'm not doing that."

"I just thought—"

"I'm not."

He looks at her with an incredulity that makes her furious, that makes her want to do something utterly drastic. She pauses, thinks. "I'm fucking Martin," she says. "Or I *was* fucking Martin until quite recently." She wanted to know what it felt like to say it to her husband, and there it is. A feeling like riding and going over a jump blind, wondering whether the horse will find its footing on the other side.

"Martin?" Oleg says.

"Yes."

He seems to be working out some equation in his head. He says, "Of course, I was aware of this."

"Sorry?"

"Yes," he says.

"You were aware, and you didn't say anything?"

"We're grown-ups, Marinka. You think I've always been faithful myself?" He takes one of the glasses of water from the bedside table and drinks. His face is red. A vein stands out in a zigzag at his left temple. She doesn't believe him, doesn't believe in this deflection of his. And with this comes a sinking realization she didn't anticipate: he is keener to show himself knowing than admit a moment of hurt, or concede that he cares about her fidelity. He regards her. He says, "We're all flawed creatures, my darling." He lies back in the bed.

You are not allowed to do this, she wants to say. She doesn't want him furious, exactly, but she wants something other than this.

HE FALLS asleep. He snores. Since he's become heavier in these weeks of hanging around the house, plotting, his snoring is worse. It builds until a point at which he seems to have stopped breathing, after which comes a choking sound, and then the spluttering return of a normal, quieter breathing pattern; the restarting of the cycle.

She stands and dresses in tracksuit trousers and a T-shirt. She descends the stairs, slips out the back door onto the rear lawn. She circles the house in the moonlight, her eyes adjusting. It is like being at boarding school again. She half-expects to find Jane behind a bush with a menthol cigarette between her lips.

She walks to the lower wall line and looks out at the farmland beyond. There are cows in the field, clustered under some bushes near the far fence.

She hears an exhalation and experiences an animal certainty that it was a sound made by a human being. She turns back to the house, her pulse jumping, and sees that walking across the lawn is a man. She takes a moment to realize that it is her bodyguard, Chris. The house behind is lit white in the moonlight. "Fucking hell," she says. "You scared me."

He says something quietly into his two-way radio. He says, "I'm going to need to follow you if you're going to be walking around out here."

41

HEAT AS Martin drives out of the city. Hot concrete and people out in T-shirts and shorts. The parks and green spaces dry and trees within them full-leafed and heaving in the warm winds. People are dining al fresco, and drinking, of course, packing the pubs though it's barely past noon on Saturday.

The motorway, when he reaches it, is jammed with the vehicles of people seeking to escape the capital. Traffic creeps, stops, moves again. Out in the countryside, he drives through stone-built villages, past war memorials and quiet churchyards. A cricket game, even: an elderly bowler lopes across the field as Martin passes by. Wind turbines turn patiently on the ridgeline.

It is as if the sunny day ends at Oleg's gate, however. Not the heat itself, because the air is still warm, but the hysteria of it all: the sense the rest of Britain seems to have that this is all wonderfully too much.

A suited security guard walks across the gravel to greet Martin and to scan him with a small metal detector. "We have enhanced security procedures," the man says.

Martin is led by the man into the house, into the tang of artificially cooled air. He ascends the broad stairs, up through pockets of heat on the landings. A fly buzzes against the tall stained-glass window that overlooks the staircase The security man directs Martin to a living room. "Mr. Gorelov will see you soon," he says. He departs.

One of Oleg's house staff brings Martin a cup of tea, and Martin holds and sips it and listens to the complicated quiet of the old house:

creaks of movement in rooms above, the shifting of trees outside, the gravel crunching under the tread of the security men.

The day has dimmed a little when Oleg finally enters the living room. Outside there are shadows on the hills. Martin has drunk three cups of tea. The oligarch wears a navy-blue suit with burgundy tasseled loafers. His shirt collar is open. He looks tired but purposeful. Martin notes that he's trimmed his beard. "I'm sorry," he says. He waves his hand at the door through which he has just entered. "We have many things to do right now."

"With the political campaign?"

"Naturally," he says. He takes a seat in an armchair facing Martin. He waits for Martin to speak.

Martin takes out the draft pages of the sale catalogue. "We've discussed these with Lord Waterforth," he says. "Things are coming together nicely. We just want to check whether you wish to have any input." He slides the papers across the coffee table.

Oleg looks at the pages. He says, "Fine. No problems for me. Maybe you make my foundation logo bigger here?"

"I'm sure we can manage that."

The oligarch nods. He is eager to be done with this, Martin thinks. The placid lack of interest chafes Martin a little. They are preparing a grand sale to flatter this man. They're being tactful and discreet. "We completed the provenance research," he says.

"It was as I said," says Oleg. "Am I right?"

"Of course," says Martin. "It was interesting."

"Yes?"

"Galina, my colleague, verified your purchase of the picture."

Oleg nods coolly.

Martin feels irritated, he realizes, vexed enough to press the specifics, to ask a little more of the man's attention. "You bought it from a competitor's widow?" he says.

Oleg glowers. "Competitor? I wouldn't say that. I knew him. He was a businessman. She confirmed this, did she not?"

"Yes."

Oleg leans forward from the armchair. His heavy hands grip his knees. He says, "It was an accident, you know."

"The car crash?"

Oleg suddenly looks furious. "Who is talking about the car crash?" He catches himself. He goes to the window. When he turns back, his eyes are focused fiercely on Martin. He sits again. He rubs his hands together and grimaces. "The paintings," he says. "*That* was what I was talking about." He exhales. "They were an accident. I started collecting by mistake. I knew nothing about painting. I bought mining interests. I bought some pieces of furniture. I saw the *Supremus* picture. I was interested. I thought, *Why not?*"

"I see."

"And yet you want to speculate about the car crash—"

"I misunderstood."

Oleg's steady glare is terrible. Martin wouldn't have thought Oleg would care so much about what Martin thinks of him. Yet that is, of course, the way men like Oleg work. Martin thinks of Marina speaking of the Peter Doig painting of the Ping-Pong playing man. They let nothing go, she'd said. Martin's pulse is jumping in his neck. He realizes that his jaw is clenched. The oligarch flashes his eyes. "I warned him, in fact. I knew that there were some people with plans against him. I warned him but he didn't act."

Martin nods silently.

"Maybe I could have protected the man better, but he could have protected himself." He shrugs. He looks Martin in the eye. "To stay silent is not the same as to do."

"I didn't mean . . ." says Martin. "It's not my intention to ask questions of you."

"But you suspect me?"

Why did I not just go? Martin wonders. Why didn't he take the oligarch's first assent to the catalogue and leave? He says, "You've been nothing but kind to me."

"But you still think, maybe this man is a gangster. I know how this is. You cannot come through a life like mine without mistakes."

Martin gestures at the papers on the coffee table. "I just want to help you with this sale."

"Is that right?" says Oleg. He fixes his eyes on Martin. "I know you fucked my wife, by the way."

Briefly, Martin feels he will dissolve. He is barely there, yet then he is lurchingly *too* present, stifled by the dry, warm room, gripping the arms of the chair he sits in with sweaty hands, his head throbbing. His heart is fluttering, and then a strange calm thought in the midst of this: this is another thing he has been waiting for. This is the *worst thing*. It is happening and there is nothing he can do, and the firmness of this fact is a sort of comfort. *It is over,* Martin thinks. It will soon be over. The thought has a certain attraction.

The oligarch's big hands clasp and unclasp, yet otherwise he is very still, and looking keenly at Martin. He is tracking Martin's expression closely. An odd little smile appears on his thick lips in response to what he sees. He has gained the balance of control again. "Maybe you think that I am a gangster, but I know you fucked my wife. I know you fucked my wife and yet I sit here talking to you like a civilized man. Is that what a gangster would do?"

Eventually, Martin manages to say, "I don't think so." His mouth is dry.

Oleg nods. "I just thought you should know that I know."

"I'm sorry."

"I suspected it. I am busy. Preoccupied. A little adventure for her." Oleg waits, looks at Martin. "Lucky for you, I am very reasonable. Civilized. It was just a little thing, yes?"

The silence of the room again. The great long summer day between them. The man is waiting, and Martin speaks in reaction, as he so often speaks. He says, "Yes." Though he now thinks, as he says it, that it wasn't so necessarily a little thing. It was a risk. He suspected that this reckoning was coming. He thinks of the morning in Switzerland, when he sat at the mirror in her hotel room, preparing to leave, and Marina arrived behind him to touch his back, and the feeling of that, of turning to see her, some sense of recovering something, of recognition of an old affection, the blessing of seeing qualities in a person that others miss. He stood and they kissed, and then they went on with their days, and he never thought, even then, that it would last, but it wasn't unimportant.

Oleg's expression is greedy. The expression, Martin thinks, with which the man ate in that restaurant in Switzerland, before all of this. He nods and smiles, and Martin feels that Oleg has gained something from him. He knows Martin is lying, yet Martin senses he wanted the lie, the false fearful denial, and the humiliation it implies.

Martin can hear the faint sound of a dog barking outside. Oleg still looks at him steadily. Then Oleg stands. He puts his hands on his knees as he rises from the chair. He exhales through his nose. Martin stands too. He waits for everything to break. And yet, Oleg puts out his hand to shake. "The catalogue is good. I will draft my statement for it."

The realization takes a moment to settle. Oleg is giving him the sale still. Just like that. Despite all this. *Or because,* Martin thinks. Oleg grips his hand firmly, looks at Martin with narrowed eyes and a grin. There is something Martin has given for this, he thinks, something he has handed to the man without a moment of negotiation.

42

THE WEATHER is an accomplice to the deceptions of memory. On the afternoon of the farewell party at Huntley Hall, Martin drives the last ten miles along winding country roads with the windows fully open, feeling ecstatic to be back in this landscape. It's August. The blackberries are plumping out in the hedgerows, weighing down thorny tendrils that swing like the arms of some green crowd lining the edges of the lanes. He follows the tree-lined driveway to the house. There are cars parked on the lower lawn, tire tracks indented in the yellowy summer grass. He finds a space there. He ascends the steps between flower borders, onto the main lawn on which people stand around with drinks, many familiar faces amongst those that turn to note Martin's arrival. He looks at the house and can't help but think of Oleg and Marina's mansion and feel a stab of regret. Up on the lawn, several children are playing in a paddling pool, kicking water, squealing. He was one of those children once. It's hard to hold in mind that days here were not always like this: the skies so clear, the air so warm, the breeze rising up the valley, a distant tractor baling hay, moving across parched fields with the steadiness of a model train.

It's all going: the house behind this crowd, their easy way of being in this place. The face of the house looks lighter in the brilliant sunlight. The windows have been cleaned.

Carol, one of the old residents of the place—moved now, Martin seems to recall, to a cottage in Cornwall—comes over to him first.

"Look at you," she says. She shakes her head, smiling, adding nothing more, as if the change in him is beyond the need for remarking.

"You look well," he says. "It's great to see you."

"Your mother," she says. She exhales. She gestures toward the drinks table. "Your mother has done a wonderful job with all this."

And she has. Martin's mum emerges from the crowd and approaches him with her arms spread wide. "We were worried you weren't coming," she says. She beams.

He embraces her. "I'm only half an hour late," he says.

She steps back, looks at him with a smile. "We're counting down in minutes now."

Martin's dad ambles over wearing his Crocs, his baggy Pink Floyd T-shirt. "It was only an interlude," he says, "letting a rabble like us live in a place like this."

"I hope Mr. Donk likes it," says Martin's mother. Louis Van de Donk is the name of the retail magnate who has bought the house.

"He damn well better," says Martin's dad.

Martin's mother puts her hand over her mouth, takes a moment. "Let's not start. Let's not be serious. I'll start weeping. There'll be speeches later. There'll be time for that." She looks at Martin. "Drink?"

"Sure."

"We must all get irresponsibly drunk," says Martin's dad.

They do so, slowly, as the day cools. The children kick a football. The adults circulate and talk. At some point, someone lights up the barbecue. Many people remark to Martin how he has grown, become so mature, so smart. There are stories told for no one but for the sake of their telling: punch lines and denouements so familiar they can be sung out by the assembled crowd like a chorus.

As afternoon drifts into evening, James arrives on the lawn. Martin goes over to the bar, fetches a drink, walks to James, who lingers where the terracing begins, looking over the valley toward the point at which the sun hits the easterly hills. "You've just arrived?" Martin says.

"I was here," says James. He waves his hand. "I was walking. One last look."

They stand in silence for a moment. "I'm sorry, you know," says Martin.

James raises a hand in dismissal. "You don't have to say that."

Someone calls out that the barbecue is ready. They turn without speaking and walk back to join the crowd around the table that has been set out. There are platters of blackened meat, rolls, salads. Martin recognizes people's specialties, many of which he dreaded eating as a child but which now hold a nostalgic attraction. He fills his plate and goes and sits next to his dad on the steps between flower borders. His dad recounts to him the trial of moving to the detached suburban home they have bought. "My God, that was a job!" he says.

LATER IN the evening, people move into the communal hall. There are chairs set out. There are speeches. Martin's mother talks about the house when she moved in. "I've put my hands into this earth so often," she says.

Then James comes and sits at the old upright piano. "I wrote something for today," he says.

He leans forward and begins to play, and there is something about even this simple movement that pleases Martin. He's committing to this piece, which begins haltingly, sparely, then loops and builds, gaining momentum and yet holding off resolution as it goes on. The progression is satisfying, yet there is a wistfulness in the way that the melody does not quite come home. Martin closes his eyes, opens them again. The room is totally silent. People seem to be breathing quietly in sync, drawn together by what they hear. The piece goes on until Martin is not sure how long his friend has been playing, and then the melody begins to resolve. Then there is the shock of a sudden silence and James is sitting back on the piano stool, a shy smile on his face, and everyone in the room is breaking into applause.

Martin goes out to the lawn and looks at the hills, the cooler evening light on them. His mother comes out. She smiles at him. He says,
"You've done a great job."

"It's a good party."

He means more than the party, of course, but she seems keen to
push that away.

"You're well?" she says.

"Fine."

"Your work? Your Russian man? He's tied into this war?"

"It's a mess. I don't totally understand it. Their politics is crazy."

"You take their money and their politics is ours."

He looks back at the house, cast pink in the late light. "I could say
the same about your windfall."

"Indeed, you could," she says. "We're none of us untouchable."

AS THE dark comes in, a local band arrives and begins setting up at
the front of the room. People fold the chairs away. James finds Martin
outside, smoking on the lawn. "That piece was great," Martin says.

"Thanks." James smiles. He takes a long drag on his cigarette.

"Really. I didn't know you could compose like that. What are you
going to do with it?"

James looks at him, blows smoke from his nose. "That," he says.

"Sorry?"

"That was what I was going to do with it."

"Oh. Right." James offers Martin a cigarette. He'd sometimes
smoke on nights out with James. Martin shakes his head. He remembers the bottle of gin he bought as James's birthday present, which is still
in the rental car. "I have something for you," he says. "I'll be a moment."

When Martin returns, James has started another roll-up. James
puts the cigarette between his lips and works to get the wrapping off.
"Wow," he says. "Very fancy. Thank you. I should say, I'm not drinking right now."

"Really?"

"It's been good to have a break. I don't know whether I'll start again."

"That's very impressive," says Martin.

"I'm not trying to impress anyone. I just feel better for it. I'm taking better care of myself."

"That's great."

"You should have some now, though." James holds the bottle out to Martin. "Tell me whether it's nice."

Martin finds himself some tonic on the drinks table, mixes it with the gin, which he leaves for anyone who wants it. He goes out again. "It's good," he says as he comes back to James.

James turns. "Oh yes?" he says.

"Botanical," says Martin. "Or whatever."

"Right."

"You seem good."

"Thanks. I feel good."

"How's the flat?"

"Messy as usual," says James. He smiles. "How's your work?"

"Fine," says Martin. "I might secure a decent sale soon."

"Marina's husband?"

"Yes, actually. I'm lucky. It all worked out."

"You're good at it, you know," says James. "You're not lucky. I saw you working at it all."

"You're kind. I'm not enough of a salesman. Julian, my boss, has a confidence I'll never reach."

James nods. "He's slick. I talked to him at that party you took me to. He's a piece of shit. This isn't a secret. He knows it himself, I suspect. He puts on a great performance. But people trust you. They feel they understand you. You have another kind of charm. You're not a piece of shit. Don't try to be."

"That's kind."

"It's not supposed to be kind. I'm telling you something you should know. People trust you. That's important. I always trusted you. Don't lose sight of that."

Martin goes back into the house. Trusted, he thinks. That's just like James, to bury his rebuke in a tense. But he's right, there is something gone between the two of them, though they can be civil, even kind to each other still. The band leader is calling a dance: some kind of reel. Martin moves through the hall, up the stairs. The different units are cleared out now, and he walks through them. There are silhouettes on the walls where pictures have hung, carpets with depressions where sofas and beds once stood, floorboards with dark patches over which rugs have lain for years. So many kitchens and bathrooms. Complex configurations of rooms to fit all these families into this huge house. He moves through James's old unit, goes downstairs, through the door to the house in which he grew up. It is empty, but the smell of the place remains, the smell of one's family, which one doesn't notice until one leaves. The whole house is ready to come apart again. The old doors between units—turned into closets or hidden with paneling—are ready to be reopened. In its moment of breaking up, the house seems more impressive to Martin than it ever has before. "A special place," his mother always says, and though he has often replied that he visits similar properties in the course of his work, he has always understood what she means, feels it especially tonight. They made it work, for decades and decades. He reaches the top of the stairway that leads down into the hall. The music rises up. Heat comes from the crowd. He descends and sees the dancers beneath him. They form rings. They rush together. They pull apart and stamp. They rush together again. Martin pauses on the stairs and watches this: the circles spinning, halting, spinning. People he has lived with, known all his life, hurtle over the floor. They all speed up. Circles breaking. Catches in the pattern. A joyous falling into raggedness as the pace increases. Why has he not joined in with this dance? James is down there amidst the other faces, young and old. The dance stops, and Martin comes down the stairs to be among them. They are all panting and flushed. They smile past him at each other.

43

IT'S A Saturday morning, and Oleg is working and Marina is not. She wakes and walks the dogs and stops at the slope at the bottom of the garden and smokes a joint. She can smell manure on the air. The day is neither warm nor cold. The clouds scud across the sky. The dogs pad around, occasionally requesting with sad moans that she throw a tennis ball for them. She could go riding this morning, but she can't summon the impetus. She puts a hand in her jacket pocket to find that she's left the tennis ball up at the house. The dogs both watch the empty hand as she withdraws it from the pocket, expecting a little trick on her part. She goes over to the trees and picks a stick and throws that, but Gena merely trots over to it and sniffs it before turning away in dismay. Leo, the other dog, flops to the grass and looks at her with tired hooded eyes.

Chris is standing fifty yards away monitoring her and then scanning the horizon. She nods at him when she sets off to walk back to the house.

She enters the house and the dogs scamper off into the building ahead of her. She should take off their collars and dry their paws, but as it is, the staff will catch them marking the downstairs carpets and chase after them and clean up.

The weed hasn't lifted her mood, but it has steadied things. She walks up the stairs slowly. She goes into the upstairs living room where the curtains are still closed. She presses the button to open them, and the mechanism runs with a faint squeal, revealing a more elevated aspect of the same view she just smoked and looked out at. The curtains don't stop when they're fully open, however. The mechanism sings on and they begin to close again. When they've drawn themselves, they start to draw apart again. She goes back to the switch by the door and toggles it, to no effect. She stands in the room and watches this opening and closing curtain for a while. People think that wealth should insulate one from dysfunction, but actually it does the opposite. "A seventeenth-century mansion with a twenty-first-century nervous system," Oleg repeated when he planned the renovation of the place. Someone had sold him this idea via those words, played to that tendency of his to be seduced by grand language.

It was supposed to be a project for their new life together: a house organized around their particular vital statistics, their interests and needs. And yet the systems don't work together. To adjust the heating is a task beyond her. The staff hate working with the software, so much of the management falls to Oleg, who takes on this duty while muttering all the while that it is all very self-explanatory.

Marina can hear her husband talking to himself when she arrives outside the heavy door of his office. "The country's change of direction is a modern tragedy," he says. He stops, says the words again varying the intonation. He has an interview with Radio Four this afternoon, and has been practicing for it since yesterday, when Waterforth visited to coach him and stroke his ego.

Marina knocks and goes straight in. "Did you know the curtains in the second-floor living room are broken?" she says.

"No."

"They won't stop opening and closing."

"Oh," he says. "It's just a bug in the system."

"Maybe the FSB has hacked into the curtain programming."

He doesn't laugh. This is their house now: a place where even the stupidest statements are thought to be spoken seriously. He says, "I think they have other priorities."

"Right."

He looks at her and says, "The country's change of direction is a modern tragedy." He smiles proudly, waits. "I have a good feeling about this interview."

"Good."

He speaks in a different register, reciting. "We all had so many ideas about liberty. We dreamed of a strong rule of law like this country. We thronged into the city to protest for these things."

Marina nods.

"What do you think?"

"Waterforth coached you in the lines."

"Yes. Why?"

"Who dreams of a strong rule of law?"

"You know what I mean."

"It sounds like jargon. People don't know what you mean by a strong rule of law."

"I mean fairness."

"Say fairness."

"Hm. This is about my grand ideas, Marinka."

"Perhaps your grand idea could be attention to the details of day-to-day life?"

"No, no," says Oleg. He closes his eyes and rubs his forehead. "Look at Putin. Putin is good at appealing to grand things. Russia is a strong country, with a long history. My cousin speaks in these terms also."

"Maybe she speaks in these terms, but she also cares what she can buy. This is your area: hard physical facts. How much is an apartment? The weekly shopping? A holiday?"

Oleg shakes his head. "One side is fighting a war, and we talk about groceries."

"Consider the effect of sanctions on domestic prices."

"One man goes to war for the motherland, and another man talks of the price of flour."

"Flour is produced domestically. Price rises will come from other goods: foreign cheeses, spices, Italian food."

"You see," he says. "You say this and I want to fall asleep."

She shrugs.

"Why do you care?" he says. "You've made it clear you don't like this project."

HE LEAVES in the car with Victor before lunch. She eats a salad alone in the dining room. She goes to her office and opens her computer and looks at a work presentation she is supposed to be refining. She can't bring herself to concentrate on it, however. She senses that things are being said about her at work. She's doing less, and because her modus operandi has always been working harder than others, this is noticed. Yet why should she be expected to do more? Because she has done so before? She has never fully escaped that school characterization of her as a robot. She has only learned to use it.

She goes onto LiveJournal and reads articles that mention her husband. She looks at his mentions on Twitter. People generally don't like him. Why is he submitting himself to this? Why is everyone letting him? She is resolved to give his project no time at all, but instead she devotes her afternoon to its consideration. At three, his radio interview is due to start, and she connects to the Internet stream. Oleg's voice booms through the speakers of her office.

The questions are soft. The interviewer treats him with deference, and Marina wonders whether the woman feels impressed in the same way she herself once did on encountering Oleg: this big man, this bodily instantiation of so much wealth and power, who can still hold your gaze with sincerity, who can make you feel when he turns toward you that the world itself is turning your way.

He says, "Politics is not a choice I have made, but a choice that has been thrust upon me. If not me, who?"

"There's no one else standing up against the government?" says the interviewer.

"Plenty of good people," says Oleg. "But no one so relentless as me."

The interviewer laughs, and Marina feels sure that the woman is half in love with her husband, even surer that he intends this result.

He sounds more Russian than he does at home, Marina thinks. Though perhaps she hears him with different ears as he is broadcast out across the country, to the homes of her colleagues, to people she knew at school. He says, "People wanted freedom, but they do not have freedom. They have a government that goes to war and lies about that war. People wanted the rule of law, but where is that?"

"Some might say that you made your fortune avoiding the law."

Oleg clucks his tongue. "When I made my fortune," he says, "there was no law, pretty much."

"Right," says the interviewer. Marina can sense her leaving space for Oleg to clarify what he says. He only says, "We need a consistent law, like you have here in Great Britain."

"Yes, of course."

"I'm a straightforward man," he says, "with a straightforward aim."

SHE TAKES the dogs out and smokes again. She sits in the kitchen and eats carrots with hummus and watches a nature documentary about penguins.

In the early evening, she hears the gravel popping on the drive outside the house, the engine of a car puttering and cutting off.

Her husband comes in and treads heavily through the downstairs rooms. The penguin documentary is finished, and now Marina watches a program about orca whales. The footage of them underwater makes the hairs on her neck stand up: the dark arctic sea and these creatures slipping through the terrible lightless depths. She dips a carrot, chews. She hears her husband enter the room, but doesn't turn.

"There you are!" he says. "What did you think?" He assumes so readily that she listened to it, she thinks. But then, she did.

"It was good," she says. He has his tie off, his shirt collar open. He looks happy.

"Look," he says. "I know it wasn't perfect. A lot of it was—well—quite vague, frankly."

"Yes," she says. She wonders about joining him in his critique. There is something there, at least, some self-awareness in his understanding that it wasn't perfect.

The phone rings, and he turns away to answer it. It'll be Waterforth, she thinks. Her husband listens for a long time, and then he says, "Look. I think we need to focus on the details of people's lives. We must show I am in touch. Not so abstract, don't you think?" He rings off. He walks back to where Marina sits at the counter. On the screen of the kitchen TV a whale is cresting out of the sea in delicious slow motion, drops of water falling around it like shattered safety glass.

"You're taking my advice," she says.

He looks at her in brief confusion.

"I suggested you be more specific this morning."

"I suppose you did," he says.

"I did."

"I'd thought this for a while also," he says. "Waterforth's slogans are not incisive."

"You argued against this view this morning."

"No," he says. "You misunderstand."

"Do I?"

She has to stop herself. She can't argue. Shouldn't. This is the way to madness. He looks at her across the kitchen island, his arms crossed loosely. He believes what he is saying. He has no doubt about what he just said. That loop of self-creation and confidence. That weird, insidious madness that runs inside him. What use is anger against this? He has reordered the world, turned her insight to his. And she shouldn't be surprised, though he has never switched things around so quickly before.

He says, "People need to eat. They care about the details of their lives."

She thinks, *I'm a fool.*

• • •

IN THE bedroom, she packs some things into a suitcase.

He has always been like this, of course, and yet she let herself think for a time that he was different. She didn't believe that she could change him, necessarily, but she thought that he might be softened with age and circumstance. Yet if he has a true nature, it is this. He is a man alive only in his own power. When her father died, she looked back at the event like a historical war: a moment that shaded all that had happened before it, that she felt herself blind to have not anticipated, the question not *how* but *how did I not see it coming?* All she did prior to that, innocently, felt like delusion in retrospect. It is similar to recall her earlier life with her husband, her decision to join her life to his. He bends the gravity of the world around him, and yet—what?—she thought she could stay balanced next to that?

She goes downstairs and knocks on Oleg's office door. He's inside, talking on the phone. She pushes it open. He places a hand over the receiver. *Waterforth,* he mouths.

She says, "This is important."

He says, "I have to go." There must be something he reads in her expression, at least. There is a sudden acute attention in the way he looks at her that she almost wants to surrender to, because it would be easier, because maybe she wants still to believe him. He leans forward over his desk.

She says, "I'm going to London, then I'm going to go somewhere else."

He looks at her for a long time. He seems to be making a calculation. He says, "I'm sorry, Marinka. I don't have the energy for a fight right now."

She says, "I don't want a fight."

He offers the smallest shrug. His face is hard to read. She has an impulse to test this façade, and yet she will break herself, can feel a pressure behind her eyes. He can close himself off in moments like this in a way that she cannot. She says, "I don't do this lightly, you understand."

He nods, neutrally. He has a poise she can't bear. What self-degradation, she thinks, to have submitted herself to this. She turns and closes the door behind her. She walks down the stairs. She asks Victor to ready the car and drive her into the city. When she goes out to the waiting vehicle it's dark; only the upstairs living room of all the rooms in the front of the building is lit, and the curtains of the room are still opening and closing: a single eye winking as the Bentley draws away.

44

HE SITS for a long time after Marina has departed. He sits because he can think of nothing else to do, and because he needs to convince himself of the logic of his own immobility, of how futile it would have been to have risen and tried to call her back.

He was too late to this. He didn't see it. He suspected he was losing her, but not the rate, not the sudden irreversibility of it.

He is heavy-sick with the shock of not having foreseen.

This is not him. He is not the kind of man to be so suddenly surprised.

And yet, it seems, he is.

The affair, and now this.

He takes off his blazer, undoes the cuffs of his shirt. He massages his hands together, tries to think. She has not understood what he is doing. He has not been able to make her see.

HIS MIDLIFE crisis was inverted. He reached his midforties, and he felt his life to be so flimsy. He wanted solid things. He wanted to live in a house with someone who didn't always expect an apology. He had been fucking his personal trainer, Stephanie, who was staggeringly stupid and fearfully flexible. Katya found out, of course, because he hadn't ever liked going to the gym and suddenly he was going nearly every night. There had been others before: waitresses and staff and for a time the woman who had been tutoring Alexi in history. And yet this time things were different. They were done even with fighting about such things. He and Katya had an odd second-order fight, about their apathy, about the resigned, intimate way that they hated each other. They were blind to any possibility but disappointment. Once they had been young and naïve and thrilled by the simple promise of a large house and a full refrigerator, and then they gained more money than they could ever spend and it seemed that this limitlessness confirmed only their lack of imagination, their personal faults and myopias, their propensity to act predictably in the eyes of the other. He felt that success had made him brittle. He walked around his grand houses and the staff all knew exactly what he liked—the temperature, the music, the drinks on hand. And he accepted all this, felt himself solved like a human equation. Marina, when he met her, seemed like someone who could see him newly. She looked through the fortune and the reputation. She considered the possibility that he might not truly know himself. She alerted him to his own qualities, his own potential. She let him know his capacity for change, his ability to be more than just a man of great wealth.

The first thing he said to her was that he wasn't an easy man to be married to, and yet she had married him. She altered things totally. She has brought him back to life, but she doesn't seem to want to live with the man she revived. Maybe she will see in time, he thinks. The history of this, the magnitude of what he is trying to do. He is half-crazy, he knows, yet this half-craziness is *him*, the real man she reinvigorated.

There's a knock at the door, and he feels his heart juddering. "Yes," he says. He waits.

It's just Calum, though, who enters and looks at him strangely. "Dinner will be ready in ten minutes," Calum says.

"Ten minutes?" says Oleg.

"You said seven thirty, earlier. The salmon."

"I know what I said."

"Oh," says Calum. "I'm sorry."

Calum is still waiting. "What else?" says Oleg.

"Will Mrs. Gorelova be eating?"

"No." Oleg casts his hand out toward the corridor. "Do you see her here?"

"I just thought she might return."

Oleg snorts. "Please limit your speculation."

"I'm sorry, sir."

Oleg waves a hand.

"In the dining room?"

"What?"

"You'd like to be served in the dining room?"

"Of course."

"I'm sorry." Calum speaks while his own eyes display the knowledge that he should not be speaking. "It's just sometimes Mrs. Gorelova dines in the kitchen when she's alone."

"Go and get Stacy."

"She's on her break."

"Now!"

"Okay."

"And then go home. I don't want to see you ever again." A flash of satisfaction saying that, watching the boy turn and close the door behind him.

But he should stop the boy. He gets up from the desk. He lumbers to the door, opens it, looks down the hall, which is empty. He strains to hear Calum's footsteps, but the boy has gone. He walks back into the office and sits down again behind the desk.

He thinks then of Marina and the other boy, Martin. He imagines Martin with his top off. The boy lacks depth, of course, lacks definition. What can that boy have given her? He is not brave, not composed. The boy was only a distraction, he tells himself. He closes his eyes, tries to reset.

The phone on the desk rings. Waterforth's voice speaks. "Well," he says. "To resume where we left off. Your proposal for a change of direction . . ."

"Oh. Yes."

"I've been considering it, and I really think it's a great idea." Water-forth exhales happily. "You have great instincts, you know. You are a natural."

Oleg should make his excuses—tell Waterforth that now is not the time—and ring off. But he doesn't. He should stop this brittle flattery. And yet—well—it is here, within reach, like a glass of red wine poured out and set in front of him. He feels that he needs it, and while he knows he shouldn't, he allows himself to take it. He says, "I did think it was a good idea."

"Oh, my friend," Waterforth almost purrs. He is at his best, the ham actor of himself. "Really, honestly, I think that you were born for this."

45

THEY'RE HANGING the sale. The pictures are going up: these are works that Martin has been writing about for months now. Porters pace through the rooms moving packing crates. A woman walks toward a crate with an electric drill. She's new, just out of university or the Courtauld, fresh to this as Martin once was. "You're not going to open the box with that, I hope," he says.

She looks at him with concern. She looks at the drill, at the Phillips fitting in the chuck.

"Use a manual screwdriver," Martin says more softly, "when you're opening a box with a work inside."

She looks crestfallen. "Yes. Of course."

"It's okay. You can't know if you haven't been told."

Martin is looking for the woman's supervisor when Julian appears. "Come and see this," he says. He leads Martin to the front room. Four men are lifting a picture from its packing.

Martin sees a flash of the canvas, a glimpse of the old paint, slightly cracked and crazed. The *Supremus.* The colors of those shapes, lost to scholars of Malevich until now. "It's like raising the dead," says Julian. "I always say it, but it is."

THAT NIGHT, there's a meal for an old hand, Burt, who is retiring. Forty members of staff gather in the upstairs room of an old bistro. "We'd give you a carriage clock," says Julian. "But you'd only raise doubts as to its value." He smiles and accepts the laughter of the room.

Burt makes his own speech. He's a short man. His thinning gray hair is set in a side parting. He wears thick glasses and a brown tweed suit. He says, "When I started here, nearly sixty years ago, they still paid a 'gentleman's salary.' That is, a trifling symbolic sum, calculated on the assumption that the recipient didn't really need the money." He takes off his glasses and cleans the lenses with a handkerchief, puts them back on. "I'd love to say that everything has changed. . . ." The diners laugh and tap on the table in appreciation. People like all these old stories of the place, tales of the persistence of its virtues and problems. Everyone listens rapt as Burt talks about his days at the front desk, and of the men as old then as he is now, who could recall selling the treasures of great estates at the start of the twentieth century. "Hunched old men from the works of Charles Dickens," he says. "I knew nothing. I was ignorant beyond belief, but they tolerated me. I was given the chance to learn. I've valued works from lords and dukes and princes. Pop stars, even. I've been into all the most beautiful and— believe me—the most tasteless houses in this country. And what have I learned?" He pauses again to clean his glasses. "That there are treasures out there. Despite what you may hear, we are a blessed people. Ours is a nation full of the most exquisite riches. I wish you all as much happiness seeking them out as I have enjoyed."

Martin thinks of what Galina told him of Oleg acquiring his Malevich canvas. The old student of the artist himself. The icy road. The accident. Oleg's angry denials.

There are coffees and liqueurs brought in then. Everyone is getting drunk and nostalgic. Returning from the bathroom, Martin hears snippets spoken about those who worked at the house before he arrived:

"She smoked at least a couple of cigarettes while she bicycled to work."

"His father was a terrible gambler, you see, and the first he knew that the old man had sold the family silverware was when a chap brought it in to be valued."

"What a spectacular bastard Terry was! He grew up in India with lots of servants, and I think that spoiled him."

AFTERWARD, MARTIN has to go back to the office to fetch his bag. Julian, returning also, walks with him. "What a lot of nonsense," he says. There is a looseness to Julian's words. He's a little drunk, as is Martin.

"The speech was good," says Martin. "The lamb was good."

"Overdone. To be honest, I prefer more blood," says Julian. He swings his keys around his finger. "And the job wasn't noble then, and it isn't noble now. There's no use getting sentimental about it."

They greet the security guards. They go in, up the back way to the offices.

"Let's take another look at the gallery," says Julian. He goes to the door, taps his code, deactivates the alarm. He turns on the lights and they move through the rooms. "You really pulled it off, you know," he says. He slaps Martin's back.

"Thanks."

They walk past the pictures: the Freud, the Richter, the Basquiat that was sold by the house only a year before. "The man has taste," says Julian. He pauses in front of the three Bacon heads.

Martin halts with him. "Do you ever worry about the background of these people?"

"These people?"

"Oleg."

Julian moves toward the pictures, steps back again. "Galina's report on the provenance was good."

"Of course. But there are rumors about how he acquired the pictures, even if the lineage is traceable."

"I wouldn't recommend that you worry about whether these

people are *nice*." Julian laughs. "Do the staff at McDonald's worry about who they sell their burgers to?"

"He's going to do well out of this."

Julian gives an amused sigh. "In six months you won't be able to pick Mr. Gorelov's face out of a crowd." He gestures at the paintings. "You won't forget these for the rest of your life, though."

46

HE SITS at the desk. The desk is three hundred years old. He bought it at great expense. It smells of dust and wax and just a hint of the insecticide the furniture specialist applied to keep it free of woodworm. What things have been written and thought here? he wonders. What plans have been hatched behind this desk? The desk will outlast him. This idea makes him strangely melancholy. To the desk, he supposes, he is already a ghost.

He looks out of the window. The sun is out. He has a meeting with a contact of Malcolm's later in the day. He doesn't know the subject of the meeting, but whatever it is is sensitive. Malcolm came straight to Oleg, cut Waterforth out of the loop. This doesn't dismay Oleg. Waterforth has seemed too timid recently.

The meeting, in fact, is a nice distraction from the envelope Oleg received two days ago, which he opened overeagerly, hoping that it was a message from Marina, but which contained instead a photograph of a Moscow street, a tower block and a little café at its base. On the back was written "I miss you."

The picture is in the desk drawer now. He senses it in there, beneath the wood on which he rests his elbows. He knows the place exactly, knows the little café. Vasyli went there often. The *pirozhki* there were the best in town. Freshly made and cheap, apparently. Sitting at his desk, Oleg has a vision of Vasyli looming from the grave to say these words: "Freshly made and cheap." Vasyli exhibited no curiosity regarding more sophisticated delicacies. He was a greedy, childish man. It was perhaps inevitable that such a café would be where Oleg's man would catch up with Vasyli. Vasyli had employed security, but the men were not real professionals.

It was a simple, inelegant job, and yet sophistication hadn't been necessary in that era. Oleg hadn't dealt in the details, but he had asked his contact to act.

It had saddened Oleg, of course. Vasyli didn't see what Oleg had done for him. Oleg had always had a breadth of vision he lacked, yet Vasyli thought the world as he saw it was all there was. The two men couldn't work together, ultimately. Oleg was out alone, ahead.

Sometimes he thinks of Vasyli dead in the ground. The fucking idiot. Oleg went to the funeral. Maybe that is where his guilt comes from. The family knew it was him, and yet he still went. Yet Oleg really did want to mourn the man as he had known him once. They put Vasyli in the ground underneath some giant, ostentatious gravestone, like he was a gangster and not some simpleton. Vasyli had come up with precisely one intelligent notion in his whole life, and thought himself wise ever after.

There were other mistakes, of course. He thinks of Martin's questions about Grigory. The car crash. Other men initiated that one. Oleg only looked out for his interests, acquired what he could use when it was available, bought a picture that briefly felt like a salvation in itself. Men like Martin from this quiet little country cannot understand this.

Vasyli is the one who comes back to Oleg. In the churchyard, Oleg gave condolences to Vasyli's wife and his daughter. The man had hired some idiot Azerbaijanis, who let out word of their contract against Oleg before they had so much as planned a time or place. It had been straightforward enough for Oleg to hear of this, to decide to put the fool out of his misery. German had seen it years before. Vasyli had terrible judgment. And now he has been dead for over twenty years. How is it in the ground down there? What would they find were they to go to that cemetery and dig him up?

Oleg thinks of the last twenty years. Marina. This house. This tepid country. Alexi has grown and things have gotten better with the boy and Vasyli has been in the ground all this time, collapsing back into the earth, the fool.

And the photograph? Someone knows. It was never so hard to puzzle out, of course, but at the time it was easy enough to ensure the police investigation went nowhere. They couldn't convict now, surely? They couldn't link him. So many people from that era dead these days. The message of the picture is unclear anyway. Is he to understand that the accounting of that time is still ongoing? Or that such a thing as happened to Vasyli could happen to him? It's a useful ambiguity, they probably think. He gathers his resolve and pulls the photograph out of the drawer. In the picture it's an indifferent cloudy day. The café is decorated in muted colors. It looks the same all these years later as it did on the evening when Vasyli collapsed next to it in a pool of blood. Oleg had driven past a day later and it was back in business as usual. When your product is cheap, volume is everything. You must keep going. He's a businessman. He understands that.

THE MEETING happens at a horse trials. This was Malcolm's idea, and Oleg must admit it isn't bad. It's the kind of event each of them might plausibly attend. Crowds, yet also spaces. Outdoor sounds. Temporary structures. A nightmare to bug. They sit at the back of a grandstand. In front of them, some early round of the dressage. The stand is empty enough. It is dry but windy. A loose piece of canvas flapping behind them. Down at ground level, a horse is doing that funny high-stepping walk. Spanish music playing. A table of judges with their bored, drawn faces. Oleg thinks he understands the English, and then he comes to an event like this.

Marina, Oleg thinks regretfully, would be able to explain the nuances of these horse dances. The music stops, and the few people at the front of the grandstand offer a smattering of applause.

Malcolm's friend's name is David. Or, more precisely, he is called

David for this meeting, this moment. They're different from their Russian counterparts, the British spies. David sits in his seat and crosses his legs, folds his tall frame into itself. He's a thin, stretched-looking man. He has black hair with flecks of gray. He could be a waiter in a fine restaurant, Oleg thinks, with that aura of proud self-control.

Malcolm claps loudly. He is overdoing it, as usual. David says, "Do you understand my essential interest?"

"Financial gossip," says Oleg. "Malcolm has briefed me a little."

"We're preparing a new sanctions plan. The Americans are very keen now because of Ukraine, of course. It's becoming possible to tug a few threads."

"And me? What do I get?"

"I understand you have political plans?"

"I heard you weren't keen on these."

"Well, things have changed, of course."

"Of course."

"We're keen to target those close to the President. We're interested in Mr. German Bobrov. He was an acquaintance of yours?"

Oleg thinks of German, of that drafty old office of his in the cooperative days. German arriving at the tool workshop in his Swedish shoes. Moscow streets when there were so many fewer cars. The two of them walking down the road in ugly coats, their hands stuffed into their pockets. Oleg imagines himself standing, his grandstand seat flipping up behind him. He pictures himself descending the metal steps, pushing past the group of people at the rail and toward the exit. German is not simply the President's man, he could say. German is not a good man, necessarily, but not as plainly bad as David thinks. German is pragmatic, but he has a code, some things he wouldn't do, Oleg is sure.

Oleg and German lived through the nineties together—those years of chaos and double-crossing—and they came out the other side on good terms. That has to mean something.

But then, German's loyalty is directed elsewhere these days. That

was the message of their dinner together. That change in their relationship had been ongoing for a while. Oleg has felt this desertion
creeping over his skin for months. He feels so sad when he thinks of
German these days, and is this grief not a sign of something?

If you expect someone will strike, Oleg tells himself, *you must strike
yourself.*

Oleg stays sitting, and eventually he says, "I know him, yes. More
than an acquaintance, I would say."

"He has funds everywhere, from what we can ascertain."

"Oh yes. Of course."

"It's all speculative so far. We need some help working out how
things can really be traced back to him."

Now is the time to express a little concern, Oleg thinks, to stop
it rolling quite so easily on. "Excuse my language," he says. "But I am
worried about shitting in my own kitchen."

"Right. Yes. I can see that."

"Say I was securing my funds in a similar way . . ."

Malcolm is still surprisingly silent, sitting forward and watching
another dancing horse down on the rectangle of wood chippings.

"Investigating you is not a priority," says David. "I can make that
clear."

"We can make a deal?"

"Not officially," says David. He smiles: a flash of surprisingly
crooked teeth. "I'm not going to write anything down."

"Right."

"But trust me, you're not the only one hiding a bit of money away.
And you're doing it better than a lot of people we encounter, I must say."

Oleg feels a pride that he knows he shouldn't feel. David is flattering him, but David is also flattering with actual facts. The shells, the
twisted connections, the instruments. Oleg has gotten to his station
through his judgment of people, and the people who helped him set
up these things are virtuosos. They've made networks that would have
flattered Glushkov himself.

"You tell us somewhere he's put his funds and you get your own money out." David smiles. "We don't ask questions about your withdrawn investment."

There was a Spanish property company German and Oleg both invested in years ago, through London, via Belize. A whole town waiting to be built. Various incentives and kickbacks that made it all pretty profitable, though they only finished a single street of the town: a dusty avenue somewhere out in unpromising scrubland.

David looks down at the dancing horse, then back at Oleg. A picture of patience. Marinka would tell him to slow down, but Marinka is not here. It's him or German, Oleg thinks. One comes to know somehow. One must trust oneself. "He has some concerns in the property market," says Oleg.

On the wood chips the performance is concluding, and people are clapping. Malcolm hunches forward in his chair and grins and thumps his hands together.

47

HER BODY knows how to sail better than her mind does. Forgotten days of her childhood are resurrected by the way she can coil a rope, by the ease with which she walks across a pitching deck.

Marina sails under the direction of a man called Uri, in a small yacht that she bought from an old friend of Jane's. It has two cabins, a little kitchen.

"Bring the sail in," says Uri, and she gets to work. At times the activity is obliterating: the two of them scuttling over the deck, their only aim the alignment of the craft with the forces of the wind, the currents of the Mediterranean.

She quit her job so simply that she felt stupid doing so. Either this was folly, or the years before were folly. She said the ordinary things about needing to reassess, about tiredness, about perspective.

The firm gave her a small good-bye party. Lawrence, who will be taking her position, said, "I was always surprised that you didn't do this earlier." The possibility that she had been more prepared to go than she had known reassured her.

Marina and Uri sail for two days, and Marina's eyes adjust to all the colors that the ocean can be: the greens and blues and dark shadows shifting through the depths. She gets tanned. Sun is all around her, reflecting off the water, off the shiny metal fixtures of the boat. She burns the soles of her feet lying on the deck and watching the horizon. When she looks at herself in the little mirror in the small bathroom she sees that she has white patches around her eyes from wearing sunglasses. She is a new, surprised creature. On the fourth day of sailing, they reach the place.

Uri consults the GPS. "Here," he says. He drops the sea anchor.

The current turns the boat around. She looks up and sees the sparse clouds moving across the blue sky. Uri goes below. She feels what? The reflexive stuff, first of all: the sense that she *should* be feeling so much but isn't.

The coast guard found the boat here. It listed a little, a sail flapping loose. It was deserted. She has seen the photographs, studied them. The coroner spoke at length about the scene in placid jargon.

She stands and feels the boat shift with the sea, and time passes, and eventually she lets herself feel disappointment. She recalls burying the empty coffin at her father's funeral, of standing afterward and looking at the gravestone with her mother. She had a sense then that there was something more real to be done than that hollow ceremony. But maybe this isn't it. She realizes that she has held a great deal of hope for this moment, for this point on the map.

Uri comes up onto the deck and looks at her solemnly, then goes back down below. He is either very perceptive, she thinks, or dumb as a mule.

IN THE next few days, they sail on toward the Strait of Sicily. "You want to sight-see?" asks Uri in his strangely accented English. He captains boats through this part of the world often. He can play the tour guide if Marina wants (though she doesn't). These are Oleg's places, she feels. She doesn't wish to snag on all of that. They sail all day and then put down the anchor and sleep. They eat the rehydratable meals that Uri packed aboard when they departed in Spain. They speak seldom. They settle into routine.

One night they anchor off a small island in the Aeolian archipelago. The island rises from the water in craggy cliff faces that give way to steep scrub-covered hills. From where they drop anchor, there is no sign of human life, but for a ruin up near the highest point of the island and one other boat, some distance away. The busyness of the summer season has waned.

"We shouldn't strictly be here," says Uri. "It's a protected nature reserve, but no one checks this time of year."

They eat rehydratable chili con carne, and head to their bunks before ten. In the early morning, Marina is woken by a repetitive scratching noise. It sounds like the claws of a huge creature scratching against the deck. She slips out of her bunk, puts on a fleece, wraps a blanket around herself, and clambers up the companionway. Outside, she feels the grain of the treated wood that forms the cockpit floor under her bare feet, she can smell salt and iodine and a hint of the fuel of the motor. The anchorage is relatively unsheltered, and a cool wind rushes over her, grabbing at her hair. The night is moonless, nearly black. She waits, crouched, working to control her breathing, striving to really hear the sound, to fathom it. She tries to rein in an animal panic, tells herself to stand, to face and defuse her fear of the noise. She rises and is shocked, briefly, by a motion at the front of the boat. *Someone is up there,* she thinks. Yet when her eyes adjust, she sees that the jib is loose, flapping, pulling a line back and forth with its billowing. A pulley block, attached to this line, drags and rasps against the textured deck. This is the source of the noise. Yet Marina watches the block bumping and scratching and can't get a grip on the feeling of fear that climbs up her back and makes her round her shoulders. She looks out around the boat at the dark water. She feels too open to the blackness. She listens to the ghostly scratching, and behind that the lapping sea, the creaking boat, and the hissing wind. The island is a humped black silhouette. Her heart is leaping. *It's okay,* she tells herself, *there's no one there.* She has a sense of eerie weirdness, a yawning, lonely terror that she can't quite explain, which she will begin to doubt away in the morning, but which grips her for now, which she gives in to. She stays still for a long time, until the sun begins to rise from the east, cutting across the island and giving texture to the scrub, and she feels released by this new light.

The next day, they see the coast of Greece, which grows closer all afternoon. They come into Methoni at dusk. They pass the ruined fort at the head of the peninsula: the old walls of sun-beaten granite and the shallow green water beneath them, and then the new colorful jumble of the town. Marina and Uri eat that night in a taverna, on a terrace shaded by vines and paved with cracked dark tiles. They eat grilled fish and potatoes and drink tart local wine.

They sail on more slowly then. This continuation is Marina's choice (or her deferral of choice). Uri is happy, anyway. He's paid by the day. He moves about the boat with a firm economy. His salt-stiffened hair is light and wild.

THEY ROUND the most southerly point of mainland Greece. Marina sits on the cabin roof looking at the land.

"You don't want to stop?" says Uri.

"For what?"

"The Underworld." He points to the shore. "This is one of the places where the ancient Greeks believed you could enter."

"Right. I see."

"When I sail here with tour groups, we often visit. You want to?"

She chews her lip, tastes the bitter tang of sun block. This is more than they've said to each other for days, and it feels odd to form her thoughts into words. "It's not my thing," she says. "Myths. Gods. Men and their hubris. Reviving the dead . . ."

Uri smiles. "Well, what's this trip about then?"

She looks at the barren coastline, leached of color in the full sun. The gray stone lighthouse. The flat sea between. "I don't know. . . .The opposite, if anything."

Uri nods and pads back to the cockpit. They turn away from the coast, adjusting for the wind. The boat leans as the sails fill, and the bow scuds over small waves. Spray is tossed back toward Marina. If she believes in an underworld, then it is not a place in which one recognizes faces, from which stories may be recovered. It is not a place we can chart. She clambers back to Uri, and says, "What's actually there, anyway?"

"There?"

"The Underworld."

"Oh." He squints against the sun behind her. "Not much. A little temple. A small cave."

"Right." They are moving quite fast now. She enjoys the feeling. A velocity that begins to feel like flight.

"You're missing nothing, really." Uri smiles earnestly, thinking he is assuaging regrets.

"That's good to know," she says.

48

OLEG IS selecting a tie to wear to his auction in the evening when the man comes into his bedroom. At first, he thinks the man is a security guard he doesn't recognize. The man is tall and very pale and he steps around the door into the bedroom and looks at Oleg.

The man greets Oleg in Russian, and Oleg thinks, *Oh, well. Douglas thinks I want a Russian speaker. That's fine enough, though he should have cleared the idea with me and he needs to explain to this new man my boundaries. The guy can't walk right into my bedroom.*

Funny how hard it is to shift the mind from the story it has settled on. He has been feeling good this morning. He slept well. He came up with some interesting turns of phrase that he might use in describing his foundation at the auction house tonight. He let Nadja in to collect the laundry and clean the bathroom, and he thinks at first that this is where the confusion with this new man has arisen. Oleg talks in English: "Please. This space is private. I prefer you stay on the ordinary patrol route."

The man smiles widely, and Oleg wonders briefly whether the man is very stupid. The man speaks in Russian again: "I'm sure that you would."

A lurch of understanding, then. The man continues to smile as the revelation breaks. He seems to be enjoying the turn in Oleg's expression. Oleg spins and bolts toward the silent alarm next to the bed. The man follows him. He is wearing those blue plastic covers over his shoes. He wears a dark-blue shirt and a pair of black cotton trousers. "That doesn't work, of course," he says of the alarm, which Oleg has already pulled. "I've deactivated it."

"Not possible," says Oleg. He is gasping for breath now. "Only Douglas can deactivate it."

The man laughs again. He seems to be having a very pleasant time. "Yes," he says. "I suppose the company's advertising is very impressive. Not everything is totally true, though. I'm sure you understand."

Oleg doubles over and puts his hands on his knees. He breathes and stares at his feet. He expects the man to put hands on him, but the man doesn't. Oleg's breathing slows, though he can feel his heart thrashing in his chest like a landed salmon. He looks up at the man, who is waiting. The man must be seven feet tall. Oleg needs one show of composure, one moment of logical thinking. Oleg has it in him. He rises again and looks around. He seeks an opening.

The man says, "If you can think of it, we've already thought of it."

Oleg picks up a book, Tony Blair's autobiography, and hurls it at one of the windows. It flies open in the air. It flutters and slows and strikes the glass with a dull ring. The book falls onto the carpet.

"As I said," says the man.

"What are you going to do?" says Oleg.

The man shakes his head. His long nose has a notch in it, as if it has been broken before. His hair is brown and disordered, with a choppy fringe: a cheap and unbecoming cut. "You know the answer to this question," he says. There is weary disappointment creeping into his tone, as if Oleg in his resistance is being a little rude.

"We can reach an agreement," says Oleg. "I can adjust. I can make things right."

The man shakes his head with irritation. He says, "They don't send me to make agreements."

"Well, let me call them." Oleg's phone is over on the desk. Why is he only now thinking of that phone?

The man notes him glancing at the phone and steps a pace left, positioning himself between Oleg and the desk. "I can't do that," says the man. "We can't go backwards from here, believe me."

"They'll regret this."

"You know," says the man, "we've been planning this for some time. This plan has been ready for years, waiting for someone to say go. You've been a long-term project for us. Isn't that a kind of compliment?"

Oleg tries to flush the feeling of panic from his chest. He must hold this all together. He must be lucid.

"We were ready, and finally we got the call. I have to say, I was excited. It's a nice house. I'm glad we got the go-ahead to do it here. I'm glad we could make that work."

"The President?"

The man waves his hand. "He allows it, yes. But the man who is angry is the minister of defense. You fuck his property investment."

"Oh." Oleg feels the air taken out of him for a moment. "I thought . . ."

"You thought?"

"Nothing," he says. "I was confused. The President knows?"

The man smiles. "Yes. The President knows."

Oleg is making himself pitiable, he thinks.

"You're important enough," says the man. "Don't worry about that. Yours is the *deluxe* package." He isn't joking. This is a man with a trade, a pride in that trade. "I don't have to even touch you, you know."

"What?"

"If you just do what I say."

"Why would I do that?"

The man grins. He takes a phone from his pocket. He taps at the screen. He holds out the phone so Oleg can see. A video is playing. The quality is not perfect. The picture shifts. It takes Oleg some time to understand it. Some figures sit at tables. A café. Cars occasionally pass through the foreground of the shot. One of the figures, alone at

a table, leans forward and takes up a glass, and Oleg suddenly understands. The movement makes it clear to him. It's Marina.

"Go and get your phone," says the man. He gestures to the desk.
"Nothing stupid, you understand?"

Oleg grunts. He walks carefully to the desk, he picks up the phone.

"She is in danger, just to be clear," says the tall man. "If you—"

"I understand."

"Good. Send her a text."

"What?"

"Send her a text."

"Why?"

"It's live, this video." The man wants Oleg to witness his project,
to offer some reaction.

Oleg thinks of saying simply that he believes the man, but stops.
He has a chance to send a message, he thinks.

"Don't send anything without letting me see," says the man. "She's
not taking a lot of security precautions in Greece, by the way."

She's in Greece. Oleg didn't know this. He could tell the man,
work at the fact the man seems not to know the level of his estrange-
ment from Marina. Yet what would that accomplish?

He thinks. He types: I love you. Truly.

The tall man checks the message. It doesn't interest him particularly. "Fine," he says. "Send it."

Oleg presses send. The man holds his phone in front of Oleg so
he can see the video feed. After a moment, Marina picks her phone up
from the table and reads the message. She seems to be thinking. Then
she puts down her phone. She doesn't type back. The man tugs Oleg's
phone from his limp grip and throws it across the room. "You see?" he
says, smiling, too pleased. "Do you see?"

"I see." He wrote those words, and she merely noted them and
carried on.

"So, you do what I say, right?"

"Yes."

"You go where I say."

Oleg nods. The man points to the hallway. Oleg walks out of the room. He thinks of shouting out.

"There is no one to hear you," says the man, as if he has read Oleg's thoughts. "This way." Perhaps someone can only have so many thoughts in a situation like this. Perhaps we are all unoriginal when we're cornered.

Oleg thinks of Vasyli outside the café. Oleg and the tall man walk to the end of the hallway to the utility cupboard.

"How did you get in here?" says Oleg.

The man smiles again. He's happy to discuss his work, as Oleg was glad to explain the property deal that set this into motion. He opens the door of the storage cupboard. He points Oleg in. Oleg enters and the man follows, closing the door behind him.

"We have a guy. A guy on your staff whose wife is not happy here. We'll set him up. He sorted things out for us. We're both going to be giving this lady a nice life. Think about that. That's a good thing to consider. They're going somewhere warmer, away from here. We should both keep that in mind while we're doing this."

"What's this?"

The man throws Oleg one of his own belts. "You know," he says.

This is it. This certainty has come and gone in these moments. He can't quite focus. The tall man smiles and Oleg thinks of blackness. His body just a thing hanging in here. He has a vision of the hospital attendant wheeling his mother's corpse away.

"You look not so well," says the man. "Look. I'll try and make this quick." There is a stepladder on the wall. He takes it down and folds it out, gives it to Oleg. "Over by the paints," he says, pointing to the corner.

"Those aren't paints," says Oleg. "Those are varnishes." He has the sudden sense that things like this matter acutely.

"Okay," says the man. "*Varnishes.*" Oleg looks around and wonders whether there isn't something he should be trying. Could he not grab a can of varnish and bring it down into the man's skull? He feels weak. They have thought of this, he thinks. This is a plan known by the creep stalking Marina. She won't be safe until Oleg is dead. These people do not mess around.

The man is wearing gloves—silk gloves of the kind that the porters at the auction house wear while handling paintings. He indicates that Oleg should loop the belt around his neck, and Oleg does so, threading the end through the buckle, so he wears it like an ugly tie.

He can smell the leather of the belt. He has had this belt a long time, since he was a skinnier man. He has used each notch in it. He bought it in Paris with Katya, many years ago. The man points to the stepladder, and indicates that Oleg should place it down and ascend the three steps. Oleg's legs are utterly leaden, but he takes one step, then the next, then the last. When he stands on top of the little stepladder, it sways under him. He tries to prevent his legs quivering. The man looks up at him placidly. There is a bare bulb dangling from the ceiling half a meter away.

He looks around for a moment. There are a couple of mops hanging from the wall. The shelving holds spare toilet paper, candles, lightbulbs. There is a roll of carpet underlay on a shelf, next to it a clear box of curtain rings. These are the last things he will see, he tells himself. Such ugliness. He spots a shoe box and realizes that it holds the 18650 batteries he took from his old laptop months before. He had no plan for them, and here they are, never to be used now. He has been so many different men, felt himself so many different men, and yet still he has arrived here on this unsteady ladder, this end of all identities.

The man points to the beam above Oleg's head and says, "There should be a nail."

And there is, of course: a thick joinery nail driven deep into the beam. How did Oleg not hear this nail going in? Where was he? Did the man stalk through the rooms with his own hammer to tap in his own nail? Or was it here already? It doesn't matter, really. It is all flowing together now: tributaries joining a great river and pouring out into the ocean. Oleg hooks the belt to the nail as the man indicates he should. He straightens up on the ladder, and now the man's face is different, more relaxed. Oleg can imagine encountering this face on the street, thinking for not a moment about it. The man feels his task accomplished. In a few moments, hopefully, this man will call the man watching Marina and that second man will depart, leave her to that glass of wine she drinks outside that café.

And then what?

Who knows?

This has all been waiting for Oleg. This has all been coming, he tells himself. The tall man was always bound to step from behind that door, Oleg's life set to end in this dingy space. And who will know this happened? Who will not think it the suicide of a washed-out old tycoon? Marina will know, he thinks. She has understood him better than he understood himself. She foresaw this. She said, yes, that even his rebellion would lie under their control. He didn't recognize all she gave him. He should have said *thank you* in the text, he thinks. She doesn't deserve this. She was good. How did he find a woman so good at the end? The man is still looking up at Oleg. Oleg needs to hold himself together. He needs to get through this. Or not *through.* There is no *through. Concentrate,* he tells himself. She is there, in the café in the sun: he does this for her, to let her walk away from there oblivious. It's the smallest possible thing he could do for her, but he feels a slight joy to be able to do it. He senses this small satisfaction giving him strength. He tries to send her a message, out through the walls, the plaster and stone, the clear blue air, over fields and seas. She saw him, she knew him. He wants her just to understand what has happened, to under-stand that he is sorry. She has a life ahead of her. She saw something good in him. She stepped toward him. He steps himself now.

49

MARTIN IS up in the office taking a call from a collector who is running late on her way to the sale. "The lot is fifteenth, Mrs. Chatfield," he says. "I feel totally assured you will make it on time. If it looks like you won't, I'll have one of our people call you and you can bid on the phone."

Outside, it is an early autumn evening. He can see the gray rooftops of Mayfair, a little coral light from the last of the sunset in the west, beyond the buildings. Pigeons take off en masse from a ledge, like debris thrown from a slow-motion explosion. A plane moves across the darkening sky, wing lights blinking, in the direction of Heathrow. "I know it's not the same, of course, as being in the auction hall, but that's our backup should the need arise, which I'm sure it won't."

He rings off. The office is empty. A fan runs in the corner of the room, turning a slow semicircle, then halting, coming back, ruffling the papers in Martin's in-tray as it scythes by.

Martin can just make out his reflection in the window. He adjusts the collar of his shirt. He turns and walks toward the stairs.

He bought new formal shoes for the night on his credit card. He shouldn't have, as he's already doubtful of his ability to make the minimum payment at the end of the month. The shoes are bluish black, and very stiff. They pinch a little as he walks across the upper gallery. They will wear in, he thinks. They will last. They will prove an investment. He stops, lifts a foot, and rubs at his Achilles tendon where it meets the back of the shoe. He tugs his sock into place. There's the likelihood of a raise after all this, of course, though it will still take a while until he has ready money in his pocket.

He thinks, as his thoughts turn to money, of a package he received a month ago: a painting, a study for a larger work by Peter Doig. A man playing Ping-Pong, leaning too far over the table, losing himself. There was no sign of who had sent it, but he didn't need that. It sits still boxed in his small flat. He knows he will sell it. It's not just that he couldn't afford to *buy* this picture, but that he can't afford to hang such money on the wall, can't afford to not sell. Also, looking at the image twists his insides. He was making peace with the feeling that their time together was a mirage, a thing that barely happened; and then this box, this picture inside, the sense that it was, of course, more than that, and all the counterfactuals born of that awareness. There were real feelings, beneath the dissembling, the pride and confusion.

He stops at the top of the stairs, watches people entering the building, working their way into the chattering, clustering crowd of attendees. He sees Julian raising a hand to him.

He descends and moves through the crowd toward his boss, smiling and offering greetings to those he passes. "Everything is all right?" says Julian when Martin arrives at his side.

"Yes. Mrs. Chatfield should make it on time. But I've made arrangements in case she doesn't."

"Wonderful," says Julian. He grins and waves to someone who has just come through the door. "It's all going superbly, I must say. You've done so much to make this work."

"Thank you."

"At first, I just worried that you weren't our type, but you've really grown into the role. You used to be so overeager, so keen to be agreeable."

Martin thinks of Jason, the manager at the rental car location: the cheap suit, the palpable sense that the man would do anything to be liked.

"Now you've got the instinct. The right instinct. You've developed it. It's quite impressive."

"Thanks."

"We should move," says Julian. "We should do our work."

"Of course."

MARTIN SCANS the crowd before him and recognizes so many faces. It was only a year ago that Martin wouldn't have been able to definitively identify Oleg, and now he knows nearly every client. He has worked with Julian planning this event. He has met these people on their visits to the galleries, spoken to them on the phone. Everyone at the house has been working long days to line up buyers for these lots. They have guarantors for the major pieces. A Saudi prince is backing the main works up to their reserve prices.

Martin spots Mrs. Dempsey. The neck brace is gone, but now she wears an eye patch and stands with a walker. Next to her is Henry, looking uncomfortable.

"How nice to see you, Mrs. Dempsey," Martin says.

She scowls with her uncovered eye as she takes him in. "Oh. Yes. You," she says.

"I'm very glad you came," says Martin.

"It cost me." She points at her patched eye. "I'm having some issues."

"Well, I'm sorry to hear, but I'm grateful you've made such an effort." He thinks of putting a hand on Mrs. Dempsey's hand as some kind of welcoming gesture. She grips the walker fiercely though. He thinks better of the idea. "Are there any lots you're particularly interested in?" he says.

"The girl forgot the catalogue."

"Sorry?"

"The carer. She's in the bathroom. She's always in the bathroom. A very small bladder."

"I'm sorry to hear that." Martin looks at Henry. "Henry?" he says. His colleague looks up. "Could you go and fetch Mrs. Dempsey another catalogue?" A pause in Henry's response. He seems to be calculating whether he needs to take this instruction, but then he nods and moves off. "He'll get you a new one," says Martin to Mrs. Dempsey. "It'll only be a minute."

Departing from Mrs. Dempsey, Martin sees Philpot speaking to a small group. He greets Philpot, greets the others. "I was talking about the Malevich picture," says Philpot.

"You'll buy it?" says Martin. He winks.

"It's out of my price range, as you know."

"No need to apologize."

Philpot laughs. "I'm a fan, though. I was just saying that the history of this piece is monumental."

"Yes." Martin looks at the others, nods in performative agreement with Philpot.

"Lost and rediscovered. To have fought against the state to make something so incredible . . ."

"Yes."

"To live in a repressive place, and yet open such a space for self-expression . . . and such modern ideas, such a modern picture. His ideas created the impetus for so many great works."

"Right."

"Cutting back to such simple elements. Creative destruction, right?"

"Yes," says another man in the group. He wears wire-frame glasses. He has a narrow, birdlike face. He softens his expression with a grin. "Like Uber!"

"Right!" says Philpot. He laughs. "You joke, but yes!"

"Disruption," says the man.

"Yes!"

Martin joins the laughter of the others, forcing it a little. Too much, perhaps. When it has subsided, he thanks the group for coming, excuses himself, moves off.

• • •

THE HOUSE is crowded now, the air filled with a rich cacophony. He feels . . . what exactly? A blankness. A sense of anticlimax. The paintings in the show were in all the newspapers this morning. The predictable outrage, the predictable claims of madness. It's been a coup for the house.

Oleg is not here yet. He said he would be here, but Martin doubted this. Martin has done his very best to give the oligarch the grand sale he claimed to want: his collection of works all together, his name on the event, the logo of his foundation stenciled in huge letters on the wall. But Oleg is absorbed with new projects now.

OLEG WROTE a little piece about *Supremus No. 51* for the catalogue. "This picture is about new beginnings. Malevich wanted to open space for a new way of doing things. Perhaps it is appropriate that I am selling it now, as I begin a new phase of my life. This picture is about hope."

It is all always about them, of course: art, like much else, just a tool by which they know themselves. A game. You don't realize at first that these people live on a different scale. Martin found the flippant manner of men like Julian confusing when he first encountered it, but like the humor of doctors, it is a strategy for life. The key in dealing with these people is not to indulge their drama.

Martin sees Waterforth, who flashes his white teeth. The PR man is in conversation with an old woman in a flowing purple gown. Thomas is there too, and he moves from the group to greet Martin. He beams. He shakes Martin's hand. He wears a dinner jacket with velvet lapels. He says, "This is all we hoped."

"I'm glad."

"It reflects wonderfully on Mr. Gorelov. Your media work around this sale has been excellent."

"It's a shame he couldn't be here."

"I agree. I suppose his priorities have shifted. These people move on quickly."

Martin nods.

This morning Julian was on breakfast television with *Supremus No. 51.* The picture stood at the back of the set, flanked by two security guards. The presenters asked the usual incredulous questions, and Julian patiently bantered back. "There are so many ideas in this simple painting," he said.

"Just these shapes?" said the presenter.

Julian smiled at her. "Of course. The picture looks so simple, because it's already changed this world."

"Could you give an example?" said the presenter.

"These blocks, these colors, speak of modernity and cleanness because Malevich had that idea before we did. Blocks, lines, simplicity, primary colors. Modern architecture doesn't exist in the form you know without this man. Your luxury apartment looks like a Malevich picture, but then so does your laptop and so does the home screen of your search engine when you open the thing up." He grins. "The man is everywhere, like air. The man invented this world of ours."

Or we have squashed the man, Martin thought, watching, *to fit into this world of ours.*

THE HALL opens, and the clients move through the double doors. Martin stays behind the mass of bodies. He can see over heads toward the block, to the porters waiting. On the rear wall are the *Supremus,* the Bacon pictures. That is what to hold to, of course: the work and the celebration of the work.

He waits as the punters file into the auction room. The catering staff move around him, collecting glasses and clearing away dropped napkins. Chatter drifts indistinctly from the hall. He looks back to the antique glass front doors, at the light falling through crystal, the blurs of vehicles moving out on the street. The year is turning. The morning air was cool as he made his way here. The change in seasons always provokes in Martin an indulgent wistfulness. The days will draw in from here, he thinks. The light will go. Just submit to it, he thinks.

The doors to the street open, and he finds himself surprised, looking into the face of Mrs. Chatfield. "You look like you've seen a ghost," she says.

"I'm sorry," he says. "I drifted off." With some effort, he pulls himself back to the moment, smiles. "I'm so glad you made it. I knew you would. Everything is about to begin."

He gestures toward the hall. She walks off ahead of him.

One of the caterers is scrubbing at a wine stain on the carpet. Martin steps past her. He realizes that his phone is buzzing. He takes it out and looks at the screen. Marina is calling. Doesn't she know that it's the sale right now? These people. He puts the phone back into his breast pocket, where it vibrates for a few more seconds and then gives up. Martin enters the hall. He takes a place against the back wall. The doors are closed behind him. The talk of the crowd falls away. Julian strides to the block and places down his hammer. He looks out over the crowd and grins.

Sources & Acknowledgments

THE QUOTES by and about Kazimir Malevich that appear in this novel are taken from the book *Kazimir Malevich: Letters, Documents, Memoirs, Criticism*, compiled and edited by Irina A. Vakar and Tatiana N. Mikhienko, published via Tate Modern, London, 2015.

Thank you to my agent, Amelia Atlas, for your untiring support, advice, and advocacy. Thanks to my editor, Sean Manning, and to the many others at Simon & Schuster, including Tzipora Baitch, Kayley Hoffman, and Joal Hetherington, who have worked patiently to nix my typos and Britishisms, and to lay out this novel so handsomely.

Frances Leviston, Kaye Mitchell, and Peter Knight all saw early drafts of this book, and offered invaluable insight as to how it may be improved. Thank you to John McAuliffe and all the students and staff of the University of Manchester Centre for New Writing who offered a warm welcome to a vibrant writing community.

I'm grateful to the Art and Humanities Research Council North West Consortium Doctoral Training Partnership for the provision of the funding that allowed me to complete this project.

I'm thankful for the encouragement and support of my friends and family, with special gratitude, as ever, reserved for Jenny Reed.